St. Elmo

An Inspirational Victorian Romance
Annotated and Illustrated

by Augusta Jane Evans

Magnolia grandiflora.

Edited and annotated within an inch of its life
for a new generation

by Melinda R. Cordell

ROSEFIEND PUBLICATIONS.
Copyright © 2019 Melinda R. Cordell

Cover design by the amazing Monica Ford.
ISBN: 9781708753443

FROM AUGUSTA
TO J.C. DERBY

IN GRATEFUL MEMORY OF MANY YEARS OF KIND AND
FAITHFUL FRIENDSHIP, THESE PAGES ARE
AFFECTIONATELY DEDICATED.

also

From Melinda
To Brad
"My first and my last and my only love."

~ ST. ELMO ~

My 1896 copy of St. Elmo, found in a box that my grandpa brought back from an auction.

FOREWORD BY THE EDITOR
(THAT'S ME)

I have contemplated editing *St. Elmo*, seriously, since 1993, and I am very happy to have gotten this edited book out into the world at last.

Here's how this project came to be:

When I was in junior high, Grandpa Vance would go to consignment sales just like his dad did, and sometimes he'd have boxes of stuff that we (the kids) would dig through. After one such auction, I got an *Oxford Book of English Verse*, a very small volume that traversed all of English poetry from its beginning, and a copy of *St. Elmo*. I still have both books, and both have long been a part of my life.

I read *St. Elmo* shortly thereafter. I was a freshman in high school at the time and was not very impressed. All the characters seemed to do was sit around talking about MSS (manuscripts) in a very lofty tone.

But the next year I reread the book. And
Oh
My
Goodness.

Utterly swept away by the love story – what a love story! – I devoured that book. I read it again and again all through high school. I lent it book to my favorite English teacher, Kay Tucker, and she stayed up until 2 a.m. that weekend reading it. A winner!

I spent a lot of time in the library, trying to find the poems and references Augusta had sprinkled liberally through the book. I also wrote my stories like Augusta, all flowery and erudite, until I bought a copy of *The Elements of Style*. This book's admonitions to "Omit needless words" and "Do not overwrite" kept my own writing in balance – mostly.

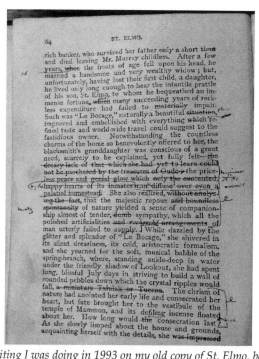

Some of the editing I was doing in 1993 on my old copy of St. Elmo, because I was a dedicated word nerd. In fact, I still am.

Hey Melinda, why are you editing this book?

Mainly because St. Elmo is a damn good story, and I'll be the first to be tackling people in the street saying READ THIS BOOK. You know, *St. Elmo* was the third top-selling novel in the 1800s, up there with *Uncle Tom's Cabin* and *Ben-Hur*. When it first came out, the publisher had fifteen cylinder presses running day and night to keep up with the demand. But there are some issues with this novel that caused it to fall out of favor over the years.

A parody of *St. Elmo*, called, *St. Twel'mo, or, The Cuneiform Cyclopedist of Chattanooga*, explains that Edna discovered a dictionary, and "she acquired in consequence a fatal fondness for polysyllables, a trick of speaking them trippingly, and a contempt for Common English, from which she never recovered."

That parody was on the nose. It would seem that Augusta shook an encyclopedia upside-down over the MS to add her references. You don't believe me? Well, get an eyeful of this paragraph from the original *St. Elmo*:

> "Pardon me if I remind you, *par parenthese*, of the preliminary and courteous *En garde*! which should be pronounced before a thrust. De Guérin felt starved in Languedoc, and no wonder! But had he penetrated every nook and cranny of the habitable globe, and traversed the vast zaarahs which science accords the universe, he would have died at last as hungry as Ugolino. I speak advisedly, for the true Io gad-fly, ennui, has stung me from hemisphere to hemisphere, across tempestuous oceans, scorching deserts, and icy mountain ranges. I have faced alike the bourrans of the steppes and the Samieli of Shamo, and the result of my vandal life is best epitomized in those grand but grim words of Bossuet: *'On trouve au fond de tout le vide et le néant.'* Nineteen years ago, to satisfy my hunger, I set out to hunt the daintiest food this world could furnish, and, like other fools, have learned finally, that life is but a huge, mellow, golden Ösher, that mockingly sifts its bitter dust upon our eager lips. Ah! truly, *on trouve au fond de tout le vide et le néant!*"

This whole paragraph is a marvel, requiring you to understand common French phrases; the life story of Maurice De Guérin; that the vast zaarahs are like Saharas; know the story of Ugolino from Dante's *Inferno*, who was locked in a tower with his sons to starve to death and eventually fell to eating their bodies before he died; be cognizant of the Greek myth of Io, a girl who was turned into a heifer by Zeus but Hera found out and had the poor gal chased to the ends of the earth by stinging flies.

Then we get to the obscure references. I found what the bourrans of the steppes were after about 15 minutes of online searching: an 1850s encyclopedia that said this is "the name given to the fierce snowstorms that blow from the north-east over the steppes of Russia." The Samieli of Shamo is explained this way in an article widely reprinted in a number of magazines during the early to mid-1800s: "Samieli which is felt in the deserts of Arabia ... is called in literal Arabic *sammoum*, which means *burning wind blowing at intervals and by night.*"

Now, as you can see, there's a lot to unpack in this one paragraph. The obscure references do nothing to advance the plot. They don't reveal anything new about St. Elmo, and they obscure the narrative – namely, how St. Elmo believes the world to be "weary, stale, flat, and unprofitable."[1]

So what I've done, as editor, was streamline her book. I cut unnecessary paragraphs and repetitive text. I smoothed out the tangles of references by giving them context to make them understandable – *if* they served the story. If the references hindered the story, out they went.

Augusta was also occasionally guilty of writing scenes with "talking heads," i.e., blocks of dialogue with no setting, no action. So I wrote a little action into those scenes to give the reader a "place to stand," so to speak, when reading. I've updated some of the punctuation, particularly semicolons; cleaned up a few misspelled words (gasp!), and switched her default spelling from British English to American English.

My aim is to keep this novel focused on Edna and St. Elmo and their struggles. The love story in these pages is incredible, guys, but it was buried by so much extraneous stuff. So by this streamlining, I hope the love story of Edna and St. Elmo will gain new power and vigor -- and a new generation of fans.

I also took a few liberties in some scenes. In the original story, there are a few scenes that one would think would be *very* important to Edna – for instance, St. Elmo's declaration scene, and particularly the ending of this book. But Augusta does a very odd thing in these scene: She pulls us out of Edna's point of view and

---

1 *Hamlet*, Act I, scene II – Shakespeare. I believe Augusta would have saved a lot of time and confusion by using this quote instead of all the others, to be honest.

has another character observe her reaction, instead of letting us see through her eyes. I took the liberty of giving Edna a voice in these places – even if it makes Edna herself less than perfect.

Over the years as I've edited *St. Elmo*, I've always imagined Augusta standing behind me, indignant at my editing her work with so liberal a hand. I hope she can forgive me.

All my life, I've read the 1896 edition. Imagine my surprise when I discovered that the original 1866 *St. Elmo* was slightly different in a few crucial places. For instance, Augusta had cut a few lines during St. Elmo's declaration scene that showed his scorn toward poor Annie. Feeling that he should not be let off the hook -- especially as Edna is, in fact, acting much like a confessor in this scene -- I included in this book the lines that Augusta had originally cut. After all, St. Thomas Aquinas states, "Three conditions are necessary for penance: contrition (which is sorrow for sin together with a purpose of amendment), confession of sins without any omission, and satisfaction by means of good works." Read on to see if St. Elmo lives up to this.

About the footnotes

For years I've been trying to look up the provenance of all the quotations in *St. Elmo*. When I was in high school, I spent many hours in the library combing through books of Victorian poetry, looking for the poems that Augusta had sprinkled through the text. I was able to find some of the Tennyson and Browning and Whittier poems, but many of the quotes were mysteries to me.

Not anymore! Thanks to the internet, I was able to find the majority of the references and poems via Google Books.

The Jean Ingelow poems, in particular, had not even crossed my radar back in the old days. Now, 32 years later, I'm excited to have finally found who wrote them. As a result, nearly all the books and poems that Augusta quoted in *St. Elmo* are now cited. I'm a happy gal. (And now I need to read Ingelow's works.)

I used footnotes to list the sources of the quotes in this book. I'm not crazy about footnotes, but it was the best way I could think of to list these references, and I tried to make them small and unobtrusive. Now you can read the poems that Augusta loved!

At any rate, I am very happy to bring *St. Elmo* to a new audience. I sincerely hope you enjoy reading this great old favorite.

all best,
Melinda R. Cordell
Savannah, Mo.

CHAPTER I
HONORABLE SATISFACTION

"He stood and measured the earth: and the everlasting mountains were scattered, the perpetual hills did bow."[2]

A slender girl of fourteen years steadied a pail of water on her head, with both dimpled arms thrown up. Pausing a moment beside the spring, Edna Earl stood fronting the great golden dawn – watching for the first level ray of the coming sun and chanting the prayer of Habakkuk. Behind her in silent grandeur towered the huge outline of Lookout Mountain, shrouded at summit in gray mist; while its center and base showed dense masses of foliage, dim and purplish in the distance – a stern cowled monk of the Cumberland brotherhood. Low hills clustered on either side, but a wooded plain stretched before the girl, over which the sunrise brightened into fiery radiance.

Until Edna's wild song waked echoes among the far-off rocks, the holy hush of early morning had rested like a benediction upon the scene. Morning among the mountains possessed witchery and glories which filled the heart of the girl with adoration, and called from her lips exultant songs of praise.

Her large black eyes held a singular fascination in their mild, sparkling depths, full of love and childish gladness; her lips curled in lines of orthodox Greek perfection, showing remarkable versatility of expression. Her hair, black, straight, hung round her shoulders, and glistened as the water from the dripping bucket trickled through the wreath of purple morning-glories and scarlet cypress that she had twined about her head before lifting the cedar pail to its resting-place. Edna wore a short-sleeved dress of yellow striped homespun that fell nearly to her ankles, and her bare feet gleamed on the green grass and rank dewy creepers that

---

[2] Habakkuk 3:6

clustered along the margin of the bubbling spring. Her complexion was transparent, and early exercise and mountain air had rouged her cheeks until they glowed.

A few steps ahead of her stood a large yellow dog, with black, scowling face and ears cut close to his head, posed as if prepared to make good his name, Grip.

In the solemn beauty of that summer morning, the girl seemed to have forgotten the mission upon which she came – namely, drawing water for her grandparents' breakfast preparations – but just then the sun flashed up, kindling diamond fringes on every dew-beaded chestnut leaf and oak-bough, and silvering the misty mantle which enveloped Lookout.

A moment longer that pure-hearted Tennessee girl stood watching the gorgeous spectacle, drinking draughts of joy which mingled no drop of sin or selfishness in its crystal waves. She had grown up alone with nature – utterly ignorant of the roar and strife, the burning hate and cunning intrigue of the great world of men and women, where, "like an Egyptian pitcher of tamed vipers, each struggles to get its head above the other."[3]

Life stretched before the girl like the sun's path in that clear sky. As free from care or foreboding as the fair June day, Edna left the spring, her dog trotting ahead.

The chant burst once more from her lips. "He stood and measured the earth: and the everlasting mountains were scattered, the perpetual hills –"

The sudden, almost simultaneous report of two pistol-shots rang out sharply on the cool air.

The girl startled so violently that she sprang forward and dropped the bucket. The sound of voices reached her from the thick wood bordering the path. Without thinking, she followed her dog, who bounded off toward the noise.

At the verge of the forest she paused, looking into a dewy green glade. There she beheld a spectacle which would burn itself upon her memory for the rest of her life.

A group of five gentlemen stood beneath the dripping chestnut and sweet-gum arches. One leaned against the trunk of a

---

[3] Sartor Resartus – Thomas Carlyle

tree, two were conversing eagerly in undertones, and two faced each other fifteen paces apart, with pistols in their hands.

Before Edna could comprehend the scene, the brief conference ended. The seconds resumed their places to witness another fire, and like the peal of a trumpet echoed the words:

"Fire! One! – two! – three!"

The flashes and ringing gunshots mingled with the command. One of the men threw up his arm and fell.

With horror in her eyes and pallor on her lips, the girl staggered to the spot and looked on the man twitching in the grass. His hazel eyes stared blankly at the sky as his body stilled. The man's face, still flushed, made her heart bound with hope – perhaps he would survive! – But then she saw the ball had entered the heart. Shuddering, she saw the warm blood, bubbling from his breast, dripping on the dewy grass.

Two other men came running, but the surgeon was already kneeling beside the man. He took the pistol from his clenched fingers and gently pressed the lids over his glazing eyes. Not a word was uttered as the seconds, choked with grief and anger, knelt next to the stiffening form.

A movement brought the girl's eyes up from the pool of blood. The surviving man, still standing in the middle of the field, coolly drew out a cigar, lighted it, and placed it between his lips, all while gazing with complete satisfaction at the dead man.

Her shuddering cry broke the silence. "Murderer!"

The men looked around instantly, and for the first time saw her standing there in their midst. Loathing and horror was in the gaze she fixed on the perpetrator of the awful deed.

In great surprise he drew back a step or two, and asked gruffly, "Who are you? What business have you here?"

"Oh! How dared you murder him? Do you think God will forgive you on the gallows?"

He was a man probably twenty-seven years of age – singularly fair, handsome, and hardened in iniquity, and he sneered at Edna. However, before he could reply, his friend came close to him.

"Clinton, you had better be off; you have barely time to catch the Knoxville train, which leaves Chattanooga in half an hour. I

3

would advise you to make a long stay in New York, for there will be trouble when Dent's brother hears of this morning's work."

"Aye! Take my word for that, and put the Atlantic between you and Dick Dent," added the surgeon, smiling grimly, as if the hope of retributive justice pleased him.

"I will simply put this between us," replied the murderer, fitting his pistol to the palm of his hand. As he did so, a heavy antique diamond ring flashed on his little finger.

"Come, Clinton, delay may cause you more trouble than we bargained for," urged his second.

Without even glancing toward the body of the dead man, Clinton scowled at the child. "What are you going to do? Will you arrest me?" Then he turned and went with his second through the trees until they were soon out of sight.

"Oh, sir!" Edna cried. "Will you let him get away? Will you let him go unpunished?"

"He cannot be punished," answered the surgeon, looking at her with curiosity.

"I thought men were hung for murder."

"Yes – but this is not murder."

"Not murder? He shot him dead! What is it?"

"He killed him in a duel, which is considered quite right and altogether proper."

"A duel?" She had never heard the word before. "To take a man's life is murder. Is there no law to punish a duel?"

"None strong enough to prohibit the practice. It is regarded as the only method of honorable satisfaction open to gentlemen."

"Honorable satisfaction?" she repeated, weighing the words as fearfully as she would have handled the bloody garments of the victim.

The surgeon sighed, looking Edna over with kindly eyes. "What is your name?"

"Edna Earl."

"Do you live near this place?"

"Yes, sir, very near."

"Is your father at home?"

"I have no father, but grandpa has not gone to the shop yet."

"Will you show me the way to the house?"

"Do you wish to carry him there?" she asked, glancing at the corpse and shuddering violently.

"Yes, I want some assistance from your grandfather."

"I will show you the way, sir."

The surgeon spoke hurriedly to the two remaining gentlemen, then followed Edna.

Slowly she retraced her steps, refilled her bucket at the spring, and walked on before the surgeon. The glory of the morning had passed away; a bloody mantle hung between the splendor of summer sunshine and the chilled heart of the badly shocked girl. The forehead of the radiant, holy June day had been suddenly red-branded like Cain, to be henceforth an occasion of hideous reminiscences. With trembling legs, Edna followed a narrow, beaten path, which soon ended at the gate of a rough, unwhitewashed fence. A low, comfortless looking three-roomed house stood within, and on the steps sat her dear grandfather smoking a pipe and busily engaged in mending a bridle.

The creaking of the gate attracted his attention, and he looked up wonderingly at the advancing stranger.

"Oh, Grandpa! There is a murdered man lying in the grass, under the chestnut trees, down by the spring."

Her startled grandfather removed his pipe. "Why! How do you know he was murdered?"

"Good morning, sir," the surgeon said, closing the gate behind him. "Your granddaughter happened to witness a very unfortunate and distressing affair. A duel was fought at sunrise, in the edge of the woods yonder, and the challenged party, Mr. Dent of Georgia, was killed. I came to ask permission to bring the body here until arrangements can be made for its interment, and also to beg your assistance in obtaining a coffin."

Unwilling to listen further, Edna passed on to the kitchen. As she set the bucket on the table, her tall, muscular, red-haired grandmother, who was stooping over the fire, raised her flushed face.

"What upon earth have you been doing?" she said angrily. "I have been halfway to the spring to call you, and hadn't a drop of water in the kitchen to make coffee! A pretty time of day Aaron Hunt will get his breakfast! What do you mean by such idleness?"

Her grandmother advanced on Edna but stopped suddenly.

"Edna, what ails you? Have you got an ague? You are as white as that pan of flour. Are you sick?"

Edna could barely speak. "There was a man killed this morning, and the body will be brought here directly. If you want to hear about it, you had better go out on the porch. One of the gentlemen is talking to grandpa."

Stunned by what she had seen, and indisposed to narrate the horrible details, Edna went to her own room, and seating herself in the window, tried to collect her thoughts. She was tempted to believe the whole affair a hideous dream, which would pass away with vigorous rubbing of her eyes, but the crushed purple and scarlet flowers she took from her forehead, her dripping hair and wet feet assured her of the vivid reality of the vision. Every fiber of her frame had received a terrible shock, and when Mrs. Hunt bustled from room to room, calling on Edna to help put the house in order, she obeyed silently, mechanically, as if sleepwalking.

Mr. Dent's body was brought up on a rude litter of boards, and temporarily placed on Edna's bed, to her horror. Toward evening when a coffin arrived from Chattanooga, the body was moved, and the coffin rested on two chairs in the middle of Edna's room. The surgeon insisted upon an immediate burial near the scene of combat; but the gentleman who had officiated as second for the deceased was determined to carry the unfortunate man's body back to his home and family. The earliest train on the following day was appointed as the time for their departure.

Late in the afternoon Edna cautiously opened the door of her room which she had hitherto avoided. With her apron full of lilies, white poppies, and sprigs of rosemary, she approached the coffin and looked at the rigid sleeper. Judging from his appearance, not more than thirty years had gone over his handsome head, and a soft, silky brown beard fell upon his pulseless breast. Fearful lest she should touch the icy body, the girl timidly strewed her flowers in the coffin. Tears gathered and dropped with the blossoms as she noticed a plain gold ring on the little finger. Perhaps his death would leave wailing orphans in his home, and a broken-hearted widow at the desolate hearthstone.

6

Absorbed in her melancholy task, she heard neither the sound of strange voices in the passage, nor the faint creak of the door as it swung back.

A wild, despairing shriek from behind Edna made her bound, terrified, away from the side of the coffin. The light of the setting sun streamed through the window and over the convulsed face of a feeble but beautiful woman, who was supported on the threshold by a venerable, gray-haired man, down whose furrowed cheeks tears coursed rapidly. Struggling to free herself from his restraining grasp, the stranger tottered into the middle of the room.

"O Harry! My husband! My husband!" She threw up her wasted arms and fell forward senseless on the corpse.

They bore the young woman into the adjoining room, where the surgeon administered the usual restoratives. Though finally her pulse stirred and throbbed feebly, no symptom of returning consciousness greeted the anxious friends who bent over her. Hour after hour passed, during which the young woman lay as motionless as her husband's body.

At length the physician sighed, and pressing his fingers to his eyes, said sorrowfully to the grief-stricken old man beside her, "It is paralysis, Mr. Dent, and there is no hope. She may linger twelve or twenty-four hours, but her sorrows are ended; she and Harry will soon be reunited. Knowing her constitution, I feared as much. You should not have suffered her to come; you might have known that the shock would kill her. For this reason, I wished his body buried here."

The old man fought back tears as he spoke. "I could not restrain her. Some meddling gossip told her that my poor boy had gone to fight a duel, and she rose from her bed and started to the railroad depot. I pleaded, I reasoned with her that she could not bear the journey, but I might as well have talked to the winds. I never knew her obstinate before, but she seemed to have a presentiment of the truth. God pity her two sweet babes!"

The old man bowed his head upon her pillow and sobbed aloud.

Throughout the night Edna crouched beside the bed, watching the wan face of the young widow, and tenderly chafing the numb,

7

fair hands which lay so motionless on the coverlet. Edna could not believe that death would snatch from the world one so beautiful and so necessary to her fatherless infants. But morning showed no encouraging symptoms; the stupor was unbroken. At noon the wife's spirit passed gently to the everlasting reunion.

Before sunrise on the following day, a sad group clustered once more under the dripping chestnuts. Where a pool of blood had dyed the sod, a wide grave yawned. The coffins were lowered, the bodies of Henry and Helen Dent rested side by side. As the sextons filled in the grave, the solemn silence was broken by the faltering voice of the surgeon, who read the burial service.

"Man, that is born of a woman, hath but a short time to live, and is full of misery. He cometh up, and is cut down, like a flower; he fleeth as it were a shadow, and never continueth in one stay.[4] Yet, O Lord God most holy, O Lord most mighty, O holy and most merciful Savior, deliver us not into the pains of eternal death!"

The melancholy rite ended, the party dispersed, the strangers took their departure for their distant homes, and quiet reigned once more in the small, dark cottage. But days and weeks brought to Edna no oblivion of the tragic events which constituted the first great epoch of her monotonous life. A nervous restlessness took possession of her. She refused to occupy her old room and insisted upon sleeping on a pallet at the foot of her grandfather's bed. She forsook her former haunts about the spring and forest, and started up in terror at every sudden sound, while from each opening between the chestnut trees the hazel eyes of the dead man, and the wan, thin face of the golden-haired wife, looked out beseechingly at her. Frequently, in the warm light of day, before shadows stalked to and fro in the thick woods, she would steal, with an apronful of wild flowers, to the solitary grave, scatter her treasures in the rank grass that waved above it, and hurry away with hushed breath and quivering limbs.

Summer waned, autumn passed, and winter came, but the girl recovered in no degree from the shock which had cut short her chant of praise on that bloody June day. Innocent childhood had

---

[4] From the Book of Common Prayer, 1789.

for the first time stood face to face with Sin and Death and could not forget the vision.

*****

Edna Earl had lived in the Tennessee mountains all her life. An orphan, she had lost both her parents before she was old enough to remember either. Her mother was the only daughter of Aaron Hunt, the village blacksmith, and she had died suddenly while working at the loom. A short time after her mother's death, Edna's father, who was an intelligent young carpenter, slid from the roof of the house which he was shingling on one wintery day, and died from the injuries sustained. Thus Mr. Hunt, who had been a widower for nearly ten years, found himself burdened with the care of an infant only six months old.

Aaron Hunt's daughter had never left home – she, her husband, and Edna all lived in his home – and after their deaths, the loneliness of the house oppressed him painfully. For the sake of his grandchild he resolved to marry again. The middle-aged widow whom he selected was a kind-hearted and generous woman, but ignorant and exceedingly high-tempered. While Mrs. Hunt really loved the little orphan committed to her care, her outbursts of temper only tightened the bonds of union between her husband and the child. Mrs. Hunt gradually left Edna more and more to the indulgence of her own views and caprices. She made Edna do her daily work, but after the chores were finished, Edna was allowed her to amuse herself as childish whims dictated. There were no children of her own age in the neighborhood, so she grew up without companionship, except that furnished by her grandfather. Mr. Hunt doted on her, and would have spoiled her, except her temperament forbode that.

Before Edna was able to walk, he would take her to the forge, and keep her for hours on a sheepskin in one corner, whence she watched, with infantile delight, the blast of the furnace and the shower of sparks that fell from the anvil. There she often slept, lulled by the monotonous chorus of trip hammer and sledge. As she grew older, the mystery of bellows and slack-tub engaged her attention. At one end of the shop, on a pile of shavings, Edna collected a mass of curiously shaped bits of iron and steel and blocks of wood, from which a miniature shop threatened to rise in

9

rivalry. Finally, when strong enough to grasp the handles of the bellows, her greatest pleasure consisted in rendering the feeble assistance which her grandfather was always so proud to accept at her hands.

Although uneducated and uncultivated, Mr. Hunt was a man of warm, tender feelings, and rare nobility of soul. He regretted his lack of schooling, which poverty had denied him; and in teaching Edna to read and to write, and to cipher, he never failed to impress upon her the vast superiority which a thorough education confers.

Whether his urgings first kindled her ambition, or whether her aspiration for knowledge was spontaneous and irrepressible, he knew not; but Edna began reading when she was four, so he did everything he could to gratify her fondness for study and thirst for learning. The blacksmith's library consisted of the family Bible, *Pilgrim's Progress,* a copy of Irving's *Sermons on Parables,* Sir Walter Scott's *Guy Mannering,* a few tracts, and two books which had belonged to an traveling minister who preached occasionally in the neighborhood, and who, having died rather suddenly at Mr. Hunt's house, left the volumes in his saddle-bags, which were never claimed by his family, residing in a distant state. Those books were Plutarch's *Lives* and a worn school copy of Anthon's *Classical Dictionary;* Edna considered them treasures of inestimable value and exhaustless interest.

Plutarch especially was a Mt. Pisgah of knowledge, whence the vast domain of learning stretched alluringly before her the way Canaan had stretched before Moses. As often as she climbed this height and viewed the wondrous scene beyond, it seemed, indeed,

> "an arch where through
> Gleams that untraveled world, whose margin fades
> Forever and forever when we move."[5]

In after years she sometimes questioned if this mountain of observation was also that of temptation, to which ambition had led her spirit, and there bargained for and bought her future.

Love of nature, love of books, an earnest piety and deep religious enthusiasm were the characteristics of a noble young soul, left to stray through the devious, checkered paths of life without other guidance than that which she received from communion with Greek sages and Hebrew prophets. Therefore, it was no marvel that the child shivered when she saw the laws of God vetoed and was blandly introduced to murder as Honorable Satisfaction.

---

[5] "Ulysses" – Lord Alfred Tennyson

CHAPTER II
THE DIVINE COMEDY

Nearly a mile from the small, straggling village of Chattanooga stood Aaron Hunt's shop, shaded by a grove of oak and chestnut trees that grew upon the knoll where two roads intersected. Like most blacksmith's shops at country crossroads, it was a low, narrow shed, filled with dust and rubbish, with old wheels and new single-trees, broken plows, and dilapidated wagons awaiting repairs. At the rear of the shop stood a smaller shed, where Aaron Hunt's old gray horse quietly ate his corn and fodder, waiting to carry him to his home two miles away as soon as the sun had set beyond the neighboring mountain.

Early in winter, having an unusual amount of work on hand, Mr. Hunt hurried away from home one morning, forgetting to take the bucket which contained his dinner, and Edna was sent to repair the oversight.

Accustomed to ramble about the woods alone, she walked leisurely along the rocky road, swinging the tin bucket in one hand, and pausing now and then to watch the shy red-birds that flitted like flame-jets in and out of the trees as she passed. The unbroken repose of earth and sky, the cold, still atmosphere and peaceful sunshine, touched her heart with a sense of quiet happiness, and she began singing a hymn which her grandfather often sang over his anvil:

> "Lord, in the morning Thou shalt hear
> My voice ascending high;
> To Thee will I direct my prayer,
> To Thee lift up mine eye."

Ere the first verse was ended, the clatter of a horse's hoofs hushed her song. She glanced up as a harsh voice asked impatiently, "Are you stone deaf? I say, is there a blacksmith's shop near?"

The rider reined in his horse, a spirited, beautiful animal, and waited for an answer.

"Yes, sir. There is a shop about half a mile ahead, on the right-hand side, where the road forks."

He just touched his hat with the end of his gloved fingers and galloped on.

When Edna reached the shop, her grandfather was examining the horse's shoes, while the stranger walked up and down the road before the forge. He was a very tall, strong man with a gray shawl thrown over one shoulder and a black fur hat drawn so far over his face that only the lower portion was visible. His face, swarthy and harsh, left a most disagreeable impression on Edna as she passed him and went up to the spot where Mr. Hunt was at work.

Putting the bucket behind her, she stooped, kissed him on his furrowed forehead, and said, "Grandpa, guess what brought me to see you today?"

"I forgot my dinner, and you have trudged over here to bring it. Ain't I right, Pearl? Stand back, honey, or this Satan of a horse may kick your brains out. I can hardly manage him."

Here the stranger uttered an oath, and called out, "How much longer do you intend to keep me waiting?"

"No longer, sir, than I can help, as I like the company of polite people."

"Oh, grandpa!" whispered Edna, as the traveler came striding toward them, throwing his shawl down on the grass as if preparing to fight.

Mr. Hunt pushed back his old battered woolen hat, unperturbed. He looked steadily at the master of the horse, saying resolutely, "I'll finish the job as soon as I can, and that is as much as any reasonable man would ask. Now, sir, if that doesn't suit you, you can take your horse and put out, and swear at somebody else, for I won't stand it."

"It is a cursed nuisance to be detained here for such a trifle as one shoe, and you might hurry yourself," the man snapped, and Edna moved closer to her Grandpa as if afraid.

"Your horse is very restless and vicious. I could shoe two gentle ones while I am trying to quiet him." As if to prove the old man right, the horse threw back his head, showing his teeth.

The man muttered something. Laying his hand heavily on the horse's mane, he said a few stern words, which were utterly unintelligible to Edna. But the words exerted a magical influence over the fiery creature, who soon stood tranquil and contented, rubbing his head against his master's shoulder.

Repelled by the rude harshness of this man, Edna walked into the shop, and watched the silent group outside. Soon the work was finished, and Mr. Hunt threw down his tools and wiped his face.

"What do I owe you?" The impatient rider sprang to his saddle and put his hand into his vest pocket.

"I charge nothing for 'such trifles' as that."

"But I am in the habit of paying for my work."

"It is not worth talking about. Good day, sir." Mr. Hunt turned and walked into his shop.

"There is a dollar. It is the only small change I have." The man rode up to the door of the shed, and flung the small gold coin toward the blacksmith, and began to ride rapidly away.

Edna darted after him. "Stop, sir! You have left your shawl!"

He turned in the saddle. Even under the screen of her calico bonnet Edna felt the fiery gleam of his eyes as he stooped to take the shawl from her hand. Once more his fingers touched his hat, he bowed and said hastily, "I thank you, child." Then spurring his horse, he was out of sight in a moment.

"He is a rude, blasphemous, wicked man," said Mr. Hunt as Edna reentered the shop and picked up the coin, which lay glistening amid the cinders around the anvil.

"Why do you think him wicked?"

"No good man swears as he did, before you came. Didn't you notice the vicious, wicked expression of his eyes?"

"No, sir, I did not see much of his face; he never looked at me but once. I should not like to meet him again; I am afraid of him."

"Never fear, Pearl, he is a stranger, and there's little chance of your ever setting your eyes on his ugly face again. Keep the money, dear; I won't have it after all the airs he put on. If, instead of shoeing his wild brute, I had knocked the fellow down for his insolence in cursing me, it would have served him right. Politeness is a cheap thing; a poor man, if he behaves himself and does his work well, is as much entitled to it as the President."

"I will give the dollar to grandma, to buy a new coffeepot, for she said today the old one was burnt out, and she could not use it any longer. But what is that yonder on the grass? That man left something after all."

She picked up from the spot where he had thrown his shawl a handsome morocco-bound pocket copy of Dante's *Divine Comedy*. Opening it to discover the name of the owner, she saw written on the fly-leaf in a bold and beautiful hand, "S. E. M., Boboli Gardens, Florence. *Lasciate ogni speranza voi ch'entrate.*"[6]

"What does this mean, grandpa?"

Edna held up the book and pointed out the dread inscription.

Her grandfather narrowed his eyes at the words. "Indeed, Pearl, how should I know? It is Greek, or Latin, or Dutch, like the other outlandish gibberish he talked to that devilish horse. He must have spent his life among the heathens, to judge from his talk, for he has neither manner nor religion. Honey, better put the book there in the furnace; it is not fit for your eyes."

As much as she esteemed her grandfather, Edna shrank from the thought. Books were rare in her part of the world, much to her regret. "He may come back for it if he misses it pretty soon."

"Not he. One might almost believe that he was running from the law. He would not turn back for it if it was bound in gold instead of leather. It is no account, I'll warrant, or he would not have been reading it, the ill-mannered heathen!"

Weeks passed, and as the owner was not heard of again, Edna felt that she might justly claim as her own this most marvelous of books, Dante's *Divine Comedy*, which, though beyond her comprehension, furnished a source of endless wonder and delight. The copy was Cary's translation, with illustrations by

---

[6] Dante's *Commedia*, Inferno, Canto 3. These words are inscribed upon the dread entrance to hell.

Flaxman, and many of the grand, gloomy passages were underlined by pencil and annotated in the unknown tongue that so completely baffled her curiosity. Night and day she pored over this new treasure. Sometimes she would dream of the hideous faces that scowled at her from the solemn, mournful pages; and now and then, when startled from sleep by these awful visions, she would soothe herself to rest by murmuring the metrical version of the Lord's Prayer contained in the "Purgatory."[7]

On was a bright afternoon in January, the old man sat in a large rocking-chair on the porch, smoking his pipe, and sunning himself in the last rays of the sinking sun. He had complained all day of not feeling well and failed to go to his work as usual.

Edna had been reading to him for quite some time when Mrs. Hunt came out to the porch, frowning at the child and her book. Most emphatically did Mrs. Hunt disapprove of the studious habits of the ambitious child, who she said was indulging dreams far above her station in life, and well calculated to dissatisfy her with her humble home. "Education is useless to poor people," she said, looking down with some anger at Edna's book. "I've never seen anybody feed and clothe themselves with 'book learning.' If experience has shown me anything, it's that those who lounge about with books in their hands generally come to want, and always to harm."

She had said things like this before many times. Mr. Hunt lay his brawny hand fondly on Edna's head and said tenderly, "Let her alone, wife! Let her alone! You will make us proud of you, won't you, little Pearl, when you are smart enough to teach a school? I shall be too old to work by that time, and you will take care of me, won't you, my little mockingbird?"

Edna closed her book and went to his side. "Oh, Grandy! That I will. But do you really think I ever shall have sense enough to be a teacher? You know I ought to learn everything, and I have so few books."

"To be sure you will. Remember there is always a way where there's a will. When I pay off the debt I owe Peter Wood, I will see what we can do about some new books. Put on your shawl now,

<hr>

[7] Dante's *Commedia*, Paradiso, Canto 11, if you want to take a gander.

Pearl, and hunt up old Brindle. It is milking time, and she is not in sight."

Mrs. Hunt snorted and went back inside.

"Grandpa, are you sure you feel better this evening?" Edna plunged her fingers in his thick white hair, and rubbed her round, rosy cheek softly against his.

"Oh! Yes, I am better. Hurry back, Pearl, I want you to read to me some more."

Now, as Edna tied her pink calico bonnet under her chin, and wrapped herself in her faded plaid shawl, he watched her with a tender, loving light in his keen gray eyes. She kissed him, buttoned his shirt collar, which had become unfastened, and drew his homespun coat closer to his throat. Then, springing down the steps, she bounded away in search of the cow, who often strayed so far off that Edna had to drive her home.

In the peaceful, solemn woods, through which the wintry wind now sighed in a soothing monotone, Edna ran calling for Brindle. She loved trees and flowers, stars and clouds, with a warm, clinging affection, and that solace and amusement which most children find in the society of children and the sports of childhood, she found in the solitude and serenity of nature. To her, the woods and fields were indeed vocal, and every flitting bird and gurgling brook, every passing cloud and whispering breeze, brought messages of God's eternal love and wisdom, and drew her tender, yearning heart more closely to Him.

Today, in the boundless reverence, she directed her steps to a large spreading oak, now leafless, where in summer she often came to read and pray. Here, falling on her knees, she thanked God for the blessings showered upon her. Entirely free from discontent and fretfulness, she was thoroughly happy in her poor humble home. Over her life, like a consecration, shone her devoted love for her grandfather, which more than compensated for any want. Accustomed always to ask special favor for him, his name now passed her lips in earnest supplication, and she fervently thanked the Father that his threatened illness had been arrested without serious consequences.

The sun had gone down when she rose and hurried on in search of the cow. The shadows of a winter evening gathered in the forest and climbed like trooping spirits up the rocky mountain side. As she plunged deeper and deeper into the woods, the child began a wild cattle call that she used on such occasions. The echoes rang out against the mountains. At last, when she was growing impatient of the fruitless search, she paused to listen, and heard the welcome sound of the familiar lowing by which the old cow recognized her summons. Following the sound, Edna saw the missing cow coming slowly toward her, and soon both were running homeward.

As she approached the house, driving Brindle before her, and merrily singing her song, the moon rose full and round, and threw a flood of light over the porch where the blacksmith still sat. Edna took off her bonnet and waved it at him, but he did not seem to notice the signal.

She drove the cow into the yard, and called out as she latched the gate, "Grandy, dear, why don't you go in to the fire? Are you waiting for me, out here in the cold? I think Brindle certainly must have been cropping grass around the old walls of Jericho, as that is the farthest off of any place I know. If she is half as tired and hungry as I am, she ought to be glad to get home."

He did not answer. Running up the steps, she thought he had fallen asleep. The old woolen hat shaded his face. She crept on tiptoe to the chair, stooped, put her arms around him, and kissed his wrinkled cheek – and she started back in terror.

His eyes stared at the moon, his stiff fingers clutched the pipe from which the ashes had not been shaken, and his face was cold and rigid.

Aaron Hunt had indeed fallen asleep, to wake no more amid the storms and woes and tears of time.

Edna fell on her knees and grasped his icy hands. "Grandpa! Wake up! Oh, grandpa! Speak to me, your little Pearl! Wake up, dear Grandy! I have come back! My grandpa! Oh! – "

Her wild, despairing cry rent the still evening air, and shrieked dismally back from the distant hills and the gray, ghostly mountain – and the child fell on her face at the dead man's feet.

Throughout that night of agony, Edna lay on the bed where her grandfather's body had been placed, holding one of his stiffened hands folded in both hers, and pressed against her lips. She neither wept nor moaned; the shock was too terrible to admit of noisy grief. Completely stunned, she lay desolate.

For the first time in her life she could not pray. She wanted to turn away from the thought of God and heaven, for she had nothing left to pray for. That silver-haired old man was the only father she had ever known. He had cradled her in his strong arms and slept clasping her to his heart; he had taught her to walk, and surrounded her with his warm love, making a home of peace and blessedness for her young life. Giving him, in return, the whole wealth of her affection, he had become the center of all her hopes, joys and aspirations. Now what remained? Bitterness hardened her heart when she remembered that even while she was kneeling, thanking God for his preservation from illness, he had already passed away; nay, his sanctified spirit probably poised its wings close to the Eternal Throne, and listened to the prayer which she sent up to God for his welfare and happiness and protection while on earth.

So we all trust, and prate of our faith, and deceive ourselves with the fond hope that we are resigned to the Heavenly Will, and we go on with a show of Christian reliance, while the morning sun smiles in gladness and plenty, and the hymn of happy days and the dear voices of our loved ones make music in our ears; and lo! God puts us in the crucible. The light of life – the hope of all future years – is blotted out; clouds of despair and the grim night of an unbroken desolation falls on heart and brain; we dare not look heavenward, dreading another blow; our anchor drags, we drift out into a hideous Dead Sea, where our idol has gone down forever – and boasted faith and trust and patience are swept like straws from our grasp in the tempest of woe, while our human love cries wolfishly for its lost darling.

Edna had never contemplated the possibility of her grandfather's death – it was a horror she had never forced herself to confront. Now he was cut down in an instant, without even the mournful consolation of parting words and farewell kisses. She asked herself again and again: "What have I done, that God should punish me so? I thought I was grateful, I thought I was doing my duty; but oh, what dreadful sin have I committed, to deserve this awful affliction?"

During the long, ghostly watches of that winter night, she recalled her past life, gilded by the old man's love. She could remember no happiness with which he was not intimately connected, and no sorrow that his hand had not soothed and lightened. The future was now a blank, lit with no ray of hope.

At daylight, when the cold, pale morning showed the stony face of the corpse at her side, her unnatural composure broke up in a storm of passionate woe. Edna sprang to her feet, almost frantic with loss.

"All alone! Nobody to love me; nothing to look forward to! Oh, grandpa, did you hear me praying for you yesterday? Dear Grandy – my own dear Grandy! I did pray for you while you were dying – here alone! Oh, my God! What have I done, that you should take him away from me? Was not I on my knees when he died? Oh, what will become of me now? Nobody to care for Edna now! Oh, grandpa! Grandpa! Beg Jesus to ask God to take me too!"

Throwing up her clasped hands, she sank back insensible on the shrouded form of the dead.

"When some beloved voice that was to you
Both sound and sweetness, faileth suddenly,
And silence against which you dare not cry,
Aches round you like a strong disease and new –
What hope? What help? What music will undo
That silence to your senses? Not friendship's sigh,
Not reason's subtle count. Nay, none of these!
Speak Thou, availing Christ! And fill this pause."[8]

---

[8] "Substitution" – Elizabeth Barrett Browning

CHAPTER III
ORPHANED

Of all that occurred during many ensuing weeks Edna knew little. In after years, she retained a remembrance of keen anguish and utter prostration. In delirious visions she saw her grandfather now struggling in the grasp of Phlegyas, and now writhing in the fiery tomb of Uberti with jets of flame leaping through his white hair, his worn old hands stretched toward her, as she had seen in one of the illustrations in her Dante. All the appalling images evoked by the gloomy Italian poet had seized upon her fancy and were now reproduced by her disordered brain in nightmarish forms. Her wails of agony, her passionate prayers to God to release the beloved spirit from the tortures which her delirium painted, were painful beyond expression to those who watched her ravings. It was with a feeling of relief that they finally saw her sink into apathy – into a quiet mental stupor – from which nothing seemed to rouse her. She did not notice Mrs. Hunt's absence, or the presence of her neighbors, Mr. and Mrs. Wood, at her bedside.

One morning, when Edna was wrapped up and placed by the fire, Mrs. Wood told her as gently as possible that her grandmother had died from a disease which was ravaging the country and supposed to be cholera. The news produced no emotion. Edna merely looked up an instant, glanced mournfully around the room, and, shivering, drooped her head again on her hand.

Week after week went slowly by, and Edna was moved to Mrs. Wood's house, but no improvement was discernible, and the belief became general that the child's mind had sunk into hopeless imbecility. The kind-hearted miller and his wife tried to coax her out of her chair by the chimney corner, but she crouched there, a wan, mute figure of woe, asking no questions, causing no trouble, receiving no consolation.

One bright March morning she sat, as usual, with her face bowed on her thin hand, and her vacant gaze fixed on the blazing fire – when, through the open window, came the impatient lowing of a cow.

Edna came to herself and lifted her eyes, and a quiver passed over her lips. It was Brindle's voice. Slowly she rose and followed the sound, her limbs quivering through lack of use, and made her way to Brindle's side, as the old cow now furnished milk for the miller's family. The gentle cow recognized Edna and gazed at her, with an expression almost human in the mild, liquid eyes. Only then did all the events of that last serene evening sweep back into Edna's deadened memory.

Leaning her head on Brindle's horns, Edna shed the first tears that had flowed for her great loss, while sobs, thick and suffocating, shook her feeble frame.

Standing in the doorway, Mrs. Wood wiped her eyes. "Bless the poor little outcast, she will get well now. That is just exactly what she needs. I tell you, Peter, one good cry like that is worth a wagonload of physic. Now, don't go near her; let her have her cry out. Poor thing! It ain't often you see a child love her granddaddy as she loved Aaron Hunt. Poor lamb!" Mrs. Wood went back to her weaving.

After the first storm of grief left her spent, Edna turned away from the mill and walked to her deserted home, while the tears poured ceaselessly over her cheeks. As she approached the old house, she saw that it was shut up and neglected; but when she opened the gate, Grip, the fierce yellow terror of the whole neighborhood, sprang from the doorstep, where he tirelessly kept guard. With a dismal whine of welcome, he leaped up and put his paws on Edna's shoulders. Grip had been the blacksmith's pet, fed by his hand, chained when grandpa went to the shop, and released at his return. Grim and repulsively ugly though he was, Grip was the only playmate Edna had ever known. He had gamboled around her cradle, slept with her on the sheepskin, and frolicked with her through the woods in many a long search for Brindle. He alone remained of all the happy past. As precious memories crowded mournfully up, she sat upon the steps of the dreary homestead, with her arms around Grip's neck, and wept bitterly.

After an hour, she left the house, and, followed by the dog, crossed the woods in the direction of the neighborhood graveyard. In order to reach it she was forced to pass by the spring and the green hillock where Mr. and Mrs. Dent slept side by side. No nervous terror seized her now as it used to; her great present horror swallowed up all others. Though Edna trembled from physical debility, she made herself walk on until the rough fence of the burying-ground stood before her.

Oh, dreary desolation; thy name is country graveyard! Here no polished sculptured stela pointed to the Eternal Rest beyond; no classic marbles told, in gilded characters, the virtues of the dead; no flowery-fringed gravel-walks wound from murmuring waterfalls and fountains to crystal lakes, where willows threw their flickering shadows over silver-dusted lilies. No spicy perfume of purple heliotrope and starry jasmine burdened the silent air; none of the solemn beauties and soothing charms of Greenwood or Mount Auburn wooed the mourner from her weight of woe.

Here, decaying headboards, green with the lichen-fingered touch of time, leaned over neglected mounds. Last year's weeds shivered in the sighing breeze, and autumn winds and winter rains had drifted a brown shroud of shriveled leaves between them. Here and there meek-eyed sheep lay sunning themselves upon the trampled graves, and the slow-measured sound of a bell rang now and then as cattle browsed on the scanty herbage in this most neglected of God's Acres.

In one corner of the enclosure, where Edna's parents slept, she found the new mounds that covered the remains of those who had nurtured and guarded her young life. On an unpainted board was written in large letters:

"To the memory of Aaron Hunt: an honest blacksmith, and true Christian; aged sixty-eight years and six months."

Here, with her head on her grandfather's grave, and the faithful dog crouched at her feet, lay the orphan, wrestling with grief and loneliness, striving to face a future that loomed before her. Here Mr. Wood found her when anxiety at her long absence induced his wife to search for the missing invalid. The storm of sobs and tears had spent itself; fortitude took the measure of the burden imposed, shouldered the galling weight, and henceforth, with undimmed vision, walked steadily to the appointed goal.

The miller was surprised to find Edna so calm, and as they went homeward, she asked the particulars of all that had occurred, and thanked him gravely for the kind care bestowed upon her, and for the last friendly offices performed for her grandfather.

Conscious of her complete helplessness and physical prostration, Edna said nothing about the future, but waited patiently until renewed strength permitted the execution of designs now fully mapped out. Notwithstanding her feebleness, she made herself helpful to Mrs. Wood, who praised her dexterity and neatness as a seamstress, and predicted that she would make a model housekeeper.

Late one Sunday evening in May, as the miller and his wife sat upon the steps of their humble home, they saw Edna slowly approaching, and knew where she had spent the afternoon. Instead of going into the house she seated herself beside them. When she removed her bonnet, traces of tears were visible on her sad but patient face.

"You ought not to go over yonder so often, child. It is not good for you," said the miller, knocking the ashes from his pipe.

Edna hid her countenance with her hand. After a moment she said, in a low but steady tone, "I shall never go there again. I have said good-bye to everything and have nothing now to keep me here. You and Mrs. Wood have been very kind to me, and I thank you heartily; but you have a family of children, and have your hands full to support them without taking care of me. I know that our house must go to you to pay that old debt, and even the horse and cow; and there will be nothing left when you are paid. You are very good, indeed, to offer me a home here, and I never can forget your kindness; but I should not be willing to live on anybody's charity. Besides, all the world is alike to me now, and I want to get out of sight of – of – what shows my sorrow to me every day. I don't love this place now; it won't let me forget, even for a minute, and – and – "

Here Edna's voice faltered and she paused.

"But where could you go, and how could you make your bread, you poor little ailing thing?"

"I hear that in the town of Columbus, Georgia, even little children get wages to work in the factory. I know I can earn enough to pay my board among the factory people."

Mr. Wood shook his head. "But you are too young to be straying about in a strange place. If you will stay here and help my wife about the house and the weaving, I will take good care of you, and clothe you till you are grown and married."

"I would rather go away, because I want to be educated, and I can't be if I stay here."

"Fiddlestick!" the miller said. "You will know as much as the balance of us, and that's all you will ever have any use for. I notice you have a hankering after books, but the quicker you get that foolishness out of your head the better; for books won't put bread in your mouth and clothes on your back, and folks that want to be better than their neighbors generally turn out worse. The less book-learning you women have, the better."

Mrs. Wood held up a hand to her husband. "I don't see that it is any of your business, Peter Wood, how much learning we women choose to get, provided your bread is baked and your socks darned when you want 'em. A woman has as good a right as a man to get book-learning, if she wants it; and as for sense, I'll thank you, mine is as good as yours any day."

Mr. Wood made a rude sound with his lips, but his wife spoke over him. "Now, folks have said it was a blessed thing for the neighborhood when the rheumatiz laid you, Peter Wood, up, and his wife, Dorothy Elmira Wood, run the mill. It's of no earthly use to cut at us women over that child's shoulders. If Edna wants an education, why, she has as much right to it as anybody, if she can pay for it. My doctrine is, everybody has a right to whatever they can pay for, whether it is schooling or a satin frock!"

Mrs. Wood seized her snuff-bottle and plunged a stick vigorously into the contents. The miller leaned back with a good-natured smile, and, as he showed no disposition to skirmish, she continued. "I take an interest in you, Edna Earl, because I loved your mother, who was the only sweet-tempered beauty that ever I knew. I think I never set my eyes on a prettier face, with big brown eyes as meek as a partridge's; and her hands and feet were as small as a queen's. Now as long as you are satisfied to stay here, I shall be glad to have you, and I will do as well for you as for my own Tabitha. But, if you are bent on factory work and schooling, I have got no more to say; for I have no right to say where you shall go or where you shall stay. But one thing I do want to tell you: it is a serious thing for a poor, motherless girl to be all alone among strangers."

There was a brief silence, and Edna answered slowly, "Yes, Mrs. Wood, I know it is; but God can protect me there as well as here, and I have none now but Him. I have made up my mind to go, because I think it is the best for me. I hope Mr. Wood will carry me to the Chattanooga depot tomorrow morning, as the train leaves early. I have a little money – seven dollars – that – that grandpa gave me at different times, and both Brindle's calves belong to me – he gave them to me – and I thought maybe you would pay me a few dollars for them."

"But you are not ready to start tomorrow."

"Yes, sir, I washed and ironed my clothes yesterday. What few I have are all packed in my box. Everything is ready now. If I have to go, I might as well start tomorrow."

"Don't you think you will get dreadfully homesick in about a month, and write to me to come and fetch you back?"

"I have no home and nobody to love me. How then can I ever be homesick? Grandpa's grave is all the home I have, and – and – God would not take me there when I was so sick, and – and –" The quiver of Edna's face showed that she was losing her self-control. Turning away, she took the cedar piggin, and went out to milk Brindle for the last time.

Feeling that they had no right to dictate her future course, neither the miller nor his wife offered any further opposition. Very early the next morning, after Mrs. Wood had given the girl what she called "some good motherly advice," and provided her with a basket containing food for the journey, she kissed her heartily several times and saw her stowed away in the miller's covered cart, which was to carry her to the railway station.

The road ran by the old blacksmith's shop, and Mr. Wood's eyes filled as he noticed the lingering, loving gaze which the girl fixed upon it until a grove of trees shut out the view; then Edna bowed her head, and a stifled moan reached his ears.

The engine whistled as they approached the station. Edna was hurried aboard the train, while her companion busied himself in transferring her box of clothing and books to the baggage car. She had insisted on taking her grandfather's dog with her, and, notwithstanding the horrified looks of the passengers and the scowl of the conductor, he followed her into the car and threw himself under the seat, glaring at all who passed, and looking as hideously savage as a wolf from the wild.

"You can't have a whole seat to yourself, and nobody wants to sit near that ugly brute," said the surly conductor.

Edna glanced down the aisle. Two young gentlemen sat stretched at full length on separate seats, watching her curiously. The conductor didn't say a thing to them.

Observing that the small seat next to the door was partially filled with the luggage of the parties who sat in front of it, she rose and called to the dog, saying to the conductor as she did so, "I will take that half of a seat yonder, where I shall be in nobody's way."

Here Mr. Wood came forward, thrust her ticket into her fingers, and shook her hand warmly, saying hurriedly, "Hold on to your ticket, and don't put your head out of the window. I told the conductor he must look after you and your box when you left the cars; he said he would. Good-bye, Edna; take care of yourself, and may God bless you, child."

The locomotive whistled, the train moved slowly on, and the miller hastened back to his cart.

As the engine got fully under way, and dashed around a curve, the small, straggling village disappeared. Trees and hills seemed to the orphan to fly past the window. When she leaned out and looked back, only the mist-mantled rocks of Lookout, and the dim, purplish outline of the Sequatchie heights were familiar.

In the shadow of that solitary sentinel peak Edna had passed her life; she had gathered chestnuts and chinkapins among its wooded clefts, and fearlessly clambered over its gray boulders. Now, as it rapidly receded and finally vanished, she felt as if the last link that bound her to the past had suddenly snapped; the last friendly face which had daily looked down on her for fourteen years was shut out forever, and she and Grip were indeed alone, in a great, struggling world of selfishness and sin.

The sun shone dazzlingly over wide fields of grain, whose green billows swelled and surged under the freshening breeze; golden butterflies fluttered over the pink and blue morning-glories that festooned the rail-fences; a brakeman whistled merrily on the platform, and children inside the car prattled and played. And at one end, a slender girl in homespun dress and pink calico bonnet crouched in a corner of the seat, staring back in the direction of hooded Lookout, and each instant bore her farther from the dear graves of her dead.

Oppressed with an intolerable sense of desolation and utter isolation in the midst of hundreds of her own race, who were too entirely absorbed in their individual speculations, fears and aims, to spare even a glance at that solitary young mariner, who saw the last headland fade from view, and found herself, with no pilot but ambition, drifting rapidly out on the great, unknown, treacherous Sea of Life, strewn with mournful human wrecks whom the charts and buoys of six thousand years of navigation could not guide to a haven of usefulness and peace.

Endless seemed the dreary day, which finally drew to a close. Edna, weary of her cramped position, laid her aching head on the window-sill and watched the red light of day die in the west, where a young moon hung her silvery crescent among the dusky treetops, and the stars flashed out thick and fast. Far away among strangers, uncared for and unnoticed, come what might, she felt that God's changeless stars smiled down as lovingly upon her face as on her grandfather's grave; and that the language of nature knew neither the changes of time and space, the distinctions of social caste, nor the limitations of national dialects.

As the night wore on, she opened her cherished copy of Dante and tried to read, but the print was too fine for the dim lamp which hung at some distance from her corner. Her head ached violently, and, as sleep was impossible, she put the book back in her pocket, and watched the flitting trees and fences, rocky banks, and occasional houses, which seemed strange in the darkness.

As silence deepened in the car, her sense of loneliness became more and more painful. Finally, she turned and pressed her cheek against the fair, chubby hand of a baby, who slept with its curly head on its mother's shoulder, and its little dimpled arm and hand hanging over the back of the seat. There was comfort and a soothing sensation of human companionship in the touch of that baby's hand; it seemed a link in the electric chain of sympathy. After a time, the orphan's eyes closed – fatigue conquered memory and sorrow, and she fell asleep with her lips pressed to the baby's fingers, and Grip's head resting against her knee.

Diamond-powdered "lilies of the field" folded their perfumed petals under the Syrian dew, wherewith God nightly baptized them in token of his ceaseless guardianship. The sinless world of birds, the "fowls of the air,"[9] nestled serenely under the shadow of the Almighty wing. Was the all-seeing, all-directing Eye likewise upon that desolate and destitute young mourner who sank to rest with "Our Father which art in heaven" upon her trembling lips? Was it a decree in the will and wisdom of our God, or the blind fumbling of chance, that at that instant the cherubim of death swooped down on the sleeping passengers? Over the holy hills of Judea, out of crumbling Jerusalem, the message of Messiah has floated on the wings of eighteen centuries: "What I do thou knowest not now, but thou shalt know hereafter."[10]

Edna was awakened by a succession of shrill whistles as the frantic engineer tried to clear the tracks. The conductor ran bareheaded through the car; people sprang to their feet; there was a scramble on the platform. Edna rose, her heart pounding fast – and all of a sudden, the whole world heaved to the side and flung her off her feet.

There came the crash of timbers, the screams of women and children, a colossal shock and crash as if the day of doom had dawned – and all was chaos.

---

[9] Matthew 6:26-28
[10] John 13:7

31

CHAPTER IV
A SCENE OF HORROR

Viewed by the aid of lanterns and the lurid, flickering light of torches, the scene of disaster presented a ghastly debris of dead and dying, of crushed cars and wounded men and women who writhed and groaned, trapped among the shattered timbers. The cries of those who recognized relatives in the mutilated corpses that were dragged out from the wreck increased the horrors of the occasion.

When Edna opened her eyes amid the flaring of torches and the piercing wails of the bereaved passengers, she thought she had died and gone to Dante's Hell; but the pain that seized her when she attempted to move soon dispelled this illusion. By degrees the truth presented itself to her blunted senses. She was held fast between timbers, one of which seemed to have fallen across her feet and crushed them, as she was unable to move them. Her legs felt a horrible sensation of numbness; one arm, too, was pinioned at her side, and something heavy and cold lay upon her throat and chest. Lifting this weight with her uninjured hand, she cried aloud. The face of the little baby whose fingers she had clasped met her horrified gaze; her small lips were pinched and purple, her waxen lids lay rigid over the baby's eyes, and baby's dimpled hand was stiff and icy.

The confusion increased as day dawned and a large crowd collected to offer assistance. Edna watched her approaching deliverers as they cut their way through the wreck and lifted out the wretched sufferers. Finally two men, with axes in their hands, bent down and looked into her face.

"Here is a live child and a dead baby wedged in between these beams. Are you much hurt, little one?"

Edna could do little more than nod. "Please take this log off my feet," she whispered. "And please take this little baby."

It was a difficult matter, but at length strong arms raised her, carried her some distance from the ruins, and placed her on the grass, where several other persons were writhing and groaning. The collision had flung the train from trestlework over a deep ravine, but they were near a village station, and two physicians were busily engaged in examining the wounded. The sun had risen, and shone full on Edna's face, and she turned away from its glare.

Just then one of the surgeons, with a compassionate face, came to investigate the extent of her injuries, and sat down on the grass beside her. Very tenderly he handled her, and after a few moments said gently, "I am obliged to hurt you a little, my child, for your shoulder is dislocated, and some of the bones are broken in your feet; but I will be as tender as possible. Here, Lennox! Help me."

The pain was so intense that Edna fainted. After a short time, when she recovered her consciousness, her feet and ankles were tightly bandaged, and the doctor was chafing her hands and bathing her face with some powerful extract. Smoothing back her hair, he said, "Were your parents on the cars? Do you know whether they are hurt?"

"They both died when I was a baby."

"Who was with you?"

"Nobody but Grip – my dog."

"Had you no relatives or friends on the train?"

"I have none. I am all alone in the world."

"Where did you come from?"

"Chattanooga."

"Where were you going?"

"My grandpa died, and as I had nobody to take care of me, I was going to Columbus to work in the cotton factory."

"Humph! Much work you will do for many a long day."

The doctor stroked his grayish beard and mused a moment.

Edna said timidly, "If you please, sir, I would like to know if my dog is hurt?"

33

The physician looked round inquiringly. "Has anyone seen a dog that was on the train?"

A passing brakemen, a stout Irishman, took his pipe from his mouth, and answered, "Aye, aye, sir! And as vicious a brute as ever I set eyes on. Both his hind legs were smashed – dragged so – and I tapped him on the head with an axe to put him out of his misery. Yonder he now lies on the track."

Edna put her hand over her eyes and turned her face down on the grass to hide tears that would not be driven back.

Here the surgeon was called away. For a half hour Edna lay there, wondering what would become of her, in her present helpless condition. She asked in her heart why God did not take her instead of that dimpled darling, whose parents were now weeping so bitterly. Surely God had cursed and forsaken her; surely misfortune and bereavement would dog her steps through life. A hard, bitter expression settled about her mouth, and looked out gloomily from her sad eyes.

Her painful reverie was interrupted by the cheery voice of Dr. Rodney, who came back, accompanied by an elegantly-dressed middle-aged lady.

"Ah, my brave little soldier! Tell us your name."

"Edna Earl."

"Have you no relatives?" asked the lady, stooping to scrutinize her face.

"No, ma'am."

"She is a very pretty child, Mrs. Murray, and if you can take care of her, even for a few weeks, until she is able to walk about, it will be a real charity. I never saw so much fortitude displayed by one so young; but her fever is increasing, and she needs immediate attention. Will it be convenient for you to carry her to your house at once?"

"Certainly, doctor; order the carriage driven up as close as possible. I brought a small mattress and think the ride will not be very painful. What splendid eyes she has! Poor little thing! Of course you will come and prescribe for her, and I will see that she is carefully nursed until she is quite well again. Here, Henry, you and Richard must lift this child, and put her on the mattress in the carriage. Mind you do not stumble and hurt her."

During the drive neither spoke. Edna was in so much pain that she lay with her eyes closed. Even though the carriage was driven slowly and carefully, it still jolted her around. As they entered a long avenue, the rattle of the wheels on the gravel aroused the child's attention, and when the carriage stopped, she was carried up a flight of broad marble steps to a house that was astonishingly large and handsome.

"Bring her into the room next to mine," said Mrs. Murray, leading the way.

Edna was soon undressed and placed within the snowy sheets of a heavily-carved bedstead whose crimson canopy shed a ruby light down on the laced and ruffled pillows. Edna, despite her pain and exhaustion, could not help but marvel at how soft and clean everything was, and felt sorry to impose on such fine people.

Mrs. Murray administered a dose of medicine given to her by Dr. Rodney. After closing the blinds to exclude the light, she felt the girl's pulse and found that she had fallen into a heavy sleep. With a sigh, she went down to take her breakfast.

It was several hours before Edna awoke. When she opened her eyes and looked around the elegantly furnished and beautiful room, she felt bewildered. Mrs. Murray sat in a cushioned chair, near one of the windows, with a book in her hand, and Edna had an opportunity of studying her face. It was fair, proud, and handsome, but wore an expression of habitual anxiety. Gray hairs showed themselves under the costly lace that bordered her morning head-dress, while lines of care marked her brow and mouth. In reading the countenance of her hostess, Edna felt that she was a haughty, ambitious woman, with a kind but not very warm heart, who would be scrupulously attentive to the wants of a sick child, but would never dream of caressing such a charge.

Chancing to glance towards the bed as she turned a leaf, Mrs. Murray met the curious gaze fastened upon her, and, rising, approached the sufferer.

"How do you feel, Edna? I believe that is your name."

"Thank you, my head is better, but I am very thirsty."

The lady of the house gave Edna some iced water in a silver goblet, then ordered a servant to bring up the refreshments she had directed prepared.

As she felt the girl's pulse, Edna noticed how gentle and soft her hands were, and how dazzlingly the jewels flashed on her fingers. She longed for the touch of those aristocratic hands on her hot brow, where the hair clustered so heavily.

"How old are you, Edna?"

"Almost fifteen."

"Had you any luggage on the train?"

"I had a small box of clothes."

"I will send a servant for it." She rang the bell as she spoke.

"When do you think I shall be able to walk about?"

"Probably not for many weeks. If you need or wish anything you must not hesitate to ask for it. A servant will sit here, and you have only to tell her what you want."

"You are very kind, ma'am, and I thank you very much – " Edna paused, and her eyes filled with tears.

Mrs. Murray looked at her and said gravely, "What is the matter, child?"

"I am only sorry I was so ungrateful and wicked this morning."

"How so?"

Edna looked at her hands. "Oh! Everything that I love dies; and when I lay there on the grass, unable to move, among strangers who knew and cared nothing about me, I was wicked, and would not try to pray. I thought God wanted to make me suffer all my life, and I wished that I had been killed instead of that dear little baby, who had a father and mother to kiss and love it. It was all wrong to feel so, but I was so wretched. And then God raised up friends even among strangers and showed me I am not forsaken if I am desolate. I know 'He doeth all things well,' but I feel it now. I am so sorry I could not trust Him without seeing it."

Edna wiped away her tears. Mrs. Murray's voice faltered slightly as she said, "You are a good little girl, I have no doubt. Who taught you to be so religious?"

"Grandpa."

"How long since you lost him?"

"Four months."

"Can you read?"

"Oh! Yes, ma'am."

"Well, I shall send you a Bible, and you must make yourself as contented as possible. I shall take good care of you."

As the hostess left the room, a staid-looking, elderly woman took a seat at the window and sewed silently, now and then glancing toward the bed. Exhausted with pain and fatigue, Edna slept again.

It was night when she opened her eyes and found Dr. Rodney and Mrs. Murray at her pillow. The kind surgeon talked pleasantly for some time, and, after giving ample instructions, took his leave. He brushed the hair out of Edna's face with a gentle hand. "You have been brave through your awful trial," he said. "Keep up your fortitude, and all will soon be well."

Once he'd left, Edna wept quietly, the sympathy in the surgeon's words unlocking her tears. "Thank God," she prayed fervently. "Thank God for the kind hands into which I've fallen."

So passed the first day of her sojourn under the hospitable roof which appeared so fortuitously to shelter her.

Day after day wore wearily away. At the end of a fortnight, though much exhausted by fever and suffering, she was propped up in bed by pillows, while Hagar, the servant, combed and plaited her long, thick, matted hair. Mrs. Murray came often to the room, but her visits were short. Though the matron was invariably kind and considerate, Edna felt an involuntary awe of her, which rendered her manner exceedingly constrained when they were together. Hagar was almost as taciturn as her mistress, and as the girl asked few questions, she remained in complete ignorance of the household affairs, and had never seen anyone but Mrs. Murray, Hagar, and the doctor.

Edna was well supplied with books, which Mrs. Murray brought from the library, and of this amusement the invalid never wearied during the long, tedious summer days. She found it hard to believe that anybody could have so many books, and dreaded the day when she'd have to leave them.

One afternoon in June, Edna persuaded Hagar to lift her to a large, cushioned chair close to the open window which looked out on the lawn. Here, with a book on her lap, she sat gazing out at the soft blue sky, the waving elm boughs, and the glittering plumage of a beautiful Himalayan pheasant, which seemed in the golden sunshine to have forgotten the rosy glow of his native snows. Leaning her elbows on the windowsill, Edna rested her face in her palms, and after a few minutes a tide of tender memories rose and swept over her heart, bringing a touching expression of sorrow to her sweet face, and giving a far-off wistful look to the beautiful eyes where tears often gathered.

Hagar had dressed her in a new white muslin wrapper, with fluted ruffles at the wrists and throat. The young face, with its delicate features and glossy folds of black hair, was a pleasant picture that the nurse loved to contemplate. Standing with her workbasket in her hand, she watched the graceful little figure for two or three moments, and a warm, loving light shone out over her dark features.

Then, nodding her head resolutely, Hagar muttered, "I will have my way this once; she shall stay," and passed out of the room, closing the door behind her.

Edna did not notice her departure, for memory was busy among the ashes of other days, exhuming a thousand precious reminiscences of a mountain home – chestnut groves – showers of sparks fringing an anvil with fire – andher grandfather's unpainted headboard in the deserted burying-ground.

A half hour later, Mrs. Murray laid her hand gently on her shoulder. "Child, of what are you thinking?"

Edna started. For an instant she could not command her voice, which faltered; but making a strong effort, she answered in a low tone, "Of all that I have lost, and what I am to do in future."

"Would you be willing to work all your life in a factory?"

"No, ma'am; only long enough to educate myself, so that I could teach."

"You could not obtain a suitable education in that way, and besides, I do not think that the factory you spoke of would be an agreeable place for you. I have made some inquiries about it since you came here."

Edna bowed her head. "I know it will not be pleasant, but then I am obliged to work in some way, and I don't see what else I can do. I am not able to pay for an education now, and I am determined to have one."

Mrs. Murray's eyes wandered out toward the velvety lawn, and she mused for some minutes. Then, to Edna's surprise, she laid her hands on the girl's head. "Child, will you trust your future and your education to me?"

"Mrs. Murray!"

"I do not mean that I will teach you – oh, no – but I will have you thoroughly educated, so that when you are grown you can support yourself by teaching."

Edna seized her hands, unable to speak.

Mrs. Murray seated herself next to her. "I have no daughter – I lost mine when she was a babe; but I could not have seen her enter a factory. As you remind me of my own child, I will not allow you to go there. I will take care of and educate you – will see that you have everything you require, if you are willing to be directed and advised by me. Understand, I do not adopt you; nor shall I consider you exactly as one of my family; but I shall prove a good friend and protector till you have completed your studies and can provide for yourself. You will live in my house and look upon it as your home, at least for the present. What do you say to this plan? Is it not much better and more pleasant than a wild-goose chase after an education through the dust and din of a factory?"

"Oh, Mrs. Murray!" Edna cried, thinking of all those books. "You are very generous and good, but I have no claim on you – no right to impose such expense and trouble upon you. I am – "

"Hush, child! You have that claim which poverty always has on wealth. As for the expense, that is a mere trifle, and I do not expect you to give me any trouble. Perhaps you may even make yourself useful to me."

"Thank you! Oh, thank you, ma'am! I am very grateful! I cannot tell you how much I thank you; but I shall try to prove it, if you will let me stay here – on one condition."

"What is that?"

"That when I am able to pay you, you will receive the money that my education and clothes will cost you."

Mrs. Murray laughed, and stroked Edna's silky black hair.

"Where did you get such proud notions? Pay me, indeed! You poor little beggar! Ha! Ha! Ha! Well, yes, you may do as you please, when you are able; that time is rather too distant to be considered now. Meanwhile, quit grieving over the past, and think only of improving yourself. I do not like doleful faces, and shall expect you to be a cheerful, contented, and obedient girl. Hagar is making you an entire set of new clothes, and I hope to see you always neat. I shall give you a smaller room than this – the one across the hall; you will keep your books there, and remain there during study hours. At other times you can come to my room, or amuse yourself as you like. When there is company here, remember, I shall always expect you to sit quietly, and listen to the conversation, as it is very improving to young girls to be in good society. You will have a music teacher, and practice on the upright piano in the library, instead of the large one in the parlor."

Edna could not speak, barely able to comprehend the golden realities being laid before her.

Mrs. Murray continued. "One thing more. If you want anything, come to me, and ask for it. I shall be very much displeased if you talk to the servants or encourage them to talk to you. Now, everything is understood, and I hope you will be happy, and properly improve the advantages I shall give you."

Edna drew one of the hands down to her lips and cried, "Thank you – thank you! You shall never have cause to regret your goodness; and your wishes shall always guide me."

"Well, well; I shall remember this promise, and trust I may never find it necessary to remind you of it. I dare say we shall get on very happily together."

Mrs. Murray stooped, and for the first time kissed the child's forehead. Edna longed to throw her arms about the stately form, but the polished hauteur awed and repelled her.

"Don't thank me anymore, and hereafter we need not speak of the matter."

Just as Mrs. Murray was moving toward the door, it was thrown open, startling Edna.

A gentleman strode into the room. He was a tall, athletic man, and though not one white thread silvered his thick, waving, brown hair, the heavy and habitual scowl on his high, full brow had plowed deep furrows such as age claims for its monogram. His piercing, steel-gray eyes were unusually large, and beautifully shaded with long heavy, black lashes, but Edna was repelled by their cynical glare; and the finely formed mouth, which might have imparted a wonderful charm to the countenance, wore a chronic sneer.

His clothes were costly but his jacket was carelessly spattered with blood. He wore a straw hat, belted with broad black ribbon, and his spurred boots were damp and muddy.

At sight of Edna he stopped suddenly. Dropping a bag of dead ducks on the floor, exclaimed harshly, "What the devil does this mean?"

A painful thrill shot along Edna's nerves, and dread, a presentiment of coming ill, overshadowed her heart.

"My son!" Mrs. Murray cried, walking swiftly to him. "I am so glad you are at home again. I was getting quite uneasy at your long absence. This is one of the victims of that terrible railroad disaster; the neighborhood is full of the sufferers. Come to my room. When did you arrive?"

She linked her arm in his, picked up the game-bag, and led him to the adjoining room, the door of which she closed and locked.

This was the son of her friend. The first glimpse of him filled Edna with instant repugnance. Evidently the face had once been singularly handsome, in the dawn of his earthly career, when his mother's good-night kiss rested like a blessing on his smooth, boyish forehead, and the prayer learned in the nursery still crept across his pure lips. Now the chiseled lineaments were blotted by dissipation, and blackened and distorted by the baleful fires of a fierce, passionate nature, and a restless and unhallowed intellect. In the glorious flush of his youth, this man had stood facing a noble and possibly a sanctified future; but the ungovernable flames of sin had reduced him, like a desecrated temple, to a melancholy mass of ashy arches and blackened columns, where ministering priests and all holy aspirations slumbered in the dust.

What was there about this surly son of her hostess that recalled to Edna's mind her grandfather's words, "He is a rude, wicked, blasphemous man"?

Edna put a hand to her mouth. Something in the man's rude words, in the haughty step, and the proud lifting of the regal head, reminded her painfully of the man whose insolence had stirred the ire of her grandfather's gentle nature. Was this the same man who rode in on that savage horse and lost his Dante, which she still owned?

While she pondered this, voices startled her from the next room, whence the sound floated through the window.

"If you were not my mother, I should say you were a candidate for a straight-jacket and a lunatic asylum; but as those amiable proclivities are considered hereditary, I do not favor that comparison. 'Sorry for her,' indeed! I'll bet my right arm it will not be six weeks before she makes you infinitely sorrier for your deluded self. With your knowledge of this precious world and its holy crew, I confess it seems farcical in the extreme that open-eyed you can venture another experiment on human nature. Some fine morning you will rub your eyes and find your dear little acolyte vanished, along with your silver forks, diamonds, and gold spoons."

The indignant blood burned in Edna's cheeks. She could not walk without assistance, and shrank from listening to a conversation which was not intended for her ears – especially one that slandered her. She coughed several times to arrest the attention of the speakers, but apparently without effect, for the son's voice again rose above the low tones of the mother.

"Oh, carnival of shams! She is 'pious' you say? Then, I'll swear my watch is not safe in my pocket, and I shall sleep with the key of my cameo cabinet tied around my neck. A Paris police would not insure your valuables or mine. Heaven forbid that your little saint should decamp with some of my costly travel-scrapings! 'Pious' indeed! Don't talk to me about 'her being providentially thrown into your hands,' unless you desire to hear me say things which you have frequently taken occasion to inform me 'deeply grieved' you. I dare say the little vagrant whines in what she considers orthodox phraseology, that 'God tempers the wind to the shorn lamb!' and, like some other pious people whom I have heard, will saddle some Jewish prophet or fisherman with the dictum, thinking that it sounds like the Bible, whereas Sterne said it. Shorn lamb, forsooth! We, or rather you, madame ma mère, will be shorn – thoroughly fleeced! Pious! Ha! Ha! Ha!"

Here followed an earnest expostulation from Mrs. Murray, only a few words of which were audible. Once more the deep, strong, bitter tones rejoined, "Interfere! Pardon me, I am only too happy to stand aloof and watch the little wretch play out her game. Most certainly it is your own affair, but you will permit me to be amused, will you not? What the deuce do you suppose I care about her 'faith?' She may run through the whole catalogue from the mustard-seed size up, as far as I am concerned, and you may make yourself easy on the score of my 'contaminating' the sanctified vagrant!"

"St. Elmo, my son! Promise me that you will not scoff and sneer at her religion in her presence," pleaded the mother.

A ringing, mirthless laugh was the only reply that reached the girl. She put her fingers in her ears and hid her face on the windowsill.

It was no longer possible to doubt the identity of the stranger. In the son of her friend and protectress, she had found the owner of her Dante and the man who had cursed her grandfather for his tardiness, for the initials on the book's flyleaf meant "St. Elmo Murray." If she had only known this one hour earlier, she would have declined the offer, which once accepted, she knew not how to reject without acquainting Mrs. Murray with the fact that she had overheard the conversation. Yet she could not endure the prospect of living under the same roof with a man whom she loathed and feared.

The memory of the blacksmith's aversion of this stranger intensified her own. As she pondered in indignation the derogatory epithets which St. Elmo had bestowed on her, she muttered through set teeth, "Yes, Grandy, he is cruel and wicked; and I never can bear to look at or speak to him! How dared he curse my dear, good grandpa! How can I ever be respectful to him, when he is not even respectful to his own mother! Oh, I wish I had never come here! I shall always hate him!"

At this juncture, Hagar entered, and lifted her back to her couch. Noticing the agitation of her manner, the nurse said gravely, as she put her fingers on the girl's pulse, "What has

43

flushed you so? Your face is hot; you have tired yourself sitting up too long. Did a gentleman come into the room a while ago?"

"Yes, Mrs. Murray's son."

"Did Miss Ellen – that is, my mistress – tell you that you were to live here, and get your education?"

"Yes, she offered to take care of me for a few years."

"Well, I am glad it is fixed, so – you can stay; for you can be a great comfort to Miss Ellen, if you try to please her."

Hagar busied herself about the room. Remembering Mrs. Murray's injunction that she should discourage conversation on the part of the servants, Edna turned her face to the wall and shut her eyes.

But for once Hagar's habitual silence was laid aside. Stooping over the couch, the kind nurse said hurriedly, "Listen to me, child, for I like your patient ways, and want to give you a friendly warning; you are a stranger in this house, and might stumble into trouble. Whatever else you do, be sure not to cross St. Elmo's path! Keep out of his way, and he will keep out of yours; for he is shy enough of strangers, and would walk a mile to keep from meeting anybody. But if he finds you in his way, he will walk roughshod right over you – trample you. Nothing ever stops him one minute when he makes up his mind. He does not even wait to listen to his mother, and she is about the only person who dares to talk to him. He hates everybody and everything; but he doesn't tread on folks' toes unless they are where they don't belong. He is like a rattlesnake that crawls in his own track, and bites everything that meddles or crosses his trail."

Edna mutely met the nurse's eyes. Hagar nodded and continued. "Above everything, child, for the love of peace and heaven, don't argue with him! If he says black is white, don't contradict him; and if he swears water runs upstream, let him swear, and don't know it runs down. Keep out of his sight, and you will do well enough, but once make him mad and you had better fight Satan hand to hand with red-hot pitchforks! Everybody is afraid of him, and gives way to him, and you must do like the rest of us that have to deal with him. I nursed him; but I would rather put my head in a wolf's jaws than stir him up. God knows I wish he had died when he was a baby, instead of living to grow up the swearing, raging devil he is! Now mind what I say, child. I am not given to talking, but this time it is for your good. If you want to have peace, keep out of his way."

Hagar left the room abruptly. Edna lay in the gathering gloom of twilight, perplexed, distressed, and wondering how she could avoid all the angularities of this amiable character, under whose roof fate seemed to have deposited her.

CHAPTER V
OR THE DEVIL!

At length, by the aid of crutches, Edna was able to leave the room where she had been so long confined, and explore the house in which every day presented some new charm. The parlors and sitting room opened on a long, arched veranda, which extended around two sides of the building and was paved with variegated tiles. The stained-glass doors of the dining-room, with its lofty frescoed ceiling and deep bow-windows, led by two white marble steps out on the terrace, whence two more steps showed the beginning of a serpentine gravel walk winding down to an octagonal hot-house, surmounted by a richly carved pagoda-roof. Two sentinel statues – a Bacchus and Bacchante – placed on the terrace, guarded the entrance to the dining-room. In front of the house, where a sculptured Triton threw jets of water into a gleaming circular basin, a pair of crouching monsters glared from the steps. When Edna first found herself before these grim doorkeepers, she started back in terror, and could scarcely repress a cry of alarm, for the howling rage and despair of the distorted hideous heads seemed fearfully real. Years elapsed before she comprehended their significance, or the somber mood which impelled their creation. They were imitations of that monumental lion, raised on the battlefield of Chaeronea, to commemorate the Boeotians slain.

In the rear of and adjoining the library, a narrow, vaulted passage with high Gothic windows of stained-glass opened into a beautifully proportioned rotunda. Beyond this circular apartment with its ruby-tinted skylight and Moresque frescoes, extended two other rooms, of whose shape or contents Edna knew nothing, save the tall arched windows that looked down on the terrace. The door of the rotunda was generally closed, but accidentally it stood open one morning, and she caught a glimpse of the circular form and the springing dome. Evidently this portion of the mansion had been recently built, while the remainder of the house had been constructed many years earlier.

All desire to explore it was extinguished when Mrs. Murray remarked one day, "That passage leads to my son's apartments, and he dislikes noise or intrusion."

Thenceforth Edna avoided it as if the plagues of Pharaoh were pent therein.

To her dazzled eyes this luxurious home was a fairy palace, an enchanted land. With eager curiosity and boundless admiration, she gazed upon beautiful articles whose use she could not even conjecture. The furniture throughout the mansion was elegant and costly. Pictures, statues, bronzes, marble, silver, rosewood, ebony, mosaics, satin, velvet – nothing that the most fastidious and cultivated taste could suggest was lacking; while the elaborate and beautiful arrangement of the extensive grounds showed with how prodigal a hand the owner squandered a princely fortune.

The flower garden and lawn comprised fifteen acres. The subdivisions were formed entirely by hedges, except for that portion of the park surrounded by a tall iron railing, where congregated a menagerie of deer, bison, a Lapland reindeer, a Peruvian llama, some Cashmere goats, a chamois, wounded and caught on the Jungfrau, and a large white cow from Ava. This part of the enclosure was thickly studded with large oaks, groups of beech and elm, and a few enormous cedars which would not have shamed their sacred prototypes sighing in Syrian breezes along the rocky gorges of Lebanon. The branches were low and spreading, and even at mid-day the sunshine barely freckled the cool, mossy knolls where the animals sought refuge from the summer heat of the open and smoothly-shaven lawn.

Here and there on the soft, green sward stood a circlet of martinet poplars standing face-to-face to a clump of willows whose long hair threw quivering, fringy shadows when the slanting rays of dying sunlight burnished the white and purple petals nestling among the clover tufts. Rustic seats of bark, cane and metal were scattered through the grounds. Where the well-trimmed numerous hedges divided the parterre, china, marble and iron vases of varied shape held rare vines and lovely exotics. Rich masses of roses swung their fragrant chalices of crimson and gold, rivaling the glorious blooms of ancient Persia.

The elevation upon which the house was placed commanded an extensive view of the surrounding country. Far away to the northeast, purplish gray waves along the sky showed a range of lofty hills. In an easterly direction, scarcely two miles distant, glittering spires told where the village clung to the railroad and to a deep rushing creek, whose sinuous course was distinctly marked by the dense growth that clothed its steep banks. Now and then luxuriant fields of corn covered the level lands with an emerald mantle, while sheep and cattle roamed through the adjacent countryside. In the calm, cool morning air, a black smoke-serpent crawled above the tree-tops, mapping out the track over which the long train of cars thundered.

Mr. Paul Murray, the first proprietor of the estate, and father of the present owner, had early in life spent much time in France, where, espousing the royalist cause during the French Revolution, his sympathies were fully enlisted by the desperate daring of François Athanase de Charette, Jean-Nicolas Stofflet, and Jacques Cathelineau. On his return to his native land, he gave the name "Le Bocage," to his country residence, because the venerable groves that surrounded his fine home resembled the woodlands and pastures of that area of France.

While his own fortune was handsome and abundant, Paul Murray married the orphan of a rich banker, who survived her father only a short time and died, leaving Mr. Murray childless. After a few years, when the frosts of age fell upon his head, he married a handsome and very wealthy widow. Unfortunately, having lost their first child, a daughter, he lived only long enough to hear the infantile prattle of his son, St. Elmo, to whom he bequeathed an immense fortune, which many succeeding years of reckless expenditure had failed to materially impair.

Such was "Le Bocage," naturally a beautiful situation, improved and embellished with everything which refined taste and worldwide travel could suggest to the fastidious owner. Notwithstanding the countless charms of the home so benevolently offered to her, the blacksmith's granddaughter was conscious of a great need, scarcely to be explained, yet fully felt – the dreary lack of that which could not be purchased by the treasures of the world – the priceless peace which only the contented, happy hearts of its residents can bring to even a palatial homestead. She also realized that the majestic repose and boundless spontaneity of nature yielded a sense of companionship of tender sympathy that all the polished artificial arrangements of man failed to supply. While dazzled by the glitter and splendor of "Le Bocage," she shivered in its silent dreariness, its cold, aristocratic formalism. Edna yearned for the soft, musical babble of the spring-branch, where, standing ankle-deep in water under the friendly shadow of Lookout, she had spent long, blissful July days in striving to build a wall of rounded pebbles down which the crystal ripples would fall.

The chrism of nature had anointed her early life and consecrated her heart, but fate brought her to the vestibule of the temple of Mammon, and its defiling incense floated about her. How long would the consecration last?

As Edna slowly limped about the house and grounds, acquainting herself with the details, she could not help but believe that happiness had once held her court here, but had been dethroned, exiled, and now waited beyond the confines of the park, unable to renew her reign and expel usurping gloom.

For some weeks after her arrival Edna took her meals in her own room. Having learned to recognize the hasty tread of the dreaded master of the house, she invariably fled from the sound of his steps as she would have fled an ogre; consequently, her knowledge of him was limited to the brief inspection and uncomplimentary conversation which introduced him to her acquaintance on the day of his return. Her habitual avoidance and desire of continued concealment was, however, summarily thwarted when Mrs. Murray came into her room late one night, and asked, "Did not I see you walking this afternoon without your crutches?"

"Yes, ma'am. I was trying to see if I could not do without them entirely."

"Did the experiment cause you any pain?"

"No pain exactly, but I find my ankle still weak."

"Be careful not to overstrain it. By degrees it will strengthen if you use it moderately. By the by, you are now well enough to come to the table. From breakfast tomorrow you will take your meals with us in the dining-room."

A shiver of apprehension seized Edna. "Ma'am!"

"I say, in future you will eat at the table instead of here in this room."

"If you please, Mrs. Murray, I would rather stay here."

"Pray, what possible objection can you have to the dining-room?"

Edna averted her head but wrung her fingers nervously.

Mrs. Murray frowned. "Don't be silly, Edna," she said gravely. "It is proper that you should go to the table and learn to eat with a fork instead of a knife. You need not be ashamed to meet people; there is nothing clownish about you unless you effect it. Good night; I shall see you at breakfast. The bell rings at eight o'clock."

There was no escape. Edna awoke next morning oppressed with the thought of the ordeal that awaited her. She dressed herself even more carefully than usual, despite the trembling of her hands. When the ringing of the little silver bell summoned her to the dining-room, her heart seemed to stand still. But though exceedingly sensitive and shy, Edna was brave, and even self-possessed, so she advanced to meet the trial.

Entering the room, she saw that her benefactress had not yet come in, but was approaching the house with a basket of flowers in her hand. One swift glance around discovered Mr. Murray standing at the window. Unobserved, she scanned his tall, powerful figure clad in a suit of white linen. He wore no beard save the heavy but closely-trimmed moustache, which now, in some degree, concealed the harshness about the handsome mouth. Only his profile was turned toward her, and she noticed that, while his forehead was singularly pale from wearing a hat, his cheeks and chin were thoroughly bronzed from exposure.

As Mrs. Murray came in, she nodded to her young protégée, and approached the table. "Good morning! It seems I am the laggard today, but Nicholas had mislaid the flower shears, and detained me. Hereafter I shall turn over this work of dressing vases to you, child. My son, this is your birthday, and here is your button-hole souvenir."

She fastened a few sprigs of white oxalis in his linen coat. As he thanked her briefly, and turned to the table, she said, with marked emphasis, "St. Elmo, let me introduce you to Edna Earl."

He looked around, and fixed his keen eyes on the orphan, whose cheeks crimsoned.

Edna looked down and said, quite distinctly, "Good morning, Mr. Murray."

"Good morning, Miss Earl."

"No, I protest! 'Miss Earl,' indeed! Call the child Edna."

"As you please, mother, provided you do not let the coffee and chocolate get cold while you decide the momentous question."

Neither spoke again for some time. In the embarrassing silence Edna kept her eyes on the china, wondering if all their breakfasts would be like this.

At last Mr. Murray pushed away his large coffee cup and said abruptly, "After all, it is only one year today since I came back to America, though it seems much longer. It will soon be time to prepare for my trip to the South Sea Islands. The stagnation here is intolerable."

An expression of painful surprise flitted across the mother's countenance. "It has been an exceedingly short, happy year to me," she said quickly, almost pleading. "You are such a confirmed absentee that when you are at home, time slips by unnoticed."

"But few and far between as my visits are, they certainly never approach the angelic. 'Welcome the coming, speed the parting guest,' must frequently recur to you."

Before his mother could reply he rose and ordered his horse. As he drew on his gloves, and left the room, looked over his shoulder, saying indifferently, "That box of pictures from Munich is at the warehouse; I directed Henry to go after it this morning. I will open it when I come home."

A moment after he passed the window on horseback.

With a heavy sigh Mrs. Murray dropped her head on her hand, compressing her lips, and toying abstractedly with the sugar-tongs.

Edna watched the grave, troubled countenance for some seconds, and then, putting her hand on the flower-basket, she asked softly, "Shall I dress the flower-pots?"

"Yes, child, in four rooms; this, the parlors, and the library. Always cut the flowers very early, while the dew is on them."

Her eyes went back to the sugar-tongs while Edna, very much relieved, escaped the room.

Impressed by Hagar's vehement adjuration to keep out of Mr. Murray's path, she avoided those portions of the house that he preferred to inhabit. Thus, although they continued to meet at meals, no words passed between them after that brief salutation on the morning of presentation. Often, Edna was painfully conscious that his searching eyes scrutinized her; but though the blood mounted instantly to her cheeks at such times, she never looked up – dreading his gaze as she would that of a basilisk.

One sultry afternoon she went into the park and threw herself down on the long grass under a clump of cedars, near which the deer and bison were quietly browsing, while the large white merino sheep huddled in the shade and blinked at the sun. Opening a pictorial history of England that she had selected from the library, Edna spread it on the grass, and leaning her face in her palms, rested her elbows on the ground, and began to read. Now and then she paused as she turned a leaf, looking around at the beautiful animals.

Gradually the languor of the atmosphere stole into her busy brain. As the sun crept down the sky, her eyelids sunk with it. Very soon she was fast asleep, with her head on the book and her cheeks flushed almost to a vermilion hue.

From that brief summer dream she was aroused by some sudden noise. Starting up, she saw the sheep bounding far away, while a large, gaunt, wolfish dog snuffed at her hands and face.

Once before she had seen this dog chained near the stables, and Hagar told her he was "very dangerous," and was never loosed except at night. The expression of his fierce, red eyes as he stood over her made her freeze, her heart pounding.

At that instant Mr. Murray's voice thundered, "Keep still! Don't move, or you will be torn to pieces!" Then followed some rapid interjections and vehement words in the same unintelligible dialect which had so puzzled her once before, when her grandfather could not control the horse he was attempting to shoe.

The dog was sullen and unmanageable, keeping his black muzzle close to her face. Edna grew pale with terror as she realized that his shaggy breast and snarling jaws were dripping with blood.

Leaping from his horse, Mr. Murray strode up. With a quick movement he seized the heavy brass collar of the savage creature, hurled him back on his haunches, and held him thus, giving vent the while to a volley of oaths.

Pointing to a large, half-decayed elm branch lying at a little distance, he tightened his grasp on the collar and said to the trembling girl, "Bring me that stick, yonder."

Edna complied. There ensued a scene of cursing, thrashing, and howling that absolutely sickened her. The dog writhed, leaped, whined, and snarled; but the iron hold was not relaxed, and the face of the master rivaled in rage that of the brute, which seemed as ferocious as the hounds of Gian Maria Visconti, fed with human flesh.

Distressed by the severity of the punishment, and without pausing to reflect, Edna cried, "Oh, please don't whip him anymore! It is cruel to beat him so!"

Probably he did not hear her, and the blows fell thicker than before. She drew near, and, as the merciless arm was raised to strike, she seized it with both hands, and swung on with her whole weight, repeating her words.

If one of his meek sheep had sprung at his throat to throttle him, Mr. Murray would not have been more astounded. He shook her off, flung her from him, but she carried the stick in her grasp.

"Damn you! How dare you interfere! What is it to you if I cut his throat, which I mean to do!"

Edna got to her feet, still holding the branch. "That will be cruel and sinful, for he does not know it is wrong; and besides, he did not bite me." She spoke resolutely, and for the first time ventured to look straight into his flashing eyes.

"Did not bite you! Did not he worry down and mangle one of my finest Southdowns? It would serve you right for your impertinent meddling, if I let him tear you limb from limb!"

"He knows no better," she answered, firmly.

"Then, by God, I will teach him! Hand me that stick!"

"Oh, please, Mr. Murray! You have nearly put out one of his eyes already!"

"Give me the stick, I tell you, or I – "

He did not finish the threat, but held out his hand with a peremptory gesture.

Edna gave one swift glance around. There were no other branches within reach, and the dog's face was swelling and bleeding from its bruises. Bending the stick across her knee, she snapped it into three pieces, which she threw as far as her strength would permit.

There was a brief pause, broken only by the piteous howling of the suffering creature. As she began to realize what she had done, Edna's face reddened, and she put her hands over her eyes to shut out the vision of the enraged man, who was dumb with indignant astonishment.

Presently a sneering laugh caused her to look through her fingers. Ali, the dog, now released, lay fawning and whining at his master's feet.

"Aha! The way of all natures, human as well as brute. Pamper them, they turn under your caressing hand and bite you; but bruise and trample them, and instantly they are on their knees licking the feet that kicked them. Begone, you bloodthirsty devil! I'll settle the account at the kennel. Buffon is a fool, and Pennant was right after all. The blood of the jackal pricks up your ears."

He spurned the crouching dog. As it slunk away in the direction of the house, Edna found herself alone, face to face with Mr. Murray, and she wished that the earth would open and swallow her.

Mr. Murray came close to her, held her hands down with one of his, and placing the other under her chin, forced her to look at him. "How dare you defy me?"

"I did not defy you, sir, but I could not help you to do what was wrong and cruel," she said, her voice shaking.

54

"I am the judge of my actions. I neither ask your help nor permit your interference with what does not concern you."

"God is the judge of mine, sir. If I had obeyed you, I should have been guilty of all you wished to do with that stick. I don't want to interfere, sir. I try to keep out of your way, and I am very sorry I happened to come here this evening. I did not dream of meeting you; I thought you had gone to town."

He read all her aversion in her eyes, which strove to avoid his. Smiling grimly, he continued, "You evidently think that I am the very devil himself, walking the earth like a roaring lion. Mind your own affairs hereafter, and when I give you a positive order, obey it, for I am master here, and my word is law. Meddling or disobedience I neither tolerate nor forgive. Do you understand me?"

"I shall not meddle, sir."

"That means that you will not obey me unless you think proper?"

Edna was silent, and her eyes filled with tears.

"Answer me!"

"I have nothing to say that you would like to hear."

"What? Out with it!"

"You would have a right to think me impertinent if I said any more."

"No, I swear I will not devour you, say what you may."

She shook her head, and the motion brought two tears down on her cheeks.

"Oh, you are one of the stubborn sweet saints, whose lips even Torquemada's red-hot steel fingers could not open. Child, do you hate or dread me most? Answer that question."

He took his own handkerchief from his pocket and wiped away her tears.

"I am sorry for you, sir," she said in a low voice.

He threw his head back and laughed heartily.

"Sorry for me! For me? The owner of as many thousands as there are hairs on your head! Keep your pity for your poverty-stricken vagrant self! Why the deuce are you sorry for me?"

She withdrew her hands, which he seemed to hold unconsciously, and answered, "Because, with all your money, you never will be happy."

"And what the devil do I care for happiness? I am not such a fool as to expect it; and yet after all, 'Out of the mouths of babes and sucklings.' Pshaw! I am a fool nevertheless to waste words on you. Stop! What do you think of my park, and the animals? I notice you often come here."

"The first time I saw it I thought of Noah and the ark, with two of every living thing; but an hour ago it seemed to me more like the garden of Eden, where the animals all lay down together in peace, before sin came into it."

"And Ali and I entered, like Satan, and completed the vision? Thank you. Considering the fact that you are on my premises, and know something of my angelic, sanctified temper, I must say you indulge in bold flights of imagery."

"I did not say that, sir."

"You thought it nevertheless. Don't be hypocritical! Is not that what you thought of?"

She made no reply. Anxious to end an interview painfully distressing to her, Edna stepped forward to pick up the history which lay on the grass.

"What book is that?"

She handed it to him, and the leaves happened to open at a picture representing the murder of Becket.

A scowl blackened Mr. Murray's face, and he turned away, muttering, "Malice aforethought! Or the devil!"

At a little distance, leisurely cropping the long grass, stood his favorite horse, whose arched forehead and peculiar mouse-color proclaimed his unmistakable descent from the swift hordes that scour the Kirghiz steppes, and sanctioned the whim which induced his master to call him Tamerlane. As Mr. Murray approached his horse, Edna walked away toward the house, a chill creeping down her spine that he might gallop up and overtake her. But no sound of hoofs reached her ears. Looking back as she crossed the avenue and entered the flower-garden, horse and rider were standing where she left them. Edna wondered why Mr. Murray was so still, with one arm on the neck of his Tartar horse, and his own head bent down on his hand.

In reflecting upon what had occurred, her repugnance grew. How could they live in the same house without continual conflicts? She dearly wanted an education, piano lessons, books without number – would she have to leave, and abandon all of these? A ray of hope darted through her mind when she remembered his talking about a visit to the South Sea Islands, and the possibility of his long absence.

Her dislike of Mr. Murray extended to everything he handled. As much as she had enjoyed reading the Dante, she decided to lose no time in returning his lost volume, which she felt certain that his keen eyes would recognize the first time she inadvertently left it in the library or the greenhouse. The doubt of her honesty, which he had expressed to his mother, rankled in the orphan's memory, and for some days she had been nerving herself to return the book. The encounter in the park only increased her dread of addressing him; but she resolved that the rendition of Caesar's things to Caesar should take place that evening before she slept.

CHAPTER VI
PANDORA'S BOX

The narrow, vaulted passage leading to Mr. Murray's suite of rooms was dim and gloomy when Edna approached the partly opened door of the rotunda, whence issued a stream of light. Timidly she crossed the threshold and stood within on the checkered floor, whose polished tiles glistened under the glare of gas from bronze brackets representing Atlas, that stood at regular intervals around the apartment. The walls were painted in Saracenic style, and here and there hung specimens of Oriental armor – Turcoman cimeters, Damascus swords, Bedouin lances, and a crimson silk flag, with heavy gold fringe, surmounted by a crescent. The cornice of the lofty arched ceiling was elaborately arabesque, and as Edna looked up she saw through the glass roof the flickering of stars in the summer sky.

In the center of the room, immediately under the dome, stretched a billiard-table, and near it was a circular one of black marble, inlaid with red onyx and lapis lazuli, which formed a miniature zodiac similar to that at Denderah, while in the middle of this table sat a small Murano hour-glass, filled with sand from the dreary valley of El Ghor. A huge plaster Trimurti stood close to the wall, on a triangular pedestal of black rock, and the Shiva-face with its writhing cobra confronted all who entered. Just opposite grinned a red granite slab with a quaint basso-relievo taken from the ruins of Elora. Near the door were two silken divans and a richly carved urn, three feet high, which had once ornamented the facade of a tomb in the royal days of Petra, ere the curse fell on Edom, now stood in memoriam of the original Necropolis.

For what purpose this room was used Edna could not imagine. After a hasty survey of its singular furniture, she crossed the rotunda and knocked at the door that stood slightly ajar. All was silent; but the smell of a cigar told her that the owner was within, and she knocked once more.

"Come in."

"I don't wish to come in; I only want to hand you something."

"Oh! The deuce you don't! But I never meet people even halfway, so come in you must, if you have anything to say to me. I give you my word there are neither blue blazes, nor pitchforks, nor small devils shut up here to fly away with whomsoever peeps in! Either enter, I say, or be off."

The temptation was powerful to accept the alternative; but as he had evidently recognized her voice, Edna reluctantly pushed open the door and entered.

It was a long room, and at its end were two fluted white marble pillars supporting a handsome arch, where hung heavy curtains of crimson Persian silk, partly looped back, showing the furniture of the sleeping apartment beyond.

For a moment the bright gaslight dazzled the orphan, and she shaded her eyes.

In the space between the tall windows that fronted the lawn hung a weird, life-size picture that took hold of the imagination of all who looked at it. A gray-haired Cimbrian Prophetess, in white vestments and brazen girdle, with canvas mantle fastened on the shoulder by a broad brazen clasp, stood, with bare feet, on a low, rude scaffolding, leaning upon her sword, and eagerly watching, with divining eyes, the stream of blood which trickled from the throat of the slaughtered human victim down into the large brazen kettle beneath the scaffold. Her snowy locks and white mantle seemed to flutter in the wind. Those who gazed on the stony, inexorable face of the Prophetess, and into her glittering blue eyes, shuddered and almost fancied they heard the pattering of the gory stream against the sides of the brass caldron.

Mr. Murray rose from a sofa near the window and advanced a step or two, taking the cigar from his lips.

"Come to the window and take a seat." He pointed to the sofa.

Edna shook her head, and said quickly, "I have something which belongs to you, Mr. Murray, which I think you must value very much. Therefore, I wanted to see it safe in your own hands."

Without raising her eyes, she held the book toward him.

"What is it?"

He took it mechanically with his gaze fixed on the girl's face. As she made no reply, he glanced down at it - and his stern, swarthy face lighted up joyfully.

"Is it possible? My Dante! My lost Dante! The copy that has travelled round the world in my pocket, and that I lost a year ago, somewhere in the mountains of Tennessee! Girl, where did you find it?"

"I found it where you left it - on the grass near a blacksmith's shop."

"A blacksmith's shop! Where?"

"Near Chattanooga. Don't you remember the sign, under the horse-shoe, over the door, 'Aaron Hunt'?"

"No; but who was Aaron Hunt?"

For nearly a minute Edna struggled for composure. Looking suddenly up, she said falteringly, "He was my grandfather - the only person in the world I had to care for, or to love me - and - sir--"

"Well, go on."

"You cursed him because your horse fretted, and he could not shoe him in five minutes."

"Humph!"

There was an awkward silence. St. Elmo Murray bit his lip and scowled. Recovering her self-control, Edna added, "You put your shawl and book on the ground, and when you started off you forgot them. I called you back and gave you your shawl; but I did not see the book for some time after you rode out of sight."

"Yes, yes, I remember now about the shawl and the shop. Strange I did not recognize you before. But how did you learn that the book was mine?"

"I did not know it was yours until I came here by accident and heard Mrs. Murray call your name; then I knew that the initials written in the book spelt your name. And besides, I remembered your figure and your voice."

Her mission ended, Edna turned to go.

"Stop! Why did you not give it to me when you first came?"

She made no reply.

Putting his hand on her shoulder to detain her, he said, more gently than she had ever heard him speak to anyone, "Was it because you loved my book and disliked to part with it, or was it because you feared to come and speak to a man whom you hate? Be truthful."

Still Edna was silent.

Raising her face with his palm, as he had done in the park, he continued in the same low, sweet voice, which she could scarcely believe belonged to him, "I am waiting for your answer, and I intend to have it."

Her large, sad eyes were brimming with precious memories, as she lifted them steadily to meet his. "My grandfather was noble and good, and he was all I had in this world."

"And you cannot forgive a man who happened to be rude to him?"

Edna stammered slightly. "If you please, Mr. Murray, I would rather go now. I have given you your book, and that is all I came for."

"Which means that you are afraid of me, and want to get out of my sight?"

She did not deny it, but her face flushed painfully.

"Edna Earl, you are at least honest and truthful, and those are rare traits at the present day. I thank you for preserving and returning my Dante. Did you read any of it?"

"Yes, sir, all of it. Good-night, sir."

"Wait a moment. When did Aaron Hunt die?"

"Two months after you saw him."

"You have no relatives? No cousins, uncles, aunts?"

"None that I ever heard of. I must go, sir."

"Good-night, child. For the present, when you go out in the grounds, be sure that wolf, Ali, is chained up, or you may be sorry that I did not cut his throat, as I am still inclined to do."

Edna closed the door, ran lightly across the rotunda, though her legs trembled. Regaining her own room and closing her door behind her, she felt inexpressibly relieved that the ordeal was over – that in future there remained no necessity for her to address one whose very tones made her shudder, and the touch of whose hand filled her with dread and loathing.

When the echo of her retreating footsteps died away, St. Elmo threw his cigar out of the window, and walked up and down the quaint and elegant rooms, whose costly bizarre relics would more appropriately have adorned a villa of Greece or long-ago southern Italy, than a country-house in so-called "republican" America.

The floor, covered in winter with velvet carpet, was of white and black marble, now bare and polished as a mirror, reflecting St. Elmo's figure as he crossed it. Oval ormolu tables, buhl chairs, and oaken and marqueterie cabinets loaded with cameos, intaglios, and Abraxoids whose erudition would have filled the philosopher Mnesarchus with envy, and challenged the admiration of the Samian lapidary who engraved the ring of Polycrates. These and numberless articles testified to the universality of what St. Elmo called his "world-scrapings," and to the reckless extravagance and archaistic taste of the collector. On a verd-antique table lay a satin cushion holding a vellum MS., bound in blue velvet, whose uncial letters were written in purple ink, powdered with gold-dust, while the margins were stiff with gilded illuminations. Near the cushion, as if prepared to shed light on the curious cryptography, stood an exquisite white glass lamp, shaped like a vase, and richly ornamented with Arabic inscriptions in ultramarine blue – a precious relic of some ruined Christian monastery in the Nitrian desert, by the aid of whose rays the hoary hermits, whom St. Macarius ruled, broke the midnight gloom chanting, *"Kyrie eleison, Christe eleison,"* fourteen hundred years before St. Elmo's birth.

Immediately opposite, on an embossed ivory stand, and protected from air and dust by a glass case, were two antique goblets, one of green-veined agate, one of blood-red onyx; and into the coating of wax, spread along the ivory slab, were inserted amphorae, one dry and empty, the other a third full of Falerian wine from ancient Rome, whose topaz drops had grown strangely mellow and golden in the ashy cellars of Herculaneum, and had doubtless been destined for some luxurious triclinium in the days of Emperor Titus. A small Byzantine picture, painted on wood, with a silver frame ornamented with carnelian stars, and the background heavily gilded, hung over an étagère, where lay a leaf from Nebuchadnezzar's diary, one of those Babylonish bricks on which his royal name was stamped. Near it stood a pair of

Bohemian vases representing the two varieties of lotus – one velvety white with rose-colored veins, the other with delicate blue petals. This latter whim had cost a vast amount of time, trouble, and money, it having been found difficult to carefully preserve, sketch, and paint them for the manufacturer in Bohemia, who had never seen the holy lotus, and required specimens. But the indomitable will of the man, to whose wishes neither oceans nor deserts opposed successful barriers, finally triumphed, and the coveted treasures fully repaid their price as they glistened in the gaslight, perfect as their prototypes slumbering on the bosom of the Nile, under the blazing midnight stars of rainless Egypt.

Several handsome rosewood cases were filled with rare books – two in the sacred Pali language – centuries old; and moth-eaten volumes and valuable MSS. – some in parchment, some bound in boards – recalled the days of astrology and alchemy, and the somber mysteries of Rosicrucianism. Side by side, on an ebony stand, lay an Elzevir Terence, printed in red letters in 1635, and a curious Burman book, whose pages consisted of thin leaves of ivory, gilded at the edges. Here too were black rhyta from Chiusi, Italy, which were drinking horns in the shape of rams and horses; and a cylix drinking cup from Vulci with two handles, and one of those quaint Peruvian jars, which was so constructed that, when filled with water, the air escaped in sounds that resembled that of the song or cry of the animal represented on the vase or jar.

But expensive and rare as were these relics of bygone dynasties and moldering epochs, there was one other object for which the master would have given everything else in this museum of curiosities, and the secret of which no eyes but his own had yet explored. Upon a sculptured slab that once formed a portion of the architrave of the Cave Temple at Elephanta, stood a splendid marble miniature, four feet high, of that miracle of Saracenic architecture, the Taj Mahal. The elaborate carving resembled lacework, and the beauty of the airy dome and slender, glittering minarets of this miniature tomb could find no parallel, save in the superb and matchless original. The richly-carved door that closed the arch of the tomb swung back on golden hinges, and opened only by a curiously-shaped golden key that never left Mr. Murray's watch-chain; consequently, what filled the innermost part of the building was left for the conjecture of the imaginative.

When his mother asked to look inside, St. Elmo merely frowned and said hastily, "That is Pandora's box, minus imprisoned hope. I prefer it should not be opened."

Immediately in front of the tomb he had posted a grim sentinel – a black marble statuette of Mors, modeled from that hideous little brass figure which Spence saw at Florence, representing a skeleton sitting on the ground, resting one arm on an urn.

Filled though it was with sparkling bijouterie, the glitter of the room was cold and cheerless. No light, childish feet had ever pattered down the long rows of shining tiles; no gushing, mirthful laughter had ever echoed through those lofty windows. Everything pointed to a classic, storied past – dead as the mummies of the Karnac temples, and treacherously, repulsively lustrous as the waves that break in silver circles over the buried battlements, and rustling palms and defiled altars of the proud cities of the plain. These trifles documented a heart that, in wandering to and fro through the earth, had fed itself with dust and ashes, acrid and bitter, and had studiously collected only the melancholy symbols of moldering ruin, desolation, and death, and which found its best type in the Taj Mahal, that glistened so mockingly as the gaslight flickered over it.

A stranger looking upon St. Elmo Murray for the first time, as he paced the floor, would have found it difficult to realize that only thirty years had plowed those deep, rugged lines in his swarthy and colorless but still handsome face; where habitual excesses had left their unmistakable plague-spot, and Mephistopheles had stamped his signet. Blasé, cynical, scoffing, and hopeless, he was recklessly striding to his grave, trampling upon the feelings of all with whom he associated, and at war with a world in which his lordly brilliant intellect would have lifted him to any eminence he desired, and which, properly directed, would have made him the benefactor and ornament of the society he snubbed and derided.

Like all strong though misguided natures, the power and activity of his mind enhanced his wretchedness, and drove him farther and farther from the path of rectitude; while the knowledge that he was originally capable of nobler pursuits than those that now engrossed his darkened thoughts, rendered him savagely morose. For nearly twelve years, nothing but jeers and oaths and sarcasms had crossed his lips, which had forgotten how to smile. It was only when the mocking demon of the wine-cup looked out from his gray eyes that his ringing, sneering laugh struck like a dagger to the heart that loved him, that of his anxious and miserable mother.

Tonight, for the first time since his desperate plunge into the abyss of vice, conscience, which he had believed effectually strangled, stirred feebly, startling him with a faint moan. Down the murdered years came wailing ghostly memories, which even his iron will could no longer scourge to silence. Clamorous as the avenging Furies, they refused to be exorcised, and goaded him almost to frenzy.

Those sweet, low, timid tones, "I am sorry for you," had astonished him. To be hated and dreaded was not at all unusual or surprising, but to be pitied and despised was a sensation as novel as humiliating. The fact that all his ferocity failed to intimidate the "little vagrant" was unpleasantly puzzling.

For some time after Edna's departure he pondered all that had passed between them. At length he muttered, "How thoroughly she abhors me! If I touch her, the flesh absolutely writhes away from my hand, as if I were a leper. Her very eyelids shudder when she looks at me – and I believe she would more willingly confront Apollyon himself. Strange! How she detests me. What a steady, brave look of scorn there was in her eyes when she told me to my face I was sinful and cruel!"

He set his teeth hard, and his fingers clinched as if longing to crush something. Then came a great revulsion, a fierce spasm of remorse, and his features writhed.

"Sinful? Ay! Cruel? O my lost youth! My cursed and wrecked manhood! If there be a hell blacker than my miserable soul, man has not dreamed of nor language painted it. What would I not give for a fresh, pure, and untrampled heart, such as slumbers peacefully in yonder room, with no damning recollections to scare sleep from her pillow? Innocent childhood!"

St. Elmo threw himself into a chair, and hid his face in his hands; and thus an hour went by, during which he neither moved nor sighed.

Tearing the veil from the past, he reviewed it calmly, relentlessly, vindictively.

At last, rising, he threw his head back, with his old defiant air, and his face hardened and darkened as he approached the marble mausoleum and laid his hand upon the golden key.

"Too late! Too late! I cannot afford to reflect. The devil himself would shirk the reading of such a record."

He fitted the key in the lock, but paused. Then he laughed scornfully as he slung it back on his chain.

"Pshaw! I am a fool. After all, I shall not need to see them. The silly, childish mood has passed."

He filled a silver goblet with some strong spicy wine, drank it, and taking down *Candide*, brightened the gas jets, lighted a fresh cigar, and began to read as he resumed his walk.

>"Lord of himself; that heritage of woe –
>That fearful empire which the human breast
>But holds to rob the heart within of rest."[11]

---

[11] "Lara" – Lord Byron

CHAPTER VII
BLUE-STOCKING

Mrs. Murray had informed Edna that the gentleman whom she had engaged to instruct her lived in the neighboring town, and one Monday morning in August she carried her to see him, telling her, as they drove along, that he was the minister of the largest church in the county, was an old friend of her family, and that she considered herself exceedingly fortunate in having prevailed upon him to consent to undertake her education.

The parsonage stood on the skirts of the village in a square immediately opposite the church, and was separated from it by a wide handsome street, lined on either side with elm trees. The old-fashioned house was of brick, with a wooden portico jutting out over the front door, and around the slender pillars twined honeysuckle and clematis, purple with clustering bells; while the brick walls were draped with luxuriant ivy that hung in festoons from the eaves, and clambered up the chimneys and in at the windows. The daily-swept walk leading to the gate was bordered with white and purple irises – "flags," as the villagers dubbed them – and over the little gate sprang an arch of lattice-work loaded with Belgian and English honeysuckle, whose fragrant wreaths drooped till they touched the heads of all who entered.

When Mrs. Murray and Edna ascended the steps and knocked at the open door, bearing the name "Allan Hammond," no living thing was visible, except a thrush that looked out shyly from the clematis vines. After waiting a moment, Mrs. Murray entered unannounced. They looked into the parlor, with its cool matting and white curtains and polished old-fashioned mahogany furniture, but the room was unoccupied. They passed on to the library, where tiers of books rose to the ceiling, much to Edna's delight. From that room they saw, through the open window, the pastor stooping to gather the violets blooming in the little shaded garden at the rear of the house. A large white cat sunned herself in the strawberry bed, and in the myrtle tree that overshadowed the study window, a mockingbird leaned down from a branch to scold the cat.

Mrs. Murray called to the minister, and taking off his straw hat he bowed, and came to meet them at the window.

"Mr. Hammond, I hope I do not interrupt you?"

"No, Ellen, you never interrupt me. I was merely gathering some violets to strew in a child's coffin. Susan Archer, poor thing! Lost her little Winnie last night, and I knew she would like some flowers to sprinkle over her baby."

He reached through the window to shake hands with Mrs. Murray. Turning to Edna, he offered his hand, saying kindly, "This is my pupil, Edna, I presume? I expected you several days ago and am very glad to see you at last. I will come into the house so we can become acquainted at once."

He joined them in the library, talking to Mrs. Murray. Edna's eyes followed him with an expression of intense veneration. He appeared to her a living original of the pictured prophets – the Samuel, Isaiah, and Ezekiel, whose faces she had studied in the large illustrated Bible that lay on a satin cushion in the sitting-room at Le Bocage. Sixty-five years of wrestling and conquests on the Mount Quarantina of life had set upon his noble and benevolent countenance the seal of holiness, and shed over his placid features the light of a serene heart, of a sanctified soul. His white hair and beard had the silvery sheen which seems peculiar to prematurely gray heads, and the snowy mass wonderfully softened the outline of the face; while the pleasant smile on his lips, the warm, cheering light in his bright blue eyes, won the perfect trust, the profound respect, the lasting love and veneration of those who entered the charmed circle of his influence. His heart throbbed with warm, tender sympathy for all people; and while none felt his or her happiness complete until his cordial congratulations sealed it, every sad mourner realized that her burden of woe was lightened when poured into his sympathizing ears. The sage counselor of the aged among his flock, he was the loved companion of younger members, in whose juvenile sports and sorrows he was never too busy to interest himself; and it was not surprising that over all classes and denominations he wielded an influence incalculable for good.

The limits of one church could not contain his great heart, which went forth in yearning love and fellowship to his Christian brethren and co-laborers throughout the world, while the refrain of his daily work was, "Bear ye one another's burdens." So in the evening of a life blessed with the bounteous fruitage of good deeds, he walked to and fro in the wide vineyard of God, with the light of peace, faith, and hope shining in his face.

Drawing Edna to a seat beside him on the sofa, Mr. Hammond said, "Mrs. Murray has entrusted your education entirely to me; but before I decide positively what books you will require I should like to know what particular branches of study you love best. Do you feel disposed to take up Latin?"

"Yes, sir – and – "

"Well, go on, my dear. Do not hesitate to speak freely."

"If you please, sir, I should like to study Greek also."

"Oh, nonsense, Edna!" interrupted Mrs. Murray. "Women never have any use for Greek; it would only be a waste of your time."

Edna faltered, but Mr. Hammond smiled and nodded. "Why do you wish to study Greek? You will scarcely be called upon to teach it."

"I should not think that I was well or thoroughly educated if I did not understand Greek and Latin. Besides, I want to read what Solon and Pericles and Demosthenes wrote in their own language."

"Why, what do you know about those men?"

"Only what Plutarch says."

"What kind of books do you read with most pleasure?"

"History and travels."

"Are you fond of arithmetic?"

Edna shook her head. "No, sir."

"But as a teacher you will have much more use for mathematics than for Greek."

"I should think that, with all my life before me, I might study both. Even if I should have no use for it, it would do me no harm to understand it. Knowledge is never in the way, is it?"

"Certainly not half so often as ignorance." Edna felt a hiccup of joy at Mr. Hammond's words. "Very well," he said, "you shall learn Greek as fast as you please. I should like to hear you read something. Here is Goldsmith's "Deserted Village." Suppose you try a few lines. Begin here at 'Sweet was the sound.'"

She read aloud the passage designated. He expressed himself satisfied and took the book from her hand.

Mrs. Murray shook her head. "I think the child is as inveterate a bookworm as I ever knew; but for heaven's sake, Mr. Hammond, do not make her a blue-stocking."

"Ellen, did you ever see a genuine blue-stocking?"

"I am happy to be able to say that I never was so unfortunate."

"You consider yourself lucky then, in not having known Madame de Staël, Hannah More, Charlotte Brontë, and Mrs. Browning?"

"To be consistent, of course, I must answer yes; but you know we women are never supposed to understand that term, much less possess the jewel itself. Besides, sir, you take undue advantage of me, for the women you mention were truly great geniuses. I was not objecting to genius in women."

Mr. Hammond nodded. "The world flatters and crowns those successful women; but unsuccessful aspirants are strangled with an offensive sobriquet. It were better that they had mill-stones tied about their necks. After all, Ellen, it is rather ludicrous, and seems very unfair, that the whole class of literary ladies should be sneered at on account of the color of Stillingfleet's stockings, eighty years ago."

"If you please, sir, I should like to know the meaning of 'blue-stocking?'" said Edna.

"You are in a fair way to understand it if you study Greek," answered Mrs. Murray, laughing at the puzzled expression of the child's countenance.

Mr. Hammond smiled, and replied, "A 'blue-stocking,' my dear, is generally supposed to be a severe lady, neither young, pleasant, nor pretty (and in most instances unmarried); ignorant of all domestic accomplishments and truly feminine acquirements, and ambitious of appearing very learned. Such a woman's fingers are more frequently adorned with ink-spots than thimble. She detests housekeeping[12] and talks loudly about politics, science, and philosophy; who is ugly, and learned, and cross; whose hair is never smooth and whose ruffles are never fluted. Is that a correct likeness, Ellen?"

"As good as one of Mathew Brady's photographs. Take warning, Edna."

Edna could not help but wonder if every accomplished woman was jeered at and called ugly.

"The title of 'blue-stocking,'" continued the pastor, "originated in a jest, many, many years ago, when a circle of brilliant ladies in London met at the house of Mrs. Vesey to take part in the conversation of some of the most gifted and learned men in England. One of those gentlemen, Stillingfleet, who always wore blue stockings, was so exceedingly agreeable and instructive, that when he chanced to be absent the company declared the party was a failure without the 'blue stockings,' as he was familiarly called. A Frenchman gave to these conversational gatherings the name of 'bas bleu,' which means blue stocking. Hence, you see, the humorous title given to a very charming gentleman now belongs to very pedantic and disagreeable ladies."

Edna frowned. "I do not quite understand why ladies have not as good a right to be learned and wise as gentlemen."

"To satisfy you on that point would involve more historical discussion than we have time for this morning. Some day we will look into the past and find a solution. Meanwhile, you may study as hard as you please, and remember, my dear, that where one woman is considered a blue-stocking, and tiresomely learned, twenty are more tiresome still because they know nothing. I will obtain all the books you need."

At the mention of the books, Edna became even happier.

"Hereafter you must come to me every morning at nine o'clock. When the weather is good, you can easily walk over from Mrs. Murray's." He took her hand again, and she smiled at her new friend.

---

[12] Editor's Note: THIS IS ME

As they drove homeward, Edna asked, "Has Mr. Hammond a family?"

"No; he lost his family years ago. But why do you ask that question?"

"I saw no lady, and I wondered who kept the house in such nice order."

"He has a very faithful servant who attends to his household affairs. In your discussions with Mr. Hammond, be careful not to allude to his domestic afflictions."

Mrs. Murray looked earnestly, searchingly at the girl, as if striving to fathom her thoughts; then throwing her head back with the haughty air which Edna had noticed in St. Elmo, she compressed her lips, lowered her veil, and remained silent and abstracted until they reached home.

The comprehensive curriculum of studies now eagerly commenced by Edna, and along which she was guided by the kind hand of the teacher, furnished the mental sustenance for which she hungered, exercised her active intellect, and induced her to visit the quiet parsonage library as assiduously as did Horace, Valgius, and Virgil visited the gardens on Esquiline Hill where Maecenas, that great patron of literature, held his literary gatherings.

Instead of skimming a few textbooks that cram the brain with unwieldy scientific technicalities and pompous philosophic terminology, her range of thought and study gradually stretched out into a broader, grander cycle, embracing, as she grew older, the application of those great principles that underlie modern science. Edna's tutor seemed impressed with the fallacy of the popular system of acquiring one branch of learning at a time, locking it away as in drawers of rubbish, never to be opened, where it molders in shapeless confusion till swept out ultimately to make room for more recent scientific invoices. Thus in lieu of the educational plan of "finishing natural philosophy and chemistry this session, and geology and astronomy next term, and taking up moral science and criticism the year we graduate," Mr. Hammond allowed his pupil to finish and lay aside none of her studies; but sought to impress upon her the great value of Blackstone's aphorism, "For sciences are of a sociable disposition, and flourish best in the neighborhood of each other; nor is there any branch of learning but may be helped and improved by assistance drawn from other arts.[13]"

Finding that her imagination was remarkably fertile, he required her, as she advanced in years, to compose essays, letters, dialogues, and sometimes orations, all of which were not only written and handed in for correction, but he frequently directed her to recite them from memory, and invited her to assist him, while he dissected and criticized either her diction, line of argument, choice of metaphors, or intonation of voice. In these compositions he encouraged her to seek illustrations from every department of letters, and convert her theme into a focus, upon which to pour all the concentrated light which research could reflect.

His favorite plea in such instances was, "Wide as the universe and free as its winds should be the range of human mind."

Recognizing that "the proper study of mankind is man,"[14] and understanding how history tells the story of the magnificent triumphs and stupendous failures, the grand capacities and innate frailties of mankind, he fostered and stimulated his pupil's fondness for historic investigation. While in impressing upon her memory the chronologic sequence of events he not only grouped into great epochs the principal dramas, but carefully selected her miscellaneous reading, so poetry, novels, biography, and essays reflected light upon the actors of the particular epoch which she was studying.

The extensive library at Le Bocage, and the valuable collection of books at the parsonage, challenged research. With a boundless ambition, equaled only by her patient, persevering application, Edna devoted herself to the acquisition of knowledge, astonishing and delighting Mr. Hammond by her rapid progress and her restless intellect.

The noble catholicity of spirit that distinguished Mr. Hammond's character encouraged her to discuss freely the ethical and psychological problems that caught her attention as she grew

---

[13] "On the Study of the Law," from *Commentaries on the Laws of England*, Vol. 1 -- William Blackstone
[14] "An Essay on Man: Epistle II" – Alexander Pope

older, and facilitated her appreciation and acceptance of the great fact that all bigotry springs from narrow minds and ignorance. He taught her that ignorance and intolerance are the red-handed Huns that ravage society, immolating the pioneers of progress upon the shrine of prejudice – fettering science, blindly divorcing natural and revealed truth, which "God hath joined together" in holy and eternal wedlock. They battle against every innovation, lock the wheels of human advancement, and turn a deaf ear to the thrilling cry,

"Yet I doubt not thro' the ages one increasing purpose runs,
And the thoughts of men are widen'd with the process of the suns."[15]

While Christ walked among the palms and poppies of Palestine, glorifying anew a degraded human nature, he chose unlettered fishermen, who mended their nets and trimmed their sails along the blue waves of Galilee, as fit instruments in his guiding hands for the dissemination of his Gospel. When the days of the Incarnation ended and Jesus returned to the Father, this work required all the learning and the mighty genius of Saul of Tarsus to refute the scoffing Greeks who, within sight of the Parthenon, gathered on Mars Hill to defend their marble altars to the Unknown God[16].

---

[15] "Locksley Hall" – Lord Alfred Tennyson
[16] The speech that Saul (the apostle Paul) gives before the Greek court at the Areopagus can be found in Acts 17:22-31

CHAPTER VIII
THE GOLDEN KEY

During the months of September and October Mrs. Murray filled the house with company, and parties of gentlemen came from time to time to enjoy the game season and take part in the hunts to which St. Elmo devoted himself. There were elegant dinners and small suppers; there were billiard-matches and horse-races, and merry gatherings at the ten-pin alley. Laughter, music, and dancing usurped the dominions where silence and gloom had so long reigned.

Naturally shy and unaccustomed to companionship, Edna felt no desire to participate in these festivities, but became more and more absorbed in her studies. Her knowledge of the visitors was limited to the brief time of the table, where she observed the deference yielded to the opinions of the master of the house, and the dread that all manifested lest they should fall under the lash of his merciless sarcasm. An Ishmael in society, St. Elmo's uplifted hand smote all conventionalities and shams, spared neither age nor sex, and acknowledged sanctity nowhere. The scrupulous courtesy of his manner polished and pointed his satire, and when a personal application of his remarks was possible, he would bow gracefully to the lady indicated, and fill her glass with wine while he filled her heart with chagrin and rankling hate.

Since she'd returned his Dante to him, not a word had passed between him and Edna, who regarded him with increasing detestation. One evening at dinner, the conversation was general, and he sat silent at the foot of the table, but when she looked up at him, she found his eyes fixed on her face. Inclining his head slightly to arrest her attention, he handed a decanter of sherry to one of the servants, with some brief direction.

A moment after, her glass was filled. The waiter said, "Mr. Murray's compliments to Aaron Hunt's granddaughter."

Observation had taught Edna what was customary on such occasions. She knew that he had once noticed her taking wine with the gentleman who sat next to her. But now, repugnance conquered politeness, for the mention of her grandfather's name seemed an insult from his lips. Putting her hand over her glass, she looked him full in the face and shook her head.

Nevertheless, he lifted his wine, bowed, and drank the last drop in the crystal goblet; then turned to a gentleman on his right hand, and instantly entered into a learned discussion on the superiority of the wines of the Levant over those of Germany.

When the ladies withdrew to the parlor, he rose, as was his custom, and held the door open for them. Edna was the last of the party, and she dreaded what was to come.

As she passed him, he smiled mockingly and said, "It was unfortunate that my mother omitted to include etiquette in your catalogue of studies at the parsonage."

Instantly the answer sprang to her lips: *She knew I had a teacher for that branch nearer home.* But she repressed the words and said gravely, "I think only good friends should take wine together."

"This is your declaration of war? Very well, only remember I raise a black flag and show no quarter. Woe to the conquered!"

That was not at all what she'd said, but Edna hurried away to the library, and thenceforth kept out of his way more assiduously than ever. Nevertheless, he scrutinized her closely when she was forced to enter his presence, leaving her constrained and uncomfortable. Mrs. Murray well understood her hostile feeling toward her son, but she never alluded to it, and his name was not mentioned by either.

One by one the guests departed. Autumn passed, and winter was ushered in by wailing winds and drizzling rains.

One morning as Edna came out of the hothouse with a basketful of camellias, she saw St. Elmo bidding his mother good-bye as he started on his long journey to Oceania. They stood on the steps, Mrs. Murray's head rested on his shoulder, and bitter tears fell on her cheeks as she talked rapidly to him.

Edna heard him say impatiently, "You ask what is impossible; it is worse than useless to urge me. Better pray that I may find a peaceful grave in the cinnamon groves and under the plumy palms of the far south."

He kissed his mother's cheek and sprang into the saddle, but checked his horse at sight of Edna, who stood a few yards distant.

"Are you coming to say good-bye? Or do you reserve such courtesies for your 'good friends'?"

Regret for her former rudeness, and sympathy for Mrs. Murray's uncontrollable distress, softened her heart toward him. She selected the finest white camellia in the basket, walked close to the horse, and, handing him the flower, said, "Good-bye, sir. I hope you will enjoy your travels."

"And prolong them indefinitely? Ah, you offer a flag of truce? I warned you I should not respect it. You know my motto, *'Nemo me impune lacessit!'*[17] Thank you for this lovely peace-offering. Since you are willing to negotiate, run and open the gate for me. I may never pass through it again except as a ghost."

She placed her basket on the steps and ran down the avenue, while he paused to say something to his mother. Edna knew that he expected to be absent, possibly, several years. While she regretted the pain which his departure gave her benefactress, she could not avoid rejoicing at the relief she promised herself during his sojourn in foreign lands.

Slowly he rode along the venerable aisle of elms that had overarched his childish head in the sunny morning of a quickly clouded life. As he reached the gate, which Edna held open, he dismounted.

"Edna, if you are as truthful in all matters as you have proved in your dislikes, I may safely entrust this key to your keeping."

Edna shook her head, wondering if she had heard him aright.

"It belongs to that marble temple in my sitting-room, and opens a vault that contains my will and a box of papers, and – some other things that I value. There is no possibility of entering it, except with this key, and no one but myself knows the contents. I wish to leave the key with you, on two conditions: first, that you

---

[17] "No one attacks me with impunity." Remember that now.

never mention it to anyone – not even my mother, or allow her to suspect that you have it."

"Mr. Murray —"

"Secondly," he said over her, "you must solemnly promise me you will not open the tomb or temple unless I fail to return at the close of four years. This is the tenth of December. Four years from today, if I am not here, and *if you have good reason to consider me dead*, take this key (which I wish you to wear about your person) to my mother, inform her of this conversation, and then open the vault. Can you resist the temptation to look into it? Think well before you answer."

He had disengaged the golden key from his watch-chain and held it in his hand.

Edna shrank from it. "I should not like to take charge of it, Mr. Murray. You can certainly trust your own mother sooner than an utter stranger like myself."

He frowned and muttered an oath. Then he exclaimed, "I tell you, I do not choose to leave it in any hands but yours. Will you promise or will you not?"

The dreary wretchedness of his countenance awed and pained the girl. After a moment's silence, and a short struggle with her heart, she extended her hand, saying with reluctance, "Give me the key. I will not betray your trust."

"Do you promise me solemnly that you will never open that vault, except in accordance with my directions? Weigh the promise well before you give it."

"Yes, sir; I promise most solemnly."

He laid the key in her palm, then pointed back to where Mrs. Murray sat on the steps, her face in her hands. "My mother loves you. Try to make her happy while I am away; and if you succeed, you will be the first person to whom I have ever been indebted. I have left directions concerning my books and the various articles in my rooms. Feel no hesitation in examining any that may interest you, and see that the dust does not ruin them. Good-bye, child; take care of my mother."

He held out his hand, and she gave him hers for an instant only. He mounted, lifted his cap, and rode away.

Closing the ponderous gate, Edna leaned her face against the iron bars and watched the lessening form. Gradually trees intervened. Then at a bend in the road he wheeled his horse as if to return, and she stiffened, shrinking from a further interview with him. For some moments he remained, looking back, but, after a long moment, he at last cantered on, and was gone.

With a sigh of indescribable relief, she retraced her steps to the house. As she approached the spot where Mrs. Murray still sat, her face hidden in her handkerchief, the touch of the little key, tightly folded in her palm, brought a painful tinge of shame to her cheeks. It seemed in her eyes an insult to her benefactress that the guardianship of the papers should have been withheld from her.

Edna would have stolen away to her own room to hide the key; but Mrs. Murray called her. As she sat down beside her, the miserable mother threw her arms around the orphan, and resting her cheek on her head, wept bitterly. Timidly, but very tenderly, Edna strove to comfort her, caressing the hands that were clasped in almost despairing anguish.

"Dear Mrs. Murray, do not grieve so deeply; he may come back much earlier than you expect. He will get tired of traveling, and come back to his own beautiful home, and to you, who love him so devotedly."

"No, no! He will stay away as long as possible," Mrs. Murray sobbed. "It is not beautiful to him. He hates his home and forgets me! My loneliness, my anxiety is nothing in comparison to his morbid love of change. I shall never see him again."

"But he loves you very much, and that will bring him to you."

"Why do you think so?"

"He pointed to you a few moments ago, and his face was full of wretchedness when he told me, 'Make my mother happy while I am gone, and you will be the first person to whom I have ever been indebted.' Do not weep so, dear Mrs. Murray. God can preserve him as well on sea as here at home."

"Oh, but he will not pray for himself!" sobbed the mother.

"Then you must pray all the more for him; and go where he will, he cannot get beyond God's sight, or out of His merciful hands. You know Christ said, 'Whatsoever you ask in my name, I will do it[18];' and if the Canaanite woman's daughter was saved not by her own prayers but by her mother's faith, why should not God save your son if you pray and believe?"

Mrs. Murray clasped Edna close to her heart and kissed her. "You are my only comfort! If I had your faith I should not be so unhappy. My dear child, promise me one thing, that every time you pray you will remember my son, and ask God to preserve him in his wanderings, and bring him safely back to his mother. I know you do not like him, but for my sake will you not do this?"

"My prayers are not worth much, but I will always remember to pray for him. Mrs. Murray, while he is away, suppose you have family prayer, and let all the household join in praying for the absent master. I think it would be such a blessing and comfort to you. Grandpa always had prayer night and morning, and it made every day seem almost as holy as Sunday."

Mrs. Murray was silent a little while. She answered hesitatingly, "But, my dear, I should not know how to offer up prayers before the family. I can pray for myself, but I should not like to pray aloud."

There was a second pause, and finally she said, "Edna, would you be willing to conduct prayers for me?"

"It is your house, and God expects the head of every family to set an example. Even the pagans offered sacrifices every day for the good of the household, and you know the Jews have morning and evening prayer services; so it seems to me family prayer is such a beautiful offering on the altar of the hearthstone. If you do not wish to pray yourself, you could read a prayer. There is a book called *Family Prayer*, with selections for every day in the week. I saw a copy at the parsonage, and I can get one like it at the bookstore if you wish."

"That will suit my purpose much better than trying to compose them myself. You must get the book for me. But, Edna, don't go to school today, stay at home with me; I am so lonely and low-spirited. I will tell Mr. Hammond that I could not spare you. Besides, I want you to help me arrange some valuable relics belonging to my son. Now that I think of it, he told me he wished you to use any of his books or manuscripts that you might like to examine. This is a great honor, child, for he has refused many

[18] John 14:13

80

grown people admission to his rooms. Come with me. I want to lock up his curiosities."

They went through the rotunda and into the rooms together; and Mrs. Murray busied herself in carefully removing the cameos, antique vases, and goblets from the tables, and placing them in the drawers. As she crossed the room, tears fell on the costly trifles. Finally she approached the beautiful miniature temple and stooped to look at its lock. She selected the smallest key on the bunch, that contained a dozen, and attempted to fit it in the small opening, but it was too large. She tried her watch-key, but without success, and a look of chagrin crossed her sad, tear-stained face.

"St. Elmo has forgotten to leave the key with me."

Edna's face grew scarlet. Stooping to pick up a heavy cornelian seal that had fallen on the carpet, she said hastily, "What is that marble temple intended to hold?"

"I have no idea; it is one of my son's *outré* fancies. I presume he uses it as a private desk for his papers."

"Does he leave the key with you when he goes from home?"

"This is the first time he has left home for more than a few weeks since he brought this gem from the East. I must write to him about the key before he sails. He has it on his watch-chain."

An intense curiosity took possession of Edna as she looked wonderingly at the shining facade of the exquisite Taj Mahal. Only a promise stood between her and its contents, and the hand holding the key trembled.

Escaping to her own room, she proceeded to secrete the troublesome key. Not only was it her duty to pray for the wanderer, but she also had to keep always about her a souvenir of the man whom she detested and was yet forced to remember continually. It was grossly unfair.

On the following day, when she went to her usual morning recitation, and gave the reason for her absence, Mr. Hammond's face sagged, and a look of keen sorrow settled on it.

"Gone again! And so soon! So far, far away from all good influences!"

He put down the Latin grammar and walked to the window, where he stood for some time. When he returned to his armchair

81

Edna saw that his eyes were red-rimmed, as if he were on the verge of weeping.

"Mr. Hammond! You look grieved." Edna caught his hand in hers. "Did he not stop to tell you good-bye?"

"No, my dear, he never comes to the parsonage now. When he was a boy, I taught him here in this room, as I now teach you. But for about twelve years he has not crossed my threshold, and yet I never sleep until I have prayed for him."

"Oh, I am so glad to hear that! Now I know he will be saved."

The minister shook his gray head, and a tear flashed from his mild blue eyes. "A man's repentance and faith cannot be offered by proxy to God. So long as St. Elmo Murray persists in insulting his Maker, I shudder for his final end. He has the finest intellect I have ever met among living men; but it is unsanctified. In his youth he promised to prove an ornament to Christianity; now he is a curse to the world and a dreary burden to himself."

"What changed him so sadly?"

"Some melancholy circumstances that occurred early in his life. Edna, he planned and built that beautiful church where you come on Sabbath to hear me preach, and about the time it was finished he went off to college. When he returned, he avoided me, and has never yet been inside of the costly church which his taste and his money constructed. Still, while I live, I shall not cease to pray for him, hoping that in God's good time he will return to the pure faith of his boyhood."

"Mr. Hammond, is he not a very wicked man?"

"He had originally the noblest heart I ever knew, and was as tender in his sympathies as a woman, while he was almost reckless in his charity. But in his present irreligious state I hear that he has grown bitter and illiberal. Yet, however repulsive his manner may be, I cannot believe that his nature is utterly perverted. He is dissipated but not unprincipled. Let him rest, my child, in the hands of his God, who alone can judge him. We can but pray and hope. Go on with your lesson."

The recitation was resumed; but Edna was well aware that for the first time her teacher was inattentive, and the heavy sighs that passed his lips almost unconsciously told her how sorely he was distressed by the erratic course of his former pupil. Her heart ached for her dear friend.

When she rose to go home, she asked the name of the author of the *Family Prayers* which she wished to purchase for Mrs. Murray. The pastor's face flushed with pleasure as he heard of her scheme.

"My dear child, be circumspect, be prudent; above all things, be consistent. Search your own heart; try to make your life an exposition of your faith; let profession and practice go hand in hand; ask God's special guidance in the difficult position in which you are placed, and your influence for good in Mrs. Murray's family may be beyond all computation."

Laying his hands on her head, he continued tremulously, "O my God! If it be thy will, make her the instrument of rescuing St. Elmo, ere it be indeed too late. Help me to teach her aright; and let her pure life atone for all the wrongs that have well-nigh wrought eternal ruin."

Turning quickly away, he left the room before she could catch a glimpse of his countenance.

Edna, watching him leave, clutched the prayer book to her chest, shaken by Mr. Hammond fervent prayer, and deeply touched by the venerable old man's love for Mr. Murray.

As she left for home, she lingered outside the church across the street from the parsonage. Ever since she'd healed from the terrible train accident, this had become her home church, where she sang in the choir every Sunday and had started to stand in for the regular organist now and then. She'd spent many an hour sheltered in its holy warmth. To know that St. Elmo had caused it to be built seemed almost incredible. Edna gazed across the dreary gulf that stood between what he'd been as a boy and the man he'd grown into, and wondered what had happened to cause him to fall so far in so short a time.

Standing in the sight of that dear church that was her second home, Edna vowed to herself, "For your sake, dear Mr. Hammond, I will do my best to help in what you have asked – try and be worthy of the hope you have placed in me."

The strong and lasting affection that sprang up between Mr. Hammond and Edna – the sense of dependence on each other's society – rarely occurs among persons in whose ages so great a disparity exists. Spring and autumn have no affinities – age has little sympathy for the rose-hued dreams of young people; and youth shrinks from the austere companionship of those who, with snowy locks gilded by the fading rays of a setting sun, journey to the valley of the shadow of death.

Preferring Mr. Hammond's society to that of the strangers who visited Mrs. Murray, Edna spent half of her time at the quiet parsonage, and the remainder with her books and music. As a result, her progress was almost unprecedentedly rapid. Mrs. Murray watched the expansion of her mind and the development of her beauty with pride and pleasure, which, had she analyzed them, would have told her how dear and necessary to her happiness the orphan had become.

As Edna's reasoning powers strengthened, Mr. Hammond led her gradually to the contemplation of some of the gravest problems that have from time unknown perplexed and maddened humanity, plunging one half into blind, bigoted traditionalism, and scourging the other into the somber, starless wastes of Pyrrhonism. Knowing full well that of every earnest soul and honest, profound thinker these metaphysical questions would sooner or later demand audience, he placed her in the philosophic arena, cheered her on, handed her from time to time the assistance she needed, and then, when satisfied that the intellectual work had properly trained her, he invited her – to the great Greek games of speculation, where the lordly intellects of the nineteenth century gather to test their skills in logic, and bear off the crown of laurel on the point of a syllogism or the wings of a hypothesis.

Thus immersed in study, weeks, months, and years glided by, bearing Edna's young life swiftly across the flowery meads of girlhood, nearer and nearer to the portals of that mystic temple of womanhood, on whose fair shrine was to be offered a heart either consumed by the baleful fires of Baal, or consecrated by the divine presence of God, promised through Messiah.

CHAPTER IX
PEACE BE WITH THEE

During the first year of Mr. Murray's absence his brief letters to his mother were written at long intervals. In the second, they were rarer and briefer still; but toward the close of the third he wrote more frequently and announced his intention of revisiting Egypt before his return to the land of his birth. Although no allusion was ever made to Edna, Mrs. Murray sometimes read aloud descriptions of beautiful scenery, written now among the scoriae of Mauna Loa or Mauna Kea, and now from the pinnacle of Mount Ophir, whence, through waving forests of nutmeg and clove, flashed the blue waters of the Indian Ocean, or the silver ripples of Malacca. On such occasions, the orphan listened eagerly, entranced by the tropical luxuriance and grandeur of his imagery, by his gorgeous word-painting, which to her charmed ears seemed scarcely inferior to the wonderful pen-portraits of Ruskin. Those letters seemed flecked with the purple and gold, the amber and rose, the opalescent and beryline tints, of which he spoke in telling the glories of Polynesian and Malaysian skies, and the matchless plant and floral splendors of their serene spicy dells.

For many days after the receipt of each, Mrs. Murray was graver and sadder, but the ghost that had disquieted Edna was thoroughly exorcised. Only when the cold touch of the golden key startled her was she conscious of a vague dread of some far-off but slowly approaching evil.

In the fourth year of her pupilage with Mr. Hammond, Edna was possessed by an unconquerable desire to read the Talmud. In order to penetrate the mysteries and seize the treasures hidden in that exhaustless mine of myths, legends, and symbolisms, she prevailed upon Mr. Hammond to teach her Hebrew and the rudiments of Chaldee. Very reluctantly he consented, and subsequently informed her that, as he had another pupil who was also commencing Hebrew, he would class them, and hear their recitations together.

This new student was Mr. Gordon Leigh, a lawyer in the town, and a gentleman of wealth and high social position. Although quite young, he gave promise of eminence in his profession, and was a great favorite of the minister, who pronounced him the most upright and exemplary young man of his acquaintance. Edna had seen him several times at Mrs. Murray's dinners. While she considered him exceedingly handsome, polite, and agreeable, she regarded him as a stranger, until the lessons at the parsonage brought them every two days around the little table in the study.

They began the language simultaneously. Edna, knowing the flattering estimation in which Mr. Leigh was held, could not resist the temptation to measure her intellect with his, and soon threatened to outrun him in the Talmud race. Piqued pride and a manly resolution to conquer spurred him on. The venerable instructor looked on and laughed at the generous emulation thus excited. Mr. Hammond saw an friendship daily strengthening between the rivals, and knew that in Gordon Leigh's magnanimous nature there was no element which could cause an objection to the companionship to which he had paved the way.

Four months after the commencement of the new study, Edna rose at daylight to complete some exercises, which she had neglected to write out on the previous evening. As soon as she concluded the task, she went downstairs to gather the flowers. It was the cloudless morning of her nineteenth birthday and as she stood clipping geraniums, jasmine, and verbena, memory flew back to the tender years in which the grizzled blacksmith had watched her career with such fond pride and loving words of encouragement. Memory painted the white-haired old man smoking on the porch that fronted Lookout, while from his lips, tremulous with a tender smile, seemed to float the last words he had spoken to her on that calm afternoon when, in the fiery light of a dying day, he was gathered to his forefathers.

"You will make me proud of you, my little Pearl, when you are smart enough to teach a school and take care of me, for I shall be too old to work by that time."

Now, after the lapse of years, when her educational course was almost finished, she recalled every word and look and gesture; even the thrill of horror that shook her limbs when she kissed the lips that death had sealed an hour before. Mournfully vivid was her recollection of her tenth birthday, for then he had bought her a blue ribbon for her hair, and a little china cup and saucer. Now tears sprang to her eyes as she murmured, "I have studied hard and the triumph is at hand, but I have nobody to be proud of me now! Ah, Grandpa! If you could only come back to me, your little Pearl! It is so desolate to be alone in this great world; so hard to have to know that nobody cares specially whether I live or die, whether I succeed or fail. I have only myself to live for; only my own heart and will to sustain me."

Through the fringy acacias that waved their long hair across the hothouse windows, the golden sunshine flickered over the graceful figure of the orphan – over her young face with its delicate cameo features, warm, healthful coloring, and brave, hopeful expression. Four years had developed the sad-eyed child into a lovely woman with a pure heart filled with humble piety, and a vigorous intellect accustomed to study; a woman ambitious of every honorable eminence within her grasp.

Edna had endeavored to remember what her Bible first taught her, and what moralists of all creeds, climes and ages, had reiterated – that human life was at best but "vanity and vexation of spirit,[19]" that "man is born to trouble as the sparks fly upward[20]" – yet as she stood on the razor-thin line that divides girlhood and womanhood, her future seemed to her as bewitching as the magnificent panorama upon which enraptured lotus-eaters gazed from the ancient acropolis of Cyrene.

As Edna turned to leave the hothouse, the ring of horse's hoofs on the rocky walk attracted her attention. A moment after, Mr. Leigh gave his horse to the gardener and came to meet her.

---

[19] Ecclesiastes 1:14
[20] Job 5:7

"Good morning, Miss Edna. As I am bearer of dispatches from my sister to Mrs. Murray" – here he patted his coat pocket – "I have invited myself to breakfast with you."

Edna smiled. "You are an earlier riser than I had supposed, Mr. Leigh, from your lamentations over your exercises."

"I do not deny that I love my morning nap, and generally indulge myself; for, like old Sir James Herring, 'I can easily make up my mind to rise early, but I cannot make up my body.[21]' Do you know that we are both to have a holiday today?"

Edna stopped, pleasantly surprised. "No, sir; upon what score?"

"It happens to be my birthday as well as yours! As my sister, Mrs. Inge, gives a party tonight in honor of the event, I have come to insist that you shall enjoy the same reprieve that I promise myself. Mrs. Inge asked me to ensure your presence at her party."

Edna blushed slightly. "Thank you; but I never go out to parties."

"Ah! Bad precedents must not guide you any longer," he said warmly. "If you persist in staying at home, I shall not enjoy the evening, for in every dance I shall fancy my dancing partner your ghost, with an exercise in one hand and a Hebrew grammar in the other. By the way! Mr. Hammond told me to say that he would not expect you today, but would meet you tonight at Mrs. Inge's. You need not trouble yourself to decline, for I shall arrange matters with Mrs. Murray. In honor of my birthday, will you not give me a sprig of something sweet from your basket?"

"I should be happy to, my dear friend."

They sat down on the steps of the dining-room, and Edna selected some delicate oxalis cups and nutmeg geranium leaves. These she neatly tied up and handed to her companion.

He daintily sniffed them and fastened them in the buttonhole of his coat. Then Edna watched, curious, as he drew a small box from his pocket and showed it to her. "I noticed last week, when Mr. Hammond was explaining the tenets of the Basilidian gnostics, you expressed some curiosity concerning their amulets

---

[21] Augusta originally attributed this to Sydney Smith, but though I cannot find a definitive source for this line, the miscellany books of the 1850s, which contained amusing quotes, bits of poetry, historical stories, serialized novels, etc., attributed this quote to one "old Sir James Herring." Look, guys, if I'm going to look 'em up, I'm going to tell you where they came from!

and mythical stones. Now, many years ago, while an uncle of mine was missionary in Arabia, he saved the life of a son of a wealthy sheik. In token of his gratitude, he received a curious ring, which tradition said once belonged to a caliph, and had been found near the ruins of Persepolis. The ring was bequeathed to me, and is probably the best authenticated antique in this country. Presto! We are in Baghdad in the blessed reign –

'... in the golden prime
Of good Haroun Alraschid!'[22]

GOOD HARUN AL-RASHID IN HIS GOLDEN PRIME.

"I am not versed in Kufic scripts, for you know that would mean more study than I could possibly bear, but the characters engraved on this ring say, in Kufic, 'Peace be with thee,' which I believe has been, from time immemorial, the national greeting of the Arabs."

Gordon unwound the cotton that enveloped the gem and held it before Edna's astonished eyes.

A broad band of dusky, tarnished gold was surmounted by a large crescent-shaped emerald, set with beautiful pearls. Underneath the Arabic inscription was engraved a ram's head, bearing on one horn a small crescent, on the other a star.

As Edna bent forward to examine it Mr. Leigh continued, "I do not quite comprehend the symbolism of the ram's head and the star; the crescent is clear enough."

"I think I can guess the meaning." Edna's eyes kindled.

---

[22] "Recollections of the Arabian Nights" – Lord Alfred Tennyson. The caliph's name is Harun al-Rashid.

"Tell me your conjecture; my own does not satisfy me, as the Arabic love of mutton is the only solution at which I have arrived."

"Oh, Mr. Leigh! Look at it and think a moment."

He pondered a moment, and answered, gravely, "Well, I have looked at it and thought a great deal, and I tell you mutton-broth sherbet is the only idea suggested to my mind. You need not look so shocked, for, when cooled with the snows of Caucasus, I am told it makes a beverage fit for Greek gods."

She hesitated. The color deepened on her cheek as she repeated, in a low voice, "The ram's head might refer to the guardian spirit of the Persians, as their kings would wear the head of a ram, instead of a crown, when they rode into battle. It can also be considered a manifestation of the Sun God and resurrection. The crescent, of course, represents the moon and the moon gods, the lamp of heaven, and is a potent symbol of Islam. The star may be the star of the goddess Ishtar, but both crescent and star are often found together in the symbols of the great Arabic nations. 'Peace be with thee," said Islam. I am not as familiar with the tenants of their religion, but I hope I have not erred egregiously."

Mr. Leigh bowed. "I repeat 'Peace be with thee,' during the new year on which we are both entering. As you have at least attempted to read the riddle, let me beg that you will do me the honor to accept and wear this ring in memory of our friendship and our student life."

He took her hand to place the ring on her finger.

Edna, blushing again, closed her hand before he could do so, stammering, "Thank you, Mr. Leigh, I appreciate the honor, but indeed you must excuse me. Please, I cannot accept the ring."

"Why not, Miss Edna?"

"In the first place, because it is very valuable and beautiful, and I am not willing to deprive you of it. In the second, I do not think it proper to accept presents from – anyone but relatives or dear friends."

"I thought we were dear friends. Why can we not be such?"

At this moment Mrs. Murray came into the dining-room. As she looked at the two sitting there in the early sunshine, with the basket of flowers between them, she marked the heightened color and embarrassed expression on Edna's face, and the eager pleading written Gordon Leigh's, so full of manly beauty, so frank and bright. A possible destiny for both flashed before her. Pleased surprise warmed her own countenance as she hurried forward.

"Good-morning, Gordon. I am very glad to see you. How is Clara?"

"Quite well, thank you, and entirely absorbed in preparations for her party, as you will infer from this note, which she charged me to deliver in person, and for which I here pray your most favorable consideration." He pulled it from his pocket and handed it to her.

As Mrs. Murray glanced over the note, Edna turned to leave the room; but Mr. Leigh exclaimed, "Edna, do not go just yet. I wish Mrs. Murray to decide a matter for me."

"Well, Gordon, what is it?"

"First, do you grant my sister's petition?"

"Certainly. I will bring Edna with me tonight, unless she prefers staying at home with her books. You know I let her do pretty much as she pleases."

"Now then, for my little quarrel! Here is a curious old ring, which she will appreciate more highly than anyone else whom I happen to know, and I want her to accept it as a birthday memento from me, but she refused to wear it. Can you not come to my assistance, my dear Mrs. Murray?"

She took the ring, examined it. After a pause she said, "I think, Gordon, that she did exactly right." Gordon deflated slightly. "I also think that now, with my approval and advice, she need not hesitate to wear it henceforth, as a token of your friendship. Edna, hold out your hand, my dear."

The ring was slipped on Edna's slender finger. As she released her hand, Mrs. Murray bent down and kissed her forehead.

"Nineteen today! My child, I can scarcely believe it. And you – Gordon? May I ask how old you are?"

"Twenty-four – I grieve to say! You need not tell me – "

The conversation was interrupted by the ringing of the breakfast bell.

Edna felt puzzled and annoyed at breakfast every time she looked down at the ring. She thought that instead of "Peace be with thee," the Kufic characters must surely mean, "Disquiet seize thee!" for they had shivered the beautiful calm of her girlish nature, and thrust into her mind ideas unknown until that day.

Mr. Leigh took his departure after breakfast. Going to her own room, she opened her books, but ere she could fix her wandering thoughts Mrs. Murray entered.

"Edna, I came to speak to you about your dress for tonight."

"Please do not say that you wish me to go, my dear Mrs. Murray, for I dread the very thought."

"But I must tell you that I insist upon your conforming to the usages of good society. Mrs. Inge belongs to one of the very first families in the state; at her house you will meet the best people. You could not possibly make your debut under more favorable circumstances. Besides, it is very unnatural that a young girl should not enjoy parties and the society of gay young people. You are very unnecessarily making a recluse of yourself, and I shall not permit you to refuse such an invitation as Mrs. Inge has sent. It would be rude in the extreme."

Edna lay down her pen. "Dear Mrs. Murray, you speak of my debut, as if, like other girls, I had nothing else to do but fit myself for society. These people care nothing for me, and I am as little interested in them. I have no desire to move for a short time in a circle from which my work in life must soon separate me."

"Why, child! To what work do you allude?"

"The support which I must make by teaching. In a few months I hope to be able to earn all I need, and then – "

Mrs. Murray made an imperious gesture. "Then it will be quite time enough to determine what necessity demands. In the meanwhile, as long as you are in my house, you must allow me to judge what is proper for you. Clara Inge is my friend, and I cannot allow you to be rude to her. I have sent the carriage to town for Miss O'Riley, my mantua-maker, and Hagar will make the skirt of your dress. Come into my room and let her take the measure."

Edna's fingers convulsively clutched Mrs. Murray's. "Thank you for your kind thoughtfulness, but indeed I do not want to go. Please let me stay at home. You can frame some polite excuse. Mrs. Inge cares not whether I go or stay. I will write my regrets and – "

Mrs. Murray's brow clouded, and her lips contracted, as was their habit, when anything displeased her. "Don't be childish, Edna; I care whether you go or stay. That fact should weigh with you much more than Mrs. Inge's wishes, for you are quite right in supposing that it is a matter of indifference to her. Do not keep Hagar waiting."

Edna meekly followed her to the room where Hagar was at work. It was the first time the orphan had been invited to a large party, and she shrank from meeting people whose standard of gentility was confined to high birth and handsome fortunes. Mrs. Inge came frequently to Le Bocage, but Edna's acquaintance with her was comparatively slight.

But, more to the point, she dreaded seeing Mr. Leigh again so soon, for she felt that an undefinable barrier had suddenly risen between them; the frank, fearless freedom of the old friendship at the parsonage table had vanished. She began to wish that she had never studied Hebrew, that she had never heard of Basilides, and that the sheik's ring was back among the ruins of Persepolis.

Mrs. Murray saw her discomposure, but chose to take no notice of it, and superintended her toilette that night with almost as much interest as if Edna had been her own daughter.

During the drive to the party she talked on indifferent subjects, and as they went up to the dressing-room, Mrs. Murray was pleased to see that her protégée showed no agitation. They arrived rather late, so the company had assembled, and the rooms were quite full as Mrs. Murray entered.

Mrs. Inge met them at the threshold. Mr. Leigh, who seemed on the watch, came forward at the same instant, and offered Edna his arm.

"Ah, Mrs. Murray! I had almost abandoned the hope of seeing you. Miss Edna, the set is just forming, and we must celebrate our birthday by having the first dance together."

Edna heartily wished that she would not blush so often. "Excuse me, but –"

"Excuse you, indeed! You presume upon my well-known good nature and generosity, but this evening I am privileged to be selfish."

As Mr. Leigh drew her into the middle of the room, she noticed that he wore the flowers she had given him in the morning. This, in conjunction with the curious scrutiny from all the eyes around the room, brought an even greater surge of color to her cheeks.

The dance commenced, and from one corner of the room Mr. Hammond looked eagerly at his two pupils, contrasting them with the gay groups that filled the brilliant apartment.

Edna's slender, graceful figure was robed in white Swiss muslin, with a bertha of rich lace. Rose-colored ribbons formed the sash and floated from her shoulders. Her beautiful glossy hair was simply coiled in a large roll at the back of the head and fastened with an ivory comb. Scrutinizing the face lifted toward Mr. Leigh's, while he talked to her, the pastor thought he had never seen a countenance half so eloquent and lovely. Turning his gaze upon her partner, he was compelled to confess that Gordon Leigh was the handsomest man in the room. No acute observer could look at the two and fail to discover that the blacksmith's granddaughter was far superior to the pampered brother of the aristocratic Mrs. Inge.

He was so much interested in watching the couple that he did not observe Mrs. Murray's approach until she sat down beside him and whispered, "Are they not a handsome couple?"

"Gordon and Edna?"

"Yes."

"Indeed, they are! I think that child's face is the most fascinating I ever looked at. There is such a rare combination of intelligence, holiness, and serenity in her countenance; such a calm light shining in her splendid eyes; such a tender look far down in their soft depths."

"Child? Why, she is nineteen today."

"No matter, Ellen; to me she will always seem a gentle, clinging child. I look at her often when she is intent on her studies, and wonder how long her pure heart will reject the vanities that engross most women; how long mere abstract study will continue to charm her; and I tremble when I think of the future to which I know she is looking so eagerly. Now, her emotional nature sleeps, her heart is at rest – she is all intellect at present – giving her brain no relaxation. Ah, if it could always be so. But it will not! There will come a time, I fear, when her fine mind and warm heart will be arrayed against each other, will battle desperately."

"Gordon seems to admire her very much," said Mrs. Murray.

Mr. Hammond sighed, and a shadow crept over his placid features, as he answered, "Do you wonder at it, Ellen? Can anyone know the child well, and fail to love her?"

"If he could only forget her obscure birth – if he could only consent to marry her – what a splendid match it would be for her?"

"Ellen! Ellen Murray! I am surprised at you!" said the minister, turning to her. "Let me beg of you for her sake, for yours, for all parties concerned, not to raise your little finger in this matter; not to utter one word to Edna that might arouse her suspicions; not to hint to Gordon that you dream such an alliance possible; for there is more at stake than you imagine – "

He was unable to conclude the sentence, for the dance had ended. As soon as Edna caught a glimpse of the beloved countenance of her teacher, she slipped her fingers from Mr. Leigh's arm and hastened to the pastor's side, taking his hand between both hers.

"O, sir! I am glad to see you," she cried with evident relief. "I have looked around so often; hoping to catch sight of you. Mrs. Murray, I heard Mrs. Inge asking for you."

When the lady walked away, Edna glided into the seat next to the minister, and continued in a low voice, "I want to talk to you about a change in some of my studies."

"Wait till tomorrow, my dear. I came here tonight only for a few moments to gratify Gordon, and now I must slip away."

"But, sir, I only want to say, that as you objected at the outset to my studying Hebrew, I will not waste any more time on it just now, but take it up again after a while, when I have plenty of leisure. Don't you think that would be the best plan?"

"My child," Mr. Hammond said, taken aback. "Are you tired of Hebrew?"

"No, sir; on the contrary, it possesses a singular fascination for me; but I think, if you are willing, I shall discontinue it – at least, for the present. I shall take care to forget nothing that I have already learned."

"You have some special reason for this change, I presume?"

She lowered her eyes. "Yes, sir, I have."

Mr. Hammond nodded sagely. "Very well, my dear, do as you like. Good-night."

"I wish I could go now with you."

"Why? I thought you appeared to enjoy your dance very much. Edna, look at me."

She hesitated – then obeyed him. Tears glistened on her long lashes.

Very quietly the old man drew her arm through his, and led her out on the dim veranda, where only an occasional couple promenaded.

"Something troubles you, Edna. Will you confide in me?"

"I feel as if I were occupying a false position here, and yet I do not see how I can extricate myself without displeasing Mrs. Murray, whom I cannot bear to offend – she is so very kind and generous."

"Explain yourself, my dear."

"You know that I have not a cent in the world except what Mrs. Murray gives me. I shall have to make my bread by my own work just as soon as you think me competent to teach. Despite this, she thinks I ought to visit and associate as she does with these people, who tolerate me now, simply because they know that while I am under her roof, she will exact it of them."

Edna paused to gather herself. "Tonight, during the dance, I heard two of her fashionable friends sneering at me; ridiculing her for 'attempting to smuggle that spoiled creature of unknown parentage and low origin into really first circles.' Other things were said which I cannot repeat, that showed me plainly how I am regarded here, and I will not remain in a position which subjects me to such remarks. Mrs. Murray thought it best for me to come; but it was a mistaken kindness. I thought so before I came – I was right in my forebodings."

"Can you not tell me all that was said?"

"I shrink, sir, from repeating it, even to you."

"Did Mr. Leigh hear it?"

"I hope not."

Mr. Hammond's fingers gently clasped hers. "My dear child, I am very much pained to learn that you have been so cruelly wounded; but do not let your mind dwell upon those weak, heartless people. Try to fix your thoughts on nobler themes, and waste no reflection on the idle words of those poor gilded moths of fashion and folly. Remember Virgil's admonition to Dante: 'Speak not of them, but look, and pass them by.'"[23]

"I do not care particularly what they think of me," Edna said, leaning her head against his arm. "But I am anxious to avoid hearing their hurtful comments upon me, and therefore I am determined to keep as much out of sight as possible. To me, poverty is no stigma. My grandfather was very poor, but he was noble and honest, and as courteous as a nobleman; and I honor his dear, dear memory as tenderly as if he had been reared in a palace. I am not ashamed of my parentage, for my father was as honest and industrious as he was poor, and my mother was as gentle and good as she was beautiful."

There was no faltering in the sweet voice, and no bitterness poisoning it. Mr. Hammond could not see her face, as she had bowed her head; but her tone said all, and he was satisfied.

"I am glad, my dear little Edna, that you look at the truth so bravely. If you have any difficulty in convincing Mrs. Murray of the correctness of your views, let me know, and I will speak to her on the subject. Good night! May God watch over and bless you."

When the orphan reentered the parlor, Mrs. Inge presented her to several gentlemen who had requested an introduction. Though Edna's heart was heavy and her cheeks burned, she exerted herself, dancing and talking constantly until Mrs. Murray announced herself ready to depart.

Joyfully Edna ran upstairs for her wrappings, bade adieu to her hostess, who complimented her on the sensation her beauty had created, and felt relieved when the carriage door closed and she found herself alone with her benefactress.

"Well, Edna, notwithstanding your repugnance to going, you acquitted yourself admirably, and seemed to have a delightful time."

[23] Inferno, Canto 3, *Divine Comedy* -- Dante

97

"I thank you, ma'am, for doing all in your power to make the evening agreeable to me. I think your kind desire to see me enjoy the party made me happier than everything else."

Edna drew Mrs. Murray's hand to her lips. In the darkness, her benefactress little dreamed that at that instant, tears were rolling over Edna's flushed face, while the words of the conversation which she had overheard rang mockingly in her ears.

"Mrs. Murray and even Mr. Hammond are scheming to make a match between her and Gordon Leigh. Studying Hebrew indeed! Much Hebrew she will learn! Her eyes are set on Gordon's fortune, and Mrs. Murray is silly enough to think he will step into the trap. She will have to bait it with something better than Hebrew and pretty eyes, or she will miss her game. Gordon will make a fool of her, I dare say, for, like all other young men, he can be flattered into paying her some little attention at first. I am surprised that Mrs. Inge even allowed the girl to show her face here among the likes of us."

Such was Edna's initiation into the charmed circle of fashionable society.

CHAPTER X
A SPIDER'S WEB

When Mr. Hammond mentioned Edna's determination to discontinue Hebrew, Mr. Leigh expressed no surprise and asked no explanation, but he bit his lip and beat a hurried tattoo with the heel of his boot on the stony hearth. As he studiously avoided all allusion to her, Mr. Hammond felt assured that the conversation which she had overheard must also have reached the ears of her partner and supplied him with a satisfactory reason for her change of purpose.

For several weeks Edna saw nothing of her former schoolmate, and she fixed her thoughts more firmly than ever on her studies, attempting to make the painful recollection of the birthday fete fade from her mind.

One morning, as Edna was preparing to walk home from the parsonage, Mr. Leigh joined her. "May I have your kind permission to attend you home?" he asked.

The sound of his voice, the touch of his hand, brought back all the embarrassment and constraint of her birthday, and her face flushed with confusion.

After a few commonplace remarks as they walked, he asked, "When is Mr. Murray coming home?"

"I have no idea. Even his mother is ignorant of his plans."

"How long has he been absent?"

"Four years today."

"Indeed! So long? Where is he?"

"I believe his last letter was written at Edfu, in Egypt, where he was seeing the Temple of Horus. He said nothing about returning."

"What do you think of his singular character?"

"I know almost nothing about him," Edna stammered. "I was too young when I last saw him to form an estimate of him."

"Do you not correspond?"

Edna looked up with astonishment and could not avoid smiling at the inquiry. "Certainly not."

A short silence followed, and then Mr. Leigh said, "Do you not frequently ride on horseback?"

"Yes, sir."

"Will you permit me to accompany you tomorrow afternoon?"

"I have promised to make a visit with Mr. Hammond."

"Tomorrow morning then, before breakfast?"

She hesitated – the blush deepened. After a brief struggle, she said hurriedly, "Please excuse me, Mr. Leigh; I prefer to ride alone."

He bowed, and was silent for a minute, but she saw a smile lurking about the corners of his handsome mouth, threatening to run riot over his features.

"By the by, Miss Edna, I am coming tonight to ask your assistance in a Chaldee quandary. For several days I have been engaged in a controversy with Mr. Hammond on the old battlefield of ethnology. In order to establish my position of diversity of origin, I have been comparing the Septuagint with some passages from the Talmud. I heard you say that there was a Rabbinical Targum in the library at Le Bocage. I must beg you to examine it for me and ascertain whether it contains any comments on the first chapter of Genesis. Mr. Hammond tells me that in some of those early Targums was the declaration that 'God originally created men red, white and black[24].' I was charitable enough to say that he must have smoked an extra cigar and dreamed the sentence I am so anxious to authenticate. Will you help me by searching for the passage?"

---

[24] Augusta pulled this idea from a book written by a southern slaveholder who states that sometimes the holy texts are wrong (because he doesn't like the idea that God created all races), there is no evidence for the equality of all races (because he rejects that evidence), and the oft-mistaken theory of the Declaration of Independence is mistaken (because profiting off slavery is more important than any moral imperative). I will not cite this man or his text. Bury him in the ash-heap of history.

"Certainly, Mr. Leigh, with great pleasure. Though perhaps you would prefer to take the book and look through it yourself? My knowledge of Chaldee is very limited."

"Pardon me! My mental laziness vetoes the bare suggestion. I study by proxy whenever I can, for laziness is the only hereditary taint in the Leigh blood."

"I shall enter into the search with great eagerness."

"Thank you. Do you take the unity or diversity side of the discussion?"

Her laugh rang out through the forest that bordered the road. "Oh, Mr. Leigh!" Then she became serious. "I don't need to read Chaldee to know that all humans are equal."

Mr. Leigh began with a justification for "human diversity," but Edna had often heard former slaveowners using these selfsame arguments in their endless justifications for slavery. Fortunately, Edna saw her goal in sight. "I must stop here, Mr. Leigh, at Mrs. Carter's, for I am on an errand for Mrs. Murray. Good morning, sir. I will seek out the passage you require. That should settle the argument for you." *In Mr. Hammond's favor,* she thought.

"How have I offended you, Miss Edna?" He took her hand and detained her.

Edna felt the blush rise in her cheeks. "I am not offended, Mr. Leigh," she said, drawing back, though in truth his views on humanity also added to her discomfort regarding him.

"Why do you dismiss me in such a cold, unfriendly way?" His voice trembled – only very slightly, but she heard it.

"If I sometimes appear rude, pardon my unfortunate manner. Believe me when I say that it results from no unfriendliness."

"You will be at home this evening?" His blue eyes gazed at her with unusual intensity, as if drinking in her face.

Edna swallowed. "Yes, sir, unless something very unusual occurs."

They parted. During the rest of her walk, Edna could think of nothing but the revelation written in Gordon Leigh's eyes; that startling truth that opened a new vista in life. In his eyes she saw that she was no longer a child. He saw her as a woman, and she realized that she now reigned over the generous heart of one of the highest members of fine society.

101

Mr. Leigh loved her.

Despite herself, Edna shook her head. She trusted his honor implicitly. Yet the discovery of his affection brought regret. They had been such good friends, but to have him feel this way toward her made her feel that in future he would prove a source of endless disquiet. Hitherto she had enjoyed his society, henceforth she felt that she must shun it.

She endeavored to banish the recollection of that strange expression in his generally laughing eyes, and bent over the Targum, hoping to cheat her thoughts into other channels; but his face would not "down at her bidding." As the day drew near its close and the room grew darker, she grew nervous and restless.

At last Edna left the Targum to go downstairs. The chandelier had been lighted, and Mrs. Murray was standing at the window of the sitting-room, watching for the return of a servant whom she had sent to the post-office.

Edna joined her at the window. "I believe Mr. Leigh is coming here to tea; he told me so this morning."

"Where did you see him?"

"He walked with me as far as Mrs. Carter's gate, and asked me to look up a reference which he thought I might find in one of Mr. Murray's books."

Mrs. Murray smiled. "Do you intend to receive him in that calico dress?"

"Why not?" Edna asked, looking down at it. "I am sure it is very neat; it is perfectly new and fits me well."

"And is very suitable to wear to the parsonage, but not quite appropriate when Gordon Leigh takes tea here. You will oblige me by changing your dress and rearranging your hair, which is twisted too loosely."

When Edna re-entered the room a half-hour later, she found Mrs. Murray leaning against the mantelpiece, with an open letter in her hand and dreary disappointment on her face.

"I hope you have no unpleasant tidings from Mr. Murray. May I ask why you seem so much depressed?"

The mother's features twitched painfully as she returned the letter to its envelope. "My son's letter is dated Philoe, just two months ago. He says he intended starting next day to the interior of Persia. He says, too, that he did not expect to remain away so long, but finds that he will probably be in Central Asia for another year. The only comforting thing in the letter is the assurance that he weighs more and is in better health than when he left home."

The ringing of the doorbell announced Mr. Leigh's arrival. As Edna led the way to the parlor, Mrs. Murray hastily fastened a drooping spray of coral berries in her hair.

Before tea was ended, other visitors came in, and the orphan found relief from her confusion in the general conversation.

While Dr. Rodney, the family physician, was talking to Edna about some discoveries of Ehrenberg about which she was very curious, Mr. Leigh engrossed Mrs. Murray's attention. For some time, their conversation was exceedingly earnest; then Mrs. Murray rose and approached the sofa where Edna sat, saying gravely, "Edna, give me this seat, I want to have a little chat with the doctor. By the way, my dear, Mr. Leigh is waiting for you to show him some book you promised to find for him. Go into the library – there is a good fire there."

The room was tempting indeed to students, and the two sat down before the glowing grate, Edna warming her hands, which were cold again. Mr. Leigh took in the warm, rich curtains sweeping from ceiling to carpet, the black-walnut bookcases girding the walls on all sides, and the sentinel bronze busts keeping watch. He rubbed his fingers and exclaimed, "Certainly this is the most delightful library in the world! It makes me want to dedicate myself to a recluse life and studious habits." Edna smiled. "How incomprehensible it is that Murray should prefer to pass his years roaming over deserts and wandering about comfortless khans, when he might spend them in such an Elysium as this! The man must be demented! How do you explain it?"

"To each his own tastes! I consider it none of my business, and as I suppose he is the best judge of what contributes to his happiness, I do not meddle with the mystery."

Not to mention that, while Mr. Murray was gone, Edna had the whole library all to herself.

"Poor Murray! His wretched disposition is a great curse. I pity him most sincerely."

Edna shook her head ruefully. "From what I remember of him, I am afraid he would not thank you for your pity, or admit that he needed it. Here is the Targum, Mr. Leigh, and here is the very passage you want."

She opened the ancient Chaldee manuscript she'd been looking at earlier. Spreading it on the library table, they examined it together, spelling out the words, and turning frequently to a dictionary which lay near. Neither knew much about the language; now and then they differed in the interpretation, and more than once Edna referred to the rules of her grammar to establish the construction of the sentences.

Engrossed in the translation, she forgot all her apprehensions of the morning, and her old ease of manner came back. Her eyes met his fearlessly, her smile greeted him as in the early months of their acquaintance. While she bent over the pages she was deciphering, his eyes dwelt on her beaming countenance with a tender look. Most girls of her age would have found such a look hard to resist, and pleasant to recall in after days.

Neither suspected that an hour had passed until Dr. Rodney peeped into the room and called them back to the parlor, to make up a game of whist.

It was quite late when Mr. Leigh rose to say good night. As he drew on his gloves he looked earnestly at Edna. "I am coming again in a day or two, to show you some plans for a new house which I intend to build before long. Clara differs with me about the arrangement of some columns and arches, and I shall claim you and Mrs. Murray for my allies in this architectural war."

Edna looked down at her folded hands, but the lady of the house replied promptly. "Yes, come as often as you can, Gordon, and cheer us up; for it is terribly dull here without St. Elmo."

"Suppose you throw out that incorrigible Vandal and adopt me in his place? I would prove a model son."

"Very well," Mrs. Murray laughed. "I shall tell him about your proposition, and threaten an immediate compliance with it if he does not come home soon."

Mrs. Murray rang the bell for the servant to lock up the house, saying to herself, "What a noble fellow Gordon is! If I had a daughter I would select him for her husband." She lifted her head. "Where are you going, Edna?"

"I left a manuscript on the library table," Edna called down. "It is very rare and valuable, so I need to replace it in the glass box where it belongs before I go to sleep."

Lighting a candle, she lifted the heavy Targum from the library and slowly approached the suite of rooms that she was now in the habit of visiting almost daily.

Earlier in the day she had bolted the door, but left the key in the lock, expecting to bring the Targum back as soon as she had shown Mr. Leigh the passage over which the controversy raged. Now, as she crossed the rotunda, an unexpected sound, as of a chair sliding on the marble floor, issued from the inner room.

She stopped dead in her tracks to listen. Under the flare of the candle, the vindictive face of Shiva, and the hooded viper twined about his arm, warned her not to approach. Though Edna strained her ears, all was silent, save the tinkling of a bell far down in the park where the sheep clustered under the elms.

Opening the door, which was ajar, she entered, held the light high over her head, and peered nervously around the room. Here, too, all was quiet as the grave, and quite as dreary. The only moving thing seemed her shadow that flitted from the candlelight over the cold, gleaming white tiles. The carpets and curtains – even the rich silk hangings of the arch – were all packed away, and Edna shivered as she looked through both rooms. Finally, certain that she had mistaken the source of the sound, she opened the glass box where the manuscripts were kept.

At sight of them her mind reverted to the theme she had been investigating. Remembering the importance attached by ethnologists to the early Coptic inscriptions, she took from the bookshelves a volume containing many of these characters, along with drawings of the triumphal processions representing the captives of various nations torn from their homes and families to swell the pompous retinue of some barbaric Rhamses or Sesostris. She felt a nettle of annoyance with Mr. Leigh, wondering if the pharaohs had used the same tired arguments that the slaveholders used all those dreary years ago.

She pulled her mind back to her topic, drifting back over the gray, tideless sea of centuries, until she stood, in imagination, upon the steps of the Serapeum, a temple dedicated to Serapis, at Memphis. When the wild chant of the priests had died away under the huge propylaeum, she listened to the sighing of the wind in the tamarind and cassia trees, and the low babble of the sacred Nile as it rocked the lotus leaves under the glowing purple sky. A full moon flooded the ancient city with light, and kindled like a beacon the vast placid face of the Sphinx – rising solemn from its desert lair, and staring across arid yellow sands at the dim colossi of centuries ago.

Following the sinuous stream of Egyptian civilization to its source in the date-groves of Meroe, further down the banks of the Nile, the girl's thoughts were borne away to the Golden Fountain of the Sun, where Jupiter Ammon's black doves fluttered and cooed over the shining altars and amid the mystic symbols of the marvelous friezes. Edna bent over the drawings in the book, oblivious of everything else.

Suddenly she had the feeling that someone was in the room with her, though perfect stillness reigned. With a start she looked up, expecting to meet a pair of eyes fastened upon her.

But no living thing confronted her. The tall, bent figure of the Cimbri Prophetess gleamed like a ghost upon the wall, and her bright blue eyes seemed to count the dripping blood-drops. The unbroken, solemn silence of night brooded over all things, hushing even the chime of sheep-bells that had died away among the elm arches.

Knowing that no superstitious terrors had ever seized her before, the young student rose, took up the candle, and proceeded to search the two rooms, but as unsuccessfully as before.

"There certainly is somebody here, but I cannot find out where."

The echo of her own voice seemed sepulchral; then the chill silence again fell upon her. She smiled at her folly. Her imagination had been excited by the pictures she had been examining, and her shiver was the result of the cold.

Just then the candlelight flashed over the black marble statuette of Mors the skeleton, grinning horribly as it kept guard over the miniature Taj Mahal. Edna walked up to it, placed the candle on the slab that supported the tomb, and, stooping, scrutinized the lock. A spider had ensconced herself in the golden keyhole and spun a fine web across the front of the temple. Edna swept the airy drapery away and tried to drive the little weaver from her den; but she shrank further and further, and finally she took the key from her pocket and put it far enough into the opening to eject the intruder. The spider slung herself down one of her silken threads and crawled sullenly out of sight.

Withdrawing the key, she toyed with it, and glanced curiously at the mausoleum. Using her handkerchief, she carefully brushed off the cobwebs that festooned the minarets, and murmured that fragment of Persian poetry which she once heard Mr. Murray repeat to his mother, and which she had found, only a few days before: "The spider hath woven his web in the imperial palaces; and the owl hath sung her watch-song on the towers of Afrasiab."[25]

"It is exactly four years tonight since Mr. Murray gave me this key," Edna said to herself, "but he charged me not to open the Taj unless I had reason to believe that he was dead. His letter states that he is alive and well; consequently, the time has not come for me to unseal the mystery. It is strange that he trusted me with this secret; strange that he, who doubts all of humanity, could trust a girl of whom he knew so little. I have no interest in the contents of that vault, yet I wish the key was back in his hands. It annoys me to conceal it. I feel all the while as if I were deceiving his mother."

She stood there, wondering what luckless influence had so early blackened Mr. Murray's life. Would he return to Le Bocage soon, or had the traveler met his end somewhere? It was impossible to say.

The candlelight danced over the rich folds of her crimson merino dress, with the gossamer lace surrounding her throat and wrists; it seemed to linger on her shining black hair, her beautiful, polished forehead, and her firm lips, and made her large eyes look elfish under their heavy jet lashes.

There, again, came the same tantalizing conviction of a human presence; of some powerful influence which baffled analysis.

---

[25] Upon conquering Constantinople, Sultan Mehmed II, brokenhearted at the sight of the ruined imperial palaces, spoke these words, written by the medieval poet Saadi.

Again, Edna started and glanced over her shoulder. Snatching the candle, she put the gold key in her pocket and turned to leave the room, but stopped. This time an unmistakable sound, like the shivering of a glass or the snapping of a musical string, fell on her strained ears. She could trace it to no particular spot.

"Perhaps a mouse ..." she whispered, glancing up at the many glass ornaments on the étagère.

Perhaps a ghost! Edna thought, though she'd never seen one.

Nerves prickling, she quickly replaced the book she had taken from the shelves and fastened the glass box that contained the manuscripts. She examined the cabinets, found them securely closed, and hurried out of the room. Locking the door behind her and taking the key, Edna returned to her own room with nerves more unsettled than she felt disposed to confess.

For some time after she laid her head on her pillow, she racked her brain for an explanation of the singular sensation she had experienced. At last, annoyed by her restlessness and silly superstition, she was just sinking into dreams of Jupiter Ammon and Serapis when the fierce barking of Ali caused her to start up in terror.

A ghost! she thought.

Edna sighed at herself and put her pillow over her head. The dog seemed almost wild, running frantically to and fro, howling and whining. Finally the dog calmed down after one of the servants shouted at him. Quiet was restored, and Edna fell asleep soon after the scream of the locomotive and the rumble of the cars told her that the four o'clock train had just started to Chattanooga.

Modern zoology shows how some chameleons can change into the color of the substance on which they rest or feed. It is respectfully submitted that the mental chameleon – human thought – certainly takes its changing hues, day by day, from the books through which it crawls.

After all, if Mezzofanti's work-bench had not stood beneath the teacher's window, where the ears of the young carpenter were regaled from morning till night with the rudiments of Latin and Greek, he would never have forsworn carpentry, never would have mastered forty dialects. Instead, Mezzofanti proved a scarlet-capped polygot who spoke other languages for the sheer enjoyment of it, and received an honorary nomination for the office of interpreter-general at the Tower of Babel.

The numerous relics that crowded Mr. Murray's rooms seized upon Edna's fancy, linked her sympathies with the huge pantheistic systems of the world, and filled her mind with visions from the dusky realm of a mythology that seemed to predate the memory of man. To the East, the mighty alma mater of the human races – of letters, religions, arts, and politics – her thoughts wandered in wondering awe. As day by day she yielded more and more to this fascinating influence, and bent over the granite sarcophagus in one corner of Mr. Murray's museum, where lay a shrunken mummy shrouded in gilded cloths, the wish strengthened to understand the symbols in which subtle Egyptian priests masked the origins and stories of the gods.

While morning and afternoon hours were given to those branches of study in which Mr. Hammond guided her, she generally spent her evening in Mr. Murray's sitting-room, reading endlessly. Sometimes the clock in the rotunda struck midnight before she locked up the manuscripts and illuminated papyri.

Two nights after the examination of the Targum, she was seated near the bookcase looking over the plates in that rare but very valuable book, Spence's Polymetis, a guide to classical learning, when an idea flashed across her mind. Could she write a book analyzing and comparing all the mythologies of the world, and throw some light on them?

Pushing the Polymetis aside, Edna sprang up and paced the long room. Gradually her eyes kindled, her cheeks burned, as ambition pointed to a possible future, of which, till this hour, she had not dared to dream. Hope, o'erleaping all barriers, grasped a victory that would make her name imperishable.

In her miscellaneous reading she had stumbled upon odd correspondences in the customs and religions of nations separated by surging oceans and by ages. Many nations were separated by continents and oceans, and no possible bridge existed between them. Yet traditions and symbols were shared between them, eerily and mysteriously alike. During the past week several of these coincidences had attracted her attention.

The Druidic rites and the festival of Beltein, the Gaelic May Day in Scotland and Ireland, she found traced to their source in the worship of Phrygian Baal. The figure of the Scandinavian Disa, at Uppsala, wore a net precisely like that which surrounds some statues of Isis in Egypt. The sails made of rushes used by the Peruvians on Lake Titicaca, and their mode of handling them, were identical with those depicted upon the sepulcher of Ramses III at Thebes. The head of a Mexican priestess was ornamented with a veil similar to that carved on Egyptian sphinxes, while her robes resembled those of a Jewish high priest. A very quaint and puzzling pictorial chart of the chronology of the Aztecs contained an image of Coxcox in his ark, surrounded by rushes similar to those that overshadowed Moses, and also a likeness of a dove distributing tongues to those born after the deluge. Perhaps mythologies shared a language common to all mankind, for all nations shared a yearning to understand life and existence.

Edna was seized and mastered by the idea of gathering up these mythological links and establishing a chain of unity that would girdle the world.

To firmly grasp the Bible for a talisman, as Ulysses did his sprig of moly, and to stand in the Pantheon of the universe, examining every shattered idol and crumbling altar where worshipping humanity had bowed; to lift the veil from oracles and sibyls, and show the world the links between every system of religion -- all of this seemed to her a mission grander far than the conquest of empires, and infinitely more to be desired than the crown and heritage of Solomon.

The night wore on as Edna planned the work of coming years, but she still walked up and down the floor, with slow, uncertain steps, like one who, peering at distant objects, sees nothing close at hand. Flush and tremor passed from her countenance; for the first gush of enthusiasm, like the jets of violet flame flickering over the simmering mass in alchemic crucibles, had vanished – her thought became a crystallized and consecrated purpose.

At last, when the feeble gaslight admonished her that she would soon be in darkness, she retreated to her own room. The first glimmer of dawn struggled in at her window as she knelt at her bedside praying, "Be pleased, O Lord, to make me a fit instrument for Thy work. Sanctify my heart; quicken and enlighten my mind; grant me patience and perseverance and unwavering faith; guide me into paths that lead to truth; enable me in all things to labor with an eye single to thy glory, caring less for the applause of the world than for the advancement of the cause of Christ. O my Father and my God, bless the work on which I am about to enter, crown it with success, accept me as a humble tool for the benefit of my race. And when the days of my earthly pilgrimage are ended, receive my soul into that eternal rest which Thou hast prepared from the foundations of the world, for the sake of Jesus Christ."

CHAPTER XI
THE TAJ MAHAL

One afternoon, about a week after Mr. Leigh's last visit, Edna returned from the parsonage where she had been detained beyond her usual time.

As soon as she came in the door, Mrs. Murray, dressed beautifully, met her and placed in her hand a note from Mrs. Inge, inviting both to dine with her that day, and meet some distinguished friends from a distant state.

"Lose no time in getting ready," Mrs. Murray said. "Mrs. Inge is expecting us in less than an hour."

Edna took off her hat and laid her books down on a table. "Please offer my excuses to Mrs. Inge. I cannot accept the invitation and hope you will not urge me."

"Nonsense! Let me hear no more such childish stuff and get ready at once. We shall be too late, I am afraid."

The orphan leaned against the mantelpiece and shook her head.

Mrs. Murray colored angrily and drew herself up. "Edna Earl, did you hear what I said?"

"Yes, madam, but this time I cannot obey you. Allow me to give you my reasons, and I am sure you will forgive me. On the night of the party given by Mrs. Inge I decided, under no circumstances, to accept any future invitations to her house, for I overheard a conversation between Mrs. Hill and Mrs. Montgomery which I believe was intended to reach my ears, that wounded and mortified me very much. I was ridiculed and denounced as a 'poor upstart and interloper,' who was being smuggled into society far above my position in life. They called me a greedy schemer, intent on thrusting myself upon Mr. Leigh's notice, and ambitious of marrying him for his fortune. They sneered at the idea that we should study Hebrew with Mr. Hammond, and declared it a mere trap to catch Mr. Leigh."

Mrs. Murray pressed her lips together, and Edna, taking heart, continued. "Now, Mrs. Murray, you know that I never had such a thought. I have resolved to study Hebrew by myself, and to avoid meeting Mr. Leigh at the parsonage; for if his sister's friends entertain such an opinion of me, I know not what other people, even Mrs. Inge, may think. As I see that they are also invited to dine today, it would be very disagreeable for me to meet them in Mr. Leigh's presence."

Mrs. Murray frowned, and her lips curled, as she clasped a diamond bracelet on her arm. "I have long since ceased to be surprised by any manifestation of Mrs. Montgomery's insolence. She doubtless judges your motives by those of her snub-nosed and excruciating daughter, Maud, who rumor says, is paying most devoted attention to that same fortune of Gordon's. I shall avail myself of the first suitable occasion to suggest to her that it is rather unbecoming in persons whose fathers were convicted of forgery, and hunted out of the state, to lay such stress on the mere poverty of young aspirants for admission into society."

"My goodness," Edna said.

"As for Mrs. Hill, whose parents were respectable, even genteel, I expected more courtesy and less malice; but, poor thing, nature denied her any individuality, and she serves 'her circle' in the same capacity as those tin reflectors fastened on locomotives. All that you heard was beneath your notice, and unworthy of consideration. I would not gratify them by withdrawing from a position which you can so gracefully occupy."

"Mrs. Murray, it is no privation to me to stay at home," Edna said. "On the contrary, I prefer it, for I would not exchange the companionship of the books in this house for all the dinners that ever were given."

"There is no necessity for you to make a recluse of yourself simply because two rude, silly gossips disgrace themselves. You have time enough to read and study, and still go out with me when I consider it advisable."

"But, my dear Mrs. Murray, my position in your family, as an unknown dependent on your charity, subjects me to – "

"Your position in my family is a matter which does not concern Mesdames Hill and Montgomery, as I shall most unequivocally intimate to them. I insist that you dismiss the whole affair from your mind. How much longer do you intend to keep me waiting?"

"I am very sorry, but hereafter I cannot accompany you to dinners and parties. Whenever you desire me to see company in your own house, I shall be happy to comply with your wishes and commands; but my self-respect will not permit me to go out to meet people who barely tolerate me through fear of offending you. It is exceedingly painful, dear Mrs. Murray, for me to have to appear disrespectful and stubborn toward you, but in this instance, I cannot comply with your wishes."

They looked at each other steadily. Finally, Mrs. Murray's brow cleared and her lip unbent. "What do you expect me to tell Mrs. Inge?"

"That I return my thanks for her very kind remembrance, but am closely occupied in preparing myself to teach, and have no time for gayeties."

Mrs. Murray smiled significantly. "Do you suppose that excuse will satisfy your friend Gordon? He will fly for consolation to the simpering smile and delicious flattery of Miss Maud."

"I care not where he flies, provided I am left in peace."

"Stop, my dear child! You do not mean what you say. You know very well that you earnestly hope Gordon will escape the tender mercies of silly Maud and the machinations of her most amiable mamma. If you don't, I do. You are not to visit Susan Montgomery's sins on Gordon's head."

"Yes, madam," Edna said.

"I shall come home early, and make you go to bed at nine o'clock, to punish you for your obstinacy. By the by, Edna, Hagar tells me that you frequently sit up till three or four o'clock, poring over those heathenish documents in my son's cabinet. This is absurd and will ruin your health. Besides, I doubt if what you learn is worth your trouble. You must not sit up longer than ten o'clock. Give me my furs."

Edna ate her dinner alone and went into the library to practice a difficult music lesson; but the spell of her new project was stronger than the witchery of music. Closing the piano, she ran into the "Egyptian Museum," as Mrs. Murray termed her son's sitting room.

The previous night Edna had been reading a book about the doctrines of Zoroaster, in which the author attempted to trace all the chief features of the Zend-Avesta to the Old Testament and the Jews. Now she returned to the subject with unflagging interest.

Pushing a cushioned chair close to the window, Edna wrapped her shawl around her, put her feet on the seat of a neighboring chair to keep them from the icy floor, and blissfully gave herself up to the perusal of the volume.

The sun went down in a wintry sky. The solemn red light burning on the funeral pyre of day streamed through the undraped windows, flushed the fretted facade of the Taj Mahal, glowed on the marble floor, and warmed and brightened the serene, lovely face of the earnest young student.

As the flame faded in the west, where two stars leaped from the pearly ashes, the fine print of Edna's book grew dim. She turned the page to catch the mellow, silvery radiance of the full moon, which, shining low in the east, threw a ghastly luster on the awful form and floating white hair of the Cimbrian woman on the wall.

But between Edna and the light, close beside her chair, stood a tall, dark figure with uncovered head and outstretched hands.

She sprang to her feet, dropping the book, and uttering a cry of mingled alarm and delight. She knew that stately form and regal head could belong to but one person.

"Oh, Mr. Murray!" Edna cried, clasping her hands tightly in the first instant of surprise. "Can it be possible that you have come home to your sad, desolate mother? Oh, for her sake I am so glad!"

She stood looking at him, fear and pleasure struggling for mastery in her eloquent face.

"Edna, have you no word of welcome, no friendly hand to offer a man who has been wandering for four long years among strangers in distant lands?"

This was not the harsh, bitter voice whose mocking echoes had haunted her ears during his absence. He spoke in a tone so low and mournful, so inexplicably sweet, that she could not recognize it as his.

Unable to utter a word, she put her hand in his outstretched palm.

His fingers closed over it with a pressure that was painful. Edna's eyes fell beneath the steady, searching gaze St. Elmo fixed on her face.

For fully a minute they stood motionless. Then he took a match from his pocket, lighted a gas globe that hung over the Taj, and locked the door leading into the rotunda.

"My mother is dining out, Hagar informed me," Mr. Murray called across the room to her. "Tell me, is she well? And have you made her happy while I was far away?" He came back, leaned his elbow on the carved top of the cushioned chair, and, partly shading his eyes with his hand from the gaslight, looked down into the girl's face.

"Your mother is very well indeed, but anxious and unhappy on your account. I think you will find her thinner and paler than when you saw her last."

"Then you have not done your duty, as I requested?"

Edna opened her hands pleadingly. "I could not take your place, sir, and your last letter led her to believe that you would be absent for another year. She thinks that at this instant you are in the heart of Persia. Last night, when the servant came from the post-office without the letter which she confidently expected, her eyes filled with tears, and she said, 'He has ceased to think of his home, and loves the excitement of travel better than his mother's peace of mind.' Why did you deceive her? Why did you rob her of all the joy of anticipating your speedy return?"

The old scowl settled heavily between Mr. Murray's eyes, and the harshness crept back to his voice. "I did not deceive her. It was a sudden and unexpected circumstance that determined my return. Moreover, she should long since have accustomed herself to find happiness from other sources than my society, for no one knows better my detestation of settling down in any fixed habitation."

Edna felt all her old childish repugnance sweeping over her as she saw the swift hardening of his features. She turned toward the door.

"Where are you going?"

"To send a messenger to your mother, acquainting her with your arrival. She would not forgive me if I failed to give her such good tidings at the very earliest moment."

"You will do no such thing. I forbid any message. She thinks me in the midst of Persian ruins, and can afford to wait an hour longer among her friends. How happened it that you also are not at Mrs. Inge's?"

Either the suddenness of the question, or his intense scrutiny, or the painful consciousness of the true cause of her failure to accept the invitation, brought back the blood which surprise had driven from her cheeks.

"I preferred remaining at home."

"Home! Home!" he repeated, and continued vehemently, "Do you really expect me to believe that a girl of your age, who could attend a dinner-party among the elite, with lace, silk, and feathers, champagne, and scandal, flattering speeches and soft looks from young gentlemen, biting words and hard looks from old ladies, could possibly choose to spend a dull evening in this cold den of mine, shut up with mummies, ancient manuscripts, and musty books? Such an anomaly in nature might occur in some undiscovered and unimagined realm, where the men are all brave, honest, and true, and the women conscientious and constant. But here? And now? Ah, pardon me! Impossible!"

Edna felt as if Momus' suggestion to Vulcan, of a window in the human heart, whereby one's thoughts might be rendered visible, had been adopted. Under his impaling eye, the secret motives of her conduct seemed spread out as on a scroll.

"I preferred a quiet evening at home to a noisy one elsewhere."

"Indeed! Unless human nature here in America has undergone a radical change, nay, a most complete transmogrification since I left it some years ago, I will stake all my possessions to say that some very peculiar reason, something beyond the desire to prosecute archaeological researches, has driven you to decline the invitation."

Edna made no reply. She opened the bookcase, replaced the volume which she had been reading, and glanced uneasily toward the door, longing to escape.

"Are you insulted at my presumption?"

"I am sorry, sir, to find that you have lost none of your cynicism in your travels."

"Do you regard traveling as a cure for minds diseased?"

She looked up and smiled in his face – a smile so arch and merry, even a stone might have caught the glow. "Certainly not, Mr. Murray, as you are the most incorrigible traveler I have ever known."

But there was no answering gleam on his darkening countenance. The silence that ensued annoyed Edna, who, it was true, had made an excellent jest. She felt less at ease every moment, knowing all her peaceful, happy days at Le Bocage were drawing to a close. "Mr. Murray, I am cold. I should like to go to the fire if you have no more questions to ask. Do be so kind as to unlock the door."

He glanced round the room, and, taking his grey traveling shawl from a chair where he had thrown it, laid it in a heap on the marble tiles.

"Yes, this floor is icy. Stand on the shawl, though I am well aware you are more tired of me than of the room."

Another long pause followed, as Edna, much disappointed, took her place upon his shawl. St. Elmo Murray came close to her, saying, "For four long years I have been making an experiment – one of those experiments which men frequently attempt, believing all the time that it is worse than child's play, and half hoping that it will sanction their skepticism concerning the result. When I left home I placed in your charge the key of my private desk, exacting the promise that only upon certain conditions would you venture to open it."

"Mr. Murray, it was a confidence which I never solicited, which has caused me much pain," Edna protested.

St. Elmo shrugged slightly, continuing as if she had not spoken. "Those contingencies have not arisen; consequently, there can be no justification for your having made yourself acquainted with the contents of the vault. I told you I trusted the key in your hands; I did not. I felt assured you would betray the confidence. It was not a trust – it was a temptation, which I believed no girl ... or woman," he added as if suddenly realizing that she was now four years older, "would successfully resist. I am here to receive an account of your stewardship, and I tell you now I doubt you. Where is the key?"

Edna took from her pocket a small ivory box. Opening it, she drew out the little key and handed it to him. "You should have given the key to your mother, but– God is my witness – I have not betrayed your confidence. There is the key, but of the contents of the tomb I know nothing. It was ungenerous in you to tempt me as you did, by whetting my curiosity and then placing in my own hands the means of gratifying it. Of course, I have wondered what the mystery was, and why you selected me to guard it; and I have often wished to inspect the interior of that marble cabinet. But child though I was, I think I would have gone to the stake sooner than violate my promise."

As he took the key, his hand trembled. A sudden pallor overspread St. Elmo's face.

"Edna Earl, I give you one last chance to be truthful with me. If you yielded to the temptation – and what woman would not? – it would be no more than I expected, and you will scarcely have disappointed me; for, as I told you, I put no faith in you. But even if you succumbed to a natural curiosity, be honest and confess it!"

Edna looked steadily into his inquisitorial eyes. "I have nothing to confess."

He laid his hand heavily on her shoulder. His tone was vehement, pleading. "Can you look me in the eye – so – and say that you never put this key in yonder lock? Edna! More hangs on your words than you dream of. Be truthful, as if you were indeed in the presence of the God you worship. I can forgive you for prying into my affairs, but I cannot and will not pardon you for trifling with me now."

"Sir, I never unlocked the vault. I never had the key near it but once – about a week ago – when I found the tomb covered with cobwebs, and twisted the key partly into the hole to drive out the spider. I give you my most solemn assurance that I never unlocked it, never saw the interior. Your suspicions are ungenerous and unjust – derogatory to you and insulting to me."

"The proof is at hand. If I have indeed unjustly suspected you, atonement full and ample shall be made."

Clasping one of her hands so firmly that she could not extricate it, he drew her before the Taj Mahal. Stooping, he fitted the key to the lock. There was a dull click as he turned it.

At this moment, St. Elmo paused and scrutinized her face. Edna felt her face flush, but she gazed at him, proud, defiant, but grieved.

St. Elmo's face was colorless as the marble that reflected it. Through his hand, she felt the heavy, rapid beating of his blood, and saw the cords thickening on his brow.

"If you have faithfully kept your promise, there will be an explosion when I open the vault."

Slowly he turned the key a second time with a click. As the arched door opened and swung back on its golden hinges, there was a flash and sharp explosion from a pistol within.

Edna started involuntarily, notwithstanding the warning, and clung to his arm.

He took no notice. St. Elmo's fingers relaxed their iron grasp of hers, and his hand dropped to his side. Leaning forward, he bowed his head on the marble dome of the little temple.

How long he stood there she knew not; but the few moments seemed to her an eternity as she watched his motionless figure.

He was so still, that finally she wondered if he might have fainted. Averse though she was to addressing him, she asked timidly, "Mr. Murray, are you ill? Give me the key of the door and I will bring you some wine."

There was no answer. Alarmed, Edna put her hand on his.

Tightly he clasped it, and drawing her suddenly close to his side, he said without raising his face, "Edna Earl, I have been ill – for years – but I shall be better henceforth. O child, child! Your guileless soul cannot comprehend the blackness of mine. Better that you should lie down now in death, with all the unfolded freshness of your life gathered in your grave, than live to know the world as I have proved it. For many years I have lived without trust or faith in anything – in anybody. Tonight I stand here and my confidence in human nature was dead; but, child, you have galvanized the corpse."

Again, the mournful music of his voice touched her heart. Edna felt her tears rising as she answered in a low, hesitating tone, "It was not death, Mr. Murray, it was merely syncope, and this is a healthful reaction from disease."

"No, it will not last. It is but a will o' the wisp that will lure me to deeper gloom and darker morasses. 'I have swept and garnished, and the seven other devils will dwell with me forever[26]! ' My child, I have tempted you, and you stood firm. Forgive my suspicions. Twenty years hence, if you are so luckless as to live that long, you will not wonder that I doubted you, but that my doubt proved unjust. This little vault contains no skeleton, no state secrets; only a picture and a few jewels, my will, and the history of an utterly ruined life. Perhaps if you continue true, and make my mother happy, I may put all in your hands someday, when I die; and then you will not wonder at my hopeless life."

Now St. Elmo lifted his haggard head, and met Edna's eyes. "One thing I wish to say now. If at any time you need assistance of any kind – if you are troubled – come to me. I am not quite as selfish as the world paints me, and even if I seem rude and harsh, do not fear to come to me. You have conferred a favor on me, and I do not like to remain in anybody's debt."

Edna's heart trembled to meet his eyes, and she looked down at her hands. "I am afraid, sir, we never can be friends."

"Why not?"

"I shall not be here much longer to trouble you; but while we are in the same house, I trust no bitter or unkind feelings will be entertained. I thank you, sir, for your polite offer of assistance, but hope I shall soon be able to maintain myself without burdening your mother any longer."

"How long have you burdened her?"

"Ever since that night when I was picked up lame and helpless, and placed in her kind hands."

"Do you really love my mother?"

"Next to the memory of my grandfather, I love her and Mr. Hammond; and I feel that my gratitude is beyond expression.

---

[26] Matthew 12:43-45

There, your mother is coming! I hear the carriage. Shall I tell her you are here?"

St. Elmo took the key of the door from his pocket and placed it into her hands. "No. I will meet her in her own room."

Edna hastened to the library, and throwing herself into a chair, tried to collect her thoughts and reflect upon what had passed in the "Egyptian Museum."

Very soon Mrs. Murray's cry of joyful surprise rang through the house. Tears of sympathy rose to Edna's eyes as imagination pictured the happy meeting in the neighboring room.

But now she was now disquieted to discover that Mr. Murray's bronzed face suddenly possessed an indescribable fascination to her. In striving to analyze the interest she was for the first time conscious of feeling, she soothed herself with the belief that it arose from curiosity concerning his past life, and sympathy for his evident misanthropy. It was in vain that she endeavored to fix her thoughts on a book; his eyes met hers on every page. When the bell summoned her to a late supper, she was glad to escape from her own confused reflections.

Mrs. Murray and her son were standing on the rug before the grate. As Edna entered, the mother held out her hand.

"Have you seen my son? Come and congratulate me." She kissed the girl's forehead, and continued, "St. Elmo, has she not changed astonishingly? Would you have known her had you met her away from home?"

"I should certainly have known her under all circumstances."

He did not look at her, but resumed the conversation with his mother which her entrance had interrupted.

During supper Edna could scarcely realize that the cold, distant man, who took no more notice of her than of one of the salt cellars, was the same whom she had left leaning over the Taj. Not the faintest trace of emotion lingered on his dark, stony features, over which occasionally flickered the light of a sarcastic smile as he outlined the course of his wanderings. Now that she could, without being observed, study his countenance, she saw that he looked much older, more haggard, than when last at home, and that the thick, curling hair that clung in glossy rings to his temples was turning grey.

When they arose from the table, Mrs. Murray took an exquisite bouquet from the mantelpiece and said, "Edna, I was requested to place this in your hands as a token of the regard and remembrance of your friend and admirer, Gordon Leigh. He wanted me to assure you that your absence spoiled his enjoyment of the day. As he seemed quite inconsolable because of your non-attendance, I promised that you should ride with him tomorrow afternoon."

As Edna glanced up to receive the flowers, she met the merciless gaze she so much dreaded. In her confusion she let the bouquet fall on the carpet.

Mr. Murray picked it up, inhaled the fragrance, rearranged some of the geranium leaves that had been crushed, and, smiling bitterly all the while, bowed and put it securely in her hand.

"Edna, you have no other engagement for tomorrow?"

"Yes, madam, I have promised to spend it with Mr. Hammond," Edna stammered.

"Then you must excuse yourself, for I will not have Gordon disappointed again."

Too much annoyed to answer, Edna left the room, but paused in the hall and beckoned to Mrs. Murray, who joined her. "Of course, you will not have prayers tonight, as Mr. Murray has returned?"

Mrs. Murray pleaded, "For that very reason I want to have them, to make a public acknowledgment of my gratitude that my son has been restored to me. Oh, if he would only consent to be present!"

"It is late, and he will probably plead fatigue."

"Leave that with me. When I ring the bell, come to the library."

Edna went to her room and diligently copied an essay which she intended to submit to Mr. Hammond for criticism on the following day. She soon became absorbed by Grecian politics, and was only reminded of the events of the evening when the bell sounded, calling the household to prayer.

She laid down her pen and hurried to the library. Mrs. Murray had indeed enticed her son to come, for he was standing before one of the bookcases, looking over the table of contents of a new scientific work. The servants came in and ranged themselves near the door.

Mrs. Murray said, "You must take my place tonight, Edna; I cannot read aloud."

Edna looked up appealingly, but an imperative gesture silenced her, and so she sat before the table, bewildered and frightened. Mr. Murray glanced around the room, and with a look of scorn threw the book down on the floor and turned to leave.

His mother's hand seized his.

"My son, for my sake, do not go! Out of respect for me, remain here the first evening of your return. For my sake, St. Elmo!"

He frowned, shook off her hands, and strode to the door. His hand was on the knob when he paused and reconsidered. After a moment he came back and stood at the fireplace, leaning his elbow on the mantel, looking gloomily at the coals.

Although painfully embarrassed as she took her seat and prepared to conduct the services in his presence, Edna felt a great calm steal over her spirit when she opened the Bible and read her favorite chapter, the fourteenth of St. John.

Her sweet, flexible voice, gradually losing its tremor, rolled soothingly through the room; and when she knelt and repeated the prayer selected for the occasion – a prayer of thanks for the safe return of a traveler to the haven of home – her tone was full of pathos and an earnestness that stirred the proud heart of the wanderer as he stood there, looking through his fingers at her uplifted face, and listening to the first prayer that had reached his ears for nearly sixteen weary years of sin and scoffing.

When Edna rose from her knees, he had left the room. His swift steps echoed drearily through the rotunda.

CHAPTER XII
A MORTAL DRIVEN BY THE DESTINIES

"I do not wish to interrupt you. There is certainly room enough in this library for both, and my entrance need not prove the signal for your departure."

Mr. Murray closed the door as he came in. Walking up to the bookcases, he examined the titles of the many volumes.

Edna had risen to leave the room when the master of the house entered, but at his request resumed her seat and continued reading.

It was a cold, dismal morning, and sobbing wintry winds and the ceaseless pattering of rain made the outer world seem dreary in comparison with the genial atmosphere and the ruddy glow of the cozy, luxurious library, where exotic flowers breathed their fragrance and early hyacinths exhaled their rich perfume. In the center of the morocco-covered table stood a tall glass bowl, filled with white camellias, and from its scalloped edges drooped a fringe of scarlet fuchsias; while near the window was a china statuette, in whose daily adornment Edna took unwearied interest. It was a lovely Flora, whose slender fingers held aloft small tulip-shaped vases, into which fresh blossoms were inserted every morning. The head was so arranged as to contain water, and thus preserve the wreath of natural flowers which crowned the goddess. Today golden crocuses nestled down on the streaming hair, and purple pansies filled the fairy hands, while the tiny, rosy feet sank deep in the cushion of fine, green mosses, studded with double violets.

After searching the shelves unavailingly, Mr. Murray glanced over his shoulder and asked, "Have you seen my copy of De Guerin's *Centaur* anywhere about the house? I had it a week ago."

"I beg your pardon, sir, for causing such a fruitless search; here is the book. I picked it up on the front steps, where you were reading a few afternoons since, and it opened at a passage that attracted my attention."

She closed the volume and held it toward him, but he waved it back.

"Keep it if it interests you. I have read it once, and merely wished to refer to a particular passage. Can you guess what sentence most frequently recurs to me? If so, read it to me." St. Elmo drew a chair close to the hearth and lighted his cigar in the coals.

Hesitatingly Edna turned the leaves. "I am afraid, sir, that my selection would displease you."

"I will risk it, as, notwithstanding your flattering opinion to the contrary, I am not altogether so unreasonable as to take offense with you for complying with my request."

Still she shrank from the task he imposed. Her fingers toyed with the scarlet fuchsias; but after eyeing her for a while, he leaned forward and pushed the glass bowl beyond her reach.

"Edna, I am waiting."

"Well, then, Mr. Murray, I should think that these two passages would impress you with peculiar force."

Raising the book, she read with much emphasis:

"Thou pursuest after wisdom, O Melampus! which is the science of the will of the gods; *and thou roamest from people to people like a mortal driven by the Destinies.* In the times when I kept my night-watches before the caverns, I have sometimes believed that I was about to surprise the thoughts of the sleeping Cybele, and that the mother of the gods, betrayed by her dreams, would let fall some of her secrets; but I have never yet made out more than sounds which faded away in the murmur of night, or words inarticulate as the bubbling of the rivers.
 ****

"Seekest thou to know the gods, O Macareus, and from what source men, animals, and the elements of the universal fire have their origin? The aged Ocean, the father of all things, keeps locked within his own breast these secrets; and the nymphs who stand around sing as they weave their eternal dance before him, to cover any sound which might escape from his lips half opened by slumber. The mortals dear to the gods for their virtue have received from their hands lyres to give delight to man, or the seeds of new plants to make him rich; but from their inexorable lips – nothing!"

Edna closed the book. "Mr. Murray, am I correct in my conjecture?"

"Quite correct," he answered, smiling grimly.

Taking the book from her hand he tossed it on the table, adding in a defiant tone, "The mantle of wisdom did not fall on the shoulders of Maurice de Guérin. After all, he was a wretched hypochondriac, and a tinge of jealousy doubtless crept into his eyes."

"Yet he understood the wholesome value of traveling. Do you forget, sir, that he said, 'When one is a wanderer, one feels that one fulfills the true condition of humanity'? and that among his last words are these, 'The stream of travel is full of delight. Oh, who will set me adrift on this Nile?'"

"Pardon me if I remind you that De Guérin was not himself a traveler. He felt starved in Languedoc, and no wonder! But even if he had penetrated every nook and cranny of the habitable globe, and wandered the vast deserts that fill the universe, he would have died at last, hungry and unfulfilled. I know this, for the true gadfly, ennui, has stung me from hemisphere to hemisphere, across tempestuous oceans, scorching deserts, and icy mountain ranges. I have faced alike the deadly snowstorms of the steppes, and the fiery desert winds of the Sahara, but the result of my vandal life is best epitomized in those grim words of Bossuet: "At the bottom of everything one finds emptiness and nothingness."[27] Sixteen years ago, to satisfy my hunger, I set out to hunt the daintiest food this world could furnish to feed my starving heart. But, like other fools, I learned that life is but a golden apple of

---

[27] "On trouve au fond de tout le vide et le néant" – Augusta picked up this line from an essay about Eugénie de Guérin published in the *Cornhill Magazine* in 1863. Thanks, Google Books.

Sodom, that, as Josephus tells us, looks fair and delicious to the eye, but when plucked, it bursts, leaving dust and ashes in your hand."

"Mr. Murray, if you insist upon your bitter simile, why shut your eyes to the analogy suggested? Naturalists suggest that the apple of Sodom contains in its normal state neither dust nor ashes, until an ichneumon wasp punctures the rind to lay its eggs within. This converts the whole of the inside into dust, leaving nothing but the rind. Human life is as fair and tempting as the apples of Eden, until they are stung and poisoned by the wasps of sin.[28]"

St. Elmo smiled mockingly as he inclined his haughty head.

"Will you favor me by lifting upon the point of your dissecting-knife the stinging sin of mine to which you refer? The noxious brood swarm so teasingly about my ears that they deprive me of your cool philosophic discrimination."

"Of your history, sir, I am entirely ignorant. Even if I were not, I should not presume to bring it up in discussions with you. However vulnerable you may possibly be, a character assassination is the weakest weapon in the armory of discourse, a weapon too often dipped in the venom of personal malevolence. I merely express my belief that miserable lives are sinful lives; that when God framed the world and created humans, he made the most generous provision for all healthful hunger, whether physical, intellectual, or moral. Only a diseased nature would wear out its years on earth in bitter carping and dissatisfaction. The Greeks recognized this truth in the myth of Tantalus. You are a scholar, Mr. Murray; look back and consider the significance of that fable. Tantalus was 'a wanderer from happiness,' and he was a man abounding in wealth, but whose appetite was so insatiable, even at the ambrosial feast of the gods, that it doomed him to eternal unsatisfied thirst and hunger in Tartarus. The same truth crops out in the legend of Midas, who found himself starving while his touch converted all things to gold."

---

[28] Hi, friendly neighborhood horticulturist here. This analogy is not quite correct, as the apple of Sodom, *Calotropis procera*, is actually a variety of milkweed, so the plant has what looks like a nice fruit growing on it, but when you pop it open, it's full of milkweed fluff. Edna's wasp analogy pertains to different creatures (this is actually more pertinent to caterpillars) but at the time Augusta didn't have Google to check this information, so go easy on her.

He sneered and threw his cigar into the grate. "I see by your argument that you have arrived at the charitable conclusion that I shall inevitably join the snarling Dives Club in Hades, and swell the howling chorus. I shall not disappoint your kind and eminently Christian expectations; nor will I deprive you of the gentle satisfaction of hissing across the gulf of perdition that will then divide us, 'I told you so!'"

A tremor crept across Edna's lips. "You torture my words into an interpretation of which I never dreamed, and look upon all things through the lenses of your own moodiness. It is worse than useless for us to attempt a friendly discussion, for your bitterness never slumbers, your suspicions are ever on the alert."

She rose, but he quickly laid his hand on her shoulder, and pressed her back into the chair. "You will be so good as to sit still and hear me out."

"I should prefer to go," she said quietly.

"I should prefer you not go," St. Elmo replied, his words heated. "After all, I have a right to all my charming, rose-colored views of this world. I have gone to and fro on the earth, and life has proved a Barmecide's banquet of just thirty-four years' duration, an imaginary feast."

"But, sir, Schacabac humored the old gentleman through the entire imaginary feast, and as a result was awarded real food and a home in his palace. If you shared his patience and resolution, you too would have finally grasped the splendid realities. The world must be conquered, held in bondage to God's law and man's reason, before we can hope to levy tribute that will support our moral and mental natures; and it is only when humanity finds itself in the inverted order of serfdom to the world, that it dwarfs its capacities, and even then dies of famine."

Edna saw the scornful gleam die out of Mr. Murray's eyes, and mournful compassion stole in.

"Ah, how impetuously youth springs to the battlefield of life!" he said. "The youth dream of burnished eagles and streaming banners, spoils of victory and paeans of triumph; but slow-stepping experience, pallid, blood-stained, lays her icy hand on the rosy veil that floats before brave young eyes, and lo, the swelling corpses, the bleaching bones, the grinning horrors that strew the silent battlefield!, only silence and gloom and death – slow-sailing vultures – and a voiceless desolation! You talk of 'conquering the world – holding it in bondage.' What do you know of its perils and subtle temptations – of the glistening quicksands whose smooth lips already gape to engulf you? Ah, you remind me of an innocent child, playing on some shining beach when the sky is quiet, the winds are hushed, and all things wrapped in rest, save

> "The ripple washing in the reeds
> And the wild water lapping on the crag"[29]

a fearless child, gathering shells with which to build fairy palaces. Suddenly, as she catches the murmur of the immemorial sea that echoes in the flushed chambers of the stranded shells, her face pales with wonder – the childish lips part, her young eyes are strained to discover the mystery. While the whispering shell admonishes of howling storms and sinking ships, she smiles and listens, hears only the music of the sea sirens – and the sky blackens, the winds leap to their track of ruin, the great deep rises wrathful and murderous, bellowing for victims, and Cyclone reigns! Thundering waves sweep over and bear away the frail palaces that decked the strand. Even while the shell symphony still charms the ear, the child's rosy feet are washed from their sandy resting-place; she is borne on howling billows far out to a lashed and maddened sea, strewn with human victims; and numb with horror she sinks to her final rest among purple algae. Even so, Edna, you stop your ears with shells, and my warning falls like snow-flakes that melt and vanish on the bosom of a stream."

"No, sir, I am willing to be advised. Against what would you warn me?"

"The hollowness of life, the fatuity of your hopes, the treachery of that human nature of which you speak so tenderly and reverently. So surely as you put faith in the truth and nobility of humanity, you will find it as soft-lipped and vicious as Paolo Orsini, who folded his wife, Isabella de Medici, most lovingly in his arms, then slipped a cord around her neck and strangled her."

---

[29] "Morte d'Arthur" by Lord Alfred Tennyson

"I know, sir, that human nature is weak, selfish, sinful. But the law of compensation operates here as well as in other departments, and brings to light faithful friends. Even if the world were bankrupt in morality and religion – which, thank God, it is not – one grand shining example, like Mr. Hammond, whose sublime unselfishness all people revere, ought to –."

"Mr. Hammond?" St. Elmo cried so abruptly that Edna startled. "Sublime unselfishness? Spare me a repetition of the rhapsodies of Madame Guyon! I am not surprised that such a novice as you prove yourself should swear by that hypocritical wolf, that Tartuffe, Allan Hammond – "

Furious, Edna interrupted him with an imperious wave of her hand. "Stop, Mr. Murray! You must not, shall not use such language in my presence concerning Mr. Hammond, who I love and revere above all other human beings! How dare you malign that noble Christian, who daily lifts your name to God, praying for pardon and for peace? Oh, how ungrateful, how unworthy you are of his affection and his prayers!"

Mr. Murray snapped, "I neither possess nor desire his affection or his prayers."

"Sir, you know that you do not deserve them, but you most certainly have both."

"How did you obtain your information?"

"Accidentally, when he was so surprised and grieved to hear that you had started on your long voyage to Oceanica."

"Ah! He availed himself of that occasion to acquaint you with all my heinous sins, my youthful crimes and follies, my —"

"No, sir! He told me nothing, except that you no longer loved him as in your boyhood; that you had become estranged from him; and then he wept, and added, 'I love him still; I shall pray for him as long as I live.'"

Mr. Murray rose and stood before the grate with his face averted. "Impossible! You cannot deceive me! In the depths of his heart he hates and curses me. Even a brooding dove – pshaw! Allan Hammond is but a man, and it would be unnatural – utterly impossible that he could still think kindly of his old pupil. Impossible!"

~ ST. ELMO ~

Edna seized the opportunity to speak. "Of the causes that caused your estrangement, I am absolutely ignorant. Nothing has been told me, and it is a matter about which I have conjectured little. But, sir, I have seen Mr. Hammond every day for four years, and I know what I say. I tell you that he loves you as well as if you were his own son. Moreover, he –"

"Hush!" Mr. Murray said in a low voice. "You talk of what you do not understand. Believe in him if you will, but be careful not to chant his praises in my presence, and do not parade your credulity before my eyes, if you do not want me to disenchant you. Just now you are duped – so was I at your age. Your judgment slumbers, experience is in its swaddling-clothes, but I shall bide my time. The day will come ere long when these hymns of hero-worship shall be hushed, and you stand clearer-eyed, darker-hearted, before the moldering altar of your god of clay."

Edna clasped her hands. Though she was nearly shaking, her eyes flashed. "From such an awakening may God preserve me! Even if our religion were not divine, I should clasp to my heart the system and the faith that make Mr. Hammond's life serene. Oh, that I may be 'duped' into that perfection of character which makes his example beckon me ever onward and upward. If you have no gratitude, no reverence left, at least remember the veneration with which I regard him, and do not in my hearing couple his name with sneers and insults."

"'Ephraim is joined to idols; let him alone!'[30]" muttered the master of the house, with one of those graceful, mocking bows that always disconcerted Edna.

She was nervously twisting Mr. Leigh's ring around her finger. As it was too large, it slipped off, rang on the hearth, and rolled to Mr. Murray's feet.

Picking it up, he examined the emerald. After a moment he repeated the inscription and asked, "Edna Earl, do you understand these words?"

"I only know that they have been translated, 'Peace be with thee,' or 'upon thee.'"

"How came Gordon Leigh's ring on your hand? Has Tartuffe's Hebrew scheme succeeded so soon?"

---

[30] Hosea 4:17

132

Edna felt the blood coloring her cheeks yet again. "I do not understand you, Mr. Murray."

"My dear mother proves an admirable ally in this clerical matchmaker's deft hands, and Gordon's pathway is widened and weeded. Happy Gordon, blessed with such able assistants!"

The cold, sarcastic glitter of his eyes wounded Edna. "You deal in innuendoes which I cannot condescend to notice," she said haughtily. "Mr. Leigh is my friend, and he gave me this ring as a birthday present. Your mother advised me to accept it, and indeed placed it on my finger. Her sanction should certainly exempt me from your censure."

"Censure?" Mr. Murray laid a hand upon his heart. "Censure? Pardon me! It is no part of my business; but I happen to know something of gem symbols, and must be allowed to suggest that this selection is scarcely in accordance with custom for a betrothal ring."

Edna's face crimsoned, and the blood tingled to her fingers' ends. "As it was never intended as such, your carping criticism loses its point."

He stood with the jewel between his thumb and forefinger, eyeing her fixedly. On his handsome features shone a smile, treacherous and chilling as the Arctic. "It was particularly unkind, nay, cruel to put it on the hand of a woman, who of course will follow the example of all her sex, and go out fishing most diligently in the matrimonial sea. If you have chanced to look into gem history, Pliny relates how, on the coast of Cyprus, a marble lion had emerald eyes that glared down so brilliantly that the fishermen could catch nothing until they removed those jewels. Do you recollect the account?"

"No, sir, I never read it."

"Indeed! How deplorably your education has been neglected! I thought your adored Dominie Sampson down yonder at the parsonage was teaching you a prodigious amount?"

Edna compressed her lips, for she had read *Guy Mannering* when she was very small, and Mr. Hammond was nothing like Dominie Sampson. She held out her hand. "Give me my ring, Mr. Murray, and I will leave you."

Mr. Murray crooked an eyebrow. "Shall I not enlighten you on the subject of emeralds?"

"Thank you, sir, I believe not, as what I have already heard does not tempt me to prosecute the subject."

"You think me insufferably presumptuous?"

"That is a word which I should scarcely be justified in applying to you."

"You regard me as meddlesome and tyrannical?"

Edna shook her head. The edge was coming off her anger, and now she only wanted to leave.

"I generally prefer to receive answers to my questions. Pray, what do you consider me?"

Edna hesitated a moment, and sighed. "Mr. Murray, is it generous in you to question me thus in your own house?"

"I do not claim to be generous, and the world would indignantly defend me from such an accusation. Generous? On the contrary, I declare explicitly that, unlike some 'whited sepulchers[31]' of my acquaintance, I humbly beg you to recollect that I am not a perambulating advertisement of Christianity."

Raising her face, Edna looked steadfastly at him. Pain, compassion, shuddering dread filled her eyes.

"Well, you are reading me. What is the verdict?"

A long, heavily-drawn sigh was her only response.

"Will you be good enough to reply to my questions?"

"No, Mr. Murray. In lieu of perpetual strife and biting words, let there be silence between us. We cannot be friends, and it is painful to wage war here under your roof; consequently, I hope to disarm your hostility by assuring you that in future I shall not attempt to argue with you, shall not pick up the verbal gauntlets you seem disposed to throw down to me. Surely, sir, you are at least sufficiently courteous to abstain from attacks which you have been notified will not be resisted?"

"You wish me to understand that hereafter I, the owner and ruler of this establishment, shall on no account presume to address my remarks to Aaron Hunt's grandchild?"

"My words were very clear, Mr. Murray, and I meant what I said. But one thing I wish to add: while I remain here, if at any

---

[31] Matthew 23:27

134

time I can aid or serve you, Aaron Hunt's grandchild will most gladly do so. I do not flatter myself that you will ever require or accept my assistance in anything; nevertheless, I would cheerfully render it should occasion arise."

He bowed and returned the emerald, and Edna turned to leave the library.

"Before you go, examine this bauble."

He took from his vest pocket a velvet case containing a large ring, which he laid in the palm of her hand.

Edna suppressed her gasp. It was composed of an oval jacinth with a splendid scarlet fire leaping out as the light shone on it, and the diamonds that clustered around it were very costly and brilliant. There was no inscription, but upon the surface of the jacinth was engraved a female head crowned with oak leaves, among which serpents writhed and hissed, and just beneath the face grinned a dog's head. The small but exquisitely carved human face was sinister, and fiery rays seemed to dart from its relentless eyes.

Edna held it toward the grate, flashed the flame now on this side, now on that. "Is it a Medusa?"

"No."

"It is certainly very beautiful, but I do not recognize the face. Interpret for me."

"It is Hecate, Brimo, Empusa – all phases of the same malignant power; and it remains a mere matter of taste which of the titles you select. I call it Hecate."

"I have never seen you wear it."

"You never will."

"It is exceedingly beautiful." She handed it back to Mr. Murray.

"Edna, I bought this ring in Naples, intending to ask your acceptance of it in token of my appreciation of your care of that little gold key, provided I found you trustworthy. After your proclamation uttered a few minutes since, I presume I may save myself the trouble of offering it to you. Besides, Gordon might object to having his emerald over-shadowed by my matchless jacinth. Of course, your tender conscience will veto the thought of your wearing it?"

135

"I thank you, Mr. Murray; the ring is, by far, the most beautiful I have ever seen, but I certainly cannot accept it."

The room rang with Mr. Murray's mirthless laugh that made Edna shrink back a few steps.

Holding the ring at arm's length above his head, he continued, "To the 'infernal flames,' your fit type, I devote you, my costly Queen of Samothrace!"

Leaning over the grate, he dropped the jewel in the glowing coals.

"Oh, Mr. Murray, save it from destruction!"

She seized the tongs and sprang forward, but he put out his arm and held her back.

"Stand aside, if you please. Cleopatra quaffed liquid pearl in honor of Antony, Nero shivered his precious crystal goblets, and Suger pounded up sapphires to color the windows of old St. Denis! To each his own taste! If I choose to indulge myself in a diamond cremation in honor of my tutelary goddess Hecate, who has the right to stop me? See what a tawny, angry glare leaps from my royal jacinth! Old Hecate holds high carnival down there in her congenial flames."

He stood with one arm extended to bar Edna's approach, the other rested on the mantel; and a laughing, reckless demon looked out of his eyes, which were fastened on the fire.

Before the orphan could recover from her sorrowful amazement the library door opened and Henry looked in.

"Mr. Leigh is in the parlor and asked for Miss Edna."

Perplexed, irresolute, Edna stood still, watching the red coals.

After a brief silence, Mr. Murray smiled, and turned to look at her. "Pray, do not let me detain you, and rest assured that I understand your decree. You have entrenched yourself and hung out your banner, 'noli me tangere[32]!' Withdraw your pickets; I shall attempt neither siege nor escalade. Good morning. I have changed my mind about the de Guérin – leave the book on the table; it will be at your disposal after today."

He stooped to light a cigar in the coals. She walked away to the parlor, his laughter ringing out once again as the door closed behind her.

---

[32] Touch me not!

CHAPTER XIII
MISS HARDING'S ARRIVAL

The darling scheme of authorship had seized upon Edna's mind with a tenacity that conquered all other purposes. Though timidity and a haunting dread of failure prompted her to conceal the matter, even from her beloved pastor, she pondered it in secret, and bent every faculty to its successful accomplishment. Her veneration for books extended to those who created them; and her imagination invested authors with peculiar sanctity, as the true hierophants anointed with the chrism of truth.

The glittering pinnacle of consecrated and successful authorship seemed to Edna's longing gaze as sublime, and well-nigh as inaccessible, as the everlasting and untrodden Himalayan solitudes appear to some curious child of Tibet or Nepal; who, gamboling among pheasants and rhododendrons, shades her dazzled eyes with her hand, and looks up awe-stricken at the ice-domes and snow-minarets of lonely Mt. Everest, earth's loftiest and purest altar, nimbused with the dying light of day.

There were times when the thought of presenting herself as a candidate for admission into the band of literary heroes seemed to Edna unpardonably presumptuous, even sacrilegious, and she shrank back, humbled and abashed. She considered writers to be teachers, interpreters, expounders, discoverers, and creators – what could she, stumbling through the alphabet of science and art, hope to donate that would ennoble human motives or elevate aspirations? Was she, an unknown and inexperienced girl, worthy to be crowned with laurel?

Solemnly and prayerfully she weighed the subject. Having finally resolved to make one attempt, Edna looked trustingly to heaven for aid and went vigorously to work. To write without deep reflection for the mere pastime of author and readers, without aiming to inculcate some regenerative principle, or to photograph some valuable truth, was in her estimation ignoble. Her high standard demanded that all books should wander like evangels among the people, making some man, woman, or child happier, or wiser – more patient or more hopeful – by their utterances. Edna applied herself diligently to the task of gathering, from various sources, the data required for her projected work: a vindication of the unity of mythologies.

The vastness of the cosmic field she was now compelled to traverse required unwearied research, as she lifted the veils which various nations and successive epochs had woven before the shining features of truth. Today peering into the golden Gardens of the Sun at Cuzco; tomorrow clambering over Tibet glaciers to find the mystic lake of Yamuna; now delighted to recognize in Teoyamiqui, the Aztec Goddess of War, the unmistakable features of Scandinavian Valkyries; and now surprised to discover the Greek Fates sitting under the Norse tree Yggdrasil, deciding the destinies of mortals, and calling themselves Norns. She spent her days in pilgrimages to moldering shrines, and midnight often found her pacing through the classic dust of extinct mythologies.

Having grappled with her theme, she wrestled as obstinately as Jacob for the blessing of a successful solution. In order to popularize the subject, she cast it in the mold of fiction. The information and pleasure which she had derived from reading Robert Vaughan's delightful *Hours with the Mystics* suggested the idea of adopting a similar plan for her own book, and giving it the additional interest of a plot and interesting characters. To avoid anachronisms, she endeavored to treat the religions of the world in their chronological sequence, and brought in many pagan personages. A fair young Egyptian priestess of the temple of Neith, in the sacred city of Sais – where people of all climes collected to witness the festival of lamps – becoming skeptical of the miraculous attributes of the statues she had been trained to serve and worship, and impelled by an earnest love of truth to seek a faith that would satisfy her reason and purify her heart, begins to question minutely the religious tenets of travelers who visited the temple, and thus familiarized herself with all existing creeds and hierarchies. The lore so carefully garnered is finally analyzed, classified, and inscribed on papyrus. The delineation of scenes and sanctuaries in different latitudes, from the Dalai Lama's palace in Tibet, to the Mayan civilization in the western Honduras, gave full exercise to Edna's descriptive power, but imposed much labor in the departments of physical geography and architecture.

Verily! An ambitious literary program for a girl over whose head scarcely nineteen years had hung their dripping drab wintry skies, and pearly summer clouds.

One March morning, as Edna entered the breakfast room, she saw unusual gravity printed on Mrs. Murray's face; and observing an open letter on the table, conjectured the cause of her changed countenance. A moment after, St. Elmo came in, humming some British drinking song. As he seated himself his mother said, "St. Elmo, your cousin Estelle's letter contains bad news. Her father is dead; the estate is wretchedly insolvent; and she is coming to reside with us."

He at once dropped his napkin back on the table. "Then I am off for Hammerfest and the midnight sun! Who the deuce invited her I should like to know?"

"Remember, she is my sister's child. She has no other home, and I am sure it is very natural that she should come to me, her nearest relative, for sympathy and protection."

"Write to her by return mail that you will gladly allow her three thousand a year, provided she ensconces herself under some other roof than this." Mr. Murray began eating his bacon.

"Impossible. I could not wound her so deeply."

"You imagine that she entertains a most tender and profound regard for both of us?"

"Certainly, my son; we have every reason to believe that she does."

Leaning back in his chair, St. Elmo laughed. "I should really enjoy stumbling upon something that would overtax your most marvelous and indefinitely extensible credulity! When Estelle Harding becomes a resident of this house I shall pack my valise, and start to Tromso!"

Edna thought that northern Norway this time of year would be very dark and cold, but did not volunteer the information. Perhaps he would go. She wished he would.

Mr. Murray, having conquered his bacon, fell to his eggs and biscuits. "Estelle approaches like Discord, uninvited, armed with an apple or a dagger. I am perfectly willing to share my fortune with her, but I'll swear I would rather prowl for a month through the plague-stricken district of Constantinople than see her domesticated here!"

"My son, that is quite enough. She will come."

"You tried the experiment when she was a child, and we fought and scratched indefatigably. Of course, we shall renew the battle at sight."

Mrs. Murray laid aside her butter knife. "But, my dear son, there are claims urged by natural affection which it is impossible to ignore. Poor Estelle is very desolate, and has a right to our sympathy and love."

"Poor Estelle! Hoeredipetoe! The frailties of old Rome survive her virtues and her ruins!" Mr. Murray laughed again, beat a tattoo with his fork on the edge of his plate, and, rising, left the room without finishing his food.

Mrs. Murray looked annoyed. "Edna, do you know what he meant? He often amuses himself by mystifying me, and I will not gratify him by asking an explanation."

"Hoeredipetoe were legacy-hunters in Rome, where their sycophantic devotion to people of wealth furnished a constant theme for satire."

Mrs. Murray sighed heavily. Edna well understood how she felt.

Edna asked, "When do you expect your niece?"

"Day after tomorrow. I have not seen her for some years, but report says she is very fascinating, and even St. Elmo, who met her in Europe, admits that she is handsome. As you heard him, they used to quarrel most outrageously, and he took an unaccountable aversion to her; but I trust all juvenile reminiscences will vanish when they know each other better." Mrs. Murray looked at her blue enameled watch. "My dear, I have several engagements for today, and I must rely upon you to superintend the arrangement of Estelle's room. She will occupy the one next to yours. See that everything is in order. You know Hagar is sick, and the other servants are careless."

Sympathy for Miss Harding's recent affliction prepared Edna's heart to receive her cordially, and the fact that an irreconcilable feud existed between the stranger and St. Elmo filled her with hope that she might find a congenial companion in her.

On the afternoon of Estelle's arrival, Edna leaned eagerly forward to catch a glimpse of her face. As she threw back her long mourning-veil, and received her aunt's affectionate greeting, Edna's first impression was, "How exceedingly handsome – how commanding she is!"

Estelle Harding was no longer young; years had hardened the outline of her features, and imparted a certain staidness or fixedness to her calm countenance, where strong feeling or passionate impulse was never permitted to slip the elegant mask of polished suavity. She was surprisingly like Mrs. Murray, but not one line of her face resembled her cousin's.

But a few minutes later, when Mrs. Murray introduced them, and Estelle's keen eyes fell upon Edna's face, she drew back involuntarily, and a slight shiver crept over her, for an unerring instinctive repulsion told her they could never be friends.

Fixing her eyes on Edna, with a cold, almost stern scrutiny more searching than courteous, Estelle said, "I was not aware, Aunt Ellen, that you had company in the house."

"I have no company at present, my dear. Edna resides here. Do you not remember one of my letters in which I mentioned the child who was injured by the railroad accident?"

"True. I expected to see a child, certainly not a woman."

"She seems merely a child to me. But come up to your room; you must be very much fatigued by your journey."

When they left the sitting-room Edna sat down on one corner of the sofa, disappointed.

"She does not like me, that is patent; and I certainly do not like her. She is handsome and very graceful, and quite heartless. There is no inner light from her soul shining in her eyes; nothing tender in their clear depths; they are cold eyes, but not soft, winning, womanly eyes. They might, and doubtless would, hold an angry dog in check, but never draw a tired child to lean its drooping head on her lap. If she really has any feeling, her eyes should be indicted for slander. I am sorry I don't like her, and I am afraid we never shall be nearer each other than touching our finger-tips."

Such was Edna's unsatisfactory conclusion. Dismissing the subject, she picked up a book about the Mayans and read until the ladies returned and seated themselves around the fire.

To Mrs. Murray's great chagrin and mortification, St. Elmo had positively declined going to meet his cousin. He had been absent since breakfast and proved himself shamefully derelict in the courtesy demanded of him. It was almost dark when the quick gallop of his horse announced his return, and, as he trotted on horseback past the window on his way to the stables, Edna noticed Estelle's countenance brighten. During the next quarter of an hour her eyes never wandered from the door, though her head was turned to listen to Mrs. Murray's remarks. Soon after, Mr. Murray's rapid footsteps sounded in the hall, and as he entered, she rose and advanced to meet him.

He held out his hand, shook hers vigorously, and said, as he dropped it, "Mine ancient enemy, declare a truce and quiet my apprehensions; for I dreamed last night that, on sight, we flew at each other's throats, and renewed the bloody scuffles of our juvenile years. Most appallingly vivid is my recollection of a certain scar here on my left arm, where you set your pearly teeth some years ago."

"My dear cousin, as I have had no provocation since I was separated from you, I believe I have grown harmless and amiable. How very well you look, St. Elmo."

"Thank you. I should like to return the compliment, but facts forbid. You are thinner than when we dined together in Paris. Are you really in love with that excruciating Beau Brummell of a Count who danced such indefatigable attendance upon you?"

"To whom do you allude?"

"That youth with languishing brown eyes, who parted his 'hyacinthine tresses' in the middle of his head; whose moustache required a most powerful microscope - and who absolutely believed that the diva Adelaide Ristori singled him out of her vast audiences as the most appreciative of her listeners; who was eternally humming music from *Ernani* and raving about *La Traviata*. Your memory is treacherous – as your conscience? Well, then, that man, who I once told you 'that he abused the permission men have to be ugly.'[33]"

"Ah, you mean poor Victor! He spent the winter in Seville. I had a letter last week."

"When do you propose to make him my cousin?"

"Not until I become an inmate of a lunatic asylum."

"Poor wretch! I swear you played fiancée to perfection. Your lavish expenditure of affection seemed to me altogether uncalled for, considering the fact that the fish already floundered at your feet."

The reminiscence evidently annoyed Estelle though her lips smiled. While his words were pointed with a sarcasm lost upon Edna, it was fully appreciated by his cousin.

Standing at his side, Estelle put her hand on his shoulder. "St. Elmo, I am sorry to see that you have not improved one iota; that all your wickedness clings to you like Sinbad's burden."

As he looked down at her, his lips curled. "Nevertheless, I find a pale ghost of pity for you wandering up and down what was once my heart. After the glorious intoxication of Parisian life, how can you endure the tedium of this most moral and stupid of all country towns? Little gossip, few flirtations, neither witty people nor gourmands – what will become of you? I shall, with exemplary hospitality, dedicate myself to your service – shall try to make amends for your beloved Victor's absence, and solemnly promise to do everything in my power to assist you in strangling time, except parting my hair in the middle of my head, and making love to you. With these reservations, command me as you wish."

Her face flushed as she withdrew her hand and sat down.

Taking his favorite position on the rug, with one hand thrust into his pocket and the other dallying with his gold watch-chain, Mr. Murray continued, "Entire honesty on my part, and an amiable weakness for talking tediously on the charms of my native village, compel me to assure you, that, notwithstanding the deprivation of opera and theatre, the masquerade balls and the

---

[33] From The Letters of Madame de Sévigné to her Daughter and Friends, Letter XXXIV

Bois de Bologne and the many beauties of Paris, I believe you will be surprised to find that the tone of society here is quite up to the lofty standard of the Academy of Sciences. Our pastors are erudite as Abelard, and rigid as Trappists; our young ladies are learned as that ancient blue-stocking daughter of Pythagoras, and as pious as St. Salvia, who never washed her face. Girls yet in their teens are much better acquainted with Hebrew than Miriam was when she sung it on the shore of the Red Sea. You look incredulous, my fair cousin. Nay, permit me to complete the inventory of the acquirements of your future companions. They quote fluently from the five scrolls of the Megillot. If an incidental allusion is made about archeology, lo, they bombard you with a broadside of authorities, and cite obscure terminology that would absolutely make the hair of actual archeologists on end. I assure you the scholars of the Old World would catch their breath with envious amazement, if they could only enjoy the advantage of the conversation of these very learned refugees from the nursery!"

Although his eyes had never wandered from his cousin's face, toward the corner where Edna sat embroidering some mats, she felt the blood burning in her cheeks, and forced herself to look up.

At that moment, as St. Elmo stood in the soft glow of the firelight, he was handsomer than she had ever seen him. When he glanced swiftly over his shoulder to mark the effect of his words, their eyes met, and she smiled involuntarily.

"For shame, St. Elmo. I will have you presented by the grand jury of this county for wholesome defamation of the people thereof," said his mother, shaking her finger at him.

Estelle laughed and shrugged her shoulders. "My poor cousin, how I pity you. Henceforth the sole study of my life shall be to forget my alphabet. Miss Earl, do you understand Hebrew?"

"Oh, no; I have only begun to study it."

"Estelle, it is the popular and fashionable amusement here. Young ladies and young gentlemen form classes for mutual aid and 'mutual admiration' while they clasp hands over the Masora. If the members of the 'Society for the Diffusion of Useful Knowledge[34],' could only have been persuaded to investigate the

---

[34] This society was created to publish informative books and periodicals for people who didn't have the money or means to obtain a formal education – as Edna would have been if she'd

intellectual status of the 'rising generation' of our village, there is little room to doubt that they would have disbanded because there was no more work for them to do. I imagine Tennyson is a clairvoyant, and was looking at the young people of this vicinage, when he wrote:

'Knowledge comes, but wisdom lingers.'[35]

Not even pretentious and infallible 'Brain Town,' which mere mortals call Boston, can show a more ambitious covey of literary fledglings!"

"Your random firing seems to produce no confusion on the part of your game," answered his cousin, withdrawing her gaze from Edna's tranquil features, on which a half-smile still lingered.

Mr. Murray did not seem to hear her words, but his eyebrows thickened, as he drew a couple of letters from his pocket and looked at the superscription.

Giving one to his mother, who sat looking over a newspaper, he crossed the room and silently laid the other on Edna's lap.

It was postmarked in New York and addressed in a gentleman's large, round business handwriting. Edna's face flushed with pleasure as she broke the seal, glanced at the signature, and without pausing for a perusal, hastily put the letter into her pocket.

"Who can be writing to you, Edna?" asked Mrs. Murray, when she had finished reading her own letter.

"Oh, doubtless some Syrian scribe has written a Chaldee love letter which she cannot spell out without the friendly aid of dictionary and grammar. Permit her to withdraw and decipher it. Meantime here comes Henry to announce dinner, and a plate of soup will strengthen her for her task." Mr. Murray offered his arm to his cousin.

During dinner he talked constantly, rapidly, brilliantly of men and things abroad; now hurling a sarcasm at Estelle's head, now laughing at his mother's protests, and studiously avoiding any

never left her old home.
[35] "Locksley Hall" – Lord Alfred Tennyson

further notice of Edna, who was never so thoroughly at ease as when he seemed to forget her presence.

Estelle sat at his right hand. As he refilled his glass with bubbling champagne, he leaned over and whispered a few words in her ear that brought a look of surprise and pleasure into her eyes. Edna only saw the expression of his face, and the tenderness, the pleading written there puzzled her. The next moment they rose from the table. As Mr. Murray drew his cousin's hand under his arm, Edna hurried away to her own room.

Among the numerous magazines to which St. Elmo subscribed was one renowned for the lofty tone of its articles and the sharpness of its criticisms. This periodical Edna always singled out and read avidly.

The name of the editor roused fear in the imagination of all humble authorlings, and had become a synonym for merciless critical censure.

To this literary lion Edna had daringly written some weeks before, stating her determination to attempt a book, and asking permission to submit the first chapter to his searching inspection. She wrote that she expected him to find faults – he always did; and she preferred that her work should be roughly handled by him, rather than smeared with faint praise by men of inferior critical astuteness.

The anxiously expected reply had come at last, and as she locked her door and sat down to read it, she trembled from head to foot.

In the center of a handsome sheet of tinted paper she read,

"MADAM: In reply to your very extraordinary request I have the honor to inform you, that my time is so entirely consumed by necessary and important claims, that I find no leisure at my command for the examination of the embryonic chapter of a contemplated book.
"I am, madam,
"Very respectfully,
"DOUGLASS G. MANNING."

Tears of disappointment filled her eyes and for a moment she bit her lip with uncontrolled vexation. Refolding the letter, she put it in a drawer of her desk, and said sorrowfully, "I certainly had no right to expect anything more polite from him. He snubs even his popular contributors, and of course he would not be particularly courteous to an unknown scribbler. Perhaps someday I may make him regret that letter; and such a triumph will more than compensate for this mortification. One might think that all literary people, editors, authors, reviewers, would sympathize with each other, and stretch out their hands to aid one another, but they wage an internecine war among themselves, though it certainly cannot be termed 'civil strife,' judging from Mr. Douglass Manning's letter."

Chagrined and perplexed, Edna walked up and down the room, wondering what step to take next. She had been trying to persuade herself that she ought to consult Mr. Hammond. But she preferred to surprise him and hear his impartial opinion of a printed article which he could not suspect that she had written. Finally, she resolved to say nothing to anyone, to work on in silence, relying upon herself. With this determination she sat down before her desk, opened the manuscript of her book, and settled into writing the second chapter.

But before she had finished even the first sentence, a hasty rap summoned her to the door.

She opened it, and found Mr. Murray standing in the hall with a candle in his hand. "Where is that volume of chess problems which you had last week?"

"It is here, sir."

She took it from the table. As she approached him, Mr. Murray held the light close to her countenance, and gave her one of his keen looks. Something in the curious expression of his face, and the evident satisfaction which he derived from his investigation, told Edna that the book was a mere pretext.

She drew back. "Have I any other book that you need?"

"No; I have all I came for." Smiling half mischievously, half maliciously, he turned and left her.

"What did he see in my face that amused him?" Edna walked up to the bureau and examined her own image in the mirror.

There, on her cheeks, were the unmistakable traces of her tears of vexation.

Much annoyed, she said to herself, "At least he can have no idea of the cause, and that is some comfort, for he is too honorable to open my letters."

But a doubt flashed into her mind.

"How do I know that he is honorable? Can any man be worthy of trust who holds nothing sacred, and sneers at all religions? No; he has no conscience; and yet – "

She sighed and went back to her manuscript.

For a while, St. Elmo Murray's mocking eyes seemed to glitter on the pages, but her thoughts ere long were anchored once more with the olive-crowned priestess in the temple at Sais.

CHAPTER XIV
AN UNSATISFACTORY MAY DAY

Domestic traditions and household customs are the great arteries in which beat the social life of humanity. Roman women suffered no first day of May to pass without celebrating the festival of the woman's goddess Bona Dea. Two thousand years later, girls who know nothing of the manners and customs of ancient Italy lie down to sleep on the last day of April, and kissing their mother's face that bends above their pillows, eagerly repeat,

"You must wake and call me early, call me early, mother dear:
Tomorrow'll be the happiest time of all the glad new-year;
Of all the glad new-year, mother, the maddest, merriest day,
For I'm to be Queen o' the May, mother; I'm to be Queen o' the May."[36]

For a fortnight Edna had been busily engaged in writing colloquies and speeches for the Sabbath-school children of the village for the May Day festivities, and she had been attending the rehearsals for the perfection of the various parts. Assisted by Mr. Hammond and the ladies of his congregation, she had prepared a varied program, and was almost as much interested in the success of the youthful orators as the superintendent of the school or the parents of the children.

The day was clear, balmy, all that could be asked of the blue-eyed month – and as the festival was to be celebrated in a beautiful grove of elms and chestnuts, almost in sight of Le Bocage, Edna went over very early to aid in arranging the tables,

---

[36] "The May Queen" – Lord Alfred Tennyson.

decking the platforms with flowers, and training one juvenile orator, whose May Day speech was unpromising.

Despite her patient teaching, this boy's awkwardness threatened to spoil everything, and as she watched the nervous wringing of his hands and desperate shuffling of his feet, she was tempted to give him up in despair. The dew hung heavily on grass and foliage, and the morning carol of the birds still swelled through the leafy aisles of the grove, when she took the trembling boy to a secluded spot, directed him to stand on a mossy log, where two lizards lay blinking, and repeat his speech.

He stammered most unsatisfactorily through it. Intent on his improvement, Edna climbed upon a stump and delivered his speech for him, gesticulating and emphasizing just as she wished him to do. As the last words of the speech passed her lips, and while she stood on the stump, a sudden clapping of hands startled her.

Gordon Leigh's cheerful voice exclaimed, "Encore! Encore! You have not your equal among female elocutionists. I would not have missed it for any consideration, so pray forgive me for eavesdropping." Mr. Leigh came forward, held out his hand and added, "Allow me to assist you in dismounting from your temporary rostrum, whence you bear your 'blushing honors thick upon you[37].' Jamie, do you think you can do as well as Miss Edna when your time comes?"

"Oh, no, sir; but I will try not to make her ashamed of me."

He snatched his hat from the log and ran off, leaving his friends to walk back more leisurely to the spot selected for the tables.

Edna had been too much disconcerted by Mr. Leigh's unexpected appearance to utter a word until now. Annoyed, she said, "I am very sorry you interrupted me, for Jamie needed more guidance. Have you nothing better to do than stray about the woods like a satyr?"

"I am quite willing to be satyrized even by you on this occasion. What man, whose blood is not curdled by cynicism, can prefer to spend May Day among musty law books and red tape, when he has the alternative of listening to such a speech as you

---

[37] Henry VIII: Act 3, Scene 2 -- Shakespeare

favored me with just now, or of participating in the sports of one hundred happy children? Besides, some little bird told me that I should find you here; and I wanted to see you before the company assembled. Edna, why have you avoided me of late?"

They stood close to each other in the shade of the elms. Gordon thought that never before had Edna looked so beautiful, as the mild perfumed breeze stirred the folds of her dress and fluttered the blue ribbons that looped her hair and girdled her waist.

Just at that instant, ere she could reply, a rustling of the undergrowth arrested further conversation. Mr. Murray stepped out of the adjoining thicket, with his gun in his hand, and his grim pet Ali at his heels. Whatever surprise he may have felt, his countenance certainly betrayed none, as he lifted his hat and said, "Good morning, Leigh. I shall not intrude upon your tête-à-tête, on which I have happened to stumble, longer than is necessary. Are you so fortunate as to have a match with you? I find my case empty."

Mr. Leigh took a match from his pocket. While Mr. Murray lighted his cigar, his eyes rested on Edna's flushed face. She averted her eyes.

"Are you not coming to the children's celebration?" asked Gordon.

"No, indeed! While I am constitutionally and habitually opposed to labor, I swear I should prefer to plough or break stones till sundown, sooner than listen to all the rant and fustian that spectators will be called on to endure this morning. I have not sufficient courage to remain and witness what would certainly recall 'the manner of Bombastes Furioso making love to Distaffina.'[38] Will you have a cigar? Good morning."

Mr. Murray lifted his hat, shouldered his gun, and calling to his dog, disappeared among the thick undergrowth.

---

38 The original quote from the literature is "Falling on one knee, he put both hands on his heart and rolled up his eyes, much after the manner of Bombastes Furioso making love to Distaffina." In those days, "making love" meant flirting and making eyes. This particular quote is from a book called *An Explanatory and Pronouncing Dictionary of the Noted Names of Fiction*, and from a look at the contents (a definition for *Bona Dea* is on the same page), I suspect that Miss 'Gusta made good use of this handy little manual for some of her references in *St. Elmo*.

"What an incorrigible savage!" muttered Mr. Leigh, replacing the match-case in his pocket.

Edna made no answer and tried to slip away, but he caught her dress and detained her.

"Do not go until you hear what I have to say to you. More than once you have denied me an opportunity of expressing what you must long ago have suspected. Edna, you know very well that I love you better than everything else. I have loved you from the first day of our acquaintance; and I have come to tell you that my happiness is in your dear little hands; that my future will be joyless unless you share it; that the one darling hope of my life is to call you my wife. Edna, do not draw your hand from mine! Dear Edna, let me keep it always. Do I mistake your feelings when I hope that you return my affection?"

"You entirely mistake them, Mr. Leigh, in supposing that you can ever be more to me than a very dear and valued friend. It grieves me very much to be forced to give you pain or cause you disappointment; but I should wrong you even more than myself, were I to leave you in doubt concerning my feeling toward you. I like your society, and you have my entire confidence and highest esteem; but I cannot be your wife."

"Why not?"

"Because I do not love you as I think I ought to love the man I marry."

Mr. Leigh blew out his cheeks. "My dear Edna, answer one question candidly. Do you love anyone else better than you love me?"

"No, Mr. Leigh."

"Does Mr. Murray stand between your heart and mine?"

Edna nearly made a face. "Oh, no, Mr. Leigh!"

"Then I will not yield the hope of winning your love. If your heart is free, I will have it all my own one day! O Edna, why cannot you love me? I would make you very happy. My darling's home should possess all that fortune and devoted affection could supply; not one wish should remain ungratified."

Edna met his eyes. "I am able to earn a home; I do not intend to marry for one."

"Ah, your pride is your only fault, and it will cause us both much suffering, I fear. Edna, I know how sensitive you are, and how deeply your delicacy has been wounded by the malicious meddling of ill-mannered gossips. I know why you abandoned your Hebrew study. A wish to spare your feelings prevented me from punishing certain scandalmongers as they deserved. But, dearest, do not visit their offences upon me. Because they dared ascribe their own ignoble motives to you, do not lock your heart against me and refuse me the privilege of making your life happy."

"Mr. Leigh, you are not necessary to my happiness. While our tastes are in many respects congenial, and it is pleasant to be with you, my heart is not yours. I will not marry a man that I do not love."

"O Edna, you are cruel, unlike yourself!"

Suddenly catching both his hands in hers, Edna stooped and pressed her lips to them. "Forgive me, sir, if I seem so. No woman should marry a man whose affection and society are not absolutely essential to her peace of mind and heart. Applying this test to you, I find that mine is in no degree dependent on you; and, though you may have no warmer friend, I must tell you it is utterly useless for you to hope that I shall ever love you as you wish. Mr. Leigh, I regret that I cannot; and if my heart were only puppet of my will, I would try to return your affection, because I appreciate so fully all that you generously offer me. Today you stretch out your hand to a poor girl, of unknown parentage, reared by charity – a girl considered by your family and friends an obscure interloper in aristocratic circles. With a noble magnanimity, for which I shall thank you always, you say, 'Come, take my name, share my fortune, wrap yourself in my love, and be happy. I will give you a lofty position in society, whence you can look down on those who sneer at your poverty and lineage.' O, Mr. Leigh, God knows I wish I loved you as you deserve! Ambition and gratitude alike plead for you; but I cannot consent to be your wife."

Her eyes were full of tears as she looked in his handsome face, hitherto so bright and genial; now clouded and saddened by a bitter disappointment.

"Although you refuse to encourage, you cannot crush the hope that my affection will, after a while, win yours in return. You are very young, and as yet scarcely know your own heart. Unshaken constancy on my part will plead for me in coming years. I will be patient, and as long as you are Edna Earl – as long as you remain mistress of your own heart – I shall cling fondly to the only hope that gladdens my future. Over my feelings you have no control; you may refuse me your hand – that is your right – but while I shall abstain from demonstrations of affection, I shall certainly cherish the hope of possessing it. Meantime, permit me to ask whether you still contemplate leaving Mrs. Murray's house? Miss Harding told my sister yesterday that in a few months you would obtain a situation as governess or teacher in a school."

"Such is certainly my intention; but I am at a loss to conjecture how Miss Harding obtained her information, as the matter has not been alluded to since her arrival."

Mr. Leigh came a little closer and lowered his voice. "I trust you will pardon me the liberty I take, in warning you to be exceedingly circumspect in your discussions with her. I have reason to believe that her sentiments toward you are not as friendly as might be desired."

"Thank you, Mr. Leigh. I am aware of her antipathy, though of its cause I am ignorant. Our communication is limited to the salutations of the day, and the courtesies of the table."

Drawing from her finger the emerald which had occasioned so many disquieting reflections, Edna continued, "You must allow me to return the ring, which I have hitherto worn as a token of friendship, and which I cannot consent to keep any longer. 'Peace be with you,' dear friend, is the earnest prayer of my heart. Our paths in life will soon diverge so widely that we shall probably see each other rarely; but none of your friends will rejoice more sincerely than I to hear of your happiness and prosperity. Good-bye, Mr. Leigh. Think of me hereafter only as a friend."

She gave him both hands for a minute, left the ring in his palm, and, with tears in her eyes, went back to the tables and platforms.

Chattering groups of happy children gathered here: red-cheeked boys clad in white linen suits, with new straw hats belted with black, and fair-browed girls robed in spotless muslin, garlanded with flowers, and bright with rosy badges. Sparkling eyes, laughing lips, sweet, mirthful voices, and shadowless hearts filled the grove.

The celebration was a complete success. Even awkward Jamie acquitted himself with more ease and grace than his friends had dared to hope. Speeches and songs were warmly applauded, proud parents watched their merry darlings with eyes that brimmed with tenderness; and the heart of Semiramis, Queen of Assyria, never throbbed more triumphantly than that of the delighted young Queen of May, who would not have exchanged her floral crown for all the jewels that glittered in the diadem of the Assyrian sovereign.

Late in the evening of that festal day Mr. Hammond sat alone on the portico of the old-fashioned parsonage. The full moon, rising over the arched windows of the neighboring church, shone on the marble monuments that marked the rows of graves. The golden beams stole through the thick vines which clustered around the wooden columns, embroidered in glittering arabesque the polished floor at the old man's feet.

That solemn, mysterious silence which nature reverently folds like a velvet pall over the bier of the pale, dead day, when the sky is

"Filling more and more with crystal light,
As pensive evening deepens into night,"[39]

was now hushing the hum and stir of the village. Only the occasional far-off bark of a dog, and the clear, sweet vesper-song of a mockingbird singing in the myrtle tree, broke the repose so soothing after the bustle of the day. To labor and to pray from dawn till dusk is the only legacy which sin-stained man brought through the flaming gate of Eden. In the gray twilight, Mother Earth stretches her vast hands tenderly over her drooping, toil-spent children, and mercifully murmurs, "Lord, now lettest thou thy servant depart in peace."

---

[39] from *Sonnets: To Lady Fitzgerald*, "In Her Seventieth Year" – William Wordsworth

Close to the minister's armchair stood a small table covered with a snowy cloth, on which was placed the evening meal, consisting of strawberries, honey, bread, butter and milk. At his feet lay the white cat, bathed in moonlight and playing with a fragrant spray of honeysuckle which trailed within reach of her paws, and swung to and fro as the soft breeze stole up from the starry south. The supper went untasted. Mr. Hammond's silvered head leaned wearily on his hand, and through a tearful mist his mild eyes looked toward the churchyard, where gleamed the monumental shafts that guarded his white-robed, darling dead.

His past was a fruitful field of hallowed labor, bounteous with promise for that prophetic harvest whereof God's angels are reapers. His future, whose near horizon was already rimmed with the light of eternity, was full of that blessed 'peace which passeth all understanding.' Yet tonight, precious reminiscences laid their soft, mesmerizing fingers on his heart. Before him, all unbidden, floated visions of other May Days, long, long ago, when the queen of his boyish affections had worn her crown of flowers; and many, many years later, when, as the queen of his home, and the proud mother of his children, she had stood with her quivering hand nestled in his, listening breathlessly to the May Day speech of their golden-haired daughter, Annie.

"Why does the sea of thought thus backward roll?
Memory's the breeze that through the cordage raves,
And ever drives us on some homeward shoal,
As if she loved the melancholy waves
That, murmuring shoreward, break o'er a reef of graves."[40]

The song of the mockingbird still rang from the downy cradle of myrtle blossoms, and a whip-poor-will answered from a cedar in the churchyard, when the sudden slamming of the parsonage gate startled the shy thrush that slept in the vines that overarched it. A moment later, Mr. Leigh came slowly up the walk, which was lined with purple and white irises.

[40] "Summer Morning" – Thomas Miller. From a book called "Under Green Leaves: A Book of Rural Poems" edited by Richard Henry Stoddard.

As he ascended the steps and removed his hat, the pastor rose and placed a chair for him near his own. "Good evening, Gordon. Where did you hide yourself all day? I expected to find you taking part in the children's festival and hunted for you in the crowd."

"I expected to attend, but this morning something occurred which unfitted me for enjoyment of any kind; consequently, I thought it best to keep myself and my moodiness out of sight."

"I trust nothing serious has happened?"

"Yes, something that threatens to blast all my hopes, and make my life one great disappointment. Has not Edna told you?"

"She has told me nothing relative to yourself, but I noticed that she was grieved about something. She went home very early, pleading fatigue and headache."

"I wish I had a shadow of hope that her heart ached also. Mr. Hammond, I am very wretched, and have come to you for sympathy and counsel. Of course, you have seen for a long time that I loved Edna very devotedly, that I intended if possible to make her my wife. Although she was very shy and guarded, and never gave me any reason to believe she returned my affection, I thought – I hoped she would not reject me, and I admired her even more because of her reticence, for I could not value a love which I knew was mine unasked.

"Today I mentioned the subject to her, told her how entirely my heart was hers, offered her my hand and fortune, but she refused me most decidedly. Her manner more than her words discouraged me. She showed so plainly that she felt only friendship for me and entertained only regret for the pain she gave me. She was kind and delicate, but oh, so crushingly positive. I had no more place in her heart than that whip-poor-will in the cedars yonder. And yet I shall not give her up; while I live I will cling to the hope that I may finally win her. Thousands of women have rejected a man again and again and at last yielded and accepted him. I do not believe Edna can withstand the devotion of a lifetime."

"Do not deceive yourself, Gordon. It is true some women are flattered by a man's perseverance. They first reproach themselves for the suffering they inflict, then gratitude for constancy comes to plead for the inconsolable suitor, and at last they persuade themselves that such devotion cannot fail to make them happy. I must add that such an approach is cruel to the woman, who only accepts the suitor against the dictates of her own heart. Such a woman Edna is not. I sympathize with you, Gordon. It is because I love you so sincerely that I warn you against a hope destined to cheat you."

"But she admitted that she loved no one else. I can see no reason why, after a while, she may not give me her heart."

"I have watched her for years. I think I know her nature better than any other human being, and I tell you, Edna Earl will never persuade herself to marry any man, no matter what his position and endowments may be. She is not a dependent woman; while she loves her friends tenderly, she feels the need of no one. If she ever marries, it will not be from gratitude or devotion, but because she learned to love, almost against her will, some strong, vigorous thinker, some man whose will and intellect masters hers, who compels her heart's homage, and without whose society she cannot persuade herself to live."

"And why may I not hope that such will, one day, be my good fortune?"

For a few minutes Mr. Hammond was silent, walking up and down the wide portico. When he resumed his seat, he laid his hand affectionately on the young man's shoulder.

"My dear Gordon, your happiness as well as hers is very dear to me. I love you both, and I pray you forgive me if what I am about to say should mortify you. Gordon, you will never be Edna's husband, because intellectually she is your superior. To rule the man she married would make her miserable. She could only find happiness in being ruled by an intellect to which she looked up admiringly. I know that many very gifted women have married their inferiors, but Edna is peculiar, and in some respects totally unlike any other woman whose character I have studied. Gordon, you are not offended with me?"

Mr. Leigh put out his hand, grasped that of his companion, and his voice was marked by unwonted tremor. "You pain me beyond expression, but I could never be offended at words which are dictated by genuine affection. Mr. Hammond, might not years of thought and study remove this obstacle? I would dedicate my life to attain knowledge, to improve my faculties."

Mr. Hammond's eyes were sad. "I am afraid that erudition would not satisfy her. Do you suppose she could wed a mere walking encyclopedia?"

"But, sir, women listen to the promptings of heart much oftener than to the cold, stern dictates of reason."

"Very true, Gordon; but she already has been listening to her heart. I grieve to say that it seems to have decided against you. I know no man whose noble, generous heart renders him so worthy of her as yourself. If she could only love you as you deserve, I should be rejoiced."

"Do you know how soon she expects to leave Le Bocage?"

"Probably about the close of the year."

With a deep sigh, Mr. Leigh gazed at the moon for a moment, and the white light showed the distinct pain in his noble face. "I cannot bear to think of her as going among strangers – being buffeted by the world, while she toils to earn a living. It is inexpressibly bitter for me to reflect that the girl whom I love above everything upon earth, who would preside so gracefully, so elegantly over my home, and make my life so proud and happy, should prefer to shut herself up in a school-room, and wear out her life in teaching fretful, spoiled children. Oh, Mr. Hammond, can you not prevail upon her to abandon this scheme?"

"If she feels that the hand of duty points out this destiny as hers, I shall not attempt to dissuade her; for peace of mind and heart is found nowhere, save in accordance with the dictates of conscience. Now that Miss Harding has arrived at Le Bocage, I fear Edna will feel that Mrs. Murray does not need her as a companion, and her proud spirit will rebel against the surveillance to which she is subjected. She has always expressed a desire to maintain herself by teaching, but I suspect that she will do so by her pen. When she prepares to quit Mrs. Murray's house I shall offer her a home in mine; but I have little hope that she will accept it. She wishes to go to some large city, where she can command advantages beyond her reach in this quiet little place, where her own exertions will pay for the roof that covers her.

However we may deplore this decision, certainly we cannot blame her for the feeling that prompts it."

"I have racked my brain for some plan by which I could share my fortune with her without her suspecting the donor; for if she rejects my hand, I know she would not accept one cent from me. Can you suggest any feasible scheme?"

After some reflection Mr. Hammond shook his head. "We can do nothing but wait and watch for an opportunity of aiding her. I confess, Gordon, her future fills me with serious apprehension. She is so proud, so sensitive, and yet so boundlessly ambitious. Should her high hopes be destined to the sharp and summary defeat which frequently overtakes ambitious men and women early in life, I shudder for her closing years and the almost unendurable bitterness of her disappointed soul."

"Mr. Hammond, you may be correct in your predictions, but I hope you are wrong. I cannot believe that any woman whose heart is as warm as my dear Edna's will continue to reject such love as I shall always offer her. Of one thing I feel assured. No man will ever love her as well, or better than I do, and to this knowledge she will awake someday. God bless her! She is the only woman I shall ever want to call my wife."

"I sympathize most keenly with your severe disappointment, my dear young friend. I shall earnestly pray that God will overrule all things for your happiness as well as hers. He who notes the death of sparrows, and numbers even the hairs of our heads, will not doom your noble, tender heart to lifelong loneliness and hunger."

With a long, close clasp of hands they parted. Gordon Leigh walked sadly between the royal rows of irises, hoping that the future would redeem the past. The old man sat alone in the serene, silent night, watching the shimmer of the moon on the marble that covered his dead.

CHAPTER XV
EDNA'S CORRESPONDENCE

Flushed and angry, Mrs. Murray walked up and down the floor of the sitting-room. "It is impossible, Estelle. The girl is not a fool, and nothing less than idiocy can explain such conduct!"

Playing with the jet bracelet on her rounded arm, Miss Harding replied, "As Mrs. Inge happens to be his sister, I presume she knows whereof she speaks, and she certainly expressed great delight at the failure of Gordon Leigh's suit. She told me that he was much depressed in consequence of Edna's rejection, and manifested more feeling than she had deemed possible. Of course, she is much gratified that her family is saved from the disgrace of such a mésalliance."

"You will oblige me by being more choice in the selection of your words, Estelle," Mrs. Murray snapped. "It is a poor compliment to me to remark that any man would be disgraced by marrying a girl whom I have raised and educated as carefully as if she were my own daughter. Barring her obscure birth, Edna is as worthy of Gordon as any dainty pet of fashion who lounges in Clara Inge's parlors, and I shall take occasion to tell her so if ever she hints at 'mésalliance' in my presence."

"In that event she will doubtless retort by asking you in her bland and thoroughly well-bred style, whether you intend to give your consent to Edna's marriage with my cousin, St. Elmo?"

Mrs. Murray stopped suddenly. Confronting her niece, said sternly, "What do you mean, Estelle Harding?"

"My dear aunt, the goodness of your heart has blinded you to the character of the girl you have taken into your house and honored with your confidence and affection. Be patient with me while I unmask this shrewd little schemer. She is poor and unknown. If she leaves your roof, as she pretends is her purpose,

161

she must work for her own maintenance, which no one will do from choice when an alternative of luxurious ease is within reach. Mr. Leigh is very handsome, very agreeable, wealthy and intelligent, and is considered a fine match for any girl; yet your protégée discards him most positively, alleging that she does not love him, and prefers hard labor as a teacher to securing an elegant home by becoming his wife. That she can decline so brilliant an offer seems to you incredible, but I knew from the beginning that she would not accept it. My dear Aunt Ellen, she aspires to the honor of becoming your daughter-in-law, and can well afford to refuse Mr. Leigh's hand, when she hopes to be mistress of Le Bocage."

"What?"

"She is pretty, and she knows it, and her cunning handling of her cards would really amuse and interest me if I were not grieved at the deception she is practicing upon you. It has, I confess, greatly surprised me that, with your extraordinary astuteness in other matters, you should prove so obtuse concerning the machinations which the girl carries on in your own house. Can you not see how adroitly she flatters St. Elmo by poring over his stupid manuscripts and professing devotion to his favorite authors? It is unnatural for a pretty young girl like Edna to sympathize so intensely with my cousin's outlandish studies and tastes. Before I had been in this house twenty-four hours, I saw the game she plays so skillfully. I only wonder that you, my dear aunt, should be victimized by the cunning of one on whom you have lavished so much kindness."

Mrs. Murray shook her head. "I do not believe a word of it!"

"Look at the facts," Estelle said calmly. "She certainly has refused to marry Mr. Leigh, and situated as she is, how else can you explain the mystery? The solution is patent to everyone save yourself."

Painful surprise kept Mrs. Murray silent for some moments. At last she exclaimed, "I know her much better than you possibly can. So far from wishing to marry my son, she dislikes him exceedingly. Her aversion to him has even caused me regret, and at times they scarcely treat each other with ordinary courtesy. She systematically avoids him. Occasionally, when I request her to take a message to him, I have been amused at the expression of her face, and her maneuvers to find a substitute. No, no, she is too conscientious to wear a mask. You must come up with a better solution."

Estelle chuckled. "She is shrewd enough to see that St. Elmo is satiated with flattery and homage. She suspects that pique alone can force an entrance into the citadel of his heart, and her demonstrations of aversion are only a ruse. My poor aunt! I pity the disappointment and mortification to which you are destined, when you discover how complete is the imposture she practices."

"I tell you, Estelle, I am neither blind nor in my dotage. That girl has no more intention of – "

The door opened, and Mr. Murray came in. Glancing round the room, and observing the sudden silence – his mother's flushed cheeks and angry eyes, his cousin's lurking smile – he threw himself on the sofa, saying, "Can rage so great dwell in celestial minds? Pray what dire calamity has raised a feud between you two? Has your little French Count grown importunate? Does my mother refuse to speedily bestow upon him that pretty hand of yours, which has so often been surrendered to his tender clasp? If you need me to intercede on your behalf for Count Victor, pray command me, Estelle."

Mrs. Murray looked keenly at Estelle. "My son, did it ever occur to you that your eloquence might be more successfully and agreeably exercised in your own behalf?"

"My profound humility never permitted the ghost of such a suggestion to affright my soul! Judging from the confusion which greeted my entrance, I am forced to conclude that I am not wanted. But prudent regard for the reputation of the household urged me to venture near enough to the line of battle to inform you that the noise of the conflict proclaims it to the servants, and your unmistakable tones arrested my attention even in the yard. Family feuds become really respectable if only waged in a whisper," he said emphatically in a whisper.

He rose as if to leave the room, but his mother motioned him to remain. "I am very much annoyed at a matter which surprises me beyond expression. Do you know that Gordon Leigh has made

Edna an offer of marriage, and she has been insane enough to refuse him?"

"Refused him!"

"Was ever a girl so stupidly blind to her true interest? She cannot hope to make half so brilliant a match, for he is certainly one of the most promising young men in the state, and would give her a position in the world that otherwise she can never attain."

"Refused affluence, fashionable social stains! Diamonds, laces, rose-curtained boudoir, and hot-houses! Refused the glorious privilege of calling Mrs. Inge 'sister,' and the opportunity of snubbing *le beau monde* who persistently snub her. Impossible! You are growing old and oblivious of the strategy you indulged in when throwing your toils around your devoted admirer, whom I ultimately had the honor of calling my father. Your pet vagrant, Edna, is no simpleton; she can take care of her own interests, and, accept my word for it, intends to do so. She is only practicing a little harmless coquetry – toying with her victim, as fish circle round and round the bait which they fully intend to swallow."

Mrs. Murray frowned. "St. Elmo, it is neither respectful nor courteous to be eternally sneering at women in the presence of your own mother. As for Edna, I am intensely provoked at her deplorable decision, for I know that when she once decides on a course of conduct neither persuasion nor argument will move her one iota. She is incapable of the contemptible coquetry you imputed to her, and Gordon may as well look elsewhere for a bride."

"You are quite right, Aunt Ellen; her refusal was most positive," Estelle added.

"Did she inform you of the fact?" asked Mr. Murray.

"No, but Mr. Leigh told his sister that she gave him no hope whatever."

"Then, for the first time in my life, I have succeeded in slandering human nature, which, hitherto, I deemed quite impossible."

"Hush, St. Elmo!" Mrs. Murray said, annoyed.

"And she absolutely, positively declines to sell herself?" St. Elmo asked, fishing a cigar out of his pocket. "Why, I would have bet half my estate on Gordon's chances; I imagined the girl was clay in the experienced hands of matrimonial potters such as you, my dear mother, and the schemer at the parsonage. Accept, my dear mother, my most heartfelt sympathy in your ignominious defeat. Permit me to comfort you with the assurance that your campaign has been conducted with distinguished ability on your part. You have displayed topographical accuracy, wariness, and an insight into the character of your antagonist, which entitle you to an exalted place among modern tacticians; and you have the consolation of knowing that you have been defeated most unscientifically, and in direct opposition to every well-established maxim and rule of strategy, by this rash, incomprehensible, feminine Napoleon! Believe me – "

"That is enough," Mrs. Murray said imperiously. "I don't wish to hear anything more about the miserable affair. Edna is exceedingly ungrateful after all the interest I have manifested in her welfare, and henceforth I shall not concern myself about her future. If she prefers to drudge through life as a teacher, I shall certainly advise her to commence as soon as possible; for if she can so entirely dispense with my counsel, she no longer needs my protection."

"Have you reasoned with her?"

"No. She knows my wishes, and since she defies them, I certainly shall not condescend to open my lips to her on this subject."

Mr. Murray took his cousin's hand and drew her to a seat beside him on the sofa. "Women arrogate such marvelous astuteness in reading each other's motives, that I should imagine Estelle's ingenuity would allow us to peep into the locked chamber of this girl's heart and supply some satisfactory explanation of her incomprehensible course."

"The solution is very easy, my dear cynic," Estelle said smoothly. "Edna can well afford to decline Gordon Leigh's offer when she maneuvers to sell herself for a much higher sum than he can command."

As Miss Harding uttered these words, Mrs. Murray turned quickly to observe their effect.

The cousins looked steadily at each other. Then St. Elmo laughed bitterly, and patted Estelle's cheek, saying, "Bravo! 'Set a thief to catch a thief!' I knew you would hit the nail on the head! But who the devil is this fellow who is writing to her from New York? This is the second letter I have taken out of the post-office. There is no telling how often they come; for, on both occasions, when I troubled myself to ride to the post-office, I have found letters directed to her in this same handwriting."

He drew a letter from his pocket and laid it on his knee. As Estelle looked at it, and then glanced with a puzzled expression toward her aunt's equally curious face, Mr. Murray passed his hand across his eyes to hide their malicious twinkle.

Mrs. Murray stepped forward. "Give me the letter, St. Elmo. It is my duty to examine it; for as long as she is under my protection she has no right to carry on a clandestine correspondence with strangers."

Very coolly he put the letter back in his pocket. "Pardon me, but it is neither your business nor mine to dictate with whom she shall or shall not correspond, now that she is no longer a child. I have no intention of turning spy at this late day and assisting you in the eminently honorable work of waylaying letters from her distant swain."

Mrs. Murray bit her lip, and held out her hand, saying, "I insist upon having the letter. Since you are so exceedingly scrupulous, I will carry it immediately to her and demand a perusal of the contents. St. Elmo, I am in no mood for jesting."

He only shook his head and laughed. "The dictates of filial respect forbid that I should subject my mother's curiosity to so severe an ordeal. Moreover, were the letter once in your hands, your conscience would persuade you that it is your imperative duty to a 'poor, inexperienced, motherless' girl, to inspect it ere her eager fingers have seized it. Besides, she is coming, and will save you the trouble of seeking her. I heard her run up the steps a moment ago."

Before Mrs. Murray could frame her indignation in suitable words, Edna entered, holding in one hand her straw hat, in the other, a basket lined with grape leaves and filled with remarkably large and fine strawberries. Exercise had deepened the color in her fair, sweet face as she approached her benefactress, holding up the fragrant, tempting fruit.

"Mrs. Murray, here is a present from Mr. Hammond, who desired me to tell you that these berries are the first he has gathered from the new bed, next to the row of lilacs. It is the variety he ordered from New York last fall, and some roots of which he says he sent to you. Are they not the most perfect specimens you ever saw? We measured them at the parsonage and six filled a saucer."

She was selecting a cluster to hold up for inspection and had not noticed the cloud on Mrs. Murray's brow.

"The strawberries are very fine. I am much obliged to Mr. Hammond."

The severity of the tone astonished Edna, who looked up quickly, saw the stern displeasure written on her face, and glanced inquiringly at the cousins. There was an awkward silence. Feeling the eyes of all fixed upon her, Edna picked up her hat, which had fallen on the floor, and asked, "Shall I carry the basket to the dining-room, or leave it here?"

"You need not trouble yourself to carry it anywhere."

Mrs. Murray laid her hand on the bell-cord and rang sharply. Edna placed the fruit on the center table, and suspecting that she must be unwanted, moved toward the door, but Mr. Murray rose and stood before her.

"Here is a letter which arrived yesterday."

He put it in her hand. When she recognized the peculiar superscription, a look of delight flashed over her features. Raising her beaming eyes to his, she murmured, "Thank you, sir," and retreated to her own room.

Mr. Murray turned to his mother and said carelessly, "I neglected to tell you that I heard from Clinton today. He has invited himself to spend some days here, and wrote to say that he might be expected next week. At least his visit will be welcome to you, Estelle, and I congratulate you on the prospect of adding to your list of admirers the most fastidious exquisite it has ever been my misfortune to encounter."

"St. Elmo, you ought to be ashamed to mention your father's nephew in such terms. You certainly have less respect and affection for your relatives than any man I ever saw."

"Which fact is entirely attributable to my thorough knowledge of their characters. I have generally found that high appreciation and intimate acquaintance are in inverse ratios. As for Clinton Allston, were he my father's son, instead of his nephew. I imagine my flattering estimate of him would be substantially the same. Estelle, do you know him?"

"I have not that pleasure, but report prepares me to find him extremely agreeable. I am rejoiced at the prospect of meeting him. Some time ago, just before I left Paris, I received a message from him, challenging me to a flirtation at sight as soon as an opportunity presented itself."

"For your sake, Estelle, I am glad Clinton is coming. St. Elmo is so shamefully selfish and oblivious of his duties as host, that I know time often hangs very heavily on your hands."

Mrs. Murray was too thoroughly out of humor to heed the dangerous sparkle in her son's eyes.

"Very true, mother. Clinton's amiable disposition commends him strongly to your affection. Knowing what is expected of him, he will declare himself Estelle's most devoted lover before he has been thirty-six hours in her society. Now, if she can accept him for a husband, and you will consent to receive him as your son, I swear I will reserve a scanty annuity for my traveling expenses. That done, I will gladly divide the estate between them and transport myself permanently beyond the criticism on my inherited sweetness of temper. If you, my dear coz, can only coax Clinton into this arrangement, you will render me eternally grateful, and smooth the way for a trip to Tibet and Siberia which I have long contemplated. Bear this proposition in mind, will you, especially when the charms of Le Bocage most favorably impress you? If my terms are not sufficiently liberal, confer with Clinton as soon as maidenly propriety will permit, and acquaint me with your ultimatum; for I am so thoroughly weary and disgusted with this place that I am anxious to get away on almost any terms."

"St. Elmo, my son," Mrs. Murray began, but here St. Elmo interrupted her.

"Here come the autocrats of the neighborhood, the new rich, your friends the Montgomeries and Hills! I hear Madame Montgomery asking if I am not at home, as well as the ladies. Tell her I am in Spitzbergen or Manchuria, where I certainly intend to be ere long."

As the visitors approached the sitting-room, St. Elmo sprang through the window opening on the terrace and disappeared. His beleaguered mother rubbed her temples and wished heartily for a headache powder.

The contents of the unexpected letter surprised and delighted Edna much more than she would willingly have confessed. Mr. Manning wrote that upon the eve of leaving home for a tour of some weeks' travel, he chanced to stumble upon her letter, and in a second perusal some peculiarity of style induced him to reconsider the offer it contained. He determined to permit her to send the manuscript (as far as written) for his examination. If promptly forwarded it would reach him before he left home, he would reply as speedily as possible.

Drawing all happy hopes from this second letter, and trembling with pleasure, Edna hastened to prepare her manuscript for mailing. Carefully enveloping it in a thick paper, she sealed and addressed it, then fell on her knees, and, with clasped hands resting on the package, prayed earnestly, vehemently, that God's blessing would accompany it, would crown her efforts with success.

Afraid to trust it to the hand of a servant, she put on her hat and walked back to town, clutching her manuscript to her chest.

The express agent gave Edna a receipt for the parcel, assured her that it would be forwarded by the evening train. With a sigh of relief, she turned her steps homeward.

Ah, it was a frail paper boat, freighted with the noblest, purest aspirations that ever possessed a woman's soul, launched upon the tempestuous sea of popular favor, with ambition at the helm, hope for a compass, and the gaunt specter of failure grinning in the sails. Would it successfully weather the gales of malice, envy and detraction? Would it battle valiantly and triumphantly with the piratical hordes of critics who prowl hungrily along the track over which it must sail? Would it become a melancholy wreck on the mighty ocean of literature, or would it proudly ride at anchor in the harbor of immortality, with Edna's name floating forever at the masthead?

It was an experiment such as had stranded the hopes of hundreds and thousands. The pinched, starved features of Chatterton, and the pale, pleading face of Keats, stabbed to death by reviewers' poisoned pens, rose like friendly phantoms and whispered ghostly warnings.

But today the world wore only rosy garments, unspotted by shadows, and the silvery voice of youthful enthusiasm sung only of victory and spoils.

When Edna returned to her room, she sat down before her desk to re-read the letter which had given her so much gratification. As she refolded it, Mrs. Murray came in and closed the door after her.

Her face was stern and pale; she walked up to the orphan, looked at her suspiciously, and when she spoke her voice was hard and cold. "I wish to see that letter which you received today.

It is very improper that you should, without my knowledge, carry on a correspondence with a stranger. I would not have believed that you could be guilty of such conduct."

Edna's fingers tightened on her letter, but she said, as calmly as possible, "I am very much pained, Mrs. Murray, that you should even for a moment have supposed that I had forfeited your confidence. The nature of the correspondence certainly sanctions my engaging in it, even without consulting you. This letter is the second I have received from Mr. Manning, the editor of *Iconoclast* Magazine, and was written in answer to a request of mine, with reference to a literary matter which concerns nobody but myself. I will show you the signature; there it is – Douglass G. Manning. You know his literary reputation and his high position. If you demand it, of course, I cannot refuse to allow you to read it. But, dear Mrs. Murray, I hope you will not insist upon it, as I prefer that no one should see the contents, at least at present. As I have never deceived you, I think you might trust me when I assure you that the correspondence is entirely restricted to literary subjects."

"Why, then, should you object to my reading it?"

"For a reason which I will explain at some future day, if you will only have confidence in me. Still, if you are determined to examine the letter, of course I must submit, though it would distress me exceedingly to know that you cannot, or will not, trust me in so small a matter."

Edna laid the open letter on the desk and covered her face with her hands.

Mrs. Murray took up the sheet, glanced at the signature, and said, "Look at me; don't hide your face, that argues something wrong."

Edna raised her head and lifted her eyes full of tears to meet the scrutiny from which there was no escape.

Mrs. Murray sighed and stroked Edna's hair. "Mr. Manning's signature somewhat reassures me, and besides, I never knew you to attempt to deceive me. Your habitual truthfulness encourages me to believe you, so I will not insist on reading this letter, though I cannot imagine why you should object to it. But, Edna, I am disappointed in you, and in return for the confidence I have always reposed in you, I want you to answer candidly the question I am about to ask. Why did you refuse to marry Gordon Leigh?"

Edna wiped her eyes. "Because I did not love him."

"Oh, pooh! That seems incredible, for he is handsome and very attractive, and some young ladies show very plainly that they love him, though they have never been requested to do so. There is only one way in which I can account for your refusal, and I wish you to tell me the truth. You are unwilling to marry Gordon because you love somebody else better. Child, whom do you love?"

"No, indeed, no! I like Mr. Leigh as well as any gentleman I know; but I love no one except you and Mr. Hammond."

Mrs. Murray put her hand under the girl's chin, looked at her for some seconds, and sighed heavily, caressing her cheek with her thumb. "Child, I find it difficult to believe you."

"Why, whom do you suppose I could love? Mr. Leigh is certainly more agreeable than anybody else I know."

"But girls sometimes take strange whims in these matters. Do you ever expect to receive a better offer than Mr. Leigh's?"

"As far as fortune is concerned, I presume I never shall have so good an opportunity again. But, Mrs. Murray, I would rather marry a poor man whom I truly loved, and who had to earn his daily bread, than be Mr. Leigh's wife and live in that beautiful house he is building. I know you think me very unwise, very short-sighted; but it is a question which I have settled after consulting my conscience and my heart."

"And you give me your word of honor that you love no other gentleman better than Gordon?"

"Yes, Mrs. Murray, you have my word. I assure you that I do not."

As the mistress of the house looked down into the girl's beautiful face, and passed her hand tenderly over the thick folds of hair that crowned her brow, she wondered if it were possible that her son could ever regard the orphan with affection; and she asked her own heart why she could not willingly receive her as a daughter.

Verily, when human friendships are analyzed, it seems a mere poetic fiction that –

> "Love took up the harp of Life,
> and smote on all the chords with might;
> Smote the chord of Self, that, trembling,
> passed in music out of sight."[41]

---

[41] "Locksley Hall" – Lord Alfred Tennyson

CHAPTER XVI
IMPLACABLE VENUS

One afternoon, about ten days after Mr. Manning's letter had arrived, Edna returned from the parsonage to find the family assembled on the front veranda. The expected visitor had arrived, and Edna hurried across the veranda, curious, to meet the stranger.

Mrs. Murray brought Edna forward and introduced her to Mr. Allston. He rose, advanced a few steps, and held out his hand.

Edna was in the act of giving him hers, when a heart-shaped diamond cluster on his finger flashed.

One swift glance at his face and figure made her snatch away her hand before it touched his, and she drew back with a half-smothered exclamation.

He bit his lip, looked inquiringly around the circle, smiled wanly, and returned to his seat beside Estelle, to resume the merry conversation in which he had been engaged.

Mrs. Murray had turned her back; she was leaning over the iron balustrade, twining a wreath of multiflora roses around one of the fluted columns, and did not witness what had happened. But when she had secured the rose, she turned back and noticed the unusual pallor and troubled expression of the girl's face.

"What is the matter, child? You look as if you were either ill or dreadfully fatigued."

"I am tired, thank you," was Edna's rather abstracted reply, and she walked into the house and sat down before the open window in the library.

The sun had just gone down behind a fleecy cloud-mountain and kindled a volcano, from whose silver-rimmed crater fiery rays of scarlet shot up, almost to the clear blue zenith. Here and there, through clefts and vapory gorges, the lurid lava light streamed down toward the horizon.

Vacantly Edna's eyes rested on these clouds, and its sunset splendor passed away unheeded, for she was looking far beyond the western gates of day.

She saw a pool of blood – a ghastly, dead face turned up to the sky – a coffined corpse strewn with white poppies and rosemary – a wan, dying woman, whose waving hair braided Edna's pillow with gold – a wide, deep grave under the rustling chestnuts, from whose green arches rang the despairing wail of a broken heart:

"Oh, Harry! My husband!"

Imagination traveled into the past, painted two sunny-haired, prattling babes, suddenly robed in mourning garments for parents whose loving eyes were closed forever under wild clover and trailing brambles. Again she saw the awful grief of that veritable old father, bowed in tears by his daughter's deathbed.

Absorbed in retrospection of that June day, when she stood by the spring, and watched

"God make himself an awful rose of dawn,"[42]

she sat with her head resting against the window-facing, and was not aware of Mr. Murray's entrance until his harsh voice startled her.

"Edna Earl! What apology have you to offer for insulting a relative and guest of mine under my roof?"

Edna jumped. "None, sir."

"What! How dare you treat with unparalleled rudeness a visitor, whose claim upon the courtesy and hospitality of this household is certainly more legitimate and easily recognized than that of – "

He stopped and kicked out of his way a stool upon which Edna's feet had been resting.

She rose, and they stood face to face. "I am waiting to hear the remainder of your sentence, Mr. Murray."

He uttered an oath and hurled his cigar through the window. "Why the devil did you refuse to shake hands with Allston? I

[42] "The Vision of Sin" – Lord Alfred Tennyson

intend to know the truth, and it may prove an economy of trouble for you to speak it at once."

"If you demand my reasons, you must not be offended at the plainness of my language. Your cousin is a murderer, and ought to be hung! I could not force myself to touch a hand all smeared with blood."

Mr. Murray leaned down and looked into her eyes. His savage glare, and a thickening scowl that bent his brows till they met, told of the brewing of no slight tempest of passion. "You are either delirious or utterly mistaken with reference to the identity of the man. Clinton is no more guilty of murder than you are. Ancient lore has turned your brain; 'too much learning hath made thee mad.[43]'"

Though Mr. Murray's aspect was frightening, Edna stood firm. "No, sir, it is no hallucination; there can be no mistake; it is a horrible, awful fact, which I witnessed, which is burned on my memory, and which will haunt me as long as I live. I saw him shoot Mr. Dent, and witnessed all that passed on that dreadful morning. He is doubly criminal – is as much the murderer of Mrs. Dent as of her husband, for the shock killed her. Oh, That I could forget her look and scream of agony as she fainted over her husband's coffin!"

A puzzled expression crossed Mr. Murray's face. Then he muttered, "Dent? Dent? Ah, yes; that was the name of the man whom Clinton killed in a duel. Pshaw! You have whipped up a syllabub storm in a teacup. Allston only took 'satisfaction' for an insult offered publicly by Dent."

Mr. Murray's tone was sneering and his lip curled, but a strange pallor crept from chin to temples.

"I know, sir, that custom tolerates that relic of barbarous ages – that blot upon Christian civilization which, under the name of 'dueling,' I recognize as a crime, a heinous crime, which I abhor and detest! Sir, I call things by their proper names. You say 'honorable satisfaction'; I say murder! Aggravated, unpardonable murder; murder without even the poor palliation of the sudden heat of anger."

"No," said Mr. Murray.

---

[43] Acts 26:24

"Yes. Cool, deliberate, willful murder, that stabs the happiness of wives and children! Oh, save me from the presence of that man who can derive 'satisfaction' from knowing that he has laid Henry and Helen Dent in one grave, under the quiet shadow of Lookout, and brought desolation and orphanage to their two innocent babies! Shake hands with Clinton Allston? I would sooner stretch out my fingers to clasp those of Ravaillac, reeking with the blood of his victims!"

The room was dusky with the shadow of coming night; but the fading flush of sunset, low in the west, showed St. Elmo's face colorless, rigid, repulsive in its wrathful defiance.

He seized her hands, folded them together, and grasping them in both his, crushed them against his breast.

"Ha! I knew that hell and heaven were leagued to poison your mind! That your childish conscience was frightened by tales of horror, and your imagination was harrowed up, your heart lacerated by the cunning devices of that maudlin old hypocrite! The seeds of clerical hate fell in good ground, and I see a bountiful harvest nodding for my sickle!"

"You cannot, must not say such things about Mr. Hammond, my dearest friend!" Edna cried. "Let me go!"

Mr. Murray scoffed. "Oh, you are more pliable than I had fancied! You have been thoroughly trained down yonder at the parsonage. But I will be--"

There was a trembling pant in his voice like that of some wild creature driven from its jungle, hopeless of escape, holding its hunters temporarily at bay, waiting for death.

Edna's hands ached in his unyielding grasp. After two useless efforts to free them, a sigh of pain passed her lips. She said proudly, "No, sir; my hatred of that form of legalized murder, politely called 'dueling,' was not taught me at the parsonage. I learned it in my early childhood, before I ever saw Mr. Hammond. Though I am sure he agrees with me, I have never heard him mention the subject."

"Hypocrite! Hypocrite! Meek little wolf in lamb's wool! Do you dream that you can deceive me? Do you think me an idiot, to be cajoled by your low-spoken denials of a fact which I know? A fact, the truth of which I will swear till every star falls!"

"Mr. Murray, I never deceived you. However incensed you may be, I know that in your heart you do not doubt my truthfulness. Why you invariably denounce Mr. Hammond when you happen to be displeased with me, I do not know; but I tell you solemnly that he has never even alluded to dueling since I have known him. Mr. Murray, I know you do entirely believe me when I utter these words."

A tinge of red leaped into his cheek. Something that would have been called hope in any other man's eyes looked out shyly under his heavy black lashes. A tremor shook off the sneering curl of his bloodless lips.

Drawing her so close to him that his hair touched her forehead, he whispered, "If I believe in you, my – it is in defiance of judgment. Some day you will make me pay a most humiliating penalty for my momentary weakness. Tonight I trust you as implicitly as Samson did the smooth-lipped Delilah. Tomorrow I shall realize that, like him, I richly deserve to be shorn for my credulity."

He threw her hands rudely from him, turned hastily, and left the library.

Edna sat down and covered her face with her bruised and benumbed fingers, but she could not shut out the sight of something that astonished and frightened her – of something that made her shudder from head to foot, and crouch down in her chair cowed and humiliated.

Hitherto she had fancied that she thoroughly understood and sternly governed her heart – that conscience and reason ruled it. But within the past hour it had suddenly risen in dangerous rebellion, thrown off its allegiance to all things else, and proclaimed St. Elmo Murray its king.

She could not analyze her new feelings, for they would not obey the summons to the tribunal of her outraged self-respect. With bitter shame, she realized that she loved the sinful, blasphemous man who had insulted her revered grandfather, and who barely tolerated her presence in his house.

This danger had never once occurred to her, for she had always believed that love could only grow where high esteem and unbounded reverence prepared the soil. Ten days before she had positively disliked and feared him. Now, to her amazement, she found him throned in her heart, defying ejection. The sudden revulsion bewildered and mortified her, and she resolved to crush out the feeling at once, cost what it might.

When Mr. Murray had asked if she loved anyone else better than Mr. Leigh, she thought – nay, she knew – she answered truly in the negative. But now, when she attempted to compare the two men, such a strange, yearning tenderness pleaded for St. Elmo, and palliated his grave faults, that the girl's self-accusing severity wrung a groan from the very depths of her soul.

When the sad discovery was first made, conscience lifted its hands in horror, because of the man's reckless wickedness. A still louder clamor was raised by womanly pride, which bled at the thought of tolerating a love unsought, unvalued.

Until this hour, although conscious of many faults, Edna had not supposed that there was anything especially contemptible in her character; but now the feeling of self-abasement was unutterably galling. She despised herself, and the dignity of life which she had striven to attain appeared hopelessly shattered.

While the battle of reason versus love was at its height, Mrs. Murray put her head in the room. "Edna! Where are you, Edna?"

"Here I am."

"Why are you sitting in the dark? I have searched the house for you." She groped her way across the room, lighted the gas, and came to the window, where Edna was sitting.

"What is the matter, child? Are you sick?"

"I think something must be the matter, for I do not feel at all like myself," stammered the orphan, as she hid her face on the windowsill.

"Does your head ache?"

"No, ma'am."

She might have said very truly that her heart did.

"Give me your hand, let me feel your pulse. It is very quick, but shows nervous excitement rather than fever. Child, let me see your tongue, I hear there are some typhoid cases in the neighborhood. Why, how hot your cheeks are!"

"Yes, I shall go up and bathe them. Perhaps I may feel better." Edna made an effort to rouse herself.

"I wish you would come into the parlor as soon as you can, for Estelle says Clinton thought you were very rude to him. Though I apologized on the score of indisposition, I prefer that you should make your appearance this evening. Stop, you have dropped your handkerchief."

Edna stooped to pick it up and saw Mr. Murray's name embroidered in one corner. Her first impulse was to thrust it into her pocket; but instantly she held it towards his mother. "It is not mine, but your son's. He was here about an hour ago and must have dropped it."

"I thought he had gone out over the grounds with Clinton. What brought him here?"

"He came to scold me for not shaking hands with his cousin."

"Indeed! You must have been singularly rude if he noticed any want of courtesy. Change your dress and come down."

It was in vain that Edna bathed her hot face and pressed her cold hands to her cheeks. She felt as if all curious eyes read her troubled heart. She was ashamed to meet the family – above all things to see Mr. Murray. Heretofore she had shunned him from dislike; now she wished to avoid him because she began to feel that she loved him. She dreaded that his inquisitorial eyes would discover her contemptible, and, in her estimation, unwomanly weakness.

Taking the basket which contained her sewing utensils and a piece of light needlework, she went into the parlor and seated herself near the center table, over which hung the chandelier.

Mr. Murray and his mother were sitting on a sofa. He was cutting the leaves of a new book, while Estelle Harding was describing in glowing terms a scene in *Phèdre*, which owed its charm to Mademoiselle Rachel's marvelous acting. As Estelle repeated the soliloquy beginning, *"O toi, qui vois la honte ou je suis descendue, Implacable Vénus, suis-je assez confondue!*[44]*"* Edna felt as if her own great weakness were known to the world. She bent her face close to her sewing basket and tumbled the contents into inextricable confusion.

Tonight, Estelle seemed in unusually fine spirits, and talked on rapidly, till St. Elmo suddenly appeared to become aware of the import of her words. In a few cutting sentences he refuted the criticism on *Phèdre*, advising his cousin to confine her comments to dramas with which she was better acquainted.

His tone and manner surprised Mr. Allston, who remarked, "Were I Czar, I would chain you to the steepest rock on the crest of the Ural, till you learned the courtesy due to ladies. One would suppose that you had been in good society long enough to discover that your overbearing style is not allowable in discussions with ladies."

"When women put on boxing-gloves and show their faces in the ring, they challenge rough handling. I am sick of pretension, especially where it crops out in shallow criticism, and every day something recalls the reprimand of Apelles to the shoemaker – critique only what you know! If a worthy and able literary tribunal and critical code could be established, it would be well to revive an ancient Locrian custom, which required that the originators of new laws or propositions should be brought before the assembled wisdom, with nooses around their necks, ready for speedy execution if the innovation proved to be utterly unsound or puerile."

---

[44] Translation: "Venus implacable, who seest me shamed and sore confounded, have I not enough been humbled? How can your cruelty be stretch'd farther?

Mr. Murray bowed to his cousin as he spoke, and rising, took his favorite position on the rug.

"Really, Aunt Ellen, I would advise you to have him re-christened under the name of Timon," said Mr. Allston.

Estelle walked up to her cousin and stood at his side. "No, no. I decidedly object to any such gratification of his would-be classic freaks. I would suggest, as a more suitable nickname, that bestowed on Louis the Tenth, 'Le Hutin' – freely translated, The Quarrelsome!' What say you, St. Elmo?"

St. Elmo frowned. "It is very bad policy to borrow somebody else's boxing-gloves, because I happened to overhear Edna Earl when she made that same suggestion to Gordon Leigh, with reference to my amiable temperament."

Estelle laughed lightly and answered, "So much for eavesdropping! Of all the gentlemen of my acquaintance, I should fancy you were the very last who could afford to indulge in that amusement."

A blush rose in Edna's face. So both Estelle *and* Mr. Murray had been eavesdropping on her and Mr. Leigh at the same time? It was amazing that they had not managed to collide in the shrubbery.

Mr. Allston drawled, "Miss Estelle, is this your first, second or third Punic war? You and St. Elmo, or rather, my cousin, 'The Quarrelsome,' seem to wage it in genuine Carthaginian style."

"I never signed a treaty, sir, and, consequently, keep no records."

"Clinton, we continually wage war upon each other, the original spring of which antedates my memory. But at present, Estelle is directing all her genius and energy to effect, for my individual benefit, a practical reenactment of the lex Papia Poppoea, which Augustus hurled at the heads of all peaceful, happy bachelordom!"

For the first time during the conversation Edna glanced up at Estelle, for, much as she disliked her, she regretted this thrust. Her pity was utterly wasted, and she was surprised to find her countenance calm and smiling.

Mr. Allston shrugged his shoulders.

Mrs. Murray exclaimed, "I sound a truce! For heaven's sake, St. Elmo, lock up your learning with your mummies, and when you will say barbarous things, use language that will enable us to understand that we are being snubbed. Now, who do you suppose comprehends Papia Poppoea? You are insufferably pedantic!"

"My dear mother, do you remember ever to have read or heard the celebrated reply of a certain urbane lexicographer to the rash individual who attempted to find fault with his dictionary? 'I am bound to furnish good definitions, but not brains to comprehend them.'[45]"

Miss Harding tapped his hand with her fan. "I think, sir, that it is a very great misfortune that you were not raised in Sparta, where it was everybody's privilege to whip their neighbor's vicious, spoiled children. Such a regimen would doubtless have converted you into an amiable, or at least endurable, member of society."

"That is problematical, my fair cousin, for if my provocative playmate had accompanied me, I think the supply of Spartan birch would have utterly failed to sweeten my temper."

Her mother answered laughingly, "Estelle is quite right; you contrived to grow up without the necessary healthful quota of sound whipping which you richly deserved."

Mr. Murray did not seem to hear her words; he was looking down intently, smiling into his cousin's handsome face. Passing his arm around Estelle's waist, drew her close to his side. He murmured something that made her throw her head quickly back against his shoulder and look up at him.

"If such is the end of all your quarrels, it offers a premium for unamiability," said Mr. Allston, who had been studying Edna's face, and now turned again to his cousin. Curling the end of his moustache, he continued, "St. Elmo, you have travelled more extensively than any one I know, and under peculiarly favorable circumstances. Of all the spots you have visited, which would you pronounce the most desirable for a permanent residence?"

---

[45] One would think that this is from Samuel Johnson, but I cannot find this blessed quote anywhere, under his name or anybody else's.

"Have you an idea of 'quitting your country for your country's good'?"

"One never knows what contingencies may arise. I should like to avail myself of your knowledge; for I feel assured only very charming places would have detained you long."

Edna frowned at her embroidery, thinking of how Clinton had fled to New York after he'd shot Harry Dent in that duel. She wondered who he was planning to kill this time.

Mr. Murray had his mind on other things. "Were I at liberty to select a home, tranquil, blessed beyond all expression, I should certainly lose no time in domesticating myself in the Peninsula of Mount Athos."

"Ah, yes; the scenery all along that coast is described as surprisingly beautiful and picturesque."

"Oh, bah! The scenery is quite as grand in fifty other places. Its peculiar attraction consists in something far more precious."

"To what do you refer?"

"Its marvelous and bewildering charm is to be found entirely in the fact that, since the days of Constantine, no woman has set foot on its peaceful soil. The happy dwellers in that sole remaining earthly Eden are so vigilant, dreading the entrance of another Eve, that no female animal is permitted to intrude upon the sacred precincts. The embargo extends even to cats, cows, and dogs, lest the innate female proclivity to make mischief should be found dangerous in the brute creation. Constantine lived in the latter part of the third and the beginning of the fourth century. Think of the divine repose, the unapproachable beatification of residing in a land where no woman has even peeped for fifteen hundred years!"

Estelle laughed. "For shame, St. Elmo! A stranger listening to your gallant diatribe would inevitably conclude that your mother was as unnatural and unamiable as Lord Byron's; and that I, your most devoted, meek, and loving cousin, was quite as angelic as Miss Edgeworth's *Modern Griselda*!"

Affecting great indignation, Estelle attempted to quit his side; but, tightening his arm, Mr. Murray bowed and resumed,

"Had your imaginary stranger ever heard of the science of logic, the conclusion would, as you say, be inevitable. I found a happy spot where the names of women are never called, where the myth of Pandora is forgotten, and where the only females that have successfully run the rigid blockade are the tormenting fleas that wage a ceaseless war with the unoffending men, and justify their nervous horror lest any other creature of the same sex should smuggle herself into their blissful retreat."

Estelle laughed. "May all good angels help me to steer as far as possible from such a nest of cynics. I would sooner confront an army of Amazons than trust myself among a people uncivilized by the refining influence and companionship of women!"

Mr. Murray ignored her. "I have seen crowned heads, statesmen, great military chieftains, and geniuses, whose names are destined to immortality; but standing here, reviewing my certainly extended acquaintance, I swear I envy above all others that handsome monk whom Curzon found at Simopetra, who had never seen a woman! He was transplanted to the Holy Mountain while a mere infant, and though assured he had had a mother, he accepted the statement with the same blind faith, which was required for some of the religious dogmas he was called on to swallow."

"How I do long to meet some woman brave and wily enough to marry and tame you, my chivalric cousin. I want to see her revenge the insults you have heaped upon her sisterhood!"

"By fully establishing the correctness of my estimate of their amiability? That were dire punishment indeed. If I could realize the possibility of such a calamity, I should certainly bewail my fate in the mournful words of that most astute of female wits, who is reported to have exclaimed, in considering the angelic idiosyncrasies of her gentle sisterhood, 'The only thought which can reconcile me to being a woman is that I shall not have to marry one[46]."

The expression with which Mr. Murray regarded Estelle reminded Edna of the account given by a traveler of the playful mood of a lion, who, having devoured one gazelle, kept his paw on another, and, amid occasional growls, teased and toyed with his victim.

---

[46] attributed to Lady Mary Wortley Montagu.

As Edna sat bending over her sewing, listening to the conversation, she asked herself scornfully, "What hallucination has seized me? The man is a mocking devil, unworthy of the respect or toleration of any Christian woman. What redeeming trait can even my partial eyes discover in his distorted, sinful nature? Not one. No, not one!"

She rejoiced when he uttered a sarcasm or an opinion that shocked her, for she hoped that his irony would cauterize what she considered a cancerous spot in her heart.

"Edna, as you are not well, I advise you to put aside that embroidery, which must try your eyes very severely," said Mrs. Murray.

She folded up the piece of cambric and was putting it in her basket, when Mr. Allston asked, with more effrontery than she was prepared for, "Miss Earl, have I not seen you before today?"

"Yes, sir." Her face blanched.

"May I ask where?"

"In a chestnut grove, where you shot Mr. Dent."

"Indeed! Did you witness that affair? It happened many years ago."

There was not a shadow of pain or sorrow in his face or voice.

Rising, Edna said, with unmistakable emphasis, "I saw all that occurred, and the death of Mr. Dent – and of his precious wife after she arrived – has been burned into my mind until I die. May God preserve me from ever witnessing another murder so revolting!"

In the silence that ensued she turned toward Mrs. Murray, bowed, and said as she quitted the parlor, "Mrs. Murray, as I am not very well, you will please excuse my retiring early."

"Just what you deserve for bringing the subject up; I warned you not to allude to it." St. Elmo pushed Estelle from him and nodded to Mr. Allston.

Mr. Allston merely shrugged and seemed as nearly nonplussed as his habitual impudence rendered possible.

Thoroughly dissatisfied with herself, and too restless to sleep, Edna passed the weary hours of the night in endeavoring to complete a chapter on Buddhism, which she had commenced some days before. The birds were chirping their reveille, and the sky blanched and reddened ere she lay down her pen and locked up her manuscript. Throwing open the blinds of the eastern window, she stood for some time looking out, gathering strength from the holy calm of the dewy morning, resolving to watch her own heart ceaselessly, to crush promptly the feeling she had found there, and to devote herself unreservedly to her studies.

At that moment the sound of horse's hoofs on the stony walk attracted her attention, and she saw Mr. Murray riding from the stables. As he passed her window, he glanced up and their eyes met. He lifted his hat and rode on.

Were those the same sinister, sneering features she had looked at the evening before? His face was paler, sterner, and sadder than she had ever seen it.

Covering her face with her hands, she murmured, "God help me to resist that man's wicked magnetism! Oh, Grandpa, are you looking down on your poor little Pearl? Will you forgive me for allowing myself ever to have thought tenderly of this strange temptation which Satan has sent to draw my heart away from God and my duty? Ah, Grandpa, I will crush it – I will conquer it! I will not yield!"

CHAPTER XVII
THE PRINCE

Avoiding as much as possible the society of Mrs. Murray's guests, as well as that of her son, Edna turned to her books with increased energy and steadfastness, while her manner was marked by a studied reticence hitherto unnoticed. The house was thronged with visitors, and families residing in the neighborhood were frequently invited to dinner; but Edna generally found a way on these occasions to have an engagement at the parsonage. As Mrs. Murray no longer seemed to desire her presence, Edna spent much of her time alone, and rarely saw the members of the household except at breakfast. She noticed that Mr. Allston either felt or feigned unbounded admiration for Estelle, who graciously received his devoted attentions; while Mr. Murray now and then sneered openly at both, and appeared daily more impatient to quit the home, of which he spoke with undisguised disgust.

As day after day and week after week slipped by without bringing tidings of Edna's manuscript, her heart became oppressed with anxious forebodings, and she found it difficult to wait patiently for the verdict upon which hung all her hopes.

One Thursday afternoon, when a number of persons had been invited to dine at Le Bocage, and Mrs. Murray was engrossed by preparations for their entertainment, Edna took her Greek books and stole away unobserved to the parsonage, where she spent a quiet evening in reading aloud from the *Organon* of Aristotle.

It was quite late when Mr. Hammond took her home in his buggy and bade her good night at the doorstep. As she entered the house, she saw several couples promenading on the veranda, and heard Estelle and Clinton Allston singing a duet from *Il Trovatore*. Passing the parlor door, one quick glance showed her Mr. Murray and Mr. Leigh standing together under the chandelier. Mr. Leigh was talking earnestly. Mr. Murray's gaze was fastened on the carpet, a chilling smile was fixed on his lips.

The faces of the two presented a painful contrast – one fair, hopeful, bright with noble aims, and youthful yet manly beauty; the other swarthy, cold, repulsive as some bronze image of Abaddon. For more than three weeks Edna had not spoken to Mr. Murray, except to say "good-morning," as she entered the dining-room or passed him in the hall.

It would be only fair to eavesdrop on him the way that he apparently did to Mr. Leigh and me, she thought. What she would have given to know what he and Mr. Leigh were discussing now!

Instead, with a sigh which she did not possess the courage to analyze, she went up to her room and sat down to read.

Among the books on her desk was Machiavelli's *The Prince* and *History of Florence*. The copy, which was an exceedingly handsome one, contained a portrait of the author. Edna found that the Florentine satirist bore a striking resemblance to St. Elmo. One day she mentioned the subject to Mrs. Murray, who, after a careful examination of the picture, was forced to admit, rather ungraciously, that, "they certainly looked somewhat alike." Tonight, as Edna lifted the volume from its resting-place, it opened at the portrait. She looked long at the handsome face which, had the lips been thinner, and the hair thicker and more curling at the temples, might have been daguerreotyped from that one downstairs under the chandelier.

Niccolò Machiavelli

One maxim of the Prince had certainly been adopted by Mr. Murray: "It is safer to be feared than to be loved." Edna detested the crafty and unscrupulous policy of Niccolò Machiavelli, and her reason told her that the character of St. Elmo Murray was scarcely more worthy of respect.

She heard the guests take their departure, heard Mrs. Murray ask Hagar whether "Edna had returned from the parsonage," and then doors were closed and the house grew silent.

Vain were the girl's efforts to concentrate her thoughts on her books or upon her manuscript, for they wandered toward the portrait. Finally remembering that she needed a book of reference, she lighted a candle and took the copy of Machiavelli, which she determined to return to the library and put it out of her sight.

The smell of a cigar aroused her suspicions as she entered, and, glancing nervously around the room, she saw Mr. Murray seated before the window.

His face was turned from her. Hoping to escape unnoticed, she was sneaking backward out the door when he rose. "Come in, Edna. I am waiting for you, for I knew you would be here sometime before day."

She deflated slightly. *How well he knows me,* she thought.

Taking the candle from her hand, he held it close to her face, and compressed his lips tightly for an instant.

"How long do you suppose your constitution will endure the tax you impose upon it? Midnight toil has already robbed you of your color, and converted a rosy, robust child into a pale, weary, hollow-eyed woman. What do you want here?"

"The Edda."

"What business have you with Norse myths, with runes and skalds and sagas?"

Edna gave him a blank look. She certainly was not about to tell him.

"Anyway, you can't have the book. I carried it to my room yesterday, and I am in no mood tonight to play errand-boy for anyone."

Disappointed, Edna turned to place the copy of Machiavelli on the shelves. He continued, "It is a marvel that your saintly tutor does not taboo the infamous doctrines of the greatest statesman of

Italy. I am told that you do me the honor to discover a marked likeness between his countenance and mine. May I flatter myself so highly as to believe the statement?"

"Even your mother admits the resemblance," Edna admitted grudgingly.

"Think you the analogy extends further than the mere physique, or do you trace it only in the corporeal development?"

"I believe, sir, that your character is as much a counterpart of his as your features; that your code is quite as lax as his."

She had abstained from looking at him, but now her eyes met his. In their beautiful depths, St. Elmo read an expression of helpless repulsion, such as a bird might evince for the serpent whose glittering eyes enchanted it.

"Ah, at least your honesty is refreshing in these accursed days of hypocritical sycophancy. How much training will your lips require before they learn fashionable lying tricks?"

"I have better things to do than that," she assured Mr. Murray as she searched the book titles for the *Kalevala*.

"Anyway, you understand me as little as the world understood poor Machiavelli, of whom Burke justly remarked, 'He is obliged to bear the iniquities of those whose maxims and rules of government he published. His speculation is more abhorred than their practice.' We are both painted blacker than – "[47]

Edna sighed, deciding to look for her books later. "I came here, sir, to discuss neither his character nor yours. It is a topic for which I have as little leisure as inclination. Good night, Mr. Murray."

He bowed low and spoke through set teeth. "I regret the necessity of detaining you a moment longer, but I believe you have been anxiously expecting a letter for some time, as I hear that you every day anticipate my inquiries at the post office. This afternoon the express agent gave me this package."

He brought a parcel from his interior pocket. Edna startled, but then dismay and keen disappointment rushed into her face.

The frail boat had struck the reefs. She felt her hopes sinking to ruin, and her lips quivered with pain as she recognized Mr. Manning's bold handwriting on the paper wrapping.

---

[47] A Vindication of Natural Society – Edmond Burke

Mr. Murray merely smiled at her distress. "What is the matter, child?"

"Something that concerns only me," she said quietly, accepting the package from his hands.

"Are you unwilling to trust me with your secret, whatever it may be? I would sooner find betrayal from the grinning skeletons in monastic crypts than from my lips."

Smothering a sigh, she shook her head impatiently.

"That means that red-hot steel could not pinch it out of you; and that, despite your boasted charity and love of humanity, you really entertain as little confidence in humanity as it is my pleasure to indulge. I applaud your wisdom, but certainly did not credit you with so much craftiness. My reason for not delivering the parcel more promptly was simply the wish to screen you from the Argus scrutiny with which we are both favored by some now resident at Bocage."

And now, to her surprise, he took a letter from his pocket and gave it to her. "As your letters subjected you to suspicion, I presumed it would be more agreeable to you to receive them without witnesses."

She had to admit that this was, like it or not, an act of mercy on his part. "Thank you, Mr. Murray; you are very kind."

"Pardon me, that is indeed a novel accusation!" he said, placing a hand on his heart. "Kind, I never professed to be. I am simply not quite a brute, nor altogether a devil of the most malicious variety, as you doubtless consider it your religious duty to believe. Child, you are in trouble; and your truthful countenance reveals it unmistakably. Of course, it is not my business – you certainly have as good a right as any other child, to pout over your girlish griefs, to sit up all night, ruin your eyes, and grow prematurely old and ugly. But whenever I chance to stumble over a wounded creature trying to drag itself out of sight, I generally either wring its neck, or set my heel on it to end its torment; or else, if there is a fair prospect of the injury healing, I take it gently on the tip of my boot, and help it out of my way. Something has hurt you, and I suspect I can aid you. Your anxiety about those letters proves that you doubt your idol. You and your lover have quarreled? Be frank with me; tell me his name, and I swear upon the honor of a gentleman I will rectify the trouble – will bring him in contrition to your feet."

Whether St. Elmo dealt in irony, as was his habit, or really meant what he said, she was unable to determine. Her quick glance at his countenance showed her only a dangerous sparkle in his eyes.

"Mr. Murray, you are wrong in your conjecture; I have no lover."

"Oh, call him what you please. I shall not presume to dictate your terms of endearment. I merely wish to say that if poverty stands forbiddingly between you and happiness, why, command me to the extent of half my fortune, I will give you a dowry that shall equal the expectations of any ambitious suitor in the land. Trust me with your sorrow and I will prove a faithful friend. Who has your heart?"

Edna stared into his face, startled, but she remembered herself and closed her open mouth and looked back down at her package. A shivering dread possessed her that he suspected her real feelings and was laughing at her folly. Treacherous blood began to paint confusion in her face, and vehement and rapid were her words.

"God and my conscience own my heart. I know no man to whom I would willingly give it; and the correspondence to which you allude contains not a syllable of love. My time is rather too valuable to be frittered away in such trifling."

"Edna, would you prefer to have me a sworn ally or an avowed enemy?"

"I should certainly prefer to consider you as neither."

"Did you ever know me fail in any matter which I had determined to accomplish?"

"Yes, sir; your entire life is a huge, hideous, woeful failure, which mocks and maddens you."

Apparently, that was not the answer he had expected. "What the devil do you know of my life?" he snapped. "It is not ended yet, and it remains to be seen whether a grand success is not destined to crown it. Mark you, the grapple is not quite over, and I may yet throttle the furies whose cursed fingers clutched me in my boyhood. If I am conquered finally, take my oath for it, I shall die so hard that the howling hags will be welcome to their prey. Single-handed, I am fighting the world, the flesh, and the devil, and I want neither sympathy nor assistance. Do you understand me?"

"Yes, sir. And as I certainly desire to thrust neither upon you, I will bid you good-night."

"One moment. What does that package contain?"

Edna pressed it to her chest. "The contents belong exclusively to me – would only challenge your sarcasm and furnish food for derision. Consequently, Mr. Murray, you must excuse me if I decline your question."

"I'll wager my title to Le Bocage that I can guess so accurately that you will regret that you did not make a grace of necessity and tell me."

She examined the seals on the package. "That, sir, is impossible, if you are the honorable gentleman I have always tried to force myself to believe."

"Silly child. Do you imagine I would soil my fingers with the wax that secures that trash? That I could stoop to an inspection of the correspondence of a village blacksmith's granddaughter? I will give you one more chance to close the breach between us by proving your trust. Edna, have you no confidence in me?"

"None, Mr. Murray."

"Will you oblige me by looking me full in the face, and repeating your flattering words?"

Edna raised her head. Though her heart throbbed fiercely as she met his sparkling eyes, her voice was cold, steady, and resolute.

"None, Mr. Murray."

"Thank you. Someday those same red lips will humbly, tremblingly crave my pardon for what they utter now; and then, Edna Earl, I shall take my revenge, and you will look back to this night and realize the full force of my parting words – woe to the vanquished!"

He stooped and picked up a bow of rose-colored ribbon which had fallen from her throat, handed it to her, smiled, and, with one of those low, haughty bows so indicative of his imperious nature, he left the library. A moment after, she heard his peculiar laugh, mirthless and bitter, ring through the rotunda; then the door was slammed violently, and quiet reigned once more through the mansion.

Taking the candle from the table where Mr. Murray had placed it, Edna fled back to her own room and sat down before the window.

On her lap lay the package and letter, which she no longer felt any desire to open, and her hands drooped listlessly at her side. The fact that her manuscript was returned rung a knell for all her rosy hopes, for such was her confidence in the critical acumen of Mr. Manning that she deemed it utterly useless to appeal to any other tribunal. A higher one she knew not; a lower she scorned to consult.

She felt like Alice Lisle on that day of doom, when Judge Jeffreys sentenced her to death. After a time, when Edna summoned courage to open the letter, her cheeks were wan and her lips compressed so firmly that their curves of beauty were no longer traceable.

"MISS EARL: I return your manuscript, not because it is devoid of merit, but from the conviction that were I to accept it, the day would inevitably come when you would regret its premature publication. While it contains evidence of extraordinary ability, and abounds in descriptions of great beauty, your style is characterized by more strength than polish, and is marred by crudities which a dainty public would never tolerate. The subject you have undertaken is beyond your capacity – no woman could successfully handle it – and the sooner you realize your overestimate of your powers, the sooner you will succeed in your treatment of some theme better suited to your feminine ability. Burn the enclosed MS., which would fatally nauseate the intellectual dyspeptics who read my *Iconoclast*, and write sketches of home life – descriptions of places and things that you understand better than imaginings of ethical creeds and mythologic systems. Remember that women never write histories or epics; never compose oratorios that go sounding down the centuries; never paint 'Last Suppers' and 'Judgment Days'; though now and then one gives the world a pretty ballad that sounds sweet and soothing when sung over a cradle, or another paints a pleasant little genre sketch which will hang appropriately in some quiet corner and rest and refresh eyes that are weary with gazing at the sublime spiritualism of Fra Bartolomeo, or the gloomy grandeur of Salvator Rosa.

If you have any short articles that you desire to see in print, you may forward them, and I will select any for publication, which I think you will not blush to acknowledge in future years.

"Very respectfully,

"Your obedient servant,

"DOUGLASS G. MANNING."

Unwrapping the manuscript, Edna laid it with its death-warrant in a drawer, then sat down, crossed her arms on the top of her desk, and rested her head upon them. Her face was not concealed, and, as the light shone on it, her large, thoughtful eyes were sad but dry, and none who looked into them could have imagined for an instant that she would follow the advice she had so eagerly sought.

During her long reverie, she wondered whether all women were browbeaten for aspiring to literary honors; whether the poignant pain and mortification gnawing at her heart was the inexorable initiation-fee for entrance upon the arena where fame adjudges laurel crowns, and sullenly drops one now and then on female brows. To possess herself of the golden apple of immortality was a purpose from which she had never swerved; but how to baffle the dragon critics who jealously guarded it was a problem whose solution puzzled her.

To abandon her right to authorship formed no part of the program which she was mentally arranging as she sat there watching a moth singe its filmy, spotted wings in the gas-flame; for she was obstinately wedded to the unpardonable heresy that, in the nineteenth century, it was a woman's privilege to be as learned, provided the learning was accurate, and gave out no

196

hollow, counterfeit ring under the merciless hammering of the dragons.

If a man had written the same MS, Mr. Manning would not have told him that he should burn it, would not have told him that writing was not suited to his masculine ability.

Gradually the expression of pain passed from Edna's face. Lifting her head, she took from her desk several small manuscripts that she had carefully written from time to time, as her reading suggested the ideas embodied in the articles. Among the number were two upon which she had bestowed much thought, which she determined to send to Mr. Manning.

One was an elaborate description of that huge iconoclasm attributed to Alcibiades, considered by some students of history to contribute to the ruin of Athens. On one spring night just before Alcibiades' fleet was about to sail, all the hermai in Athens were vandalized in an act of shocking impiety. Alcibiades was blamed for the desecration. In order to reflect all possible light on this curious occurrence, Edna had most assiduously gleaned the pages of history, and had studied maps of the city and descriptions of travelers, that she might thoroughly understand the topography of the scene of the great desecration. So fearful was she of committing some anachronism, that she searched the ancient accounts to ascertain whether on that night in May, 415 BC, a full or a new moon looked down on the sleeping city as the vandals smashed and destroyed the busts of the god Hermes.

The other MS., upon which she had expended much labor, was entitled "Keeping the Vigil of St. Martin Under the Pines of Grütli." Her vivid imagination reveled in the weird and solemn surroundings of the lonely place of rendezvous where the three men took their oath to defend one another and their people, an action that ultimately led to the nation of Switzerland. The sketch ended with a glowing and eloquent tribute to the liberators of Switzerland, the three cantons of Schweiz, Uri, and Unterwalden.

Whether Mr. Manning would consider either of these articles worthy of preservation in the pages of his magazine, Edna thought exceedingly doubtful; but she had resolved to make one more appeal to his fastidious judgment, and accordingly sealed and addressed the roll of paper.

Weary but sleepless, Edna pushed back the heavy folds of hair that had fallen on her forehead, brightened the gaslight, and turned to the completion of a chapter in that MS. that the editor had recommended her to commit to the flames. So entirely was she absorbed in her work that the hours passed unheeded. Now and then, when her thoughts failed to flow smoothly into graceful sentence molds, she laid aside her pen and walked up and down the floor, turning the idea over and over, fitting it first to one phrase, then to another, until the verbal drapery fully suited her.

The whistle of the locomotive at the station told her that it was four o'clock before her task was accomplished. Praying that God's blessing would rest upon it, she left it unfinished, and threw herself down to sleep.

But slumber brought no relaxation to the busy brain that toiled on in fitful dreams. When sunshine streamed through the open window at the foot of her bed, it showed no warm flush of healthful sleep on her face, but weariness and pallor. Incoherent words stirred Edna's lips, troubled thought knitted her arched brows, and her arms were tossed restlessly above her head.

The fondest hope of Edna's heart was to be useful in "her day and generation" – to be an instrument of some good to her race. While she hoped for popularity as an avenue to the accomplishment of her object, the fear of ridicule and censure had no power to deter her from the line of labor. "Wherefore," O lonely but conscientious student! "be ye steadfast, unmovable, always abounding in the work of the Lord, forasmuch as ye know that your labor is not in vain.[48]"

The noble words of Kepler rang a ceaseless silvery chime in her soul, sustaining her, and she sought to mold her life in harmony with their sublime teachings:

"Lo, I have done the work of my life with that power of intellect which thou hast given. If I, a worm before Thine eyes, and born in the bonds of sin, have brought forth anything that is unworthy of Thy counsels, inspire me with Thy spirit, that I may correct it. If by the wonderful beauty of Thy works I have been led into boldness – if I have sought my own honor among men as I advanced in the work which was destined to Thine honor, pardon

[48] 1 Corinthians 15:58

me in kindness and charity, and by Thy grace grant that my teaching may be to Thy glory and the welfare of all men. Praise ye the Lord, ye heavenly harmonies! And ye that understand the new harmonies, praise ye the Lord![49]"

---

[49] from the ending of *The Harmony of the World* – Johannes Kepler

CHAPTER XVIII
OLD ESTRANGEMENTS

"Mr. Hammond, are you ill? What can be the matter?"

Edna threw down her books and put her hand on the old man's shoulder. His face was concealed in his arms, and his half-stifled groan told that some fierce trial had overtaken him.

"Oh, child, my heart is heavy with a sorrow which I thought I had crushed."

He raised his head, looked sadly into the girl's face, and dropped his furrowed cheek on his hand.

Edna sat next to him. "Has anything happened since I saw you yesterday?"

"Yes. I have been surprised by the arrival of some of my relatives, whose presence in my house revives very painful memories. My niece, Mrs. Powell, and her daughter Gertrude, came very unexpectedly last night to make me a visit of some length." Her old friend glanced toward the study doorway and lowered his voice. "To you, my child, I can frankly say the surprise is a painful one. Many years have elapsed since I received any tidings of Agnes Powell, and I knew not, until she suddenly appeared before me last night, that she was a widow, and bereft of a handsome fortune. She claims a temporary home under my roof. Though she has caused me much suffering, I feel that I must endeavor to be patient and kind to her and her child. I have endured many trials, but this is one of the severest I have yet been called to pass through."

Distressed by his look of anguish, Edna took his hand between both hers, and stroking it, said, "My dear sir, if it is your duty, God will strengthen and sustain you. Cheer up; I can't bear to see you looking so troubled. A cloud on your face, my dear Mr.

Hammond, is to me like an eclipse of the sun. Pray do not keep me in shadow."

Mr. Hammond smiled briefly, but his face passed back into that troubled look. "If I could know that no mischief would result from Agnes's presence, I would not regard it with such distress. I do not wish to be uncharitable or suspicious; but I fear that her motives are not such as I could – "

"May I intrude, Uncle Allan?"

The stranger's voice was very sweet and winning. As the woman entered the room, Edna could scarcely repress an exclamation of admiration; for the world sees but rarely such perfect beauty as was the portion of Agnes Powell.

She was one of those few women who seem the pets of time, whose form and features catch some new grace and charm from every passing year. But for the tall, lovely girl who clung to her hand and called her "mother," Edna would have believed her only twenty-six or eight.

With a complexion fresh as a child's, and a face faultless as a goddess's, it was impossible to resist the fascination which she exerted over all who looked upon her. Her blonde hair gleamed in the morning sunshine, and as she raised one hand to shade her large blue eyes, her open sleeve fell back, disclosing an arm exquisitely molded.

As Mr. Hammond introduced his pupil to his guests, Mrs. Powell smiled pleasantly, and pressed her offered hand, and the blue, cold eyes scanned Edna's face. When Edna had seen fully into their depths, she could not avoid recalling Heine's poem of the Lorelei, a mermaid with a golden comb who sang sailors down to a watery death.

Mrs. Powell's voice was very much like a mermaid's music. "My daughter Gertrude promises herself much pleasure in your society, Miss Earl; for my uncle's praises prepare her to expect a most charming companion. Gertrude is about your age, but I fear you will find great disparity in her attainments, as she has not been so fortunate as to receive her education from Uncle Allan. You are, I believe, an adopted daughter of Mrs. Murray?"

"No, madam. Only a resident in her house until my education is sufficiently advanced enough to justify my teaching."

"My friend, Miss Harding, has recently moved to Le Bocage. She intends to make it her home. How is she?"

Edna detected an odd note in the music of Mrs. Powell's voice that mystified her. "Quite well, I believe."

Mr. Hammond quite suddenly left the study.

As soon as he was gone, Mrs. Powell quickly leaned forward. "Her friends at the North tell me that she is to marry her cousin, Mr. Murray, very soon. Is it true?" she asked breathlessly.

Edna's pulses jumped at the very mention of his name, but she said, "I had not heard the report."

"Then you think there are no grounds for the rumor?"

"Indeed, madam, I know nothing whatever concerning the matter."

"Estelle is handsome and brilliant."

Not brilliant enough, Edna thought, her heart beating faster at the thought of Mr. Murray, but she made no reply. She very much wanted to edge toward the door but stayed firm.

After waiting a few seconds, Mrs. Powell, her face slightly vexed, asked, "Does Mr. Murray go much into society now?"

"I believe not."

"Is he as handsome as ever?"

Edna frowned. "I do not know when you saw him last, but the ladies here seem rather to dread than admire him. Mrs. Powell, you are dipping your sleeve in your uncle's inkstand."

Picking up her books, she said to Mr. Hammond, who now stood in the door, "I presume I need not wait. I suppose you will be too much occupied today to attend to my lessons."

"Yes; I must give you holiday until Monday." His eyes were troubled.

Disappointed, wishing she could whisk this woman out of her old friend's house, Edna turned to leave.

"Wait." Mrs. Powell placed a tiny envelope into Edna's hand. "Miss Earl, may I trouble you to hand this letter to Miss Harding? It was entrusted to my care by one of her friends in New York. Pray be so good as to deliver it, with my kindest regards."

It was all Edna could do to keep from knitting her brows with annoyance, but accepted the note.

As Edna left the house, the pastor took his hat from the rack in the hall and walked silently beside her until she reached the gate. She grieved to see him so cast down, and fished for something cheerful to say.

"Mr. Hammond, your niece is the most beautiful woman I have ever seen."

He sighed heavily, and answered, hesitatingly, "Yes, yes. She is more beautiful now than when she first grew up."

"How long has she been a widow?"

"Not quite a year."

The troubled expression settled once more over his placid face. When Edna bade him good-morning, and had walked some distance, she looked back. He still leaned on the little gate under the drooping honeysuckle tendrils, his gray head bent down on his hand.

That Mrs. Powell was in some way connected with Mr. Murray's estrangement from the minister Edna felt sure. Very often she had been tempted to ask Mr. Hammond why Mr. Murray shunned him; but the shadow which fell upon his countenance whenever St. Elmo's name was accidentally mentioned made her shrink from alluding to the subject.

Before she had walked beyond the outskirts of the village, Mr. Leigh dashed up to join her. She felt the color rise in her cheeks as his fine eyes rested on her face, and he caught up her hand and clasped it. "You must forgive me for telling you how bitterly I was disappointed in not seeing you two days ago. Why did you absent yourself from the table?"

"Because I had no desire to meet Mrs. Murray's guests, and preferred to spend my time with Mr. Hammond."

"If he were not old enough to be your grandfather, I believe I should be jealous of him. Oh, Edna, do not be offended. I am so anxious about you – so pained at the change in your appearance. Last Sunday as you sat in church, I noticed how very pale and worn you looked, and with what weariness you leaned your head upon your hand. Mrs. Murray says you are very well, but I know better. You are either sick in body or mind; which is it?"

"Neither, Mr. Leigh." Edna felt that quiver in her lips that she could not suppress. "I am quite well, I assure you."

"You are grieved about something, which you are unwilling to confide to me. Edna, it is keen pain that brings that quiver to your lips, and if you would only tell me what it is! Edna, I know that – "

Edna pressed her lips together. "You conjure up a specter. I have nothing to confide, and there is no trouble which you can relieve."

They walked on silently for a while. Then Gordon said, "I am going away day after tomorrow, to be absent at least for several months, and I have come to ask a favor which you are too generous to deny. I want your ambrotype or photograph. I hope you will give it to me without hesitation."

Edna shook her head. "I have never had a likeness of any kind taken."

"There is a good artist here," Mr. Leigh pleaded. "Will you not go today and have one taken for me?"

"No, Mr. Leigh."

"Oh, Edna! Why not?"

"Because the sooner you forget me entirely, save as a mere friend, the happier we both shall be."

"Edna, Edna. That is impossible." Mr. Leigh caught her hand up again, his blue eyes looking deep into hers. "If you withhold your picture it will do no good, for I have your face here in my heart. You cannot take that image from me."

"At least I will not encourage feelings which can bring only pain to me and disappointment to yourself. I consider it unprincipled in a woman to foster an affection which she knows she can never return."

"You might change your mind."

Her heart always broke whenever he said that. "My dear friend, let the past be forgotten; it saddens me whenever I think of it, and is a barrier to all pleasant discussion. Good-bye, Mr. Leigh. You have my best wishes on your journey."

"Will you not allow me to see you home?"

"I think it is best that – I prefer that you should not. Mr. Leigh, promise me that you will struggle against this feeling which distresses me beyond expression."

She turned and put out her hand. He took it and wordlessly pressed his lips to it.

Mr. Leigh shook his head mournfully, and said as he left her, "God bless you! It will be a dreary, dreary season with me till I return and see your face again. God preserve you till then!"

Walking rapidly homeward, Edna wondered why she could not return Gordon Leigh's affection – why his noble face never haunted her dreams instead of another's – of which she dreaded to think.

Thinking back over the past few weeks, she realized that before she was aware of the fact, an image to which she refused homage must have stood between her heart and Gordon's.

When she reached home she took off her wrap. "Is Miss Harding here?" she asked of dear Hagar.

"No, she is not. She and Mrs. Murray have gone visiting with Mr. Allston."

"Ah," Edna said.

"They have taken their lunch, and they won't return until late in the afternoon."

"Is Mr. Murray gone as well?"

"Oh, yes, child," Hagar said. "Mr. Murray started at daylight on an errand to a town about twelve miles away, and he will not be back in time for dinner."

Edna could not help the joy that sparked in her face, and Hagar smiled a little.

Much rejoiced at the prospect of a quiet day, Edna hurried up the stairs to her room, determined to complete the chapter which she had left unfinished two nights ago.

Needing a reference in the book which Mr. Murray had taken from the library, she went up to copy it. As she sat down and opened the volume to find the passage she required, a letter slipped out and fell at her feet. She glanced at the envelope as she picked it up – and her heart bounded painfully as she saw Mr. Murray's name written in Mr. Manning's peculiar and unmistakable handwriting.

The postmark and date corresponded exactly with the one that she had received the night Mr. Murray gave her the roll of manuscript.

The strongest temptation of her life here assailed her. She would almost have given her right hand to know the contents of that letter, and Mr. Murray's confident assertion concerning the package was now fully explained. He had recognized the handwriting on her letters and suspected her ambitious scheme. He was not a stranger to Mr. Manning, and must have known the nature of their correspondence; consequently, his taunt about a lover was entirely ironical.

She turned the unsealed envelope over and over, longing to know what it contained.

The house was deserted – there was, she knew, no human being nearer than the kitchen, and no eye but God's upon her.

She looked once more at the superscription of the letter. Then, with a groan, she put it back into the book without opening the envelope.

She copied into her notebook the reference she was seeking, and replacing the volume on the window-sill where she had found it, went back to her own room and tried unsuccessfully to banish the subject of the letter from her mind.

She felt as if she would rather face any other disaster sooner than have St. Elmo scoffing at her daring project; and more annoyed and puzzled than she chose to confess, she resolutely bent her thoughts upon her work.

It was almost dusk before Mrs. Murray and her guests returned. When it grew so dark that Edna could not see the lines of her paper, she smoothed her hair, changed her dress, and went down to the parlor.

Mrs. Murray was resting in a corner of the sofa, fanning herself vigorously. Mr. Allston smoked on the veranda, talking to her through the open window.

Mrs. Murray sat up a little as Edna entered. "Well, Edna, where have you been all day?"

"With my books."

"I am tired almost to death. This country visiting is an intolerable bore! I am worn out with small talk and back-biting. Child, let us have some music by way of variety. Play that symphony of Beethoven that I heard you practicing last week."

Mrs. Murray laid her head on the arm of the sofa and shut her eyes. Edna opened the piano and played.

The delicacy of her touch enabled her to render it with peculiar pathos and power; and she played on and on, unmindful of Miss Harding's entrance – oblivious of everything but the sublime strains of the great master.

The light streamed over her face, and showed a gladness, an exaltation of expression there, as if her soul had broken from its earthly moorings and was making its way joyfully into the infinite sea of eternal love and blessedness.

At last her fingers fell from the keys, and as she rose she saw Mr. Murray standing outside of the parlor door with his fingers shading his eyes. Edna, upon seeing him, quickly began arranging her piano music so she wouldn't have to meet his eyes.

He came in, and his mother held out her hand, saying, "Here is a seat, my son. Have you just returned?"

"No, I have been here some time."

"How are affairs in town?"

"I really have no idea."

"Why? I thought you went there today."

"I started; but found my horse so lame that I went no further than the village."

"Indeed! Hagar told me you had not returned, when I came in from visiting."

"Like some other people of my acquaintance, Hagar reckons without her host. I have been at home ever since twelve o'clock, and saw the carriage as you drove off."

Estelle leaned toward him coquettishly. "And pray how have you employed yourself, you incorrigible man?"

"Most serenely and charmingly, my fair cousin, in the solitude of my den. If my mother could give me satisfactory security that all my days would prove as quiet and happy as this has been, I would never quit the confines of Le Bocage again. Ah, the indescribable relief of feeling that nothing was expected of me; that the galling shackles of hospitality and etiquette were snapped, and that I was entirely free from all danger of intrusion. This day shall be marked with a white stone; for I entered my rooms at twelve o'clock and remained there in uninterrupted peace till five minutes ago, when I put on my social shackles once more, and hobbled down to entertain my fair guest."

Edna was arranging some sheets of music that were scattered on the piano; but as he mentioned the hour of his return, she remembered that the clock struck one just as she went into the sitting-room where he kept his books and cabinets. He would have been in the inner room, beyond the arch. She put her hand to her forehead. The silk curtains, she was sure, were hanging over the arch; for she remembered a large golden butterfly which had fluttered in from the terrace flitting over the glowing folds. But though St. Elmo had been screened from her view, he must have seen her as she sat before his bookcase, turning his letter over and over between her fingers.

She bent down to examine the music, so absorbed in her own emotions of chagrin that she heard not one word of what Miss Harding was saying. If Mr. Murray knew of her visit to the "Egyptian museum," he intended her to know it.

Gathering up her courage, she raised her eyes in the direction of the sofa, where he had thrown himself, and met just what she most dreaded: his keen gaze riveted on her face. Evidently he had been waiting for this glance; for instantly he smiled, inclined his head, and arched his eyebrows, as if much amused. Never before had she seen his face so bright and happy, so free from bitterness.

Edna's face crimsoned, and she put up her hand to shield it; but Mr. Murray turned toward the window, and coolly discussed the merits of a popular racehorse, upon which Clinton Allston lavished extravagant praise. Estelle leaned against the window, listening to the controversy.

After a time, the subject was very effectually settled by an oath from the master of the house.

Edna availed herself of the lull in the conversation to deliver the letter. "Miss Harding, I was requested to hand you this."

Estelle broke the seal, glanced rapidly over the letter and exclaimed, "Is it possible? Can she be here? Who gave you this letter?"

"Mrs. Powell, Mr. Hammond's niece."

"Agnes Powell?"

"Yes. Agnes Powell."

During the next three minutes, the ticking of two watches was very audible.

Estelle read through the letter again. But Mrs. Murray involuntarily laid her hand on her son's knee and watched his face with an expression of breathless anxiety. Though Mr. Murray's lips blanched, not a muscle moved, not a nerve twitched. Only the deadly hate that leapt into his large shadowy eyes told that the name stirred some bitter memory.

The silence was growing intolerable when Mr. Murray turned his gaze full on Estelle. "Have you seen a ghost? Your letter must contain tidings of Victor's untimely demise; for, if there is such a thing as retribution, such a personage as Nemesis, I swear that poor devil of a Count has crept into her garments to haunt you. Did he cut his white womanish throat with a penknife, or smother himself with charcoal fumes, or light a poisoned candle and let his poor soul drift out dreamily into eternity? If so, Gabriel will require a powerful microscope to find him. Is he really dead? Peace to his tiny soul! Who had the courage to write and break the melancholy tidings to you?"

Estelle laughed and shrugged her shoulders.

"How insanely jealous you are of Victor! He's neither dead nor dreaming of suicide, but enjoying himself vastly in Baden-Baden. Edna, did Mrs. Powell bring Gertrude with her?"

"Yes."

"Do you know how long she intends remaining at the parsonage?"

"I think her visit is of indefinite duration."

Mrs. Murray broke into the conversation. "Edna, will you oblige me by inquiring whether Henry intends to give us any supper tonight? He forgets we have had no dinner. St. Elmo, do turn down that gas – the wind makes it flare dreadfully."

Edna left the room to obey Mrs. Murray's command, and did not return immediately; but, after the party seated themselves at the table, she noticed that St. Elmo seemed in unusually high spirits. When the meal was concluded, he challenged his cousins to a game of billiards.

They repaired to the rotunda, and Mrs. Murray beckoned to Edna to follow her. As they entered her room, she carefully closed the door.

"Edna, when did Mrs. Powell arrive?"

"Last night."

"Did you see her?"

"Yes, ma'am."

"Is she very pretty?"

"She is the most beautiful woman I ever met."

"How did Mr. Hammond receive her?"

"Her visit evidently annoys him, but he gave me no explanation of the matter, which I confess puzzles me. I should suppose her society would cheer and interest him."

"Oh, pooh! Talk of what you understand. She surely has not come here to live?"

"I think he fears she has. She is very poor."

Mrs. Murray set her teeth together and muttered something which Edna did not understand. "Edna, is she handsomer than Estelle?"

"Infinitely handsomer, I think. Indeed, they are so totally unlike it would be impossible to compare them. Your niece is very fine-looking, very commanding; Mrs. Powell is beautiful."

"But she is no longer young. She has a grown daughter."

"True; but in looking at her you do not realize it. Did you never see her?"

"No; and I trust I never may. I am astonished that Mr. Hammond can endure the sight of her. You say he has told you nothing about her?"

"Nothing which explains the chagrin her presence seems to cause."

"He is very wise. But, Edna, avoid her society as much as possible. She is doubtless very fascinating; but I prefer that you should have little conversation with her. On the whole, you might as well stay at home now; it is very warm, and you can study without Mr. Hammond's assistance."

"You do not mean that my visits must cease altogether?"

"Oh, no; go occasionally – once or twice a week – but certainly not every day, as formerly. And, Edna, be careful not to mention that woman's name again; I dislike her exceedingly."

The orphan longed to ask for an explanation but was too proud to solicit confidence so studiously withheld.

Mrs. Murray leaned back in her large rocking-chair and fell into a reverie. Edna waited for some time, and finally rose.

"Mrs. Murray, have you anything more to say to me tonight? You look very much fatigued."

"Nothing, I believe. Good-night, child. Send Hagar to me."

Edna went back to her desk and resolutely turned to her work; for it was one of the peculiar traits of her character that she could at will fasten her thoughts upon whatever subject she desired to master. She tore her mind from the events of the day, and diligently toiled among the fragments of Scandinavian lore for the missing links in her mythologic chain.

Now and then peals of laughter from the billiard-room startled her; and more than once Mr. Murray's clear, cold voice rose above the subdued chatter of Estelle and Clinton.

After a while the game ended, good nights were exchanged, the party dispersed, doors were closed, and all grew silent.

While Edna wrote on, an unexpected sound arrested her pen. She listened, and heard the slow walk of a horse beneath her window. As it passed, she rose and looked out. The moon was up, and Mr. Murray was riding down the avenue.

The girl returned to her manuscript and worked on without intermission for another hour; then the last paragraph was carefully punctuated, the long and difficult chapter was finished. She laid aside her pen and locked her desk.

Shaking down the mass of hair that had been tightly coiled at the back of her head, she extinguished the light, and drawing a chair to the window, seated herself.

Silence and peace brooded over the world; not a sound broke the solemn repose of nature.

The summer breeze rocked itself to rest in the elm boughs, and the waning moon climbed slowly up a cloudless sky, passing starry sentinels whose mighty challenge was lost in vast vortices of blue, as they paced their ceaseless round in the mighty camp of constellations.

With her eyes fixed on the gloomy archway of elms, where an occasional slip of moonshine silvered the ground, Edna watched and waited. The blood beat heavily in her temples and throbbed sullenly at her heart; but she sat mute and motionless as the summer night, reviewing all that had occurred during the day.

Presently the distant sound of hoofs on the rocky road leading to town fell upon her strained ear; the hard, quick gallop ceased at the gate, and very slowly Mr. Murray walked his horse up the dusky avenue, and on toward the stable.

From the shadow of her muslin curtain, Edna looked down on the walk beneath. After a few moments saw him coming to the house.

He paused on the terrace, took off his hat, swept back the thick hair from his forehead, and stood looking out over the quiet lawn.

Then a heavy, heavy sigh, almost a moan, seemed to burst from the depths of his heart, and he turned and went into the house.

The night was far spent, and the moon had cradled herself on the tree-tops, when Edna raised her face all blistered with tears. Stretching out her arms she fell on her knees, while a passionate, sobbing prayer struggled brokenly across her trembling lips.

"O my God, have mercy upon him! Save his wretched soul from eternal death! Help me so to live and govern myself that I bring no shame on the cause of Christ. And if it be thy will, O my God, grant that I may be instrumental in winning this precious but wandering, sinful soul back to the faith as it is in Jesus!"

Ah, verily –

> ... "More things are wrought by prayer
> Than this world dreams of. Wherefore let thy voice
> Rise like a fountain for him night and day.
> For what are men better than sheep or goats,
> That nourish a blind life within the brain,
> If, knowing God, they lift not hands of prayer
> Both for themselves, and those who call them friend?"[50]

---

[50] "Morte d'Arthur" – Lord Alfred Tennyson

CHAPTER XIX
THE ICONOCLAST ARRIVES

"Where are you going, St. Elmo?" Estelle asked. "I know it is one of your amiable decrees that your movements are not to be questioned, but I dare to brave your ire."

It was a dark, rainy morning in July, and Mr. Murray was passing through the sitting room where the rest of the household had gathered.

Mr. Murray took a cigar out of his pocket. "I am going to that blessed retreat familiarly known as 'Murray's den,' where, secure from feminine intrusion, I surrender my happy soul to science and cigars, and revel in complete forgetfulness of that awful curse which Jove hurled against all mankind."

"There are asylums for lunatics and inebriates, and I wonder it has never occurred to some benevolent millionaire to found one for such abominable cynics as you, my most angelic cousin, where the snarling brutes can only snap at and worry one another."

"An admirable idea, Estelle, which I fondly imagined I had successfully carried out when I built those rooms of mine. Like Momus and his dissatisfaction with the house that Minerva built, I only wish that mine was movable, as he recommended, in order to escape bad neighborhoods and tiresome companions."

Mrs. Murray was winding a quantity of zephyr wool of various bright colors, which she had requested Edna to hold on her wrists. Edna was watching the rain lash against the windows.

Estelle pretended to take offence. "Upon my word, you spin some spiteful idea out of every sentence I utter. If I did not know that instead of proving a punishment it would gratify you beyond measure, I would take a vow not to speak to you again for a month; but the consciousness of the happiness I should thereby bestow upon you, vetoes the resolution. I assure you I am the victim of hopeless ennui, for Mr. Allston will probably not return until tomorrow, and it is raining so hard that I cannot wander outside, and I am shut up in this dreary house. Ugh! If there remains one spark of chivalry in your soul, do not go off to your den, but stay here and entertain me. It is said that you read bewitchingly; pray favor me this morning. I will be meek, docile, absolutely silent."

Estelle swept aside a mass of papers from the corner of the sofa, and, taking Mr. Murray's hand, drew him to a seat beside her.

"Your 'amiable silence,' my fair cousin, is but a cunningly fashioned wooden horse. I fear the Greeks, even when they bear gifts! Reading aloud is a practice in which I never indulge, simply because I detest it. Nevertheless, since read I must, I only stipulate that I may be allowed to select my book. Just now I am profoundly interested in a French work on infusoria, by Dujardin; and as you have probably not studied it, I will select those portions which treat of the animalcule that inhabit grains of sugar and salt and drops of water. By the time lunch is ready, your appetite will be whetted by a knowledge of the nature of your repast. According to Leeuwenhoek, the campaigns of Genghis Khan were not half so murderous as a single fashionable dinner; and the battle of Marengo was a farce in comparison with the swallowing of a cup of tea, which contains – "

"For shame, you tormentor! Not one line of all that nauseating scientific stuff shall you read to me. Here is a volume of poems of the *Female Poets*. Do be agreeable for once in your life and select me some sweet little gem."

"I refuse to endure the perusal of 'female poetry,' for Pegasus had an unconquerable repugnance to side-saddles. You vow you will not listen to science; and I swear I won't read poetry. Suppose we compromise on this new number of the *Iconoclast* Magazine? It is the ablest periodical published in this country. Let me see the contents."

At the mention of the magazine, Edna looked up suddenly at St. Elmo.

Holding his cigar between his thumb and third finger, his eye ran over the table of contents.

"'Who Smote the Marble Gods of Greece?' Humph! Rather a difficult question to answer after the lapse of twenty-two centuries. But doubtless our archaeologists are so much wiser than the Athenian Senate of Five Hundred, who investigated the affair the day after it happened, that a perusal will be exceedingly edifying."

Turning to the article he read it aloud, without pausing to comment. Hearing him reading her words aloud, Edna's heart bounded so rapidly that she could scarcely conceal her agitation. It was, indeed, a treat to listen to him. As his musical voice filled the room, she thought of Jean Paul Richter's description of Goethe's reading: "There is nothing comparable to it. It is like deep-toned thunder blended with whispering rain-drops."

But Edna's pleasure was cut short. As Mr. Murray finished the article, he tossed the magazine contemptuously across the room. "Pretentious and shallow! A tissue of pedantry and error from beginning to end – written, I will wager, by some scribbler who never saw Athens. Moreover, the whole article is based upon a glaring blunder; for, according to Plutarch and Diodorus, on the memorable night in question there was a new moon. Pshaw! It is a tasteless, insipid plagiarism from Grote. If I am to be bored with such insufferable twaddle, I will stop my subscription."

He did not even glance toward Edna, but the peculiar emphasis of his words left no doubt in her mind that he suspected – nay, felt assured, that she was the luckless author.

Raising her head which had been drooped over the woolen skeins, she said, firmly, yet very quietly, "If you will permit me to differ with you, Mr. Murray, I will say that it seems to me all the testimony is in favor of the full-moon theory. Besides, Grote is the latest and best authority; he has carefully collected and sifted the evidence, and certainly sanctions the position taken by the author of the article which you condemn."

"Ah, how long since you investigated the matter? The affair is so essentially Paganish that I should imagine that it possessed no charm for so orthodox a Christian as yourself. Estelle, what say you concerning this historic sphinx?"

"That I have a vague impression that it is not worth a quarrel with you; that the article is the merest matter of moonshine – new moon versus full moon – and must have been written by a lunatic. But, one thing I do intend to say most decidedly, and that is, that your lunge at female intellect was as unnecessary and ill-timed and ill-bred as it was ill-natured. The mental equality of the sexes is now as unquestioned, as universally admitted, as any other well-established fact in science or history; and the sooner you men gracefully concede us our rights, the sooner we shall cease wrangling, and settle back into our traditional amiability."

"Pardon me, I always bow before facts, no matter how unflattering, but those are not facts. Without doubt, the most thoroughly ludicrous scene I ever witnessed was furnished by a 'woman's rights' meeting,' which I looked in upon one night in New York, as I returned from Europe. The speaker was an angular, short-haired, lemon-visaged female of very certain age, with a hand like a bronze gauntlet, and a voice as distracting as the shrill squeak of a cracked cornet. Over the wrongs and grievances of her down-trodden, writhing sisterhood she ranted and raved and howled. The whole time, she gesticulated with a marvelous grace, which I can compare only to the antics of those inspired goats who strayed too near the Pythian cave and were thrown into convulsions.

"I pulled my hat over my eyes, clapped both hands to my ears, and rushed out of the hall after a stay of five minutes. But the vision of horror followed me. For the first and only time in my life, I had such a hideous nightmare that night that the man who slept in the next room broke open my door to ascertain who was strangling me. Heaven grant us a Bellerophon to relieve the age of these noisy Amazons!"

"'Lay on, Macduff[51]!' My toes are not bruised in the slightest degree. I am entirely innocent of any attempt at authorship, and the sole literary dream of my life is to improve the present popular recipe for *biscuit glacé*. But mark you, sir, I must bark a little under my breath at your inconsistencies. Now, if there are two living men whom, above all others, you swear by, they are John Stuart Mill and John Ruskin. Well do I recollect your eulogy of both, on that ever-memorable day in Paris, when we dined with that French encyclopedia, Count de Falloux, and the leading

---

[51] *Macbeth*, Act 5, Scene 8 -- Shakespeare

lettered men of the day were discussed. I was frightened out of my wits and dared not raise my eyes higher than the top of my wineglass, lest I should be asked my opinion of some book or subject of which I had never even heard. At that time, I had never read either Mill or Ruskin; but my profound reverence for the wisdom of your opinions taught me how shamefully ignorant I was, and thus, to fit myself for your companionship, I immediately bought their books. Lo, to my indescribable amazement, I found that Mill claimed for women what I never once dreamed we were worthy of – not only equality, but the right of suffrage. He, the foremost dialectician of England and the most learned of political economists, demands that we women should be allowed to vote. Were I to follow his teachings, I should certainly clamor for the lady-like privilege of elbowing you away from the ballot-box at the next election."

"The clearest thinkers of the world have had soft spots in their brains; and you have laid your finger on the softened spot in Mill's skull, 'suffrage.' When I read his *Representative Government*, I saw that his reason had dragged anchor, the prestige of his great name vanished, and I threw the book into the fire and eschewed him henceforth. *Sic transit.*"

Here Mrs. Murray looked up and said, "John Stuart Mill – let me see – Edna, is he not the man who wrote that touching dedication of one of his books to his wife's memory? You quoted it for me a few days ago, and said that you had committed it to memory because it was such a glowing tribute to the intellectual capacity of woman. My dear, I wish you would repeat it now. I should like to hear it again."

With her fingers full of purple woolen skeins, and her eyes bent down, Edna recited in a low, sweet voice the most eloquent panegyric which man's heart ever pronounced on woman's intellect:

"To the beloved and deplored memory of her who was the inspirer, and in part, the author, of all that is best in my writings, the friend and wife whose exalted sense of truth and right was my strongest incitement, and whose approbation was my chief reward, I dedicate this volume. Like all that I have written for many years, it belongs as much to her as to me; but the work as it

218

stands has had, in a very insufficient degree, the inestimable advantage of her revision; some of the most important portions having been reserved for a more careful re-examination, which they are now never destined to receive. Were I but capable of interpreting to the world one half the great thoughts and noble feelings which are buried in her grave, I should be the medium of a greater benefit to it than is ever likely to arise from anything that I can write unprompted and unassisted by her all but unrivalled wisdom."

"Where did you find that dedication?" asked Mr. Murray.

"In Mill's book *On Liberty*," Edna said.

"It is not in my library."

"I borrowed it from Mr. Hammond."

"Strange that a plant so noxious should be permitted in such a sanctified atmosphere. Do you happen to recollect the following sentences? 'I regard utility as the ultimate appeal on all ethical questions!' 'There is a Greek ideal of self-development, which the Platonic and Christian ideal of self-government blends with, but does not supersede. It may be better to be a John Knox than an Alcibiades, but it is better to be a Pericles than either.'"

"Yes, sir. They occur in the same book; but, Mr. Murray, I have been advised by my teacher to bear always in mind that noble maxim, 'I can tolerate everything else but every other man's intolerance'; and it is with his consent and by his instructions that I go like Ruth, gleaning in the great fields of literature."

"Take care you don't find Boaz instead of barley. After all, the universal mania for match-making schemes and maneuvers which continually stir society from its dregs to the painted foam-bubble dancing on its crested wave, is peculiar to no age or condition, but is an immemorial and hereditary female proclivity. I defy Paris or London to furnish a more perfectly developed specimen of a 'maneuvering mamma' than was crafty Naomi, when she sent that pretty little Moabitish widow out husband-hunting.[52]"

"I heartily wish she was only here to outwit you!" laughed his cousin, nestling her head against his arm as they sat together on the sofa.

"Who? The widow or the match-maker?"

---

[52] Y'all read the book of Ruth in the Bible, right?

"Oh, the match-maker, of course. There is more than one Ruth already in the field."

The last clause was whispered so low that only St. Elmo heard it.

Any other woman but Estelle Harding would have shrunk away in utter humiliation from the eye and the voice that answered, "Yourself and Mrs. Powell! Eat Boaz's barley as long as you like – nay, divide Boaz's broad fields between you; but if you love your lives, keep out of Boaz's way."

"You ought both to be ashamed of yourselves. I am surprised at you, Estelle, to encourage St. Elmo's irreverence," said Mrs. Murray, severely.

Estelle pulled herself away from Mr. Murray and went to the bookshelf. "I am sure, Aunt Ellen, I am just as much shocked as you are; but when he does not respect even your opinions, how dare I presume to hope he will show any deference to mine? Now, St. Elmo, what think you of the last Sibylline leaves of your favorite Ruskin? In looking over his new book, I was surprised to find this strong assertion ... Here is the volume now – listen to this, will you? –

"'Shakespeare has no heroes; he has only heroines. In his labored and perfect plays you find no hero, but almost always a perfect woman; steadfast in grave hope and errorless purpose .... The catastrophe of every play is caused always by the folly or fault of a man; the redemption, if there be any, is by the wisdom and virtue of a woman, and failing that, there is none!'[53]"

"For instance, Lady Macbeth, Ophelia, Regan, Goneril, and last, but not least, Petruchio's sweet and gentle Kate. *De gustibus!*" answered Mr. Murray.

"Those are the exceptions, and of course you pounce upon them. Ruskin continues: 'In all cases with Scott, as with Shakespeare, it is the woman who watches over, teaches and guides the youth; it is never by any chance the man who watches over or educates her; and thus – '"

"Meg Merrilies, Madge Wildfire, Mause Headrigg, Effie Deans, and Rob Roy's freckle-faced, red-haired, angelic Helen!" interrupted her cousin.

---

[53] Sesame and Lilies – John Ruskin

"Don't be rude, St. Elmo. You fly in my face like an exasperated wasp. I resume: 'Dante's great poem is a song of praise for Beatrice's watch over his soul; she saves him from hell, and leads him star by star up into heaven – '"

"Permit me to suggest that conjugal devotion should have led him to apostrophize the superlative charms of his own wife, Gemma, from whom he was forced to separate; and that his vision of hell was a faint reflex of his domestic felicity."

Edna shook her head over her embroidery. She was certain that the male scholars were too hard on Gemma, for very little was known about her life beside the fact that, when Dante had been exiled from Florence, she had stayed behind.

"Mask your battery, sir, till I finish this page, which I am resolved you shall hear: 'Greek literature proves the same thing, as witness the devoted tenderness of Andromache, the wisdom of Cassandra, the domestic excellence of Penelope, the love of Antigone, the resignation of Iphigenia, the faithfulness of – '"

"Allow me to assist him in completing the list: the world-renowned constancy of Helen to Menelaus, the devotion of Clytemnestra to her Agamemnon, the sublime filial affection of Medea, and the bewitching – "

"Hush, sir. Thank heaven, here comes Mr. Allston; I can smooth the ruffled plumes of my self-love in his sunny smiles and forget your growls. Good morning, Mr. Allston; what happy accident brought you again so soon to Le Bocage?"

Edna picked up the magazine, which lay in one corner, and made her escape.

The gratification arising from the acceptance and prompt publication of her essay was marred by Mr. Murray's sneering comments about her article; but still her heart was happier than it had been for many weeks. She turned to the Editor's Table where she read a few lines complimenting "the article of a new contributor." The editor promised another article from the same pen for the ensuing month, and Edna's face flushed joyfully.

While she felt it difficult to realize that her writings had found favor in Mr. Manning's critical eyes, she thanked God that she was considered worthy of communicating with her public through the medium of a magazine so influential and celebrated. She thought it probable that Mr. Manning had written her a few lines, and wondered whether at that moment a letter was not hidden in St. Elmo's pocket.

Taking the magazine, she went into Mrs. Murray's room, and found her resting on a lounge. Her face wore a troubled expression, and Edna saw traces of tears on the pillow.

"Come in, child; I was just thinking of you."

Mrs. Murray put out her hand, drew the girl to a seat near the lounge, and sighed heavily.

"Dear Mrs. Murray, I am very, very happy, and I have come to make a confession and ask your congratulations."

Edna knelt beside her, and, taking the fingers of her benefactress, pressed her forehead against them.

Mrs. Murray started up and lifted the blushing face. "A confession, Edna? What have you done?"

"Some time ago you questioned me concerning some letters which excited your suspicion, and which I promised to explain at some future day. I dare say you will think me very presumptuous when I tell you that I have been aspiring to authorship; that I was corresponding with Mr. Manning on the subject of a manuscript which I had sent for his examination. Now I have come to show you what I have been doing. You heard Mr. Murray read an essay this morning from the *Iconoclast* Magazine, which he ridiculed very bitterly, but which Mr. Manning at least thought worthy of a place in his pages. Mrs. Murray, I wrote that article."

"Is it possible? Who assisted you – who revised it, Mr. Hammond? I did not suppose that you, my child, could ever write so elegantly, so gracefully."

"No one saw the manuscript until Mr. Manning gave it to the printers. I wished to surprise Mr. Hammond, and therefore told him nothing of my ambitious scheme. I was very apprehensive that I should fail, and for that reason was unwilling to acquaint you with the precise subject of the correspondence until I was sure of success. Oh, Mrs. Murray, I have no mother, and I feel that I owe everything to you – that without your generous aid and protection I should never have been able to accomplish this one hope of my life. I come to you to share my triumph, for I know you will fully sympathize with me. Here is the magazine containing Mr. Manning's praise of my work, and here are the letters which I was once so reluctant to put into your hands. When I asked you to trust me, you did so nobly and freely. I thank you more than my feeble words can express, and I want to show you that I was not unworthy of your confidence."

She laid magazine and letters on Mrs. Murray's lap. In silence the proud, reserved woman wound her arms tightly around the orphan, pressing the bright young face against her shoulder, and resting her own cheek on the girl's fair forehead.

The door was partly ajar, and at that instant St. Elmo entered.

He stopped, looked at the kneeling figure locked so closely in his mother's arms. Over his stern face broke a light that transformed it into such beauty as Lucifer's might have worn before his sin and banishment, when God –

> "'Lucifer' – kindly said as 'Gabriel,'
> 'Lucifer' – soft as 'Michael'; while serene
> He, standing in the glory of the lamps,
> Answered, 'My Father,' innocent of shame
> And of the sense of thunder!"[54]

Yearningly he extended his arms toward the two, who, absorbed in their low talk, were unconscious of his presence. Then his hands fell heavily to his side, the brief smile was swallowed up by scowling shadows, and he turned silently away and went to his own gloomy rooms.

---

[54] from *A Drama of Exile* – Elizabeth Barrett Browning

CHAPTER XX
ANGEL AT THE GATES OF EDEN

"Mrs. Powell and her daughter to see Miss Estelle and Miss Edna."

"Why did you not say we were at dinner?" cried Mrs. Murray, darting an angry glance at the servant.

"I did, ma'am, but they said they would wait."

As Estelle folded up her napkin and slipped it into the silver ring, she looked furtively at St. Elmo. He was holding up a bunch of purple grapes, said in an indifferent tone to his mother, "The vineyards of Spain show nothing more perfect. This cluster might challenge comparison with those from which Red Hermitage is made, the seeds of which are said to have been brought from Schiraz, in Iran. Even on the sunny slopes of Cyprus and Naxos I found no finer grapes than these. I want a basketful this afternoon. Henry, tell old Simon to gather them immediately."

Estelle came to the back of his chair and leaned over his shoulder. "Pray, what use have you for them? I am sure the courteous idea of sending them as a present never could have forced an entrance into your mind, much less have carried the outworks of your heart."

"I shall go out on the terrace and I shall crown and pelt my marble Bacchus yonder with the grapes till his sculptured limbs are bathed in their purple sacrificial blood. What other use could I possibly have for them?"

He threw his head back and added something in a lower tone, at which Estelle laughed, and put up her red, full lip.

Mrs. Murray frowned and said sternly, "Estelle, if you intend to see those persons, I advise you to do so promptly."

Her niece moved toward the door, but glanced over her shoulder. "I presume Gertrude expects to see Edna, as she asked for her."

Edna had been watching Mr. Murray's face, but could detect no change in its expression, save a brief gleam as of triumph when the visitors were announced.

Rising, Edna approached Mrs. Murray, whose clouded brow betokened extraordinary displeasure, and whispered, "Gertrude is exceedingly anxious to see the house and grounds; have I your permission to show her over the place? She is particularly anxious to see the deer."

"Of course, if she requests it; but their effrontery in coming here, to this house, caps all the impudence I ever heard of. Have as little to say as possible."

Edna went to the parlor, leaving mother and son together.

Mrs. Powell had laid aside her mourning garments and wore a dress of blue muslin which heightened her beauty. As Edna looked from her to Gertrude, she found it difficult to decide who was the loveliest.

After a few desultory remarks she rose, saying to Gertrude, "As you have repeatedly expressed a desire to examine the park and hothouses, I will show you the way this afternoon."

"Take care, my love, that you do not fatigue yourself," were Mrs. Powell's low, tenderly spoken words as her daughter rose to leave the room.

Edna went first to the greenhouse, and though Gertrude chattered ceaselessly, she took little interest in her exclamations of delight, for she was conjecturing the cause of Mrs. Murray's great indignation.

For some weeks, Edna had been thrown frequently into the society of Mr. Hammond's guests. While her distrust of Mrs. Powell, and her aversion to her melting, musical voice, increased, a genuine affection for Gertrude had taken root in her heart.

They were the same age, but Edna was an earnest woman, and Gertrude was a careless, enthusiastic child. Although Edna found it impossible to make a companion of this warm-hearted girl, who hated books and turned pale at the mention of study, still Edna liked to watch her radiant face, with its cheeks tinted like sea-shells, and her soft blue eyes sparkling with joyousness.

As they stood hand in hand, admiring some goldfish in a small aquarium in the center of the greenhouse, Gertrude exclaimed, "The place is as fascinating as its master. Do tell me something about him; I wonder very often why you never mention him. I know I ought not to say it; but really, after he has talked to me for a few minutes, I forget everything else, and think only of what he says for days and days after."

"You certainly do not allude to Mr. Murray?" said Edna.

"I certainly do. What makes you look so astonished?"

"I was not aware that you knew him."

"Oh, I have known him since the week after our arrival here. Mamma and I met him at Mrs. Inge's. Mr. Inge had some gentlemen to dinner, and they came into the parlor while we were calling. Mr. Murray sat down and talked to me then for some time, and I have frequently met him since, for it seems he loves to stroll about the woods almost as well as I do. Sometimes we walk together. You know, he and my uncle are not friendly, and I believe mamma does not like him, so he never comes to the parsonage, and he never seems to notice me if I am with her or Uncle Allan. But is he not very fascinating? If he were not a little too old for me, I believe I should really be very much in love with him."

An expression of disgust passed swiftly over Edna's pale face. She dropped Gertrude's hand, and asked coldly, "Does your mother approve of your walks with Mr. Murray?"

"For heaven's sake, don't look so solemn! I – she – really, I don't know! I never told her a word about it. Once I mentioned having met him, and showed her some flowers he gave me, but she took very little notice of the matter. Several times since he has sent me bouquets, and though I kept them out of uncle's sight, she saw them in my room, and must have suspected where they came from. Of course, he cannot come to the parsonage to see me, since he does not speak to my uncle or to mamma; but I do not see any harm in his walking and talking with me when I happen to meet him. Oh, how lovely those lilies are, leaning over the edge of the aquarium. Mr. Murray said that someday he would show me all

226

the beautiful things at Le Bocage, but he has forgotten his promise. I am afraid that I – "

"Ah, Miss Gertrude, how could you doubt me? I am here to fulfill my promise."

Edna stopped as if struck by lightning, for that warm, resonant voice could belong to only one man.

Mr. Murray pushed aside the boughs of a guava which stood between them. Coming forward, he took Gertrude's hand, drew it under his arm, and looked down eagerly, admiringly, into her blushing face.

"Oh, Mr. Murray! I had no idea you were anywhere near me. I am sure I could – "

"Did you imagine you could escape my eyes, which are always seeking you? Permit me to be your chaperone over Le Bocage, instead of Miss Edna here, who looks as if she had been scolding you. Perhaps she will be so good as to wait for us, and I will bring you back in a half-hour at least."

"Edna, will you wait here for me?" asked Gertrude.

"Why cannot Mr. Murray bring you to the house? There is nothing more to see here."

"Allow us to judge for ourselves, if you please. There is a late Paris paper, which will amuse you till we return."

St. Elmo threw a newspaper at Edna's feet, and led Gertrude away through one of the glass doors into the park.

Edna sat down on the edge of the aquarium, and the hungry little fish crowded close to her, looking up wistfully for the crumbs she would scatter there daily; but now their mute appeal went unheeded.

Her colorless face and clasped hands grew cold as the marble basin on which they rested. The great, hopeless agony that seized her heart came to her large eyes and looked out drearily.

It was in vain that she said, "St. Elmo Murray is nothing to me; why should I care if he loves Gertrude? She is so beautiful and confiding and winning. Of course, if he knows her well he must love her. It is no business of mine. We are not even friends; we are worse than strangers; and it cannot concern me whom he loves or whom he hates."

Her own heart laughed her words to scorn, and answered defiantly, "He is my king! My king! I have crowned and sceptered him, and right royally he rules!"

In pitiable humiliation she acknowledged that she had found it impossible to tear her thoughts from him; that his dark face followed - haunted her, sleeping and waking. While she shrank from his presence, and dreaded his character, she could not witness his fond manner to Gertrude without a pang of the keenest pain she had ever endured.

The suddenness of the discovery shocked her into a thorough understanding of her own feelings. The grinning fiend of jealousy had swept aside the flimsy veil which she had never before fully lifted. Now she gazed down into the bared holy of holies and saw, standing between the hovering wings of golden cherubim, an idol of clay demanding homage, daring the wrath of conscience, the high priest.

She saw all now. She saw, too, at the same instant, where her line of duty led.

The air in the hothouse was hot and humid, but Edna shivered. If a mirror could have been held before her eyes, she would have started back from the gray, stony face so unlike hers.

It seemed so strange that the heart of the accomplished misanthrope - the man of letters and science, who had ransacked the world for information and amusement - should surrender itself to the prattle of a pretty young thing, who could sympathize in no degree with his pursuits, and was as utterly incapable of understanding his nature as his Tartar horse or his dog Ali.

Sternly Edna faced the future, and pictured Gertrude as Mr. Murray's wife. If he loved her (and did not his eyes declare it?), of course he would sweep every objection, every obstacle to the winds, and marry her speedily. She tried to think of him - the cold, harsh scoffer - as the fond husband of that laughing child. Though the vision was indescribably painful, she forced herself to dwell upon it.

The idea that he would ever love anyone or anything had never until this hour occurred to her. While she could neither tolerate his opinions or respect his character, she found herself smitten with a great, voiceless anguish at the thought of his giving his sinful bitter heart to any woman.

"Why did she love him? Curious fool! – be still –
Is human love the growth of human will?"[55]

Pressing her hand to her eyes she murmured, "Gertrude is right. He is fascinating, but it is the fascination of a tempting demon. Ah, if I had never come here, if I had never been cursed with the sight of his face. But I am no weak, silly child like Gertrude Powell; I know what my duty is, and I am strong enough to conquer, and if necessary to crush my foolish heart. Oh! I know you, Mr. Murray, and I can defy you. Today, shortsighted as I have been, I look down on you. You are beneath me, and the time will come when I shall look back to this hour and wonder if I were bewitched. Wake up, wake up! Come to your senses, Edna Earl! Put an end to this sinful folly; blush for your unwomanly weakness!"

As Gertrude's merry laugh floated up through the trees, Edna lifted her head. The blood came back to her cheeks while she watched the two figures sauntering across the smooth lawn. Gertrude leaned on Mr. Murray's arm, and as he talked to her his head was bent down, so that he could see the flushed face shaded by her straw hat.

Gertrude drew her hand from his arm when they reached the greenhouse, and looking much embarrassed, said hurriedly, "I am afraid I have kept you waiting a long time, but Mr. Murray had so many beautiful things to show me that I quite forgot we had left you here alone."

Edna's voice was firm and quiet. "I dare say your mother thinks I have run away with you. As I have an engagement, I must either bid you good-bye and leave you here with Mr. Murray, or go back at once with you to the house."

As she handed the French paper to St. Elmo, she turned her eyes full on his face.

"Have you read it already?" he asked, giving her one of his steely, probing glances.

[55] from *Lara*, Canto II, verse XXII – Lord Byron

229

"No, sir, I did not open it, as I take little interest in continental politics. Gertrude, will you go or stay?"

Mr. Murray put out his hand, took Gertrude's, and said in a low, thrilling voice, "Good-bye till tomorrow. Do not forget your promise."

Turning away, he went in the direction of the stables.

In silence Edna walked on to the house, trying to calm her rapid heartbeat. Presently Gertrude's soft fingers grasped hers.

"Edna, I hope you are not mad with me. Do you really think it is wrong for me to talk to Mr. Murray, and to like him so much?"

Edna tried to temper her anger, for though she was angry, it was not Gertrude's fault. "Gertrude, you must judge for yourself concerning the propriety of your conduct. I shall not presume to advise you; but the fact that you are unwilling to acquaint your mother with your course ought to make you look closely at your own heart. When a girl is afraid to trust her mother, I should think there were grounds for uneasiness."

They had reached the steps, and Mrs. Powell came out to meet them.

"Where have you two runaways been? I have waited a half hour for you. Estelle, do come and see me. It is very dreary at the parsonage, and your visits are cheering and precious. Come, Gertrude."

When Gertrude kissed her friend, she whispered, "Don't be mad with me, dearie. I will remember what you said, and talk to mamma this very evening."

Edna watched mother and daughter descend the long avenue. Then, running up to her room, she tied on her hat and walked rapidly across the park in an opposite direction.

About a mile and a half from Le Bocage, on a winding and unfrequented road leading to a sawmill, stood a small log-house containing only two rooms. The yard was full of rank weeds, and the gate was falling from its rusty hinges.

Edna walked up the decaying steps, and without pausing to knock, entered one of the comfortless-looking rooms.

On a cot in one corner lay an elderly man in the last stage of consumption. By his side, busily engaged in knitting, sat a girl about ten years old, whose face wore that look of patient placidity peculiar to the blind. Huldah Reed had never seen the light, but a marvelous change came over her countenance when Edna's light step and clear voice fell on her ear.

"Huldah, how is your father today?"

"Not as well as he was yesterday, but he is asleep now, and will be better when he wakes."

"Has the doctor been here today?"

"No, he has not been here since Sunday."

Edna stood for a while watching the labored breathing of the sleeper. Then, laying her hand on Huldah's head, she whispered, "Do you want me to read to you this evening? It is late, but I shall have time for a short chapter."

"Oh, please do, if it is only a few lines. It will not wake him."

The girl rose, spread out her hands, and groped her way across the room to a small table, whence she took an old Bible.

The two sat down together by the western window. Edna asked, "Is there any particular chapter you would like to hear?"

"Please read about blind Bartimeus sitting by the roadside, waiting for Jesus[56]."

Edna turned to the verses and read in a subdued tone for some moments. In her eager interest Huldah slid down on her knees, rested her thin hands on her companion's lap, and raised her sweet face, with its filmy hazel eyes.

When Edna read the twenty-fourth verse of the next chapter, the small hands were laid upon the page to arrest her attention.

"Edna, do you believe that? 'What things soever you desire, when ye pray believe that ye receive them, *and ye shall have them!*[57] Jesus said that: and if I pray that my eyes may be opened, do you believe I shall see? They tell me that – that pa will not live. Oh, do you think if I pray day and night, and if I believe, and oh, I do believe, I will believe! Do you think Jesus will let me see him – my father – before he dies? All my life I have felt his face, and I knew it by my fingers; but oh, I can't feel it in the grave! Last night I dreamed Christ came and put his hands on my eyes, and said to me, 'Thy faith hath made thee whole'; and I waked up crying, and my fingers were pulling my eyes open; but it was all dark, dark.

---

[56] Matthew 10:46-52
[57] Mark 11:24

Edna, won't you help me pray? And do you believe I shall see him?"

Edna took Huldah's quivering face in her palms and tenderly kissed her.

"My dear Huldah, you know the days of miracles are over, and Jesus is not walking in the world now to cure the suffering and the blind and the dumb – though I wish he were, for your dear sake."

"But he is sitting close to the throne of God. He could send some angel down to touch my eyes, and let me see my dear, dear pa once – ah, just once! Oh, he is the same Jesus now as when he felt sorry for Bartimeus. And why won't He pity me, too?"

Edna felt her own eyes fill with sympathetic tears. "I think that the promise relates to spiritual things, and means that when we pray for strength to resist temptation and sin, Jesus sends the Holy Spirit to assist all who earnestly strive to do their duty. But, dear Huldah, one thing is very certain. Even if you are blind in this world, there will come a day when God will open your eyes, and you shall see those you love, face to face; 'for there shall be no night there[58] in that city of rest – no need of sun or moon, for 'the Lamb is the light thereof.'"

"Huldah – daughter!"

The child swiftly felt her way to the cot. Looking up, Edna doubted the evidence of her senses; for in the dark room, by the side of the sufferer, stood a figure so like Mr. Murray that her heart began to throb painfully.

His strong, deep voice dispelled all doubt.

"I hope you are better today, Reed. Here are some grapes which will refresh you, and you can eat them as freely as your appetite prompts."

Mr. Murray placed a luscious cluster into the old man's thin hands and set the basket down on the floor near the cot. As he drew a chair from the wall and seated himself, Edna stealthily crossed the room, her pulses all a-flutter, and, laying her hand on Huldah's shoulder, led her out to the front steps.

"Huldah, has Mr. Murray ever been here before?"

---

[58] Revelation 22:5

"Oh, yes – often and often; but he generally comes later than this. He brings all the wine poor pa drinks, and very often peaches and grapes. He is so good to us. I love to hear him come up the steps; and many a time, when pa is asleep, I sit here at night, listening for the gallop of Mr. Murray's horse. Somehow I feel so safe, as if nothing could go wrong, when he is in the house."

"Why did you never tell me this before? Why have you not spoken of him?"

"Because he charged me not to speak to anyone about it – said he did not choose to have it known that he ever came here. There! pa is calling me. Won't you come in and speak to him?"

"Not this evening. Good-bye. I will come again soon."

Edna stooped, kissed the child hastily, and walked away very quickly, hoping to make her escape so she wouldn't have to talk to Mr. Murray.

She had only reached the gate where Tamerlane was fastened when Mr. Murray came out of the house.

"Edna!"

Reluctantly she stopped and waited for him.

"Are you not afraid to walk home alone?" he asked, walking up to her side.

"No, sir; I am out frequently even later than this."

"It is not prudent for you to go home now alone, for it will be quite dark before you can possibly reach the park gate."

He passed his horse's reins over his arm and led him along the road.

"I am not going that way, sir. There is a path through the woods that is much shorter than the road and I can get through an opening in the orchard fence. Good evening."

She turned abruptly from the beaten road, but he caught her dress and detained her again before she could escape.

"I told you some time ago that I never permitted espionage in my affairs; now with reference to what occurred at the greenhouse, I advise you to keep silent. Do you understand me?"

Edna frowned. "In the first place, sir, I could not condescend to play spy on the actions of anyone. In the second, you may rest assured I certainly have no interest in your affairs. Your estimate of me must be contemptible indeed, if you imagine that I can only employ myself in watching your career."

"My only desire is to shield my pretty Gertrude's head from the wrath that may be bottled up for her."

Edna looked up fixedly into his deep, glittering eyes and answered quietly, "Mr. Murray, if you love her half as well as I do, you will not subject her to the opening of the vials of wrath."

He laughed contemptuously. "You are doubtless experienced in such matters, and fully competent to advise me."

"No, sir. Please be so good as to detain me no longer. I have no intention whatever of meddling with any of your affairs, or reporting your actions."

Putting his hands suddenly on her shoulders, St. Elmo stooped, looked keenly at her, then muttered an oath. When he spoke again it was through set teeth. "You will be wise if you adhere to that decision. Tell them at home not to wait supper for me."

He sprang into his saddle and rode toward the village.

Edna hurried homeward, asking herself, "What first took Mr. Murray to the blacksmith's hovel? Why is he so anxious that his visits should remain undiscovered? Is there some latent nobility in his character after all? Perhaps his love for Gertrude has softened his heart. Perhaps that love may be his salvation. God grant it! God grant it!"

The evening breeze rose and sang solemnly through the pine trees, but to her it seemed only to chant the melancholy refrain, "My pretty Gertrude, my pretty Gertrude."

The chill light of stars fell on Edna's pathway. Now a silent desolation settled over her heart, a desolation such as she had seldom felt since her grandfather had died. She passed through the orchard, startling a covey of partridges that nestled in the long grass, and a rabbit that had stolen out under cover of dusk.

When Edna came to the fountain, she paused and looked out over the dark, quiet grounds.

Hitherto duty had worn a smiling, loving countenance, and walked gently by her side as she crossed the flowery vales of girlhood. Now, the guide was transformed into an angel of wrath, pointing with drawn sword to the gate of Eden.

234

As the girl's light fingers locked themselves tightly, she uttered mournfully:

"What hast thou done, O soul of mine
That thou tremblest so?
Hast thou wrought His task, and kept the line
He bade thee go?
Ah, the cloud is dark, and day by day
I am moving thither:
I must pass beneath it on my way –
God pity me! Whither?"[59]

When Mrs. Murray went to her own room later than usual that night, she found Edna sitting by the table, her Bible lying open on her lap and her eyes fixed on the floor.

"I thought you were fast asleep before this. I sat up waiting for St. Elmo, as I wished to speak to him about some engagements for tomorrow."

The lady of the house threw herself wearily upon the lounge and sighed as she unclasped her bracelets and took off the diamond cross that fastened her collar. "Edna, ring for Hagar."

"Will you not let me take her place tonight? I want to talk to you before I go to sleep."

"Well, then, unlace my gaiters and take down my hair. Child, what makes you look so very serious?"

"Because what I am about to say saddens me very much. My dear Mrs. Murray, I have been in this house five peaceful, happy, blessed years. I have become warmly attached to everything about the home where I have been so kindly sheltered during my girlhood, and the thought of leaving it is exceedingly painful to me."

"What do you mean, Edna?" Mrs. Murray said, suddenly sitting up. "Leaving it? Have you come to your senses at last, and consented to make Gordon happy?"

"No, no. I am going to New York to try to make my bread."

For a moment, Mrs. Murray fought to speak. "New York? You are going to a lunatic asylum! Stuff! Nonsense! What can you do

---

[59] "My Soul and I" – John Greenleaf Whittier

in New York? It is already overstocked with poor men and women who are on the verge of starvation. Pooh, pooh! You look like making your bread. Don't be silly."

Edna continued to take down Mrs. Murray's hair. "I know that I am competent now to take a situation as teacher in a school, or family, and I am determined to start immediately. I want to go to New York because I can command advantages there which no poor girl can obtain here, and the magazine for which I expect to write is published there. Mr. Manning says he will pay me liberally for such articles as he accepts, and if I can only get a situation which I hear is now vacant, I can support myself. Mrs. Powell received a letter yesterday from a wealthy friend in New York who desires to secure a governess for her young children, one of whom requires crutches to walk. She said she was excessively particular as to the character of the woman to whose care she committed her children, and that she had advertised for one who could teach him Greek. I shall ask Mrs. Powell and Mr. Hammond to telegraph to her tomorrow and request her not to engage any one till a letter can reach her from Mr. Hammond and me. I believe he knows the lady, who is very distantly related to Mrs. Powell. Still, before I took this step, I felt that I owed it to you to acquaint you with my intention."

"Edna, it is a step which I cannot sanction," Mrs. Murray said haughtily. "I detest that Mrs. Powell – I utterly loathe the sound of her name, and I should be altogether unwilling to see you domesticated with any of her 'friends.' I am surprised that Mr. Hammond could encourage any such foolish scheme on your part."

"As yet, he is entirely ignorant of my plan, for I have mentioned it to no one except yourself; but I do not think he will oppose it. Dear Mrs. Murray, much as I love you, I cannot remain here any longer, for I could not continue to owe my bread even to your kind charity. You have educated me, and only God knows how inexpressibly grateful I am for all your goodness; but now, I could no longer preserve my self-respect or be happy as a dependent on your bounty."

Edna had taken Mrs. Murray's hand. Tears gathered in her eyes as she kissed the fingers and pressed them against her cheek.

"Child, child, if you are too proud to remain here as you have done for so many years, how do you suppose you can endure the affronts when you accept a hireling's position in the family of a stranger? I loved you and shielded you from slights and insults as if you were my niece or my daughter. Edna, you could not endure the lot you have selected. Your proud, sensitive nature would be galled to desperation. Stay here and help me keep house; write and study as much as you like, and do as you please. Only don't leave me."

She drew the girl to her bosom, and while she kissed her, tears fell on Edna's face.

"Oh, Mrs. Murray, it is hard to leave you! For indeed I love you more than you will ever believe or realize; but I must go. I feel it is my duty, and you would not wish me to stay here and be unhappy."

"Unhappy here! Why so? Something is wrong, and I must know just what it is. Somebody has been meddling – taunting you. Edna, I ask a plain question, and I want the whole truth. You and Estelle do not like each other; is her presence here the cause of your determination to quit my house?"

"No, Mrs. Murray. If she were not here I should still feel it my duty to go out and earn my living. You are correct in saying we do not particularly like each other. There is little sympathy between us, but no bad feeling that I am aware of, and she is not the cause of my departure."

Mrs. Murray was silent a moment, scrutinizing the face on her shoulder. "Edna, can it be my son? Has some harsh speech of St. Elmo's piqued and wounded you?"

"Oh, no. His manner toward me is quite as polite, nay, rather more considerate than when I first came here. Besides, you know, we are almost strangers. Sometimes weeks elapse without our exchanging a word."

"Are you sure you have not had a quarrel with him? I know you dislike him. I know how exceedingly provoking he is; but, child, he is bitterly rude to everybody, and does not mean to wound you particularly."

"I have no complaint to make of Mr. Murray's manner to me. I do not expect that it should be other than it is. Why do you doubt the sincerity of the reason I gave for quitting dear old Bocage? I have never expected to live here longer than was necessary to qualify myself for the work I have chosen."

"I doubt it because it is so incomprehensible that a young girl, who might be Gordon Leigh's happy wife and mistress of his elegant home, surrounded by every luxury, and idolized by one of the noblest, handsomest men I ever knew, should prefer to go among strangers and toil for a scanty livelihood. Now I know something of human nature, and I know that your course is very singular, very unnatural. Edna, my child! My dear, little girl! I can't let you go. I want you! I can't spare you! I love you too well, my sweet comforter in all my troubles. My only real companion!"

She clasped the orphan closer and wept.

"Oh, you don't know how precious your love is to my heart, dear, dear Mrs. Murray! In all this wide world, whom have I to love me but you and Mr. Hammond? Even in the great sorrow of leaving you, it will gladden me to feel that I possess so fully your confidence and affection. But I must go away. After a little while you will not miss me; for Estelle will be with you, and you will not need me. Oh, it is hard to leave you! It is a bitter trial! But I know what my duty is; and were it even more difficult, I would not hesitate. I hope you will not think me unduly obstinate when I tell you that I have fully determined to apply for that situation in New York."

Mrs. Murray pushed the girl from her, and, with a sob, buried her face in her arms.

Edna waited in vain for her to speak, and finally she stooped and kissed one of the hands, and said brokenly as she left the room, "Good-night – my dearest – my best friend. If you could only look into my heart and see how it aches at the thought of separation, you would not add the pain of your displeasure to that which I already suffer."

When Edna opened her eyes on the following morning, she found a note pinned to her pillow:

"MY DEAR EDNA: I could not sleep last night in consequence of your unfortunate resolution, and I write to beg you, for my sake if not for your own, to reconsider the matter. I will gladly pay you the same salary that you expect to receive as governess, if you will remain as my companion and assist at Le Bocage. I cannot consent to give you up. I love you too well, my child, to see you quit my house. I shall soon be an old woman, and then what should I do without my little orphan girl? Stay with me always, and you shall never know what want and toil and hardship mean. As soon as you are awake, come and kiss me good-morning, and I shall know that you are my own, my dear little Edna.

"Affectionately yours,
"ELLEN MURRAY."

Edna knelt and prayed for strength to do what she felt duty sternly dictated. Though her will did not falter, her heart bled as she wrote a few lines thanking Mrs. Murray for the affection that had brightened and warmed her whole lonely life, and assuring her that the reasons which induced her to leave Le Bocage were imperative and unanswerable.

An hour later she entered the breakfast room, and found the members of the family already assembled. While Mrs. Murray was cold and haughty, taking no notice of Edna's salutation, Estelle talked gaily with Mr. Allston concerning a horseback ride they intended to take that morning; and Mr. Murray, leaning back in his chair, seemed engrossed in the columns of the London *Times* that contained a recent speech of Gladstone's. Presently he threw down the paper, looked at his gold pocket watch, and ordered his horse.

Estelle approached her cousin and put one of her fingers through the buttonhole of his coat. "St. Elmo, where are you going? Do allow yourself to be prevailed upon to wait and ride with us," she said in a coaxing tone.

"Not for all the kingdoms that Satan pointed out from the pinnacle of Mount Quarantina! Where am I going? To that 'Sea of Serenity' which astronomers tell us is located in the moon. Where am I going? To Western Ross-shire, to pitch my tent and smoke my cigar in peace, on the brink of that blessed Loch Maree, whereof Pennant wrote."

He shook off Estelle's touch, walked to the mantelpiece, and, taking a match from the china case, drew it across the heel of his boot.

"Where is Loch Maree? I do not remember ever to have seen the name," said Mrs. Murray, pushing aside her coffee cup.

"Oh, pardon me, mother, if I decline to undertake your geographical education. Ask that incipient walking encyclopedia, sitting there at your right hand. Doubtless she will find it a pleasing task to instruct you in Scottish topography. I have an engagement that forces me most respectfully to decline the honor of enlightening you. Confound these matches! They are all damp." He left the room, calling for his horse.

Involuntarily Mrs. Murray's eyes turned to Edna, who had not even glanced at St. Elmo since her entrance. Now she looked up, and though she had not read Pennant, she remembered the lines written on the old Druidic well by an American poet, and repeated two stanzas:

> "'Oh, restless heart and fevered brain!
> Unquiet and unstable.
> That holy well of Loch Maree
> Is more than idle fable!
> The shadows of a humble will
> And contrite heart are o'er it:
> Go read its legend – "TRUST IN GOD" –
> On Faith's white stones before it.'[60]"

Mr. Murray's voice drifted in from outside. "Pious claptrap!" Edna sighed.

---

[60] "The Well of Loch Maree" – John Greenleaf Whittier

CHAPTER XXI
THE DOCTOR

Mr. Hammond's eyes filled with tears as he looked at his pupil, and his hand trembled when he stroked Edna's bowed head.

"While your decision is very painful to me, I shall not attempt to dissuade you from a resolution which I know has not been lightly taken. But, ah, my child, what shall I do without you?"

The August sun shining through the lilac and myrtle boughs that rustled close to the study-window glinted over Edna's face and showed a calm mournfulness in the eyes which looked out at the quiet parsonage garden. "I dread the separation from you and Mrs. Murray, but I know I ought to go, and I feel that when duty commands me to follow a path, lonely and dreary though it may seem, a light will be shed before my feet, and a staff will be put into my hands. Duty veils her features with a silver-lined cloud, and her unbending figure signs our way – an unerring pillar of cloud by day, of fire by night. Mr. Hammond, I shall follow that stern finger till the clods on my coffin shut it from my sight."

Far away to the low hills against the sky –

"A golden luster slept upon the hills."[61]

Just beyond the low, ivy-wreathed stone wall that marked the boundary of the garden ran a little stream, overhung with alders and willows, under whose tremendous shadows rested contented cattle – some knee-deep in water, some browsing leisurely on purple-tufted clover. From the wide, hot field, stretching away on the opposite side, came the clear metallic ring of the scythes as the

---

[61] "Churchyard Among the Mountains" – William Wordsworth

mowers sharpened them; the mellow whistle of the driver lying on top of the huge hay mass, beneath which the oxen crawled toward the lowered bars; and the sweet gurgling laughter of two romping, sunburned children, who swung on the back of the wagon.

Edna gazed at the beautiful summer day outside, already grieving to have to leave all of this.

The minister enclosed her hand in his, and said gently, "My child, your ambition is your besetting sin. It is Satan pointing to the tree of knowledge, tempting you to eat and become 'as gods.' Search your heart. I fear you will find that while you believe you are dedicating your talent entirely to the service of God, there is a spring of selfishness underlying all. You are too proud, too ambitious of distinction, too eager to climb to some lofty niche in the temple of fame, where your name, now unknown, shall shine in the annals of literature and serve as a beacon to encourage others equally as anxious for celebrity. I was not surprised to see you in print; for long, long ago, before you realized the extent of your mental powers, I saw the kindling of that ambitious spark whose flame generally consumes the women in whose hearts it burns. The history of literary females is not calculated to allay the apprehension that oppresses me, as I watch you just setting out on a career so fraught with trials of which you have never dreamed. How many of the hundreds of female writers scattered through the world in this century, will be remembered six months after the coffin closes over their weary, haggard faces? You may answer, 'They made their bread.' Ah, child, it would have been sweeter if earned at the washtub, or in the dairy, or by their needles. It is the rough handling, the tension of the heartstrings that sap the foundations of a woman's life and consign her to an early grave. A Cherokee rose-hedge is not more thickly set with thorns than a literary career with torment and disappointments. Edna, you have talent, you write well, you are conscientious; but you are not De Stael, or Hannah More, or Charlotte Bronte, or Elizabeth Browning; and I shudder when I think of the disappointment that may overtake all your eager aspirations. If I could be always near you, I should indulge less apprehension for your future; for I believe that I could help you to bear patiently whatever is in store for you. But far away among strangers you must struggle alone."

"Mr. Hammond, I do not rely upon myself; my hope is in God."

"My child, the days of miraculous inspiration are ended."

"Ah, do not discourage me. God will not forsake me; He will strengthen and guide me and bless my writing, even as He blesses your preaching. Because He gave you five talents and to me only one, do you think that in the great day of reckoning mine will not be required of me?"

She had bowed her head till it rested on his knee. Presently the old man put his hands upon her glossy hair and murmured solemnly, "And the peace of God, which passeth all understanding, shall keep your heart and mind through Christ Jesus.[62]"

A brief silence reigned in the study, broken first by the shout of the haymakers and the rippling laugh of the children in the adjacent field, and then by the calm voice of the pastor. "I have offered you a home with me as long as I have a roof that I can call my own; but you prefer to go to New York. Henceforth I shall never cease to pray that your resolution may prove fortunate in all respects. You no longer require my direction in your studies, but I will suggest that it might be expedient for you to give more attention to positive and less to abstract science. Remember those noble words of Sir David Brewster, to which, I believe, I have already called your attention, 'If the God of love is most appropriately worshipped in the Christian temple, the God of nature may be equally honored in the temple of science. Even from its lofty minarets the philosopher may summon the faithful to prayer, and the priest and the sage may exchange altars without the compromise of faith or of knowledge.[63]'"

Here Mrs. Powell entered the room, and Edna rose and tied on her hat.

"Mr. Hammond, will you go over to see Huldah this afternoon? Poor little thing! She is in great distress about her father."

---

[62] Philippians 4:7
[63] The Home Life of Sir David Brewster

"I fear he cannot live many days. I went to see him yesterday morning, and would go again with you now, but have promised to baptize two children this evening."

Edna was opening the gate when Gertrude called to her from a shaded corner of the yard. Turning, Edna saw her playing with a fawn, about whose neck she had twined a long spray of honeysuckle.

"Do come and see the beautiful present Mr. Murray sent me several days ago. It is as gentle and playful as a kitten, and seems to know me already."

Gertrude patted the head of her pretty pet and continued, "I have often read about gazelle's eyes, and I wonder if these are not quite as lovely? Very often when I look at them, they remind me of yours. There is such a soft, sad, patient expression, as if she knew perfectly well that someday the hunters would be sure to catch and kill her, and she was meekly biding her time to be turned into venison steak. I never will eat another piece. The dear little thing! Edna, do you know that you have the most beautiful eyes in the world, except Mr. Murray's? His eyes glitter like great stars under long black silk fringes."

How well Edna knew it. But she said nothing.

Gertrude stole one arm around her companion's neck and nestled her golden head against the orphan's shoulder. "By the way, how is he? I have not seen him for some days, and you can have no idea how I do want to look into his face, and hear his voice, which is so wonderfully sweet and low. I wrote him a note thanking him for this little spotted darling; but he has not answered it – has not come near me. I was afraid he might be sick."

Edna took a long breath to collect herself. "Mr. Murray is very well; at least, appears so. I saw him at breakfast."

"Does he ever talk about me?"

"No; I never heard him mention your name but once, and then it occurred incidentally."

"Oh, Edna, is it wrong for me to think about him so constantly? Don't press your lips together in that stern, hard way. Dearie, put your arms around me, and kiss me. Oh, if you could know how very much I love him! How happy I am when he is with me. Edna, how can I help it? When he touches my hand, and smiles down at me, I forget everything else! He is a great deal older than I am; but how can I remember that when he is looking at me with those wonderful eyes? The last time I saw him, he said – well, something very sweet, and I was sure he loved me, and I leaned my head against his shoulder; but he would not let me touch him; he pushed me away with a terrific frown that wrinkled and blackened his face. Oh! It seems an age since then."

Edna kissed the lovely coral lips and smoothed the bright curls that the wind had blown about the exquisitely molded cheeks. "Gertrude, when he asks you to love him, you can indulge your affection; but until then, you ought not to permit yourself to think so entirely of him."

"But do you believe it is wrong for me to love him so much?"

"That is a question which your own heart must answer."

Edna felt that her own lips were growing cold, and she disengaged the girl's clasping arms.

"Edna, I know you love me; will you do something for me? Please give him this note. I am afraid that he did not receive the other, or that he is offended with me."

She drew a dainty three-cornered envelope from her pocket.

"No, Gertrude; I can be a party to no clandestine correspondence. I have too much respect for your uncle to assist in smuggling letters in and out of his house. Besides, your mother would not sanction the course you are pursuing."

"Oh, I showed her the other note, and she only laughed, and patted my cheek, and said, 'Why, Mignonne, he is old enough to be your father.' This note is only to find out whether he received the other. I sent it by the servant who brought this fawn – oh dear me! Just see what a hole the pretty little wretch has nibbled in my new Swiss muslin dress. Won't mamma scold! There, do go away, pet; I will feed you presently. Indeed, Edna, there is no harm in your taking the note, for I give you my word mamma does not care. Please, Edna. It will reach him so much sooner if you carry it over."

"Gertrude, are you not deceiving me? Are you sure your mother read the other note and sanctions this?"

"Certainly. You may ask her if you doubt me. There, I must hurry in; mamma is calling me. Dear Edna, if you love me!"

Edna could not resist the pleading of the lovely face pressed close to hers. With a sigh she took the tiny note and turned away.

More than a week had elapsed since Mr. Hammond and Mrs. Powell had written, recommending her for the situation in Mrs. Andrews's family, and with feverish impatience she awaited the result. During this time she had not exchanged a word with Mr. Murray – had spent much of her time in writing down in her note-book such references from the library as she required in her manuscript. While Estelle seemed unusually high-spirited, Mrs. Murray watched in grieved silence Edna's preparations for departure.

Absorbed in painful reflections, the girl hurried on till she reached the cheerless home of the blacksmith and knocked at the door.

"Come in, Mr. Murray," Huldah called from within.

Glad that the little girl could not see her face, Edna pushed open the door and walked in. "It is not Mr. Murray this time."

Huldah was kneeling at the side of her father's cot, and Edna was startled out of her gloom by the look of eager, breathless anxiety printed on her trembling lips. "Oh, Edna, I am so glad you happened to come. He would not let me tell you; he said he did not wish it known. But now you are here, you will stay with me, won't you, till it is over?"

Astonished, Edna asked, "What does she mean, Mr. Reed?"

The old man reached out a hand to clasp hers in welcome. "Poor little lamb, she is so excited she can hardly speak, and I am not strong enough to talk much. Huldah, daughter, tell Miss Edna all about it."

"Mr. Murray heard all I said to you about praying to have my eyes opened. He went to town that same evening and telegraphed to some doctor in Philadelphia who cures blindness to see if he could do anything for my eyes. Mr. Murray was here this morning, and said he had heard from the doctor, and that he would come this afternoon. He said he could only stay till the cars left for Chattanooga, as he must go back at once. You know he –

hush! There, there! I hear the carriage now. Oh, Edna, pray for me! Pa, pray for my poor eyes!"

Huldah's face paled, and tears filled her filmy, hazel eyes as she clasped her hands. Her lips moved rapidly, though no sound was audible.

Edna stepped behind the door and peeped through a crack in the planks.

Mr. Murray entered first, making her heart jump, and beckoned to the stranger, who paused at the threshold, with a case of instruments in his hand.

"Come in, Hugh. Here is your patient, very much frightened, too, I am afraid. Huldah, come to the light."

He drew her to the window and lifted her to a chair. The doctor bent down, pushed back his spectacles, and cautiously examined the child's eyes.

"Don't tremble so, Huldah; there is nothing to be afraid of. The doctor will not hurt you."

"Oh, it is not that I fear to be hurt! Edna, are you praying for me?"

"Edna is not here," answered Mr. Murray, glancing round the room.

"Yes, she is here. I did not tell her, but she happened to come a little while ago. Edna, won't you hold one of my hands? Oh, Edna, Edna!"

Reluctantly the orphan came forward. Without lifting her eyes, she took one of the little outstretched hands firmly in both her own. While Mr. Murray silently appropriated the other, Huldah whispered, "Please, both of you pray for me."

The doctor raised the eyelids several times, peered long and curiously at the eyeballs, and opened his case of instruments.

"This is one of those instances of congenital cataract which might have been relieved long ago. A slight operation will remove the difficulty. St. Elmo, you asked me about the probability of an instantaneous restoration, and I had begun to tell you about that case which Wardrop mentions of a woman, blind from her birth till she was forty-six years of age. She could not distinguish objects for several days – "

"Oh, sir! Will I see? Will I see my father?" Huldah's fingers closed spasmodically over those that clasped them, and the agonizing suspense written in her countenance was pitiable to see.

"Yes, my dear, I hope so – I think so," the doctor said. "You know, Murray, the eye has to be trained; but Haller mentions a case of a nobleman who saw distinctly at various distances, immediately after the cataract was removed from the axis of vision. Now, my little girl, hold just as still as possible. I shall not hurt you."

Skillfully he cut through the membrane and drew it down. Then held his hat between her eyes and the light streaming through the window.

Some seconds elapsed. Suddenly a cry broke from Huldah's lips.

"Oh, something shines! There is a light, I believe!"

Mr. Murray threw his handkerchief over her head, caught her in his arms and placed her on the side of the cot.

"The first face her eyes ever look upon shall be that which she loves best – her father's."

As he withdrew the handkerchief, Mr. Reed feebly raised his arms toward his child, and whispered, "My little Huldah – my daughter, can you see me?"

She stooped, put her face close to his, swept her small fingers repeatedly over the emaciated features, to convince herself of the identity of the new sensation of sight with the old and reliable sense of touch. Then she threw her head back with a wild laugh, a scream of delight.

"Oh, I see! Thank God, I see my father's face! My dear pa! My own dear pa!"

For some moments Huldah hung over the sufferer, kissing him, murmuring brokenly her happy, tender words, now and then resorting to the old sense of touch.

While Edna wiped away tears of joyful sympathy, she glanced at Mr. Murray, and wondered how he could stand there watching the scene with such bright, dry eyes.

Seeming suddenly to remember the other people in the room, Huldah slipped down from the cot, turned toward the group, and shaded her eyes with her fingers.

"Oh, Edna, ain't you glad for me? Where are you? I knew Jesus would hear me. 'What things soever ye desire, when ye pray believe that ye receive them, and ye shall have them.' I did believe, and I see! I see! I prayed that God would send down some angel to touch my eyes, and He sent Mr. Murray and the doctor."

Edna kissed Huldah's face, gazing into the child's eyes as her fingers swept her face.

After a pause, during which the oculist prepared some bandages, Huldah added, "Which one is Mr. Murray? Will you please come to me? My ears and my fingers know you, but my eyes don't."

He stepped forward. Putting out her hands, she grasped his, and turned her untutored eyes upon him. Before he could stop her, she fell at his feet, threw her arms around his knees, and exclaimed, "How good you are! How shall I ever thank you enough? How good." She clung to him and sobbed hysterically.

A broken smile appeared on his face, then fled. He lifted her from the floor and put her back beside her father. The doctor bandaged her eyes as he talked to Mr. Reed and Mr. Murray. Waiting to hear no more, Edna slipped out of the house and hurried along the road.

Ere she had proceeded far, she heard the quick trot of the horses and the roll of the carriage. Leaning out as they overtook her, Mr. Murray directed the driver to stop, and swinging open the door, he stepped out and approached her.

"The doctor dines at Le Bocage. Will you take a seat with us, or do you, as usual, prefer to walk alone?"

"Thank you, sir; I am not going home now. I shall walk on."

He bowed, and was turning away, but she drew the delicately perfumed envelope from her pocket.

"Mr. Murray, I was requested by the writer to hand you this note, as she feared its predecessor was lost by the servant to whom she entrusted it."

He took it, glanced at the small, cramped, school-girlish handwriting, smiled, and thrust it into his vest pocket. "This is, indeed, a joyful surprise," he said in a low, earnest tone. "You are certainly more reliable than Henry. Accept my cordial thanks, which I have not time to reiterate. I prefer to owe my happiness entirely to Gertrude; but in this instance I can bear to receive it through the medium of your hands. As you are so prompt and trustworthy, I may trouble you to carry my answer."

The carriage rolled on, leaving a cloud of dust which the evening sunshine converted into a glittering track of glory. Seating herself on a grassy bank, Edna leaned her head against the body of a tree. All the glory passed swiftly away, and she was alone in the dust.

As the sun went down, the pillared forest aisles stretching westward filled first with golden haze, then glowed with a light redder than wine. Only the mournful cooing of doves broke the solemn silence as the pines whispered their low lament for the dead day. The cool shadow of coming night crept, purple-mantled, velvet-sandaled, down the forest glades.

"Oh, if I had gone away a week ago!" Edna whispered. "If only I'd left before I knew there was any redeeming charity in his sinful nature. If I could only despise him utterly, it would be so much easier to forget him. Ah! God pity me! God help me! What right have I to think of Gertrude's lover – Gertrude's husband! I ought to be glad that he is nobler than I thought, but I am not. Oh, I am not. I wish I had never known the good that he has done. Oh, Edna Earl! Has it come to this? How I despise – how I hate myself!"

Rising, she shook back her thick hair, passed her hands over her hot temples, and stood listening to the distant whistle of a partridge, and the plaint of the lonely dove nestled among the pine boughs high above her.

Gradually a holy calm stole over her face, fixing it as the merciful touch of death stills features that have long writhed in mortal agony. Into her struggling heart entered a strength which comes only when weary, wrestling souls turn from human sympathy to seek the hallowed cloisters of Nature, where they are folded tenderly in the loving arms of Mother Cybele, who "never did betray the heart that loved her[64]."

"Whose dwelling is the light of setting suns,
And the round ocean and the living air,

[64] "Lines Composed a Few Miles Above Tinturn Abbey" – William Wordsworth

And the blue sky * * * 'Tis her privilege,
Through all the years of this our life, to lead
From joy to joy, for she can so inform
The mind that is within us, so impress
With quietness and beauty, and so feed
With lofty thoughts, that neither evil tongues,
Rash judgments, nor the sneers of selfish men,
Nor greetings where no kindness is – nor all
The dreary intercourse of daily life,
Shall e'er prevail against us or disturb
Our cheerful faith, that all which we behold
Is full of blessing."[65]

To her dewy altars among the mountains of Gilead fled Jephthah's daughter, in the days when she sought for strength to fulfill her father's battle-vow[66]. Into her pitying starry eyes looked stricken Rizpah, from those dreary rocks where love held faithful vigil, guarding the bleaching bones of her darling dead, sacrificed for the sins of Saul[67].

[65] "Lines Composed a Few Miles Above Tintern Abbey" – William Wordsworth
[66] Judges 11
[67] 2 Samuel 21

CHAPTER XXII
A BARGAIN WITH THE DEVIL

Edna rose and took her hat from the study table. "Mrs. Andrews writes that I must go on with as little delay as possible. I shall start early Monday morning, as I wish to stop one day at Chattanooga."

Mr. Hammond asked, "Do you intend to travel alone?"

"I shall be compelled to do so, as I know of no one who is going on to New York. Of course, I dislike very much to travel alone, but in this instance I do not see how I can avoid it."

"Do not put on your hat – stay and spend the evening with me."

"Thank you, sir, but I want to go to the church and practice for the last time on the organ. After tomorrow, I might never sing again in our dear choir. Perhaps I may come back after a while and stay an hour or two with you."

During the past year she had accustomed herself to practicing every Saturday afternoon the hymns selected by Mr. Hammond for the Sunday services. The sexton had given her a key, which enabled her to enter the church whenever she was so inclined.

The churchyard was peaceful and silent as the pulseless dust in its numerous sepulchers. A red-bird sat on the edge of a marble vase that crowned the top of one of the monuments, and leisurely drank the water which yesterday's clouds had poured there, while a rabbit nibbled the leaves of a cluster of pinks growing near a child's grave.

Edna entered the cool church, went up into the gallery, and sat down before the organ. For some time, the low, solemn tones whispered among the fluted columns that supported the gallery. Gradually they swelled louder and fuller and richer as she sang:

"Cast thy burden on the Lord."

Edna's sweet, well-trained voice faltered more than once, and tears fell thick and fast on the keys. Finally she turned and looked down at the sacred spot where she had been baptized by Mr. Hammond, and where she had so often knelt to receive the sacrament of the Lord's Supper.

The church was remarkably handsome and certainly justified the pride with which the villagers exhibited it to all strangers. The massive mahogany pew-doors were elaborately carved and surmounted by small crosses. The tall, arched windows were of superb stained glass, representing the twelve apostles. The floor and balustrade of the altar, and the grand Gothic pillared pulpit, were all of the purest white marble. The capitals of the airy, marble columns that supported the organ gallery were ornamented with rich grape-leaf molding. The large window behind and above the pulpit contained a figure of Christ bearing his Cross – a noble copy of the great painting of Solario, at Berlin.

As the afternoon sun shone on the glass, a flood of ruby light fell from the garments of Jesus upon the glittering marble beneath, and the nimbus that radiated around the crown of thorns caught a glory that was dazzling.

With a feeling of adoration that no language could adequately express, Edna had watched and studied this costly painted window for five long years; had found a marvelous fascination in the pallid face stained with purplish blood-drops; in the parted lips quivering with human pain and anguish of spirit; in the unfathomable, divine eyes that pierced the veil and rested upon the Father's face. Not all the sermons of Bossuet, or Chalmers, or Jeremy Taylor, or Melville, had power to stir the great deeps of her soul like one glance at that pale, thorn-crowned Christ, who looked in voiceless woe and sublime resignation over the world he was dying to redeem.

Today she gazed up at the picture of Jesus till her eyes grew dim with tears. She leaned her head against the mahogany railing and murmured sadly, "'And he that taketh not his cross, and

---

[68] Matthew 10:38

followeth after me, is not worthy of me![68] Strengthen me, O my Savior, so that I neither faint nor stagger under mine!"

The echo of her words died away among the arches of the roof, and all was still in the sanctuary. The swaying of the trees outside of the windows threw now a golden shimmer, then a violet shadow over the gleaming altar pavement. As the sun sunk lower, and the nimbus faded, the wan Christ looked ghastly and toil-spent.

"Edna! My darling, my darling!"

The pleading cry, the tremulous, tender voice so full of pathos, rang startlingly through the silent church. Edna sprang up, knowing that voice.

Mr. Murray had appeared at her side, with his arms extended toward her, and a glow on his face and a look in his eyes which she had never seen there before.

She drew back a few steps and gazed wonderingly at him. He followed, threw his arm around her, and, despite her resistance, strained her to his heart, speaking low and thrillingly.

"Did you believe that I would let you go? Did you dream that I would see my darling leave me, and go out into the world to be buffeted and sorely tried, to struggle with poverty – and to suffer alone? Oh, silly child! I would part with my own life sooner than give you up. Of what value would my life be without you, my sole hope, my only love, my own, pure Edna – "

Astonished, wondering if she were dreaming this, Edna struggled hard to free herself, but his clasp tightened. "Such language you have no right to utter. It is dishonorable in you and insulting to me. Gertrude's lover cannot, and shall not, address such words to me. Unwind your arms instantly. Let me go!"

Mr. Murray threw his head back and laughed. "'Gertrude's lover?' Knowing my history, how could you believe that possible? Am I, think you, so meek and forgiving a spirit as to turn and kiss the hand that smote me? Gertrude's lover! Ha! Ha! Your jealousy blinds you, my – "

"Stop! I know nothing of your history. I have never asked; I have never been told one word. But I am not blind. I know that you love her, and I know, too, that she fully returns your affection. If you do not wish me to despise you utterly, leave me at once."

St. Elmo laughed again, and put his lips close to her ear, saying softly, tenderly – ah! how tenderly, "Upon my honor as a gentleman, I solemnly swear that I love but one woman; that I love her as no other woman ever was loved, with a love that passes all language; that this love is the only light and hope of a wrecked, cursed, unutterably miserable life; and that idol which I have set up in the lonely gray ruins of my heart is Edna Earl!"

Her heart hammered in a way that made Edna almost dizzy, but she fought again to force him to release her. "I do not believe you! You have no honor! With the touch of Gertrude's lips and arms still on yours, you come to me and dare to perjure yourself! Oh, Mr. Murray, Mr. Murray! I thought you too proud to play the hypocrite. If you could realize how I loathe and abhor you, you would get out of my sight! You would not waste time in words that sink you deeper and deeper in shameful duplicity. Poor Gertrude! How entirely you mistake your lover's character. How your love will change to scorn and detestation!"

In vain she endeavored to wrench away his arm. A band of steel would have been as flexible. St. Elmo's voice hardened, and his heart throbbed fiercely against her cheek. "When you are my wife you will repent your rash words, and blush at the remembrance of having told your husband that he was devoid of honor. You are piqued and jealous, just as I intended you should be – but, darling, I am not a patient man, and it frets me to feel you struggling so desperately in the arms that henceforth will always enfold you. Be quiet and hear me. Don't turn your face away from mine, your lips belong to me. I never kissed Gertrude in my life, and so help me God, I never will! Hear – "

"No! I will hear nothing!" Edna exclaimed, almost ready to weep. "Your touch is profanation. I would sooner go down into my grave, out there in the churchyard, than become the wife of a man so unprincipled. Even now you must be playing some cruel jest upon me. I would sooner feel the coil of a serpent around my waist than your arms."

Instantly they fell away. He crossed them on his chest, and his voice sank to a husky whisper, as the wind hushes itself just before the storm breaks.

"Edna, God is my witness that I am not deceiving you; that my words come from the great troubled depths of a wretched heart. You said you knew nothing of my history, but I find it difficult to believe you. Answer one question: Has not your pastor taught you to distrust me? Can it be possible that no hint of the past has fallen from his lips?"

Edna was shaking. "Not one unkind word, not one syllable of your history has he uttered. I know no more of your past than if it were buried in mid-ocean."

"Here. Sit down and listen to me." Mr. Murray placed her in one of the cushioned choir chairs, and leaning back against the railing of the gallery, fixed his eyes on Edna's face.

"Then it is not surprising that you distrust me, for you know not my provocation. Edna, will you be patient? Will you go back with me over the scorched and blackened track of an accursed and sinful life? It is a hideous waste I am inviting you to traverse. Will you?"

Edna, still trying to catch her breath, shook her head. "I will hear you, Mr. Murray, but nothing that you can say will justify your duplicity to Gertrude, and – "

"Damn Gertrude! I ask you to listen and suspend your judgment till you know the circumstances."

Edna sat back, shocked. He covered his eyes with his hand, and in the brief silence she heard the ticking of his pocket watch.

"Edna, I roll away the stone from the charnel house of the past and call forth the Lazarus of my buried youth: my hopes, my faith in God, my trust in human nature, my charity, my slaughtered manhood. My Lazarus has tenanted the grave for nearly seventeen years, and comes forth, at my bidding, a grinning skeleton.

*****

"You may or may not know that my father, Paul Murray, died when I was an infant, leaving my mother the sole guardian of my property and person. I grew up at Le Bocage under the training of Mr. Hammond, my tutor. My only associate, my companion from earliest memory, was his son Murray, who was two years my senior, and named for my father. The hold which that boy took upon my affection was wonderful, inexplicable. He wound me

256

around his finger as you wind the silken threads with which you embroider. We studied and played together. I was never contented out of his sight, never satisfied until I saw him supplied with everything that gave me pleasure. I was very precocious, and made extraordinary strides in the path of learning; at all events, at sixteen I was considered a remarkable boy.

"Mr. Hammond had six children; and because his salary was rather meager, I insisted on paying his son's expenses as well as my own when I went to Yale. I could not bear that my Damon, my Jonathan, should be out of my sight; I must have my friend always with me. His father was educating him for the ministry, and he had already commenced the study of theology; but no, I must have him with me at Yale, and so to Yale we went.

"I had fancied myself a Christian, had joined the church, was zealous and faithful in all my religious duties. In a fit of pious enthusiasm, I planned this church - ordered it built. The cost was enormous, and my mother objected, but I intended it as a shrine for the 'apple of my eye.' Where he was concerned, what mattered the expenditure of thousands? Was not my fortune quite as much at his disposal as at mine? I looked forward with fond pride to the time when I should see my idol - Murray Hammond - standing in yonder shining pulpit. Ha! At this instant it is filled with a hideous specter. I see him there! His form and features mocking me, daring me to forget! Handsome as Apollo! Treacherous as Apollyon!"

St. Elmo paused, pointing to the pure marble pulpit where a violet flame seemed flickering.

Then with a groan, he bowed his head upon the railing. When he spoke again, his face wore an ashy hue, and his stern mouth was unsteady. "Hallowed days of my blessed boyhood! Ah, they rise before me now, like holy, burning stars. So full of noble aspirations, of philanthropic schemes! I would do so much good with my money. Every needy sufferer should find relief at my hands as long as I possessed a dollar or a crust. As I look back now at that dead self, and remember all that I was, all the purity of my life, the nobility of my character, the tenderness of my heart - I do not wonder that people who knew me then, predicted that I would prove an honor, a blessing to my race. Mark you, that was St. Elmo Murray – as nature fashioned him.

"My affection for my chum, Murray, increased as I grew up to manhood, and there was not a dream of my brain, a hope of my heart which was not confided to him. I reverenced, I trusted, I almost – nay, I quite worshipped him! When I was only eighteen, I began to love his cousin, whose father was pastor of a church in New Haven, and whose mother was Mr. Hammond's sister. You have seen her. She is beautiful even now, and you can imagine how lovely Agnes Hunt was in her girlhood. She was the belle and pet of the students. Before I had known her a month I was her accepted lover.

"Edna, I loved her with all the devotion of my chivalric, ardent nature, and for me she professed the most profound attachment. Her parents favored our wishes for an early marriage, but my mother refused to sanction such an idea. She wanted me to first complete my education and visit the Old World before I married.

"As summer vacation approached, I prepared to come home, hoping to beg my mother to change her mind and allow me to marry Agnes before we sailed for Europe the ensuing year, after I left Yale.

"Murray was my confidant. In his sympathizing ears I poured all my fond hopes, and he insisted that I ought to take my lovely bride with me. It would be cruel to leave her so long, he said. Besides, he was so impatient for the happy day when he should call me his cousin. He declined coming home, telling me that he wanted to continue his theological studies with his uncle over the summer.

"Well do I recollect the parting between us. I had left Agnes in tears – inconsolable because of my departure. I flew to Murray for words of consolation. When I bade him good-bye my eyes were full of tears, and as he passed his arm around my shoulders, I whispered, 'Murray, take care of my angel Agnes for me! Watch over and comfort her while I am away.'

"Ah, as I stand here today, I hear again ringing over the ruins of the past seventeen years, his loving musical tones answering, 'My dear boy, trust her to my care. St. Elmo, for your dear sake I will steal time from my books to cheer her while you are absent.

But hurry back, for I find black-letter more attractive than blue-eyes. God bless you, my precious friend. Write to me constantly.'

"Since then, I always shudder involuntarily when I hear parting friends bless each other – for well do I know the stinging curse coiled up in those liquid words.

"I left New Haven and came home. Over summer, I busied myself in the building of this church; in plans for Murray's advancement in life, as well as my own. My impatience prevailed over my mother's sensible objections, and she finally consented that I should marry Agnes and take her to Europe with me. I had also informed Mr. Hammond that I wanted Murray to accompany us. I told him that I would gladly pay Murray's traveling expenses – I was so anxious for him to see the East, especially Palestine.

"Full of happy plans, I hurried back earlier than I had intended, and reached New Haven very unexpectedly. The night was bright with moonshine, my heart was bright with hope. Too eager to see Agnes, whose letters had breathed the most tender love for me, I rushed up the steps, and was told that she was walking in the little flower-garden.

"Down the path I hurried. I suddenly stopped as I heard her silvery laugh blended with Murray's – and she said my name in tones that petrified me.

"Under a large apple tree in the parsonage garden they sat on a wooden bench, Agnes and Murray, side by side. Only the tendrils and branches of a grapevine divided us. I stood there, grasping the vine – looking through the leaves at the two whom I had so idolized. Her golden head rested on Murray's breast. I heard and saw their kisses; heard – what wrecked, blasted me! I heard myself ridiculed – sneered at – maligned. They laughed at how I was to be a mere puppet – a cat's paw, that I was a doting, awkward fool – easily hoodwinked. Agnes said she found it almost impossible to endure my caresses. She shuddered in my arms, and flew for happiness to his! I heard that from the beginning I had been duped. They said they had always loved each other – always would; but poverty barred their marriage – and she must be sacrificed to secure my fortune for the use of both!

"All that was uttered I cannot now repeat; but it is carefully embalmed, and lies in the little Taj Mahal, among other cherished souvenirs of my precious friendships.

"But their scorn, their sneers at my credulity, and at my awkward, overgrown boyishness, stung me to desperation. I wondered if I were insane, or dreaming, or the victim of some horrible delusion.

"While I stood there, I was transformed. The soul of St. Elmo seemed to pass away – a fiend took possession of me. Love died, hope with it – and an insatiable thirst for vengeance set my blood on fire. During that time my whole nature was warped, distorted; my life blasted – mutilated – deformed. The loss of Agnes's love I could have borne, nay – fool that I was! – I think my former generous affection for Murray would have made me relinquish her almost resignedly, if his happiness had demanded the sacrifice on my part. If he had come to me frankly and acknowledged all, my insane idolatry would have made me place her hand in his, and remove the barrier of poverty; and the assurance that I had secured his lifelong happiness would have sufficed for mine.

"My veins ran fire as I listened to her silvery voice with the rich melody of his, and their kisses. At last I turned and left the garden, and walked back toward the town. The moon was full, but I staggered and groped my way, like one blind, to the college buildings. I knew where a pair of pistols was kept by one of the students, and possessing myself of them, I wandered out on the road leading to the parsonage. I was aware that Murray intended to come back into the town, and I reeled into a shaded spot near the road and waited for him.

"Oh, the mocking glory of that cloudless night! To this day I hate the cold glitter of stars, and the golden sheen of midnight moons. For the first time in my life, I cursed the world and all it held; cursed the contented cricket singing in the grass at my feet; cursed the blood in my arteries, that beat so thick and fast I could not listen for his footsteps. At last I heard him whistling a favorite tune, which all our lives we had whistled together as we hunted through the woods around Le Bocage. I sprang up with a cry that must have rung on the night air like the yell of some beast of prey.

"Of all that passed I only know that I cursed and insulted and maddened him till he accepted the pistol, which I thrust into his hand. We moved ten paces apart, and a couple of students, who happened to pass along the road and heard our altercation, stopped at our request. They gave the word of command and we fired simultaneously.

"The ball entered Murray's heart, and he fell dead without a word. I was severely wounded in the chest, and now I wear the ball here in my side. Ah, a precious relic of murdered confidence!"

Until now Edna had listened breathlessly, with her eyes upon his; but here a groan escaped her. She shuddered violently and hid her face in her hands.

Mr. Murray came nearer, stood close to her, and hurried on.

"My last memory of my old idol is as he lay with his handsome, treacherous face turned up to the moon. The hair that Agnes had been playing with was wet with dew and the blood that oozed down from his side.

"When I recovered consciousness, Murray Hammond had been three weeks in his grave. As soon as I was able to travel, my mother took me to Europe. For five years we lived in Paris, Naples, or wandered to and fro. Then she came home, and I plunged into the heart of Asia. After several years I returned to Paris, and gave myself up to every species of dissipation. I drank, gambled, and my midnight carousals would sicken your soul were I to paint all their hideousness.

"You have read in the Scriptures of persons possessed of devils? A savage devil held me in bondage. I sold myself to my Mephistopheles on condition that my revenge might be complete. I hated the whole world with an intolerable, murderous hate; and to mock and make others suffer was the only real pleasure I found. The very name, the bare mention of religion maddened me. A minister's daughter, a minister's son, a minister himself, had withered my young life, and I blasphemously derided all holy things. Oh, Edna, my darling, it is impossible to paint all the awful wretchedness of that period, when I walked in the world seeking victims and finding many. Verily,

> 'There's not a crime
> But takes its proper change out still in crime,
> If once rung on the counter of this world,
> Let sinners look to it.'[69]

"Ah, upon how many lovely women have I visited Agnes's sin of hypocrisy! Into how many ears have I poured tender words, until fair hands were as good as offered to me, when I turned their love to mockery. Even in Paris I became notorious as a heartless trifler with the affections I won and trampled under my feet. Whenever a brilliant and beautiful woman crossed my path, I attached myself to her train of admirers, until I made her acknowledge my power and give public and unmistakable manifestation of her preference for me. Then I left her – a target for the laughter of her circle. It was not vanity; oh, no, no! That springs from self-love, and I had none. It was hate of everything human, especially of everything feminine.

"One of the fairest faces that ever brightened the haunts of fashion – a queenly, elegant girl – the pet of her family and of society, now wears serge garments and a black veil and is immured in an Italian convent, because I entirely won her heart. When she asked for me to declare my affection and ask her to become my wife, I quitted her side for that of another belle, and

---

[69] from *Aurora Leigh* – Elizabeth Barrett Browning

never visited her again. On the day when she bade adieu to the world, I was among the spectators. As her mournful eyes sought mine, I laughed, and gloried in the desolation I had wrought. Sick of Europe, I came home…

'And to a part I come where no light shines.'[70]

"My tempting fiend pointed to one whose suffering would atone for much of my misery. Edna, I withhold nothing; there is much I might conceal, but I scorn to do so.

"During one fatal winter, scarlet-fever had deprived Mr. Hammond of four children, leaving him an only daughter – Annie – the image of her brother Murray. Her health was feeble; consumption was stretching its skeleton hands toward her, and her father watched her as a gardener tends a delicate orchid. She was about sixteen, very sweet and attractive. After Murray's death, I never spoke to Mr. Hammond, never crossed his path; but I met his daughter without his knowledge, and finally I made her confess her love for me. I offered her my hand; she accepted it.

"A day was appointed for an elopement and marriage. The hour came; she left the parsonage. But I did not meet her here on the steps of this church as I had promised – I merely sent a note that announced my inability to fulfill the engagement, full of scorn and derision, explaining my revengeful motives that had actuated me."

Edna's eyes widened.

"Two hours later her father found her insensible on the steps, and the marble was dripping with a hemorrhage of blood from her lungs. The dark stain is still there; you must have noticed it."

Edna covered her mouth, positively ill. *He chose a consumptive little girl to prey upon after he'd killed her big brother,* she thought, her head whirling. *He broke a consumptive girl's heart and then left her, bleeding out her life, for her father to find.*

"I never saw Annie again. She kept to her room from that day, and died three months after. When on her deathbed she sent for me, but I refused to obey the summons.

---

[70] Dante's *Commedia*, Inferno, Canto IV

"As I stand here, I see through the window the gray, granite vault overgrown with ivy, and the marble slab where sleep in untimely death Murray and Annie Hammond, the victims of my insatiable revenge. Do you wonder that I doubted you when you said that afflicted father, Allan Hammond, had never uttered one unkind word about me?"

Mr. Murray pointed to a quiet corner of the churchyard. Edna did not lift her face, fighting to smother her moans.

He put his hand on hers, but she shivered and shrank away from him. Edna thought of how Mr. Hammond often gazed out at the graveyard during their lessons, and a world of grief would come into his eyes when he thought Edna wasn't looking. And St. Elmo had blithely *killed his little girl.*

Mr. Murray continued. "Years passed. I grew more and more savage; the very power of loving seemed to have died out in my nature. My mother endeavored to drag me into society, but I was surfeited, sick of the world – sick of my own excesses. My mother is a woman of stern integrity of character and sincerity of purpose; but she is worldly and ambitious, and inordinately proud, and for her religion I had lost all respect.

"Again I went abroad, solely to kill time; was absent two years, and came back. I had ransacked the world, and was disgusted, hopeless, prematurely old. A week after my return I was attacked by a malignant fever, and my life was despaired of, but I exulted in the thought that at last I should find oblivion. I refused all remedies, and set at defiance all medical advice, hoping to hasten the end; but death cheated me. I rose from my bed of sickness, cursing the mockery, realizing that indeed:

> 'The good die first,
> And they whose hearts are dry as summer dust
> Burn to the socket.'[71]

"Some months after my recovery, while I was out on a camp-hunt, you were brought to Le Bocage. The sight of you made me more vindictive than ever. I believed you selfishly calculating, and

---

[71] from *The Excursion*, book I, "The Wanderer" – William Wordsworth

I could not bear that you should remain under the same roof with me. I hated children as I hated men and women."

Edna's cheeks burned as they had back then.

"But that day when you defied me in the park, and told me I was sinful and cruel, I began to notice you closely. I weighed your words, watched you when you little dreamed that I was present, and sometimes concealed myself in order to listen to your conversation. I saw in your character traits that annoyed me, because they were noble and unlike what I had believed all womanhood or girlhood to be. I was aware that you dreaded me; I saw that very clearly every time I had occasion to speak to you.

"How it all came to pass I cannot tell – I know not – and it has always been a mystery even to me. But, Edna, after the long lapse of years of sin and reckless dissipation, my heart stirred and turned to you, child though you were. A strange, strange, invincible love for you sprang from the bitter ashes of a dead affection for Agnes Hunt. I wondered at myself; I sneered at my idiocy; I cursed my mad folly and tried to believe you as unprincipled as I had found others; but the singular fascination strengthened day by day. Finally I determined to tempt you, certain that your duplicity and deceit would wake me from the dream into which I did not want to fall.

"Thinking that at your age curiosity was the strongest emotion, I carefully arranged the interior of the Taj Mahal so that it would be impossible for you to open it without being discovered; and putting the key in your hands, I went abroad."

Edna shook her head. She had been just a girl, and he thought it great sport to tempt her this way.

"For four years I wandered, restless, impatient, scorning myself more and more because I could not forget your pure, haunting face; because, despite my jeers, I knew that I loved you. At last I wrote to my mother from Egypt that I should go to Central Persia, and so I intended.

"But one night I sat alone, smoking, amid the temple of Isis at Philae, surrounded by crumbling red granite sphinxes. There, a vision of Le Bocage rose before me, and your dear face looked at me from the lotus-crowned columns of the ancient ruins. I forgot the hate I bore all mankind; I forgot everything but you; your

pure, calm, magnificent eyes. The longing to see you, my darling –
the yearning to look into your eyes once more, took possession of
me. I sat there till the golden, dewless dawn of the desert fell upon
Egypt, and then came a struggle long and desperate. I laughed
and swore at my folly; but far down in the abyss of my distorted
nature, hope had kindled a flickering ray. I tried to smother it, but
its flame clung to some crevice in my heart and would not be
crushed.

"While I debated, a pigeon that dwelt somewhere in the
crumbling temple fluttered down at my feet, cooed softly, looked
in my face, and after a moment rose, circled above me in the pure,
rainless air and flew westward.

"I accepted it as an omen, and started to America instead of to
Persia.

"On the night of the tenth of December, four years after I bade
you good-bye at the park gate, I was again at Le Bocage. Silently
and undiscovered I stole into my own house and secreted myself
behind the curtains in the library. I had been there one hour when
you and Gordon Leigh came in to examine the Targum. During
that hour that you two sat there bending over the same book, I
became convinced that while I loved you as I never expected to
love any one, Gordon also loved you, and intended if possible to
make you his wife. I contrasted my worn, haggard face and
grayish locks with his, so full of manly hope and youthful beauty,
and I could not doubt that any girl would prefer him to me.

"Edna, my retribution began then. I felt that my devil was
mocking me, as I had long mocked others, and made me love you
when it was impossible to win you. Then and there I was tempted
to spring upon and throttle you both before he triumphantly
called you his.

"At last Leigh left, and I escaped to my own rooms. I was
pacing the floor when I heard you cross the rotunda and saw the
glimmer of the light you carried. Hoping to see you open the little
Taj, I crawled behind the sarcophagus that holds my two
mummies, crouched close to the floor, and peeped at you across
the gilded byssus that covered them. You must have felt my eager
gaze, for you were restless, and searched the room to discover
whence that feeling of a human presence came. Darling, were you

superstitious, that you avoided looking into the dark corner where the mummies lay?

"Presently you stopped in front of the little tomb, and swept away the spider-web, and took the key from your pocket. When you put it into the lock I almost shouted aloud in my savage triumph! I absolutely panted to find Leigh's future wife as unworthy of confidence as I believed the remainder of her sex. But you did not open it. You merely drove away the spider, rubbed the marble clean with your handkerchief, and held the key between your fingers.

"Then my heart seemed to stand still as I watched the light streaming over your beautiful, holy face and crimson dress. When you put the key in your pocket and turned away, my groan almost betrayed me. I had taken out my watch to see the hour, and in my suspense I clutched it so tightly that the gold case and the crystal within all crushed in my hand. You heard the tingling sound and wondered whence it came. When you had locked the door and gone, I raised one of the windows and swung myself down to the terrace. Do you remember that night?"

"Yes, Mr. Murray." Edna's voice was tremulous and almost inaudible.

"I had business in Tennessee, no matter now, what, or where, and I went on that night. After a week I returned, that afternoon when I found you reading in my sitting-room. Still I was skeptical. Not until I opened the tomb, was I convinced that you had not betrayed the trust which you supposed I placed in you. Then, as you stood beside me and looked half-reproachfully, half-defiantly at me – it cost me a terrible effort to master myself – to abstain from clasping you to my heart, and telling you all that you were to me. Oh, how I longed to take you in my arms and feed my poor famished heart with one touch of your lips! The belief that Gordon was a successful rival sealed my lips on that occasion; and ah, the dreary wretchedness of the days of suspense that followed. I was a starving beggar who stood before what I coveted above everything else on earth, and saw it labeled with another man's name and beyond my reach. The daily sight of that emerald ring on your finger maddened me; and you can form no adequate idea of my bitterness when I noted my mother's earnest efforts to secure for Gordon Leigh the hand which her own son would have given worlds to claim in the sight of God and man.

"Continually I watched you when you least expected me; I strewed infidel books where I knew you must see them; I tempted you more than you dreamed of; I tormented and wounded you whenever an opportunity offered; for I hoped to find some flaw in your character, some defect in your temper, some inconsistency between your professions and your practice. I knew Leigh was not your equal, and I said bitterly, 'She is poor and unknown, and will surely marry him for his money, for his position – as Agnes would have married me.'

"But you did not, you did not! And when I knew that you had positively refused his fortune, I felt that a great dazzling light had broken suddenly upon my darkened life. For the first time since I parted with Murray Hammond, tears of joy filled my eyes. I ceased to struggle against my love – I gave myself up to it, and only asked, *How can I overcome her aversion to me?* You were the only tie that linked me with my race, and for your sake I almost felt as if I could forget my hate.

"But you shrank more and more from me, and my punishment overtook me when I saw how you hated Clinton Allston's blood-smeared hands, and with what unfeigned horror you regarded his career. When you declared so vehemently that his fingers should never touch yours – oh, it was the fearful apprehension of losing you that made me catch your dear hands and press them to my aching heart. I was stretched upon a rack that taught me the full import of Isaac Taylor's grim words, 'Remorse is man's dread prerogative![72]' Believing that you knew all my history and that your aversion was based upon it, I was too proud to show you my affection.

"Douglass Manning was as much my friend as I permitted any man to be; we had travelled together through Arabia, and with his handwriting I was familiar. Suspecting your literary schemes, and dreading a rival in your ambition, I wrote to him on the subject, discovered all I wished to ascertain, and requested him, for my sake, to reconsider and examine your manuscript. He did so to oblige me, and I insisted that he should treat your letters and your

---

[72] Man Responsible for His Dispositions, Opinion, and Conduct: A Lecture -- Isaak Taylor

MS. with such severity as to utterly crush your literary aspirations."

He paused, and leaned over her, putting his hand on her head, but Edna shook off his touch. "You told Manning to reject my manuscript?"

"But do you not see how entirely you fill my mind and heart? How I scrutinize your words and actions? Oh, my darling – "

"You have tormented me in every way possible, and you couldn't even leave my literary career alone?"

Discomfited, he continued with his story. "It is, perhaps, needless to tell you that Estelle came here to marry me for my fortune. She professes to love me! Has absolutely avowed it more than once in days gone by. Whether she really loves anything but wealth and luxury, I have never troubled myself to find out; but my mother fancies that if Estelle were my wife, I might be less cynical. Once or twice I tried to be affectionate toward her, solely to see what effect it would have upon you; but I discovered that you could not easily be deceived in that direction – the mask was too transparent, and beside, the game disgusted me.

"The very devil himself brought Agnes here. She had married a rich old banker only a few months after Murray's death, and lived in ease and splendor until a short time since, when her husband failed and died, leaving her without a cent. She knew how utterly she had blasted my life, and imagined that I had never married because I still loved her. With unparalleled effrontery she came here, and trusting to her wonderfully preserved beauty, threw herself and her daughter in my way. When I heard *she* was at the parsonage, all the old burning hate leaped up strong as ever. I fancied that she was the real cause of your dislike to me, and that night, when the game of billiards ended, I went to the parsonage for the first time since Murray's death."

"You mean since the first time you killed Murray," Edna said quietly.

Mr. Murray nearly lashed out, but at the sight of her eyes, he suddenly closed his mouth. A moment later, he said, "Yes. Memories met me at the gate, trooped after me up the walk, and hovered like vultures as I stood in the shadow of the trees, where my idol and I had chatted and romped in the far past. Unobserved I stood there, and looked once more, after the lapse of seventeen years, on the face that had caused my crime and ruin. I listened to her clear laugh, silvery as when I heard it chiming with Murray's under the apple tree on the night that branded me and drove me forth to wander like Cain. I resolved, if she really loved her daughter, to make her suffer for all that she had inflicted on me.

"The first time I met Gertrude I could have sworn my boyhood's love was restored to me; she is so entirely the image of what Agnes was. To possess themselves of my home and property is all that brought them here. Like mother, like daughter!"

"Oh, no, no! Visit not her mother's sins on her innocent head! Gertrude is true and affectionate, and she loves you dearly." Edna spoke with a great effort, and the strange tones of her own voice frightened her.

"Loves me? Ha! Ha! Just about as tenderly as her mother did before her. That they do both 'dearly love' – my purse, I grant you. Hear me out. Agnes threw the girl constantly and adroitly in my way. The demon here in my heart prompted revenge, and, above all, I resolved to find out whether you were indeed as utterly indifferent to me as you seemed. I know that jealousy will make a woman betray her affection sooner than any other cause, and I deliberately set myself to work to make you believe that I loved that pretty cheat over yonder at the parsonage who intercepts me almost daily to favor me with manifestations of devotion, and shows me continually that I have only to put out my hand and take her to rule over my house, and trample my heart under her pretty feet.

"Edna, when you gave me that note of hers a week ago and looked so calmly, so coolly in my face, I felt as if all hope were dying in my heart. I could not believe that, if you had one atom of affection for me, you could be so generous, so unselfish toward one whom you considered your rival.

"That night I did not close my eyes, and had almost decided to revisit South America; but next morning my mother told me you were going to New York – that all entreaties had failed to shake your resolution. Then once more a hope cheered me, and I believed that I understood why you had determined to leave those whom I know you love tenderly – to quit the home my mother offered you and struggle among strangers.

"Yesterday they told me you would leave on Monday, and I went out to seek you; but you were with Mr. Hammond, as usual. But instead of you I met – that curse of my life – Agnes! Face to face, at last! Oh, it was a scene that made jubilee down in Pandemonium! She pleaded for her child's happiness – implored me most pathetically to love her Gertrude, and that my happiness would make me forget the unfortunate past! Edna, darling, I will not tell you all she said – you would blush for your sisterhood. But my vengeance was complete when I declined the honor she was so eager to force upon me; when I overwhelmed her with my scorn, and told her that there was only one woman whom I respected or trusted; only one woman upon the broad earth whom I loved; only one woman who could ever be my wife, and her name was – Edna Earl!"

His voice died away, and all was still as the dead in their grassy graves.

Edna covered her face. Her whole heart and soul battled in fierce contest at his avowal, but she steeled herself as never before.

After a moment St. Elmo Murray opened his arms and said in a low winning tone that Edna found difficult to resist. "Come to me now, my pure, noble Edna. You whom I love, as only such a man such as myself can love."

She could reply only through a terrible effort. "No, Mr. Murray. Gertrude stands between us."

"Gertrude!" he snapped. "Do not make me swear here, in your presence – do not madden me! I tell you she is a silly child, who cares no more for me than her mother did before her. I love you; God above us is my witness that I love you as I never loved any human being, and I will not – I swear I will not live without you. You are mine, and all the legions in hell shall not part us!"

He stooped, snatched her from the chair as if she had been an infant, and folded her in his strong arms.

"Mr. Murray, I know she loves you. My poor little trusting friend! You trifled with her warm heart, as you now trifle with mine; but I know you." She raised her head from his chest. "You have shown me how utterly remorseless you are. You had no right to punish Gertrude for her mother's sins; and if you had one spark of honor in your nature, you would marry her, and try to atone for the injury you have already done."

"By pretending to give her a heart which belongs entirely to you? If I wished to deceive you now, think you I would have told all that hideous past, which you cannot abhor one half as much as I do?"

"Your heart is not mine! It belongs to sin, or you could not have so maliciously deceived poor Gertrude. Or poor Annie!" she cried, starting up in his arms and meeting his eyes. "You lied to a consumptive girl, Mr. Hammond's last little darling, and – "

"Take care, do not rouse me," he said, laying a finger upon her lips. "Be reasonable, little darling."

"I am being perfectly reasonable," cried Edna.

"You doubt my love? Well, I ought not to wonder at your skepticism after all you have heard. But you can feel how my heart throbs against your cheek, and if you will look into my eyes, you will be convinced that I am fearfully in earnest, when I beg you to be my wife tomorrow – today – now! If you will only let me send for a minister or a magistrate! You are – "

"No! You asked Annie to be your wife, and – "

"Hush, hush. Look at me. Edna, raise your head and look at me."

She tried to break away. Finding it impossible, she pressed both hands over her face and hid it against his shoulder.

He laughed, and whispered, "My darling, I know what that means. You dare not look up because you cannot trust your own eyes. Because you dread for me to see something there which you want to hide, which you think it your duty to conceal."

A long shudder crept over her. She answered resolutely, "Do you think, sir, that I could love a murderer? A man whose hands are red with the blood of the son and daughter of my best friend?"

"Look at me then."

He took her hands firmly in one of his, and placing the other under her chin, lifted her burning face close to his own.

She dreaded the power of his lustrous, mesmeric eyes, and instantly her long silky lashes swept her flushed cheeks.

"Ah, you dare not! You cannot look me steadily in the eye and say, 'St. Elmo, I never have loved – do not – and never can love you.' You are too truthful; your lips can not dissemble. I know you do not want to love me. Your reason, your conscience forbid it; you are struggling to crush your heart. You think it your duty to despise and hate me. But, my own, Edna – my darling, my darling, you do love me! You know you do love me, though you will not confess it! My proud darling!"

He drew her face tenderly to his own, and kissed her quivering lips repeatedly. At last a moan of anguish told how she was wrestling with her heart.

"Do you think you can hide your love from my eager eyes?" he murmured against her cheek. "Oh, I know that I am unworthy of you. I feel it more and more every day, every hour. I tempted and tried you, and when you proved so true and honest, you kindled a faint beam of hope that, after all, there might be truth and saving, purifying power in religion. Do you know that since this church was finished I have never entered it until a month ago, when I followed you here, and crouched downstairs – yonder, behind one of the pillars, and heard your sacred songs, your hymns so full of grandeur, so full of pathos, that I could not keep back my tears while I listened. Since then I have come every Saturday afternoon, and during the hour spent here my unholy nature was touched and softened as no sermon ever touched it. Oh, you wield a power over me – over all my future, which ought to make you tremble!"

It did make her tremble. Clasped in his arms, her cheek against his chest, his lips speaking these words into her hair – this was a paradise she had always wanted. And now Edna could imagine herself in his home, his wife, softening his nature, helping him purify his sin-stained heart. She did tremble indeed, for she did want this.

Now his voice was low in her ear. "The first generous impulse that has stirred my callous, bitter soul since I was a boy, I owe to you. I went first to see poor Reed in order to discover what took you so often to that cheerless place; and my interest in little Huldah arose from the fact that you loved the child. Oh, my darling, it is not too late for me to atone! It is not too late for me to do some good in the world; and if you will only love me, and trust me, and help me – "

His voice faltered, his tears fell upon her forehead, and stooping he kissed her lips softly, reverently, as if he realized the presence of something sacred. She wanted dearly to surrender to him, to return his kisses, which stirred her as nothing ever had before, and his tears made tears rise in her own eyes in sympathy and love. When he spoke again, his voice was hoarse.

"My precious Edna, I have been mad – I think, for many, many years, and I loathe my past life; but remember how sorely I was tried, and be merciful when you judge me. With your dear little hand in mine to lead me, I will make amends for the ruin and suffering I have wrought, and my Edna – my own wife, shall save me!"

The temptation to tell him yes was almost overpowering. But he must have held Annie this way, and showered her with kisses, and made her faint with love, before he coldly left her to bleed on the church steps.

Edna saw, too, the bent figure and white locks of her beloved pastor, as he sat in his old age in his childless, desolate home, gazing out his window at the graves of his murdered children.

"Oh, Mr. Murray!" Edna cried. "That is not how you atone! Will you call your victims from their tombs? Will you mend all the hearts you've broken? What amends can you make to Mr. Hammond, and to poor Annie, whom you left to die? I cannot help you! I cannot save you!"

"Hush! You can, you shall! Have mercy on my lonely life, my wretched, darkened soul. Lean your dear head here on my heart, and say, 'St. Elmo, what a wife can do to save her sinful husband, I will do for you.' If I am ever to be saved, you, you only can effect my redemption. Edna, as you value my soul, my eternal welfare, give yourself to me! Give your pure, sinless life to purify mine."

With a sudden bound Edna sprang from his embrace and lifted her arms toward the Christ, who seemed to shudder as the flickering light of fading day fell through waving foliage upon him.

"Look yonder to Jesus, bleeding! Do you want redemption? Only his blood can wash away your sins. You ask to give my pure, sinless life to purify yours? No, no! Purifying your life is your work, not mine; atonement is not work you can give over to another! Mr. Murray, I can never be your wife. I have no confidence in you. If I accept your honor of a betrothal, how long would it be before you leave me on the steps where poor Annie choked on her blood? How would I know that you are not trying to use me to give poor Mr. Hammond one last fatal stab to the heart?"

"Hush! Hush! To your keeping I commit my conscience and my heart."

"Conscience?" Edna cried. "I put no faith in any man whose conscience another keeps. Would I marry Lucifer to save his soul? No! Am I to immolate myself upon a pyre for your sake? Am I to sacrifice my life so that you may live? You demand that I give my life to redeem yours. Christ already did that, if only you would turn to him!"

"Edna, you do not, you can not intend to leave me? Darling – "

He held out his arms and moved toward her. Edna, weeping, sprang past him, down the steps of the gallery.

"Edna, please!"

Edna dashed the tears from her eyes. "Mr. Murray, have mercy upon yourself! Go yonder to Jesus. He only can save and purify you. Not me."

She ran out of the church, and paused only at sight of the dark, dull spot on the white steps, where Annie Hammond had lain insensible.

An hour later, St. Elmo Murray raised his face from the mahogany railing where it had rested since Edna left him, and looked around the noble church which his generosity had erected. A full moon eyed him pityingly through the stained glass, and the gleam of the marble pulpit was chill and ghostly. In that weird light the Christ was threatening, wrathful, appalling.

As St. Elmo stood there alone, confronting the picture – confronting the past – memory, like the Witch of Endor, called up visions of Murray and Annie as they had died, all for his love of revenge.

The proud man bowed his head with a cry of anguish that rose mournfully to the vaulted ceiling of the sanctuary:

"It went up single, echoless, 'My God! I am forsaken!'[73]"

[73] "Cowper's Grave" – Elizabeth Barrett Browning

CHAPTER XXIII
SAYING GOODBYE

The weather was so inclement on the following day that no service was held in the church. Despite the heavy rain, Edna went to the parsonage to bid adieu to her pastor and teacher.

When she ascended the steps, Mr. Hammond was walking up and down the portico with his hands clasped behind him, as was his habit when engrossed by earnest thought; and he greeted his pupil with a degree of mournful tenderness very soothing to her grieved heart.

Leading the way to his study, where Mrs. Powell sat with an open book on her lap, he said gently, "Agnes, will you be so kind as to leave us for a while? This is the last interview I shall have with Edna for a long time, perhaps forever, and there are some things I wish to say to her alone. You will find a better light in the dining-room, where all is quiet."

As Mrs. Powell withdrew, he locked the door, and for some seconds paced the floor; then, taking a seat on the chintz-covered lounge beside his pupil, he said eagerly, "St. Elmo was at the church yesterday afternoon. Are you willing to tell me what passed between you?"

"Mr. Hammond, he told me his melancholy history. I know all now – know why he shrinks from meeting you, whom he has injured so cruelly; know all his guilt and your desolation." Edna could not help her tears when she said this.

The old man bowed his white head on his bosom, and there was a painful silence. When he spoke, his voice was scarcely audible.

"The punishment of Eli has fallen heavily upon me. There have been hours when I thought that it was greater than I could bear – that it would utterly crush me. But the bitterness of the curse has passed away; and I can say truly of that 'meekest angel of God,' the Angel of Patience:

> 'He walks with thee, that angel kind,
> And gently whispers, Be resigned;
> Bear up, bear on; the end shall tell,
> The dear Lord ordereth all things well!'[74]

"I tried to train up my children in the fear and admonition of the Lord; but I must have failed signally in my duty, though I have never been able to discover in what respect I was negligent."

"My dear Mr. Hammond! It was not their fault that these griefs were visited upon them."

Sadly, he stroked her hand. "One of the sins of my life was my inordinate pride in my only boy – my gifted, handsome son. My love for Murray was almost idolatrous; and when my heart throbbed with proudest hopes and aspirations, my idol was broken and laid low in the dust. Like David mourning for his rebellious child Absalom, I cried out in my affliction, 'My son, my son! Would God I had died for thee!'[75] Murray Hammond was my precious diadem of earthly glory; and suddenly I found myself uncrowned, and sackcloth and ashes were my portion."

"Why did you never confide these sorrows to me? Did you doubt my sympathy?"

"No, my child, not at all," he said gently. "I thought it best that St. Elmo should lift the veil and show you all that he wished you to know. I felt assured that the time would come when he considered it due to himself to acquaint you with his sad history; and when I saw him go into the church yesterday, I knew that the hour had arrived. I did not wish to prejudice you against him; for I believe that through your agency the prayers of seventeen years would be answered, and that his embittered heart would follow you to that cross before which he bowed in his boyhood."

"Sir? What do you mean?"

"Edna, it was through my son's sin and duplicity that St. Elmo's noble career was blasted. I have hoped that through your

---

[74] "The Angel of Patience" – John Greenleaf Whittier
[75] 2 Samuel 18:33

278

influence, my beloved pupil, he would be redeemed from his reckless course. My dear little Edna, I have hoped everything from your influence. Far, far beyond all computation is the good which a Christian wife can accomplish in the heart of a husband who truly loves her."

"Oh, Mr. Hammond! You pain and astonish me. Surely you would not be willing to see me marry a man who scoffs at the very name of religion; who willfully deceives and trifles with the feelings of all who are sufficiently credulous to trust his hollow vows – whose hands are red with the blood of your children! What hope of happiness or peace could you indulge for me, in view of such a union?"

"My child, if you knew him as well as I do, if you could realize all that he was, then you will understand all he can be if he repents. Edna, if I whom he has robbed of all that made life beautiful – if I, standing here in my lonely old age, in sight of the graves of my murdered darlings – if I can forgive him, and pray for him, and, as God is my witness, love him! then you have no right to visit my injuries and my sorrows upon him."

Edna looked in amazement at his earnest countenance. "Oh, if he knew your magnanimity, surely, surely, your influence would be his salvation. But, sir," she added, her voice trembling, "I should have a right to expect Annie's sad fate if I could forget her sufferings and how he wronged her."

Mr. Hammond rose and walked to the window. After a time, when he resumed his seat, his eyes were full of tears, and his face was strangely pallid.

"My darling Annie, my sweet, fragile flower, my precious little daughter, so like her sainted mother. Ah, it is not surprising that she could not resist his fascinations. But Edna, he never loved my little lamb. You have become almost as dear to me as my lost girl." The old man put his thin hand on Edna's face and turned her toward him. "My dear little girl, you will not think me impertinently curious when I ask you a question. Do you love St. Elmo?"

Edna shuddered. "Mr. Hammond, it is not love. But I cannot deny that he exerts a very singular, a wicked fascination over me. I dread his evil influence, I avoid his presence, and know that he is utterly unworthy of any woman's trust; and yet – and yet – oh, sir, I feel that I am very weak; but I cannot despise, I cannot hate him as I ought to do!"

"Is not this feeling on your part one of the causes that hurry you away to New York?"

"That is certainly one of the reasons why I am anxious to go away as early as possible. Oh, Mr. Hammond! Much as I love, much as I owe you and Mrs. Murray, I sometimes wish that I had never come here! Never seen Le Bocage, and the mocking, jeering man who owns it!" Edna buried her head in her hands.

"Try to believe that somehow in the mysterious Divine economy it is all for the best. In reviewing the apparently accidental circumstances that placed you among us, I have thought that God in his wisdom brought you where he designed you to work. Does Mrs. Murray know that her son offered to make you his wife?"

Edna spoke into her hands, her voice muffled. "No, no! I hope she never will; for it would mortify her exceedingly to know that he could be willing to give his proud name to one of whose lineage she is so ignorant. How did you know it?"

"I knew what his errand must be when he forced himself to visit a spot so fraught with painful memories as my church. Edna, I shall not urge you; but ponder well the step you are taking; for St. Elmo's future will be colored by your decision. I have faith that he will yet lift himself out of the abyss of sin, and your hand would aid him as none other human can."

"Mr. Hammond, do not tempt me! Do not make me believe that I could restore his purity of faith and life. Oh, my dear Mr. Hammond, do not attempt to take from me the only staff which can carry me firmly away. I must not see his face; for I will not be his wife. Instead of weakening my resolution by holding out flattering hopes of reforming him, pray for me! Oh, pray for me, that I may be strengthened to flee from a great temptation. I will marry no man who is not an earnest, humble believer in the religion of our Lord Jesus Christ. If I must, I will, so help me God, live and work alone, and go down to my grave, Edna Earl!"

The minister sighed heavily.

"Bear one thing in mind. It has been said, that in disavowing guardianship, we sometimes slaughter Abel. You cannot understand my interest in St. Elmo. Remember that if his wretched soul is lost at last, it will be required at the hands of my son, in that dread day when we shall stand at the final judgment! Do you wonder that I struggle in prayer, and in all possible human endeavor to rescue him from ruin; so that when I am called from earth, I can meet the spirit of my only boy with the blessed tidings that the soul he jeopardized, and well-nigh wrecked, has been redeemed, is safe! anchored once more in the faith of Christ! But I will say no more. Your own heart and conscience must guide you in this matter."

"To the mercy of his Maker, and the intercession of his Savior, I commit him.

'As for me, I go my own way – onward, upward.'[76]"

A short silence ensued, and at last Edna rose to say good-bye.

"Do you still intend to leave at four o'clock in the morning? I fear you will have bad weather for your journey."

"Yes, sir, I shall certainly start tomorrow. And now, I must leave you. Oh, my best friend! How can I tell you good-bye?"

The minister folded her in his trembling arms, and his silver locks mingled with her black hair, while he blessed her. She sobbed as he pressed his lips to her forehead, and gently put her from him. Turning, she hurried away, anxious to escape the sight of Gertrude's accusing face; for she supposed that Mrs. Powell had repeated to her daughter Mr. Murray's taunting words.

Since the previous evening she had not spoken to St. Elmo, who did not appear at breakfast. When she passed him in the hall later, he was talking to his mother, and took no notice of her bow.

Now as Edna's carriage approached the house, she glanced up and saw St. Elmo sitting at the window, with his elbow resting on the sill, and his cheek on his hand.

Upon her return home, she went at once to Mrs. Murray, and the interview was long and painful. The latter wept freely, and insisted that if the orphan grew weary of teaching (as she knew

---

[76] *Lucile* – Owen Meredith (aka Robert Bulwer-Lytton, 1st Earl of Lytton)

would happen), she should come back immediately to Le Bocage; where a home would always be hers, and to which a true friend would welcome her.

At length, when Estelle Harding came in with some letters, Edna retreated to her own quiet room. She went to her bureau to complete the packing of her clothes, and found on the marble slab a box and note directed to her.

Mr. Murray's handwriting was remarkably graceful, and Edna broke the seal which bore his motto, *Nemo me impune lacessit.*

"EDNA: I send for your examination the contents of the little tomb, which you guarded so faithfully. Read the letters written before I was betrayed. The locket attached to a ribbon was always worn over my heart, and the miniatures which it contains are those of Agnes Hunt and Murray Hammond. Read all the record, and then judge me, as you hope to be judged. I sit alone, amid the moldering, blackened ruins of my youth; will you not listen to the prayer of my heart, and the half-smothered pleadings of your own, and come to me in my desolation, and help me to build up a new and noble life? Oh, my darling, while you read and ponder, I am praying. Aye, praying for the first time in seventeen years! Praying that if God ever hears prayer, He will influence your decision, and bring you to me. Edna, my darling! I wait for you.
"Your own,
"ST. ELMO."

Ah, how her tortured heart writhed and bled; how piteously it pleaded for him, and for itself!

Edna opened the locket. If Gertrude had stepped into the golden frame, the likeness could not have been more startling. She looked at it until her lips blanched and were tightly compressed, and the memory of Gertrude became paramount. Murray Hammond's face was extraordinary beautiful, and he stared at her like some avenging angel. With a shudder she put the locket away, and turned to the letters that St. Elmo had written to Agnes and to Murray in the early, happy days of his engagement.

Tender, beautiful, loving letters, that breathed the most devoted attachment and the purest piety; letters that were full of lofty aspirations, and religious fervor, and generous schemes for the assistance and enlightenment of the poor about Le Bocage; and especially for "my noble, matchless Murray." Among the papers were several designs for charitable buildings: a house of industry, an asylum for the blind, and a free schoolhouse.

In an exquisite ivory casket, containing a splendid set of diamonds, and the costly betrothal ring, Edna found a sheet of paper around which the blazing necklace was twisted. Disengaging it, she saw that it was a narration of all that had stung him to desperation on the night of the murder.

As she read the burning taunts, the insults, the ridicule heaped by the two under the apple tree upon the faithful, absent friend, she felt the indignant blood gush into her face; but she read on and on. Two hours elapsed ere she finished the package.

Then came a trial, a long, fierce, agonizing trial, such as few women have ever been called upon to pass through; such as the world believes no woman ever triumphantly endured. Girded by prayer, the girl went down resolutely into the flames of the furnace, and the ordeal was terrible indeed. But as often as Love showed her the figure of Mr. Murray, alone in his dreary sitting-room, waiting, watching for her, she turned and asked of Duty the portrait of Gertrude's sweet, anxious face; the mournful countenance of a nun, shut up by iron bars from God's beautiful world, from the home and the family who had fondly cherished her in her happy girlhood, ere St. Elmo trailed his poison across her sunny path; and the picture of dying Annie, lying on the church steps and coughing up blood, with St. Elmo's cruel note clutched in her hand.

After another hour, the orphan went to her desk, and while she wrote, a cold rigidity settled upon her features, which told that she was deliberately shaking hands with the expelled, the departing Hagar of her heart's hope and happiness.

"To the mercy of God, and the love of Christ, and the judgment of your own conscience, I commit you. Henceforth we walk different paths, and after tonight, it is my wish that we meet no more on earth. Mr. Murray, I cannot lift up your darkened soul; and you would only drag mine down. For your final salvation I shall never cease to pray till we stand face to face before the Bar of God.

"EDNA EARL."

Ringing for a servant, she sent back the box, and even his own note, which she longed to keep, but would not trust herself to see again. Dreading reflection, and too miserable to sleep, she went to Mrs. Murray's room, and remained with her till three o'clock.

Edna was dozing with her head on Mrs. Murray's shoulder when Mr. Murray's voice rang through the house, calling for the carriage. She heard the rain pouring against the dark windows, and the sobbing of the wind outside. Her heart sank, and she desperately longed to stay. But there was nothing to be done for that.

As Edna put on her bonnet and shawl, Mr. Murray knocked at his mother's door.

The next moment, he walked in, very pale and stern. "It is raining very hard, and you must not think of going to the train, as you intended."

"But, my son, the carriage is close and – "

"I cannot permit you to expose yourself so unnecessarily. In short, I will not take you, so there is an end of it. Of course, I can stand the weather, and I will go over with Edna, and put her under the care of someone on the train. As soon as possible send her down to the carriage. I shall order her trunks strapped on."

His voice rang coldly clear as he turned and went downstairs.

The parting was very painful, and Mrs. Murray followed the orphan to the front door.

"St. Elmo, I wish you would let me go. I do not mind the rain."

"Impossible. You know I have an unconquerable horror of scenes, and I do not at all fancy witnessing one that threatens to last until the train leaves. Go upstairs and cry yourself to sleep in ten minutes; that will be much more sensible. Come, Edna, are you ready?"

Mrs. Murray folded Edna in a last embrace. Then Mr. Murray held out his hand, drew her from his mother's arms, and taking his seat beside her in the carriage, ordered the coachman to drive on.

The night was very dark, the wind sobbed down the avenue, and the rain fell in such torrents that as Edna leaned out for a last look at the stately mansion, which she had learned to love so well, she could only discern the outline of the bronze monsters by the glimmer of the gaslight burning in the hall. She shrank far back in one corner, and her fingers clutched each other convulsively; but when they had passed through the gate and entered the main road Mr. Murray's hand was laid on hers – her cold fingers were unlocked gently but firmly, and raised to his lips.

She tried to withdraw them, but found it useless, and the trial which she had fancied was at end seemed only beginning.

"Edna, this is the last time I shall ever speak to you of myself; the last time I shall ever allude to all that has passed. Is it entirely useless to ask you to reconsider? If you have no pity for me, have some mercy on yourself. You cannot know how I dread the thought of your leaving me, and being roughly handled by a ruthless world. Already your dear face has grown pale, and your eyes have a restless, troubled look, and shadows are gathering about your spirit. My darling, you are not strong enough to wrestle with the world; you will be trodden down by the masses in this conflict upon which you enter so eagerly. Help me to make a proper use of my fortune, and you will do more real good to humanity than by all you can ever accomplish with your pen, no matter how successful it may prove. If you were selfish and heartless as other women, adulation and celebrity and the praise of the public might satisfy you. But you are not, and I have studied your nature too thoroughly to mistake the result of your ambitious career.

"My darling, ambition is the mirage of the literary desert you are anxious to traverse; it is the Bahr Sheitan, the Satan's water, which will ever recede and mock your thirsty, toil-spent soul. Dear little pilgrim, do not scorch your feet and wear out your life in the hot, blinding sands, struggling in vain for the constantly fading, vanishing oasis of happy literary celebrity. Ah, the Sahara of letters is full of bleaching bones that tell where many of your sex as well as of mine fell and perished miserably, even before the noon of life. Ambitious spirit, come, rest in peace in the cool, quiet, happy, palm-grove that I offer you. My shrinking violet, sweeter than all the world! Today I found a passage which you had marked in one of my books, and it echoes ceaselessly in my heart:

> "*My future will not copy fair my past.*
> I wrote that once; and thinking at my side
> My ministering life-angel justified
> The word by his appealing look upcast
> To the white throne of God, I turned at last,
> And there instead saw thee, not unallied
> To angels in thy soul! Then I, long tired
> By natural ills, received the comfort fast;
> While budding at thy sight, my pilgrim's staff
> Gave out green leaves with morning dews impearled.
> I seek no copy of life's first half:
> Leave here the pages with long musing curled,
> Write me new my future's epigraph.
> New angel mine – unhoped-for in the world!'[77]"

He had passed his arm around her and drawn her close to his side. The pleading tenderness of his low voice was indeed hard to resist.

"No, Mr. Murray, my decision is unalterable. If you do really love me, spare me, spare me, further entreaty. Before we part there are some things I should like to say, and I have little time left. Will you hear me?"

---

[77] Sonnet 42 from *Sonnets for the Portuguese* – Elizabeth Barrett Browning

He did not answer, but tightened his arm, drew her head to his bosom, and leaned his face down on hers.

"Mr. Murray, I want to leave my Bible with you, because there are many passages marked which would greatly comfort and help you. It is the most precious thing I possess, for Grandpa gave it to me when I was a little girl. I could not bear to leave it with anyone but you. I have it here in my hand; will you look into it sometimes if I give it to you?"

He merely put out his hand and took it from her.

She paused a few seconds, and as he remained silent, she continued, "Mr. Hammond is the best friend you have on earth. Yesterday, having seen you enter the church and suspecting what passed, he spoke to me of you, and oh, he pleaded for you as only he could! He urged me not to judge you too harshly; he asked me not to leave you. He said, 'Edna, if I, whom he has robbed of all that life made beautiful; if I, standing here alone in my old age, in sight of the graves of my murdered darlings, if I can forgive him, and pray for him, and, as God is my witness, love him, you have no right to visit my injuries and my sorrows upon him!' Mr. Murray, he can help you, and he will, if you will only permit him. If you could realize how dearly he is interested in your happiness, you could not fail to reverence that religion which enables him to triumph over all the natural feelings of resentment.

"Mr. Murray, you have declared again and again that you love me. Oh, if it be true, meet me in heaven! I am striving to do what I believe to be my duty, and I hope at last to find a home with my God. For several years, ever since you went abroad, I have been praying for you; and while I live, I shall not cease to do so. Oh, will you not pray for yourself? Mr. Murray, I believe I shall not be happy even in heaven if I do not see you there. On earth we are parted – your crimes divide us; but there! there! Oh, for my sake, make an effort to redeem yourself, and meet me there!"

She felt his strong frame tremble, and a heavy shuddering sigh broke from his lips and swept across her cheek. But when he spoke his words contained no hint of the promise she longed to receive.

"Edna, my shadow has fallen across your heart, and I am not afraid that you will forget me. You will struggle to crush your aching heart, and endeavor to be famous. But amid your ovations, the memory of a lonely man, who loves you infinitely better than all the world, will come like a breath from the sepulcher, to wither your bays; and my words will haunt you, rising above the paeans of your public worshippers. When the laurel crown you covet becomes a chaplet of thorns piercing your temples, you will think mournfully of the days gone by, when I prayed for the privilege of resting your weary head here on my heart. You cannot forget me. Sinful and unworthy as I confess myself, I am conqueror, I triumph now, even though you never permit me to look upon your face again; for I believe I have a place in my darling's heart which no other man can fill! You are too proud to acknowledge it, too truthful to deny it; but, my pure Edna, my heart feels it as well as yours, and it is a comfort of which all time cannot rob me. Without it, how could I face my future? Edna, the hour has come when, in accordance with your own decree, we part. Perhaps we may never meet again in this world. Ah, do not shrink away from me. Let me kiss you once more, my darling, my darling! I shall wear it on my lips till death stiffens them. I am not at all afraid that any other man will ever be allowed to touch lips that belong to me alone; that I have made, and here seal, all my own! Good-bye."

He strained her to him and pressed his lips twice to hers, then the carriage stopped at the railroad station.

He handed her out, found a seat for her in the cars, which had just arrived, arranged her wrappings comfortably, and went back to attend to her trunks. She sat near an open window, and though it rained heavily, he buttoned his coat to the throat, and stood just beneath it, with his eyes bent down. Twice she pronounced his name, but he did not seem to hear her. Edna put her hand lightly on his shoulder and said, "Do not stand here in the rain. In a few minutes we shall start, and I prefer that you should not wait. Please go home at once, Mr. Murray."

He shook his head, but caught her hand and leaned his cheek against her soft palm, passing it gently and caressingly over his haggard face.

The engine whistled; Mr. Murray pressed a long, warm kiss on the hand he had taken, the cars moved on.

As he lifted his hat, giving her one of his imperial, graceful bows, Edna had a last glimpse of the dark face that had thrown its baleful image deep in her young heart, and defied all her efforts to expel it.

The wind howled around the cars, the rain fell heavily, beating a dismal tattoo on the glass, and the orphan sank back and lowered her veil, and hid her face in her hands.

Henceforth she felt that in obedience to her own decision,

> "They stood aloof, the scars remaining
> Like cliffs that had been rent asunder;
> A dreary sea now flows between;
> But neither heat nor frost nor thunder
> Shall wholly do away, I ween,
> The marks of that which once hath been."[78]

---

[78] *Christabel* – Samuel Taylor Coleridge

CHAPTER XXIV
THE OBELISK

As day dawned, the drab clouds blanched and broke up in marbled masses; the rain ceased, the wind sang out of the west, heralding the coming blue and gold, and at noon not one pearly cloud dotted the sky.

During the afternoon Edna looked anxiously for the first glimpse of "Lookout," but a trifling accident detained the train for several hours, and it was almost twilight when she saw it, a purple spot staining the clear beryl horizon; spreading rapidly, shifting its Tyrian mantle for gray robes. At length the rising moon silvered its rocky crest, as it towered in silent majesty over the little village nestled at its base.

The gentlemanly conductor on the cars accompanied Edna to the hotel and gave her a parcel containing several late newspapers. As she sat in her small room, weary and yet sleepless, she tried to divert her thoughts by reading the journals, and found in three of them notices of the last number of *Iconoclast* Magazine, and especial mention of her essay: "Keeping the Vigil of St. Martin under the Pines of Grütli."

The laudations of this article surprised her, and while much curiosity was indulged concerning the authorship, one of the editors ventured to attribute it to a celebrated and very able writer whose genius had lifted him to an enviable eminence in the world of American letters. The criticisms were excessively flattering, and the young author, gratified at the complete success that had crowned her efforts, cut out the friendly notices, intending to enclose them in a letter to Mrs. Murray.

Unable to sleep, giving audience to memories of her early childhood, she passed the night at her window, watching the constellations go down behind the dark, frowning mass of rock that lifted its parapets to the midnight sky. In the morning light she saw the cold, misty cowl drawn over the venerable hoary head.

The village had changed so materially that she could scarcely recognize any of the old landmarks, and the people who kept the hotel could tell her nothing about Peter Wood, the miller. After breakfast she took a box containing some flowers packed in wet cotton and walked out on the road leading in the direction of the blacksmith's shop. Very soon the trees became familiar; she remembered every turn of the road and bend on the fences. At last the grove of oak and chestnut shading the knoll at the intersection of the roads met her eye. She looked for the forge and bellows, for the anvil and slack-tub; but shop and shed had fallen to decay, and only a heap of rubbish, overgrown with rank weeds and vines, marked the spot where she had spent so many happy hours. The glowing yellow chestnut leaves dropped down at her feet, and the oaks tossed their gnarled arms as if welcoming the wanderer whose head they had shaded in infancy. Stifling a moan, the orphan hurried on.

The timber had been cut down, and fences enclosed fields where forests had stood when she went away. At a sudden, familiar bend in the narrow road, she held her breath and leaned forward to see the old house where she was born and reared – and then a sharp cry of pain escaped her. Not a vestige of the old homestead remained, save the rocky chimney, standing in the center of a cornfield.

She leaned against the low fence, and tears trickled down her cheeks as memory rebuilt the log-house, and placed the split-bottomed rocking chair on the porch in front with her Grandpa sitting in it, his pipe in his hand and his blurred eyes staring at the moon.

Through the brown cornstalks she could see the gaping mouth of the well, now partly filled with rubbish. The wreaths of scarlet cypress which once fringed the shed above it and hung their flaming trumpets down until they almost touched her childish head, as she sang at the well where she scoured the cedar piggin, now trailed helplessly over the ground. Close to the fence, and beyond the reach of plough and hoe, a yellow four-o'clock with closed flowers marked the location of her little garden. One tall larkspur leaned against the fence, sole survivor of the blue pets that Edna had loved so well in the early years. She put her fingers through a crevice, broke the plumy spray, and as she pressed it to her face, she dropped her head upon the rails and gave herself up to the flood of precious memories.

How carefully she had worked and weeded this little plat; how proud she once was of her rosemary and pinks, her double feathery poppies, her sweet-scented lemon-grass; how eagerly she had transplanted wood violets and purple phlox from the forest; how often she had sat on the steps watching for her grandfather's return, and stringing those four-o'clock blossoms into golden crowns for her own young head; and how gaily she had sometimes swung them over Brindle's horns, when she went out to milk her.

> "Ah, sad and strange, as in dark summer dawns
> The earliest pipe of half-awakened birds
> To dying ears, when unto dying eyes
> The casement slowly grows a glimmering square;
> So sad, so strange, the days that are no more."[79]

With a sob she turned away and walked in the direction of the burying-ground; for there, certainly, she would find all unchanged; graves at least were permanent.

The little spring bubbled as of yore, the brush creepers made a tangled tapestry around it, and crimson and blue morning-glories swung their velvety, dew-beaded chalices above it, as on that June morning long ago when she stood there filling her bucket, waiting for the sunrise.

She took off her gloves, knelt beside the spring, and dipping up the cold, sparkling water in her palms, drank and wept, and drank again. She bathed her aching eyes, and almost cheated herself into the belief that she heard again Grip's fierce bark ringing through the woods, and the slow, drowsy tinkle of Brindle's bell.

---

[79] "Song" from *The Princess* – Lord Alfred Tennyson

Turning aside from the beaten track, she entered the thick grove of chestnuts, and looked around for the grave of the Dents; but the mound had disappeared. She recognized the particular tree which had formerly overhung it, and searched the ground carefully, but could discover no trace of the hillock where she had so often scattered flowers. She conjectured that the bodies had probably been disinterred by friends and removed to Georgia.

She hurried on toward the hillside, where the neighborhood graveyard was situated. The rude, unpainted paling still enclosed it, and rows of headboards stretched away among grass and weeds.

Edna suddenly squinted. Whose was that shining marble shaft, standing in the center of a neatly arranged square, around which ran a handsome iron railing? On that very spot, in years gone by, had stood a piece of pine board: "Sacred to the memory of Aaron Hunt, an honest blacksmith and true Christian."

Who had dared to disturb her grandfather's bones? Who dared violate his last resting place, and steal his grave for the interment of some wealthy stranger?

A cry of horror broke from the orphan's trembling lips. She shaded her eyes with her hand and tried to read the name inscribed on the monument of the sacrilegious interloper. Bitter, scalding tears of indignation blinded her. She dashed them away, but they gathered and fell faster. Unbolting the gate, she entered the enclosure and stepped close to the marble.

ERECTED
IN HONOR OF
AARON HUNT:
BY HIS DEVOTED
GRANDDAUGHTER.

These gilded words were traced on the polished surface of the pure white obelisk. On each corner of the square pedestal stood beautifully carved vases from which drooped glossy tendrils of ivy.

Edna looked in amazement at the glittering shaft, which rose twenty feet in the autumn air. She rubbed her eyes and re-read the golden inscription, and looked at the sanded walks, and the well-trimmed evergreens, which told that careful hands kept the lot in order. She sank down at the base of the beautiful monument and laid her hot cheek on the cold marble.

"Oh, Grandpa, Grandpa! He is not altogether wicked and callous as we once thought him, or he could never have done this! Forgive your poor little Pearl, if she cannot help loving one who, for her sake, honors your dear name and memory! Oh, Grandpa, if I had never gone away from here! If I could have died before I saw him again! Before this great pain fell upon my heart!"

She knew now where St. Elmo Murray went that night, after he had watched her from behind the sarcophagus and the mummies; knew that only his hand could have erected this noble pillar of record. Most fully did she appreciate the delicate feeling which made him so proudly reticent on this subject. He wished no element of gratitude in the love he had endeavored to win, and scorned to take advantage of her devoted affection for her grandfather by touching her heart with a knowledge of the tribute paid to his memory.

Until this moment she had sternly refused to permit herself to believe all his protestations of love. But today she felt that all he had avowed was true; that his proud, bitter heart was indeed entirely hers. This assurance filled her own heart with a measureless joy, a rapture that made her eyes sparkle through their tears and brought a momentary glow to her cheeks.

Hour after hour passed; she took no note of time, and sat there pondering her past life, thinking how the dusty heart deep under the marble would have throbbed with fond pride, if it could only have known what the world said of her writings. That she should prove competent to teach the neighbors' children had been Aaron Hunt's loftiest ambition for his darling; and now she was deemed worthy to speak through the columns of a periodical that few women were considered able to fill.

She wondered if he were not watching her struggles and her triumph. Why he was not allowed, in token of tender sympathy, to drop one palm-leaf on her head from the fadeless branch he waved in heaven?

"Oh! how far,
How far and safe, God, dost Thou keep thy saints
When once gone from us! We may call against
The lighted windows of Thy fair June heaven
Where all the souls are happy; and not one,
Not even my father, look from work or play,
To ask, 'Who is it that cries after us,
Below there, in the dusk?'"[80]

The shaft threw a long slanting shadow eastward as the orphan rose, and, taking from the box the fragrant exotics which she had brought from Le Bocage, arranged them in the damp soil of one of the vases, and twined their bright-hued petals among the dark green ivy leaves. One shining wreath she broke and laid away tenderly in the box, a hallowed souvenir of the sacred spot where it grew. As she stood there, looking at a garland of poppy leaves chiseled around the inscription, neither flush nor tremor told aught that passed in her mind, and her sculptured features were calm as the afternoon sun showed how pale and fixed her face had grown.

She climbed upon the broad base and pressed her lips to her grandfather's name, and there was a mournful sweetness in her voice as she said aloud, "Pray God to pardon him, Grandpa! Pray Christ to comfort and save his precious soul! Oh, Grandpa, pray the Holy Spirit to melt and sanctify his suffering heart!"

It was painful to quit the place. She lingered, and started away, and came back, and at last knelt and hid her face, and prayed long and silently.

---

[80] from *Aurora Leigh* – Elizabeth Barrett Browning

Then turning quickly, she closed the iron gate, and without trusting herself for another look, walked away. She passed the spring and the homestead ruins, and finally found herself in sight of the miller's house, which alone seemed unchanged. As she lifted the latch of the gate and entered the yard, it seemed but yesterday that she was driven away to the depot in the miller's covered cart.

> "Old faces glimmered through the doors,
> Old footsteps trod the upper floors.
> Old voices called me from without.[81]"

An ancient apple-tree that she well remembered stood near the house, and the spreading branches were bent almost to the earth with the weight of red-streaked apples, round and ripe. The shaggy, black dog, that so often frolicked with Grip in the days gone by, now lay on the step, blinking at the sun and the flies that now and then buzzed over the golden balsam, whose crimson seeds glowed in the evening sunshine.

Over the rocky well rose a rough arbor, where a scuppernong vine clambered and hung its rich, luscious brown clusters. Here, with a pipe between her lips, and at her feet a basket full of red pepper-pods, which she was busily engaged in stringing, sat an elderly woman. She was clad in blue and yellow plaid homespun and wore a white apron and a snowy muslin cap, whose crimped ruffles pressed the grizzled hair combed so smoothly over her temples. Presently she laid her pipe down on the top of the mossy well, where the dripping bucket sat, and lifted the scarlet wreath of peppers, eyed it satisfactorily, and, as she resumed her work, began to hum "Auld Lang Syne."

> "Should auld acquaintance be forgot,
> And never brought to mind?
> Should auld acquaintance be forgot,
> And days o' lang syne?"[82]

---

[81] *Mariana* – Lord Alfred Tennyson
[82] "Auld Lang Syne" – Robert Burns

Her countenance was so peaceful that, as Edna stood watching it, a warm, loving light came into her own eyes, and she put out both hands unconsciously, and stepped into the little arbor.

Her shadow fell upon the matronly face, and the woman rose and curtsied.

"Good evening, miss. Will you be seated? There is room enough for two on my bench."

Edna did not speak for a moment, but looked up in the brown, wrinkled face, and then, pushing back her bonnet and veil, she said eagerly, "Mrs. Wood, don't you know me?"

The miller's wife looked curiously at her visitor, glanced at her dress, and shook her head.

"No, miss; if ever I set my eyes on you before, it's more than I remember, and Dorothy Wood has a powerful memory, they say, and seldom forgets faces."

"Do you remember Aaron Hunt, and his daughter Hester?"

"To be sure I do; but you ain't neither the one nor the other, I take it. Stop – let me see. Aha! Tabitha, Willis, you children, run here – quick! But, no – it can't be. You can't be Edna Earl?"

She shaded her eyes from the glare of the sun and stooped forward and looked searchingly at the stranger. Then the coral wreath fell from her fingers, she stretched out her arms, and the large mouth trembled and twitched.

"Are you – can you be – little Edna? Aaron Hunt's grandchild?"

"I am the poor little Edna you took such tender care of in her great affliction – "

"Samson and the Philistines! Little Edna – so you are! What was I thinking about, that I didn't know you right away? God bless your pretty little face!"

She caught Edna in her strong arms and kissed her, and cried and laughed.

A young girl, apparently about Edna's age, and a tall, lank young man, with yellow hair full of meal dust, came out of the house and looked on in dull wonder.

"Why, children, don't you know little Edna that lived at Aaron Hunt's – his granddaughter? This is my Tabitha and my son Willis, that tends the mill and takes care of us, now my poor Peter

– God rest his soul – is dead and buried these three years. Bring some seats, Willis. Sit down here by me, Edna, and take off your bonnet, child, and let me see you. Umph! Umph! Who'd have thought it? What a powerful handsome woman you have made, to be sure, to be sure! Well, well! The very saints up in glory can't begin to tell what children will turn out. Lean your face this way. Why, you ain't no more like that little bare-footed, tangle-haired, rosy-faced Edna that used to run around these woods in striped homespun, hunting the cows, than I, Dorothy Elmira Wood, am like the Queen of Sheba when she went up visiting to Jerusalem to call on Solomon. How wonderful pretty you are! And how soft your hands are! Now I look at you good I see you are like your mother, Hester Earl; and she was the loveliest, mild little pink in the county. You are taller than your mother, and prouder-looking; but you have got her shining black eyes; and your mouth is sweet and sorrowful, and patient as hers always was, after your father fell off that frosty roof and broke his neck. Little Edna came back a fine, handsome woman, looking like a queen! But, honey, you don't seem healthy, like my Tabitha. See what a bright red she has in her face. You are too pale; you look as if you had just been bled. Ain't you well, child?"

Mrs. Wood felt the girl's arms and shoulders, and found them thinner than her standard of health demanded.

"I am very well, thank you, but tired from my journey, and from walking all about the old place."

"And like enough you've cried a deal. Your eyes are heavy. You know, honey, the old house burnt down one blustery night in March, and so we sold the place; for when my old man died we were hard-pressed, we were, and a man by the name of Simmons, he bought it and planted it in corn. Edna, have you been to your Grandpa's grave?"

"Yes, ma'am, I was there a long time today."

"Oh, ain't it beautiful? It would be a real comfort to die, if folks knew such lovely gravestones would cover 'em. I think your Grandpa's grave is the prettiest place I ever saw, and I wonder, sometimes, what Aaron Hunt would say if he could rise out of his coffin and see what is over him. Poor thing! You haven't got over it yet, I see. I thought we should have buried you, too, when he died; for never did I see a child grieve so."

"Mrs. Wood, who keeps the walks so clean, and the evergreens so nicely cut?"

"My Willis, to be sure. The gentleman that came here and fixed everything last December, paid Willis one hundred dollars to attend to it, and keep the weeds down. He said he might come back unexpectedly almost any time, and that he did not want to see so much as a blade of grass in the walks; so you see Willis goes there every Saturday and straightens up things. What is his name, and who is he anyhow? He only told us he was a friend of yours, and that his mother had adopted you."

"What sort of a looking person was he, Mrs. Wood?"

"Oh, child, if he is so good to you, I ought not to say; but he was a powerful, grim-looking man, with fierce eyes and a thick mustache, and hair almost pepper-and-salt; and bless your soul, honey, his shoulders were as broad as a barn-door. While he talked, I didn't like his countenance; it was dark like a pirate's, or one of those prowling cattle-thieves over in the coves. He asked a power of questions about you and your Grandpa, and when I said you had no kin on earth that I ever heard of, he laughed – that is, he showed his teeth – and said, 'So much the better! So much the better!' What is his name?"

"Mr. Murray, and he has been very kind to me."

"But, Edna, I thought you went to the factory to work? Do tell me how you fell into the hands of such rich people?"

Edna briefly acquainted her with what had occurred during her long absence and informed her of her plans for the future. While she listened, Mrs. Wood lighted her pipe. Resting her elbow on her knee, she dropped her face on her hands, and watched her visitor's countenance.

Finally she nodded to her daughter, saying, "Do you hear that, Bitha? She can write for the papers and get paid for it. And she is smart enough to teach! Well, well! That makes me say what I do say, and I stick to it, where there's a will there's a way! Some children can't be kicked and kept down; spite of all the world they will manage to scuffle up somehow; and then again, some can't be cuffed and coaxed and dragged up by the ears. Here's Edna, that always had a hankering after books, and she has made something of herself; and here's my girl, that I wanted to get book-learning, and I slaved and I saved to send her to school, and sure enough she has got no more use for reading, and knows as little as her poor mother, who never had a chance to learn. It is no earthly use to fly in the face of blood and nature. 'What is bred in the bone, won't come out in the flesh.'"

She put her brawny brown hand on Edna's forehead, and smoothed the bands of hair, and sighed heavily.

"Mrs. Wood, I should like to see Brindle once more."

"Lord bless your soul, honey! She has been dead these three years! Why, you forget cows don't hang on as long as Methuselah, and Brindle was no yearling when we took her. She mired down in the swamp, back of the millpond, and before we could find her she was dead. But her calf is as pretty a young thing as ever you saw; speckled all over, most as thick as a guinea, and the children call her 'Speckle.' Willis, step out and see if the heifer is in sight. Edna, ain't you going to stay with me tonight?"

"Thank you, Mrs. Wood, I should like very much to do so, but have not time, and must get back to Chattanooga before the train leaves, for I am obliged to go on tonight."

"Well, anyhow, lay off your bonnet and stay and let me give you some supper, and then we will all go back with you – that is, if you ain't too proud to ride to town in our cart? We have got a new cart, but it is only a miller's cart, and maybe it won't suit your fine fashionable clothes."

"I shall be very glad to stay, and I only wish it was the same old cart that took me to the depot, more than five years ago. Please give me some water."

Mrs. Wood rolled up her sleeves, put away her pretty peppers, and talking vigorously all the time, prepared some refreshments for her guest.

A table was set under the apple tree, a snowy cotton cloth spread over it, and yellow butter, tempting as Goshen's, and a loaf of fresh bread, honey amber-hued, buttermilk, cider, and stewed pears, and a dish of ripe red apples crowned the board.

The air was laden with the fragrance it stole in crossing a hayfield beyond the road. The bees darted in and out of their

300

hives, and a peacock spread his iridescent feathers to catch the level yellow rays of the setting sun. From the distant millpond came the gabble of geese, as the noisy fleet breasted the ripples.

Speckle, who had been driven to the gate for Edna's inspection, stood close to the fence, thrusting her pearly horns through the cracks and watching the party at the table with her large, liquid eyes; and afar off Lookout rose solemn and somber.

"Edna, you eat nothing. What ails you, child? They say too much brainwork is not healthy, and I reckon you study too hard. Better stay here with me, honey, and run around the woods and get some red in your face, and churn and spin and drink buttermilk, and get plump, and go chestnutting with my children. Goodness knows they are strong enough and hearty enough, and too much study will never make scholars of them: for they won't work their brains, even to learn the multiplication table. See here, Edna, if you will stay a while with me, I will give Speckle to you."

"Thank you, dear Mrs. Wood, I wish I could; but the lady who engaged me to teach her children wrote that I was very much needed. I must hurry on. Speckle is a perfect little beauty, but I would not be so selfish as to take her away from you."

Clouds began to gather in the southwest. As the covered cart was brought to the gate, a distant mutter of thunder told that a storm was brewing.

Mrs. Wood and her two children accompanied the orphan. As they drove through the woods, myriads of fireflies starred the gloom. It was dark when they reached the station, and Willis brought the trunks from the hotel, and found seats for the party in the cars, which were rapidly filling with passengers. Presently the down-train from Knoxville came thundering in, and the usual rush and bustle ensued.

Mrs. Wood gave the orphan a hearty kiss and warm embrace, and bidding her "Be sure to write soon, and say how you are getting along!" the kind-hearted woman left the cars, wiping her eyes with the corner of her apron.

At last the locomotive signaled that all was ready. As the train moved on, Edna caught a glimpse of a form standing under a lamp, leaning with folded arms against the post – a form strangely like Mr. Murray's. She leaned out and watched it till the cars swept round a curve, and lamp and figure and village vanished. How could he possibly be in Chattanooga? With a long, heavily-drawn sigh, she leaned against the window-frame and looked at the dark mountain looming behind her. After a time, when the storm drew nearer, she saw it only now and then, as

"A vivid, vindictive, and serpentine flash
Gored the darkness, and shore it across with a gash."[83]

---

[83] from *Lucile* – Robert Bulwer-Lytton, Earl of Lytton (pseudonymously known as Owen Meredith)

CHAPTER XXV
IN GOTHAM

In one of those palatial brown-stone houses on Fifth Avenue, which make the name of the street a synonym for almost royal luxury and magnificence, sat Mrs. Andrews's "new governess" a week after her arrival in New York.

Edna's reception, though cold and formal, had been quite courteous; and a few days sufficed to give the stranger an accurate insight into the characters and customs of the family with whom she was now domesticated.

Some palatial brownstones on Fifth Ave. belonging to Vanderbilts

Though good-natured and charitable, Mrs. Andrews was devoted to society, and gave to the demands of fashion much of the time which she should have been spending with her children, and making her hearth-stone rival the attractions of the club, where Mr. Andrews generally spent his leisure hours. She was much younger than her husband, was handsome, merry, and ambitious, and the polished hauteur of her bearing often reminded Edna of Mrs. Murray; while Mr. Andrews seemed immersed in business during the day and was rarely at home except at his meals.

Felix, the oldest of the two children, was a peevish, spoiled, exacting boy of twelve years of age, endowed with a remarkably active intellect, but dwarfed in body and lame due to a deformed foot. His sister Hattie was only eight years old, a bright, pretty, affectionate girl, whom Felix tyrannized unmercifully, and whom from earliest memory had been accustomed to yield both her rights and privileges to him.

The room occupied by Edna, now the governess, was small but beautifully furnished. As it was situated in the fourth story, her windows commanded a view of the trees in a neighboring park and the waving outline of Long Island.

On the day of Edna's arrival, Mrs. Andrews entered into a minute analysis of the characters of the children, indicated the course which she wished pursued toward them. Then impressing upon Edna the grave responsibility of her position, the mother gave up her children to the stranger's guardianship and whisked away to a salon, seeming to consider her maternal duties fully discharged.

Edna soon ascertained that her predecessors had found the path intolerably thorny due to Felix's uncontrollable fits of sullenness and passion. Tutors and governesses had quickly alternated. After Felix finally declared he would not tolerate any more tutors, his mother resolved to humor his caprice in the choice of a teacher.

Fortunately the boy was exceedingly fond of his books, and as the physicians forbade the constant use of his eyes, Edna was called on to read aloud at least one half of the day. From eight o'clock in the morning till eight at night, the whole care of these children devolved on Edna. She ate, talked, drove with them, accompanied them wherever their inclination led, and had not one quiet moment from breakfast until her pupils went to sleep. Sometimes her twelve-hour shift lasted longer, because Felix was often restless and wakeful, and on such occasions he demanded that his governess should read him to sleep.

Notwithstanding the boy's imperious nature, he possessed some redeeming traits, and Edna soon became much attached to him; while his affection for his new governess astonished and delighted his mother.

For a week after Edna's arrival, rainy weather prevented the customary daily drive which contributed largely to the happiness of the young man; but one afternoon as the three sat in the schoolroom, Felix threw his Latin grammar against the wall.

"I want to see the swans in Central Park, and I mean to go, even if it does rain! Hattie, ring for Patrick to bring the coupe round to the door. Miss Earl, don't you want to go?"

"Yes, for there is no longer any danger of rain, the sun is shining beautifully. Besides, I hope you will be more amiable when you get into the open air."

She gave him his hat and crutches, took his gray shawl on her arm, and they went down to the neat carriage drawn by a handsome chestnut horse, which was set apart for the use of the children.

As they entered the park, Edna noticed that the boy's eyes brightened, and that he looked eagerly at every passing face.

"Now, Hattie, you must watch on your side, and I will keep a good lookout on mine. I wonder if she will come this evening?"

"For whom are you both looking?" asked the teacher.

"Oh, for little Lila, Bro' Felix's sweetheart!" laughed Hattie, glancing at him with a mischievous twinkle in her bright eyes.

"No such thing! Never had a sweetheart in my life! Don't be silly, Hattie. Mind your window, or I guess we shan't see her."

"Well, anyhow. I heard Uncle Gray tell Mamma that he kissed his sweetheart's hand at the party, and I saw Bro' Felix kiss Lila's last week."

"I didn't, Miss Earl!" cried Felix, reddening as he spoke.

"Oh, he did, Miss Earl. Stop pinching me, Bro' Felix. My arm is all black and blue, now. There she is! Look, here on my side! Here is, Red Ridinghood!"

Edna saw a little ebony girl clad in scarlet, and led by a grave, middle-aged nurse, who was walking leisurely toward one of the lakes.

Felix put his head out of the window and called to the woman.

"Hannah, are you going to feed the swans?"

"Good evening. Yes, we are going there now."

"Well, we will meet you there."

"What is the child's name?" asked Edna.

"Lila Manning, and she is deaf and dumb. We talk to her on our fingers."

They left the carriage and approached the groups of children gathered on the edge of the water. At sight of Felix, the little girl in scarlet sprang to meet him, moving her slender dark fingers rapidly as she conversed with him. She was an exceedingly lovely but fragile child, apparently about Hattie's age. As Edna watched the changing expression of her delicate features, she turned to the nurse and asked, "Is she an orphan?"

"Yes, miss; but she will never find it out as long as her uncle lives. He treats her as if she is his own daughter."

"What is his name, and where does he live?"

"Mr. Douglass G. Manning. He boards at No. – Twenty-third street; but he spends most of his time at the office. No matter what time of night he comes home, he never goes to his own room till he has looked at Lila and kissed her good night. Master Felix, please don't untie her hat, the wind will blow her hair all out of curl."

For some time, the children were much amused in watching the swans, and when they expressed themselves willing to resume their drive, an arrangement was made with Hannah to meet at the same place the ensuing day. They returned to the carriage, and Felix said, "Don't you think Lila is a little beauty?"

"Yes, I quite agree with you. Do you know her uncle?"

"No, and don't want to know him; he is too cross and sour. I have seen him walking sometimes with Lila, and mamma has him at her parties and dinners; but Hattie and I never see the company unless we peep, and, above all things, I hate peeping! It is ungenteel and vulgar; only poor people peep."

"Oh, indeed?" Edna said, much amused.

306

"Mr. Manning is an old bachelor, and very crabbed, so Uncle Grey says. He is the editor of the *Iconoclast* Magazine, that mamma declares she can't live without. Look, look, Hattie! There goes mamma this minute. Stop, Patrick! Uncle Grey! Uncle Grey! Hold up, won't you, and let me see the new horses!"

An elegant phaeton, drawn by a pair of superb black horses, drew up close to the coupe. Mrs. Andrews and her only brother, Mr. Grey Chilton, leaned forward and spoke to the children; while Mr. Chilton, who was driving, teased Hattie by touching her head and shoulders with his whip.

"Uncle Grey, I think the bays are the handsomest."

"Which proves you utterly incapable of judging horseflesh; for these are the finest horses in the city. I presume this is Miss Earl, though nobody seems polite enough to introduce us."

Their uncle raised his hat slightly, bowed, and drove on.

"Is this the first time you have met my uncle?" asked Felix.

"Yes. Does he live in the city?"

"Why, he lives with us! Haven't you seen him about the house? You must have heard him romping around with Hattie; for they make noise enough to call in the police. I think my uncle Grey is the handsomest man I ever saw, except Edwin Booth, when he plays 'Hamlet.' What do you say?"

"As I had barely a glimpse of your uncle, I formed no opinion. Felix, button your coat and draw your shawl over your shoulders; it is getting cold."

When they reached home the children begged for some music, and placing her hat on a chair, Edna sat down before the piano, and played and sang, while Felix stood leaning on his crutches, gazing earnestly into the face of his teacher.

The song was Longfellow's "Rainy Day." When she concluded it, he laid his thin hand on hers and said, "Sing the last verse again. I feel as if I should always be a good boy, if you would only sing that for me every day. 'Into each life some rain must fall?' Yes, lameness fell into mine."

While she complied with his request, Edna watched his sallow face, and saw tears gather in the large, sad eyes. She felt that henceforth the boy's evil spirit could be exorcised.

"Miss Earl, we never had a governess at all like you. They were old, and cross, and ugly, and didn't love to play chess, and could not sing, and I hated them. But I do like you, and I will try to be good."

He rested his head against her arm, and she turned and kissed his broad forehead.

"Halloo, Felix! Flirting with your governess? This is a new phase of school life."

Mr. Chilton came up to the piano, and curiously scanned Edna's face. "You ought to feel quite honored, Miss Earl, though upon my word I am sorry for you. The excessive amiability of my nephew has driven not less than six of your predecessors in confusion from the field, leaving him victorious."

Taking her hat and veil, Edna rose and moved toward the door. "I am disposed to believe that he has been quite as much sinned against as sinning. Come, children, it is time for your tea."

From that hour her influence over the boy strengthened so rapidly that before she had been a month in the house, he yielded implicit obedience to her wishes, and could not bear for her to leave him, even for a moment. When more than usually fretful, and inclined to tyrannize over Hattie, or speak disrespectfully to his mother, a warning glance or word from Edna, or the soft touch of her hand, would suffice to restrain the threatened outbreak.

Her days were passed in teaching, reading aloud, and talking to the children. When released from her duties, Edna went invariably to her desk, devoting more than half the night to the completion of her manuscript.

Because Edna took her meals with her pupils, she rarely saw the other members of the household. Though Mr. Chilton now and then sauntered into the schoolroom and frolicked with Hattie, interrupting her lessons, his visits were coldly received by the teacher; who met his attempts at conversation with very discouraging monosyllabic replies.

His insouciant manner led her to suspect that the good-looking lounger was as vain and heartless as he was frivolous, and she felt no inclination to listen to his chatter; consequently, when he thrust himself into her presence, she either picked up a book or left him to be entertained by the children.

One evening in November, Edna sat in her own room preparing to write, and pondering the probable fate of a sketch which she had finished and dispatched two days before to the office of the magazine.

The principal aim of the tale was to portray the horrors and sin of dueling, and she had written it with great care. She was aware of the powerful current of popular opinion that she was bravely striving to stem, and fully conscious that it would subject her to severe aversion from those who defended the custom. She could not shake off her fear that her article might be rejected.

The doorbell rang, and soon after a servant brought her a card: "Mr. D.G. Manning. To see Miss Earl."

Flattered and frightened by a visit from one whose opinions she valued so highly, Edna smoothed her hair. With trembling fingers she changed her collar and cuffs and went downstairs, feeling as if all the blood in her body were beating a tattoo on the drum of her ears.

As she entered the library, into which he had been shown (Mrs. Andrews having guests in the parlor), Edna had an opportunity of looking unobserved at this critical ogre, of whom she stood in such profound awe.

Douglass Manning was forty years old, tall, and well built; wore slender, steel-rimmed spectacles which somewhat softened the light of his keen, cold, black eyes; and carried his slightly bald head with the haughty air of one who habitually hurled his gauntlet in the teeth of public opinion.

He stood looking up at a pair of bronze griffins that crouched on the top of the rosewood bookcase. The gaslight falling full on his dark face showed his stern, massive features, which reminded Edna of those Egyptian Androsphinx – vast, serene, changeless.

There were no furrows on his dark cheek or brow. No beard veiled the lines and angles about the mouth, but she marked the repose of his countenance, so indicative of conscious power and well-regulated strength. Edna's mind traveled swiftly back among the "Stones of Venice," repeating the description of the hawthorn on Bourges Cathedral: "A perfect Niobe of May." Had this man been petrified in his youth before the steady stylus of time left on his features that subtle tracery which passing years engrave on human faces? The motto of his magazine, *Veritas sine clementia*[84], ruled his life, and, putting aside the lenses of passion and prejudice, he coolly, quietly, relentlessly judged men and women and their works; looking neither to right nor left; laboring steadily as a thoroughly well-balanced, intellectual automaton.

Edna's voice trembled, and she put out her hand. "Good evening, Mr. Manning. I am very glad to meet you. I fear my letters have very inadequately expressed my gratitude for your kindness."

He turned, bowed, offered her a chair. As they seated themselves, he examined her face as he would have searched the title-page of some new book for an insight into its contents. "When did you reach New York, Miss Earl?"

"Six weeks ago."

"I was not aware that you were in the city, until I received your note two days since. How long do you intend to remain?"

"Probably the rest of my life, if I find it possible to support myself comfortably."

"Is Mrs. Andrews an old friend?"

"No, sir. She was a stranger to me when I entered her house as governess for her children."

"Miss Earl, you are much younger than I had supposed. Your writings led me to imagine that you were at least thirty, whereas I find you almost a child. Will your duties as governess conflict with your literary labors?"

"No, sir. I shall continue to write."

"You appear to have acted upon my suggestion, to abandon the idea of a book, and confine your attention to short sketches."

"No, sir. I adhere to my original purpose and am at work upon the manuscript which you advised me to destroy."

He fitted his glasses more firmly on his wide nose, and she saw the gleam of his white teeth as a half-smile moved his lips.

"Miss Earl, my desk is very near a window, and as I was writing late last night, I noticed several large moths beating against the glass which fortunately barred their approach to the flame of the gas inside. Perhaps inexperience states that it was

---

[84] "Truth without mercy," -- though I laughed when I put the phrase into Google Translate and got "Truth without dementia"!

cruel of fate to shut them out; but which heals soonest, disappointed curiosity or singed wings?"

"Mr. Manning, why do you apprehend more danger from writing a book than from the preparation of magazine articles?"

"Simply because the peril is inherent in the nature of the book you contemplate. Unless I completely misunderstand your views, you indulge in the rather extraordinary belief that all works of fiction should be eminently didactic, and inculcate not only sound morality but scientific theories. Herein, permit me to say, you entirely misapprehend the spirit of the age. People read novels merely to be amused, not educated. They will not tolerate technicalities and abstract speculation in lieu of exciting plots and melodramatic denouements. Persons who desire to learn something of astronomy, geology, chemistry, or philology, never think of finding what they require in the pages of a novel, but apply at once to the textbooks of the respective sciences. They would as soon hunt for a lover's sentimental dialogue in Newton's *Principia*, or spicy small-talk in Kant's *Critique*."

"But, sir, how many habitual novel readers do you suppose will educate themselves thoroughly from the textbooks to which you refer?"

"A modicum, I grant you. Yet it is equally true that those who merely read to be amused will not digest the scientific dishes you set before them. On the contrary, far from appreciating your charitable efforts to broaden their range of vision, they will either sneer at the author's pedantry, or skip over every thoughtful passage and rush on to the next page to discover whether the heroine, Miss Imogene Arethusa Penelope Brown, wore blue or pink tarlatan to her first ball, or whether on the day of her elopement the indignant papa succeeded in preventing the consummation of her felicity with Mr. Belshazzar Algernon Nebuchadnezzar Smith. I neither magnify nor dwarf; I merely state a simple fact."

"But, Mr. Manning, do you not regard the writers of each age as the custodians of its tastes as well as its morals?"

"Certainly not. They simply reflect and do not mold public taste. Shakespeare, Hogarth, Rabelais, portrayed men and things as they found them; not as they might, could, would, or should have been. Was Sir Peter Lely responsible for the style of dress worn by court beauties in the reign of Charles II? He merely painted what passed before him." Mr. Manning placed his hands together and leaned forward slightly. "Miss Earl, the objection I urge against the novel you are preparing does not apply to magazine essays, where an author may concentrate all the knowledge he can obtain and share it unchallenged. Review writers now serve the public in much the same capacity that cupbearers did royalty in ancient days; and they are expected to taste strong liquors as well as sweet cordials and sour light wines. At any rate, your readers expect you to help them kill time, not improve it."

"Sir, is it not nobler to struggle against than to float ignominiously with the tide of degenerate opinion?"

"That depends altogether on the earnestness of your desire for martyrdom by drowning. I have seen stronger swimmers than you go down, after desperate efforts to keep their heads above water. Literally," he added, very grave.

Edna folded her hands in her lap, and looked steadily into the calm, dark eyes of the editor. After a moment she shook her head. "At all events I will risk it. I would rather sink in the effort than live without attempting it."

"When you require ointment for singed wings, I shall have no sympathy with which to anoint them; for, like most of your sex, I see you mistake blind obstinacy for rational, heroic firmness. The next number of the magazine will contain the contribution you sent me two days since. While I do not accept all your views, I think it by far the best thing I have yet seen from your pen. It will, of course, provoke controversy, but for that result, I presume you are prepared. Miss Earl, you are a stranger in New York, and if I can serve you in any way, I shall be glad to do so."

Edna smoothed her cuffs, noting with vexation that her fingers were still trembling. "Thank you, Mr. Manning. I need some books which I am not able to purchase and cannot find in this house. If you can spare them temporarily from your library, you will confer a great favor on me."

"Certainly. Have you a list of those which you require?"

"No, sir, but – "

"Here is a pencil and piece of paper. Write down the titles, and I will have them sent to you in the morning."

She turned to the table to prepare the list. All the while Mr. Manning's keen eyes scanned her countenance. A half-smile once more stirred his grave lips when she gave him the paper, over which he glanced indifferently.

"Miss Earl, I fear you will regret your determination to make literature a profession; for your letters informed me that you are poor; and doubtless you remember the witticism concerning the 'republic of letters which contained not a sovereign[85].' Your friend, Mr. Murray, appreciated the obstacles you are destined to encounter, and I am afraid you will not find life in New York as agreeable as it was under his roof."

At Mr. Murray's name, Edna blinked. "When did you hear from him?"

"I received a letter this morning."

Edna hoped that the heat rising in her face was not noticeable. "And you called to see me because he requested you to do so?"

"I had determined to come before his letter arrived."

An incredulous smile flitted across her face. She wanted to ask Manning what Mr. Murray had written, to know everything about their relationship, but she reluctantly held her peace.

After a moment's pause, he continued. "I do not wish to discourage you; on the contrary, I sincerely desire to aid you, but Mill has analyzed the subject very ably in his *Political Economy,* and declares that 'on any rational calculation of chances in the existing competition, no writer can hope to gain a living by books; and to do so by magazines and reviews becomes daily more difficult.'"

"Yes, sir, that passage is not encouraging; but I will try nevertheless."

"I think you can command better wages for your work in New York than anywhere else on this continent. You have begun well. Permit me to say to you be careful, do not write too rapidly, and do not despise adverse criticism. If agreeable to you, I will call early next week and accompany you to the public libraries, which contain much that may interest you. I will send you a note as soon

---

[85] qtd. by Thomas Hood

as I can command the requisite leisure. Should you need my services, I hope you will not hesitate to claim them. Good-evening, Miss Earl."

He bowed himself out of the library. Edna went back to her own room, thinking of the brief interview, and confessing her disappointment in the conversation of this most dreaded of critics.

"He is polished as an icicle, and quite as cold. He may be very astute and profound, but certainly he is not half so brilliant as - "

Edna did not complete the parallel, but compressed her lips, took up her pen, and began to write.

On the following morning Mrs. Andrews came into the schoolroom. After kissing her children, she turned blandly to the governess.

"Miss Earl, I believe Mr. Manning called upon you last evening. Where did you know him?"

"I never saw him until yesterday, but we have corresponded for some time."

"Indeed! You are quite honored. He is considered very fastidious."

"He is certainly hypercritical, yet I have found him kind and gentlemanly, even courteous. Our correspondence is entirely attributable to the fact that I write for his magazine."

Mrs. Andrews dropped her ivory crochet-needle and sat, for a moment, the picture of wild-eyed amazement. "Is it possible? I had no idea you were an author. Why did you not tell me before? What have you written?"

Edna mentioned the titles of her published articles, and the lady of the house exclaimed, "Oh, that 'Vigil of Grütli' is one of the most beautiful things I ever read, and I have often teased Mr. Manning to tell me who wrote it. That apostrophe to the Swiss Confederates is so mournfully grand that it brings tears to my eyes. Why, Miss Earl, you will be famous someday. If I had your genius, I should never think of plodding through life as a governess."

"But, my dear madam, I must make my bread, and am compelled to teach while I write."

"I do not see what time you have for writing. I notice you never leave the children till they are asleep; and you must sleep enough to keep yourself alive. Are you writing anything at present?"

"I finished an article several days ago which will be published in the next number of the magazine. Of course, I have no leisure during the day, but I work till late at night."

"Miss Earl, if you have no objection to acquainting me with your history, I should like very much to know something of your early life and education."

While Edna gave a brief account of her childhood, Felix nestled his hand into hers, and laid his head on her knee, listening eagerly to every word.

When she concluded, Mrs. Andrews mused a moment, and then said, "Henceforth, Miss Earl, you will occupy a different position in my house. I shall take pleasure in introducing you to such of my friends as will appreciate your talent. I hope you will not confine yourself exclusively to my children but come down sometimes in the evening and sit with me. Moreover, you should dine with us, instead of with these nursery folks, who are not quite capable of appreciating you – "

"How do you know that, mamma?" Felix cried. "I can tell you one thing – I appreciated her before I found out that she was likely to be famous! We 'nursery folk' judge for ourselves, we don't wait to find out what other people think, and I shan't give up Miss Earl. She is my governess, and I wish you would just let her alone!" he cried scornfully.

His mother bit her lip and laughed constrainedly. "Really, Felix! Who gave you a bill of sale to Miss Earl? She should consider herself exceedingly fortunate, as she is the first of all your teachers with whom you have not quarreled most shamefully, even fought and scratched."

"And because she is sweet and good, and I love her, you must interfere and take her off to entertain your company. She came here to take care of Hattie and me, not to go downstairs to see visitors. She can't go, mamma! I want her myself. You have all the world to talk to, and I have only her. Don't meddle, mamma."

"You are very selfish and ill-tempered, my poor little boy, and I am heartily ashamed of you."

"If I am, it is because – "

"Hush, Felix!" Edna laid her fingers on Felix's pale, curling lips.

Luckily, at this instant, Mrs. Andrews was summoned from the room, much to Edna's relief.

Scarcely waiting till the door closed after her, the boy exclaimed passionately, "Felix! Don't call me Felix! That means happy, lucky, and she had no right to give me such a name. I am Infelix! Nobody loves me! Nobody cares for me, except to pity me, and I would rather be strangled than pitied. I wish I was dead and at rest in Greenwood! I wish somebody would knock my brains out with my crutch! Even my mother is ashamed of my deformity! She ought to have treated me as the Spartans did their dwarfs! She ought to have thrown me into the East River before I was a day old! I wish I was dead! Oh, I do! I do!"

"Felix, it distresses me very much to – "

"I tell you I won't be called Felix. Whenever I hear the name it makes me feel as I did one day when my crutches slipped on the ice, and I fell on the pavement before the door, and some newsboys laughed at me. Infelix Andrews! I want that written on my tombstone when I am buried."

He trembled from head to foot, and angry tears dimmed his large, flashing eyes, while Hattie sat with her elbows resting on her knees, and her chin in her hands, looking sorrowfully at her brother.

Edna put her arm around the boy's shoulder, saying tenderly, "Your mother did not mean that she was ashamed of you, but only grieved and mortified by his ungovernable temper, which made him disrespectful to her. I know that she is very proud of your fine intellect, and your ambition to become a thorough scholar, and – "

"Oh, yes, and of my handsome body! And my pretty feet!"

"My dear little boy, it is sinful for you to speak in that way, and God will punish you if you do not struggle against such feelings."

"I don't see how I can be punished any more than I have been already. To be a lame dwarf is the worst that can happen."

"Suppose you were poor and friendless – an orphan with no one to care for you? Suppose you had no dear, good little sister like Hattie to love you? Now, Felix, I know that the very fact that you are not as strong and well-grown as most boys of your age, only makes your mother and all of us love you more tenderly; and it is very ungrateful in you to talk so bitterly when we are trying to make you happy and good and useful. Look at little Lila, shut up in silence, unable to speak, or to hear a bird sing or a baby laugh, and yet see how merry and good-natured she is. How much more afflicted she is than you are. Suppose she was always complaining, looking miserable and sour, and out of humor. Do you think you would love her half as well as you do now?"

He made no reply, but his thin hands covered his face.

Hattie came close to him, sat down on the carpet, and put her head, thickly crowned with yellow curls, on his knee. Her Uncle Grey had given her a pretty ring the day before, and now she softly took it from her own finger and slipped it on her brother's.

"Felix, you and Hattie were so delighted with that little poem which I read to you from the *Journal* of Eugénie de Guérin, that I have tried to set it to music for you. The tune does not suit it exactly, but we can use it until I find a better one."

She went to the piano and sang that pretty nursery ballad, "Joujou, the Angel of the Playthings."

Hattie clapped her hands with delight, and Felix partly forgot his woes and grievances.

"Now, I want you both to learn to sing it, and I will teach Hattie the accompaniment. On Felix's birthday, which is not very distant, you can surprise your father and mother by singing it for them. Hattie, it is eleven o'clock, and time for you to practice your music-lesson."

The little girl climbed upon the piano-stool and began to count aloud. After a while Edna bent down and put her hand on Felix's shoulder.

"You grieved your mother this morning and spoke very disrespectfully to her. I know you regret it, and you ought to tell her so and ask her to forgive you. You would feel happier all day if you would only acknowledge your fault. I hear your mother in her own room; will you not go and kiss her?"

He averted his head and muttered, "I don't want to kiss her."

"But you ought to be a dutiful son, and you are not; so your mother has cause to be displeased with you. If you should ever be so unfortunate as to lose her, and stand as I do, motherless, in the world, you will regret the pain you gave her this morning. Felix, sometimes I think it requires more nobility of soul to ask pardon for our faults than to resist the temptation to commit them."

She turned away and busied herself in correcting his Latin exercise, and for some time the boy sat sullen and silent.

At length he sighed heavily, and taking his crutches, came up to the table where she sat. "Suppose you tell my mother I am sorry I was disrespectful."

She laid down her pen. "Felix, are you really sorry?"

"Yes."

"Well, then go and tell her so, and she will love you a thousand times more than ever before. The confession should come from your own lips."

He stood irresolute and sighed again. "I will go if you will go with me."

She rose and they went to Mrs. Andrew's room. The mother was superbly dressed in visiting costume, and was tying on her bonnet when they entered.

"Mrs. Andrews, your son wishes to say something which I think you will be glad to hear."

"Indeed! Well, Felix, what is it?"

"Mamma - I believe - I know I was very cross - and disrespectful to you - and oh, mamma! I hope you will forgive me!"

He dropped his crutches and stretched out his arms. Mrs. Andrews threw down the diamond cluster, with which she was fastening her ribbons, and caught the boy to her bosom.

"My precious child! My darling! Of course I forgive you gladly. My dear son, if you only knew half how well I love you, you would not grieve me so often by your temper. My darling! - "

She stooped to kiss him, and she turned to look for the girlish form of the governess just in time to see Edna vanish from the room with a smile; and mother and son were alone.

CHAPTER XXVI
A NIGHT AT THE OPERA

During the first few months after her removal to New York, Edna received frequent letters from Mrs. Murray and Mr. Hammond. As winter advanced, they wrote more rarely and hurriedly. Finally, many weeks elapsed without bringing any tidings from Le Bocage. St. Elmo's name was never mentioned by either of them. While Edna's heart ached, she crushed it more ruthlessly day by day, and in retaliation imposed additional and unremitting toil upon her brain.

Mr. Manning had called twice to escort her to the libraries and art galleries. Occasionally he sent her new books, and English and French periodicals. The brooding serenity of his grave, Egyptic face, and his imperturbable calmness oppressed and embarrassed Edna, and formed a barrier to all friendly worth in their discussions. He so completely overawed her that in his august presence she was unable to do herself justice and felt that she was not gaining ground in his good opinion.

One morning in January, as she sat listening to Felix's recitations, Mrs. Andrews came into the schoolroom with an open note in one hand, and an exquisite bouquet in the other.

"Miss Earl, here is an invitation for you to accompany Mr. Manning to the opera tonight. Here, too, is a bouquet from the same considerate gentleman. As he does me the honor to request my company also, I came to confer with you before sending a reply. Of course, you will go?"

"Yes, Mrs. Andrews, if you will go with me."

Edna bent over her flowers, recognizing many favorites that she'd used to grow in the hothouse at Le Bocage. Her eyes filled with tears, and she hastily put her lips to the snowy cups of an oxalis. How often she had seen just such fragile petals nestling in the buttonhole of Mr. Murray's coat.

"I shall write and invite him to come early and take tea with us. Now, Miss Earl, pardon my candor, I should like to know what you intend to wear? You know that Mr. Manning is quite lionized here, and you will have to face a terrific battery of eyes and lorgnettes; for everybody will stretch his or her neck to find out, first, who you are, and secondly, how you are dressed. Now I think I understand rather better than you do what is *comme il faut* in these matters and I hope you will allow me to dictate on this occasion."

"Here are my keys, Mrs. Andrews; examine my wardrobe and select what you consider appropriate for tonight."

"On condition that you permit me to supply any deficiencies which I may discover? Come to my room at six o'clock, and let Victorine dress your hair. Let me see, I expect *a la Grec* will best suit your head and face."

Edna turned to her pupils and their books, but all day the flowers in the vase on the table prattled of days gone by; of purple sunsets streaming through golden-starred acacia boughs; of languid, luxurious Southern afternoons dying slowly on beds of heliotrope and jasmine, spicy geraniums and gorgeous pelargoniums; of delicious summer mornings, forever and ever past, when standing beside a quivering snowbank of Lamarque roses, she had watched Tamerlane and his gloomy rider go down the shadowy avenue of elms.

The monotonous hum of the children's voices seemed thin and strange and far, far off, jarring the sweet bouquet babble. Still as the hours passed, and the winter day waned, the flower Fugue swelled on and on through the chambers of her heart; now rising stormy and passionate, like a battle-blast, from the deep orange trumpet of a bignonia; and now whispering and pleading from the pearly white lips of hallowed oxalis.

When she sat that night in Mr. Manning's box at the Academy of Music, the editor raised his opera-glass, swept the crowded house, scanning the beaming faces wreathed with smiles, and then his grave glance came back and dwelt on Edna's countenance at his side. The cherry silk lining and puffing on her opera-cloak threw a delicate stain of color over her exquisitely molded cheeks, and a scarlet anemone burned in the braid of black hair which rested like a coronal on her polished brow. Her long lashes drooped as she looked down at the bouquet between her fingers. Listening to the Fugue which memory played on the petals, she sighed involuntarily.

"Miss Earl, is this your first night at the opera?"

Edna raised her head. "No, sir; I was here once before with Mr. Andrews and his children."

"I judge from your writings that you are particularly fond of music."

"Yes, sir; I think few persons love it better than I do."

"What style do you prefer?"

"Sacred music – oratorios rather than operas."

The orchestra began an overture of Verdi's, and Edna's eyes went back to her flowers.

Presently Mrs. Andrews said eagerly, "Look, Miss Earl! Yonder, in the box directly opposite, is the celebrated Sir Roger Percival, the English nobleman about whom all Gotham is running mad. What a commentary on Republican Americans, that we are so dazzled by the glitter of a title. However, he really is very agreeable; I have met him several times, dined with him last week at the Coltons. He has been watching us for some minutes.

Ah, there is a bow for me; and one I presume for you, Mr. Manning."

"Yes, I knew him abroad. We spent a month together at Dresden."

Edna looked into the opposite box, and saw a tall, elegantly-dressed man, with huge whiskers and a glittering opera-glass. Then, as the curtain rose on the first act of Verdi's *Ernani*, she turned to the stage, and gave her entire attention to the music.

At the close of the second act Mrs. Andrews leaned toward Edna. "Pray, who is that handsome man down yonder in the parquet, fanning himself with a libretto? I do not think his eyes have moved from this box for the last ten minutes."

She turned her fan in the direction of the person indicated. Mr. Manning answered, "He is unknown to me."

Edna's eyes wandered over the sea of heads, and she started and leaned forward, sudden joy flashing into her face, as she met the earnest, upward gaze of Gordon Leigh.

"An acquaintance of yours, Miss Earl?"

"Yes, sir, an old friend from the South."

The door of the box opened, and Sir Roger Percival came in and seated himself near Mrs. Andrews, who in her cordial welcome seemed to forget the presence of the governess.

Mr. Manning sat close to Edna. Taking a couple of letters from his pocket he laid them on her lap, saying, "These letters were directed to my care by persons who are ignorant of your name and address. If you will not consider me unpardonably curious, I should like to know the nature of their contents."

She broke the seals and read the most flattering commendations of her magazine sketches and the most cordial thanks for the pleasure derived from their perusal.

A sudden wave of crimson surged into her face. She silently put the letters into Mr. Manning's hand and watched his undemonstrative features while he read, refolded, and returned them to her.

"Miss Earl, I have received several documents of a similar character asking for your address. Do you still desire to write incognita, or do you wish your name given to your admirers?"

"That is a matter which I am willing to leave to your superior judgment."

"Pardon me, but I much prefer that you determine it for yourself."

"Then you may give my name to those who are sufficiently interested in me to write and make the inquiry."

Mr. Manning smiled slightly and lowered his voice. "Sir Roger Percival came here tonight to be introduced to you. He has expressed much curiosity to see the author of the last article which you contributed to the magazine; and I told him that you would be in my box this evening. Shall I present him now?"

Mr. Manning was rising, but Edna put her hand on his arm, and answered hurriedly, "No, no! He is engaged in conversation with Mrs. Andrews, and I believe I do not wish to be presented to him at this time. Moreover, I believe I will have a visitor myself in a moment."

"You are right. Here comes your friend; I will vacate this seat in his favor."

He rose, bowed to Gordon Leigh, and gave him the chair which he had occupied.

"Edna! How I have longed to see you once more!"

Gordon's hand seized hers, and his handsome face was eloquent with feelings which he felt no inclination to conceal.

"The sight of your countenance is an unexpected pleasure in New York. Mr. Leigh, when did you arrive?"

"This afternoon. Mr. Hammond gave me your address, and I called to see you, but was told that you were here."

"How are they all at home?"

"Do you mean at Le Bocage or the Parsonage?"

"I mean, how are all my friends?" Edna stammered.

"Mrs. Murray is very well, Miss Estelle, ditto. Mr. Hammond has been sick, but was better and able to preach before I left. I brought a letter for you from him, but unfortunately left it in the pocket of my traveling coat. Edna, you have changed very much since I saw you last."

"In what respect, Mr. Leigh?"

The crash of the orchestra filled the house, and people turned once more to the stage. Standing with his arms folded, Mr.

Manning saw the earnest look on Gordon's face as, with his arm resting on the back of Edna's chair, he talked in a low, eager tone; and a pitying smile partly curved the editor's granite mouth as he noticed the expression of pain on the girl's face, and heard her say sadly, "No, Mr. Leigh; what I told you then I repeat now. Time has made no change."

The opera ended, the curtain fell, and an enthusiastic audience called out the popular prima donna.

While bouquets were showered upon her, Mr. Manning stooped and put his hand on Edna's. "Shall I throw your tribute for you?"

She hastily caught the bouquet from his fingers. "Oh, no, thank you! I am so selfish, I cannot spare it."

"I shall call at ten o'clock tomorrow to deliver your letter," said Gordon, as he stood, hat in hand.

"I shall be glad to see you, Mr. Leigh."

He shook hands with her and with Mr. Manning, to whom she had introduced him, and left the box.

Sir Roger Percival gave his arm to Mrs. Andrews, while the editor drew Edna's cloak over her shoulders, took her hand, and led her down the steps.

As her gloved fingers rested in his, Edna's feeling of awe and restraint melted away. Looking into his face she said, "Mr. Manning, I do not think you will ever know half how much I thank you for all your kindness to an unknown authorling. I have enjoyed the music very much indeed. How is Lila tonight?"

A slight tremor crossed his lips; the petrified hawthorn was quivering into life.

"She is quite well, thank you. Pray, what do you know about her? I was not aware that I had ever mentioned her name in your presence."

"My pupil, Felix, is her most devoted knight, and I see her almost every afternoon when I go with the children to Central Park."

They reached the carriage where the Englishman stood talking to Mrs. Andrews. When Mr. Manning had handed Edna in, he turned and said something to Sir Roger, who laughed lightly and walked away.

During the drive Mrs. Andrews talked volubly of the foreigner's ease and elegance and fastidious musical taste, and Mr. Manning listened courteously and bowed coldly in reply. When they reached home she invited him to dinner on the following Thursday, to meet Sir Roger Percival.

As the editor bade them good night, he said to Edna, "Go to sleep at once; do not sit up to work tonight."

Did she follow his sage advice? Ask the stars that watched her through the long winter night, and the dappled dawn that saw her stooping wearily over her desk.

At the appointed hour on the following morning Mr. Leigh called. After some desultory remarks he asked, rather abruptly, "Has St. Elmo Murray written to you about his last whim?"

Edna was certain she had gone red all over. "I do not correspond with Mr. Murray."

"Everybody wonders what droll freak will next seize him. Reed, the blacksmith, died several months ago and, to the astonishment of our people, Mr. Murray has taken his orphan, Huldah, to Le Bocage; has adopted her I believe; at all events, is educating her."

Edna's face grew radiant. "Oh, I am glad to hear it. Poor little Huldah needed a friend, and she could not possibly have fallen into kinder hands than Mr. Murray's."

Mr. Leigh laughed. "There certainly exists some diversity of opinion on that subject. He is rather too grim a guardian, I fancy, for one so young as Huldah Reed."

"Is Mr. Hammond teaching Huldah?"

"Oh, no. Herein consists the wonder. Murray himself hears her lessons, so Estelle told my sister. By the way, rumor announces the approaching marriage of the cousins. My sister informed me that it would take place early in the spring."

"The cousins?" Edna felt faint. "Do you allude to Mr. Murray and Miss Harding?"

"I do. They will go to Europe immediately after their marriage."

Gordon looked searchingly at his companion, but saw only a faint, incredulous smile cross her calm face.

"My sister is Estelle's confidante, so you see I speak advisedly. I know that her trousseau has been ordered from Paris."

Edna's fingers closed spasmodically over each other, but she laughed as she answered, "How then dare you betray your sister's confidence? Mr. Leigh, how long will you remain in New York?"

"I shall leave tomorrow, unless I have reason to hope that a longer visit will give you pleasure. I came here solely to see you."

He attempted to unclasp her fingers, but she shook off his hand and said quickly, "I know what you are about to say, and I would rather not hear what would only distress us both. If you wish me to respect you, Mr. Leigh, you must never again allude to a subject which I showed you last night was exceedingly painful to me. While I value you as a friend, and I rejoice to see you again, I should regret to learn that you had prolonged your stay on my account."

"You are ungrateful, Edna, and I begin to realize that you are utterly heartless."

"If I am, at least I have never trifled with or deceived you, Mr. Leigh."

"You have no heart, or you certainly could not so coldly reject an affection which any other woman would proudly accept. A few years hence, when your insane ambition is fully satiated, and your beauty fades, and your writings pall upon public taste, and your smooth-tongued flatterers forsake your shrine to bow before that of some new and more popular idol, then Edna, you will rue your folly."

She rose and answered quietly, "The future may contain only disappointments for me, but however lonely, however sad my lot may prove, I think I shall never fall so low as to regret not having married a man whom I find it impossible to love. The sooner this interview ends the longer our friendship will last. My time is not now my own. As my duties claim me in the schoolroom, I must bid you good-bye."

"Edna, if you send me away from you now, you shall never look upon my face again in this world."

Mournfully her tearful eyes sought his, but her voice was low and steady as she put out both hands. "Farewell, dear friend. God grant that when next we see each other's faces they may be overshadowed by the shining, white plumes of our angel wings, in that city of God, 'where the wicked cease from troubling and the weary are at rest.[86]' Thank God! Time brings us all to one inevitable tryst in heaven."

Gordon took her hands, bowed his forehead upon them and groaned; then drew them to his lips before he left her.

With a slow, weary step she turned and went up to her room and read Mr. Hammond's letter. It was long and kind, full of affection and wise counsel, but contained no allusion to Mr. Murray.

As she refolded it, she saw a slip of paper which had fallen unnoticed on the carpet. Picking it up, she read these words:

"It grieves me to have to tell you that, after all, I fear St. Elmo will marry Estelle Harding. He does not love her; she cannot influence him to redeem himself; his future looks hopeless indeed. Edna, my child! What have you done! Oh, what have you done!"

Her heart gave a sudden, wild bound. A spasm seemed to seize it, leaving her in agony. Presently the fluttering ceased, her pulses stopped, and a chill darkness fell upon her.

A moment later, Edna gasped awake, lifting her head heavily from her chest. She felt an intolerable sensation of suffocation, and a sharp pain stabbed her heart, whose throbs were slow and feeble.

She raised the window and leaned out, panting for breath. The freezing wind powdered her face with fine snowflakes and sprinkled its fairy flower-crystals over her hair.

The outer world was chill and dreary. The leafless limbs of the trees in the park looked ghostly and weird against the dense dun clouds which seemed to stretch like a smoke mantle just above the sea of roofs. Dimly seen through the white mist, Brooklyn's heights and Staten's hills were huge, monstrous outlines.

Physical pain blanched Edna's lips, and she pressed her hand repeatedly to her heart, wondering what caused those keen pangs. At last, when the bodily suffering passed away, she shut the window and sat down exhausted, her mind reverting to the sentence in Mr. Hammond's letter.

---

[86] Job 3:17

She knew the words were not lightly written, and that his reproachful appeal had broken from the depths of his aching heart, and was intended to rouse her to some action.

"I can do nothing, say nothing," she whispered. "Must sit still and wait patiently – prayerfully. Today, if I could put out my hand and touch Mr. Murray, and bind him to me forever, I would not. No, no! Not a finger must I lift, even between him and Estelle! But he will not marry her. I know – I feel that he will not. Though I never look upon his face again, he belongs to me! He is mine, and no other woman can take him from me."

A strange, mysterious smile settled on her pallid features, and faintly she repeated:

> "And yet I know past all doubting, truly –
> A knowledge greater than grief can dim –
> I know as he loved, he will love me duly,
> Yea, better, e'en better than I love him.
> And as I walk by the vast, calm river,
> The awful river so dread to see,
> I say, 'Thy breadth and thy depth for ever
> Are bridged by his thoughts that cross to me.'[87]"

Her lashes drooped, her head fell back against the top of the chair, and she lost all her woes.

Felix's voice roused her. When she pulled her eyes open, it was morning, and she saw the frightened boy standing at her side, shaking her hand and calling piteously upon her. "Oh! I thought you were dead! You looked so white and felt so cold. Are you very sick? Shall I go for mamma?"

For a moment Edna looked in his face, perplexed, bewildered. Then made an effort to rise.

"I – I suppose that I must have fainted, for I had a terrible pain here, and – " She laid her hand over her heart. "Felix, let us go downstairs. I think if your mother would give me some wine, it might strengthen me."

Notwithstanding the snow, Mrs. Andrews had gone out; but Felix had the wine brought to the schoolroom. After a little while

---

[87] "Divided" – Jean Ingelow

the blood showed itself shyly in the governess's white lips, and she took the boy's Latin book and heard him recite his lesson.

The day appeared wearily long, but she omitted none of the appointed tasks, and it was nearly nine o'clock before Felix fell asleep that night. Softly unclasping his thin fingers which clung to her hand, she went up to her own room, feeling the full force of those mournful words in Eugénie de Guérin's *Journal*:

"It goes on in the soul. No one is aware of what I feel; no one suffers from it. I only pour out my heart before God – and here. Oh! Today what efforts I make to shake off this profitless sadness – this sadness without tears – arid, bruising the heart like a hammer!"

There was no recurrence of the physical agony. After two days the feeling of physical exhaustion passed away, and only the memory of the attack remained.

The idea of lionizing her children's governess, and introducing her to so-called "fashionable society," had taken possession of Mrs. Andrews's mind, and she was quite as much delighted with her patronizing scheme as a child would have been with a new hobby-horse. Wild imaginings floated through her busy brain and filled her kind heart with generous anticipations. On Thursday she informed Edna that she desired her presence at dinner, and urged her request with such bulldogged earnestness that no alternative remained but to give in. Reluctantly, the governess prepared to meet a formidable party of strangers.

The dinner began badly for Edna. When Mrs. Andrews presented Sir Roger Percival, he bowed rather haughtily, and with a distant politeness, which assured Edna that he had noticed, quite pointedly, her refusal to make his acquaintance at the opera.

During the early part of dinner, he divided his gay words between his hostess and a pretty Miss Morton, who was evidently laying siege to his heart and flattering his vanity. But whenever Edna, his vis-à-vis, looked toward Sir Roger, she invariably found his fine brown eyes scrutinizing her face.

Mr. Manning, who sat next to Edna, engaged her in an animated discussion concerning the value of a small volume containing two essays by Henry Thomas Buckle, which he had sent her a few days previous.

Something she said to the editor with reference to Buckle's extravagant estimate of Mill, brought a smile to the Englishman's lip. Bowing slightly, he said, "Pardon me, Miss Earl, if I interrupt you to express my surprise at hearing Mill denounced by an American. His books on Representative Government and Liberty are so essentially democratic that I expected only gratitude from his readers on this side of the Atlantic."

Despite her efforts to control it, embarrassment unstrung Edna's nerves, and threw a quiver into her voice, as she answered, "I do not presume, sir, to 'denounce' a man whom Buckle ranks above all other living writers and statesmen, but, in anticipating the inevitable result of the adoption of some of Mill's proposed social reforms, I could not avoid recalling that wise dictum of Frederick the Great concerning philosophers: 'If I wanted to ruin one of my provinces I would make over its government to the philosopher.[88]' With due deference to Buckle's superior learning and astuteness, I confess my study of Mill's philosophy assures me that, if society should be turned over to the government of his theory of Liberty and Suffrage, it would go to ruin more rapidly than Frederick's province."

"Indeed?" asked Sir Roger.

Edna bowed slightly. "Under his teachings, the women of England might soon marshal their Amazonian legions, and storm not only Parnassus but the ballot-box, the bench, and the forum. That this should occur in a country where a woman nominally rules, and certainly reigns, is not so surprising; but I dread the contagion of such an example upon America."

Sir Roger stroked his magnificent whiskers in a thoughtful manner. "Mill's influence is powerful, from the fact that he never takes up his pen without using it to break some social shackles; and the strokes of his pen are tremendous as those of the hammer of Thor. But surely, Miss Earl, you Americans cannot upbraid England on the score of our woman's rights' movements?"

"At least, sir, our statesmen are not yet attacked by this most loathsome of political leprosies. America has no Bentham, Bailey, Hare or Mill, to lend countenance or strength to the ridiculous clamor raised by a few unamiable and wretched wives, and as

[88] qtd. in the aforementioned Buckle essay "Mill on Liberty"

many embittered old maids of New England. The noble apology which Edmund Burke once offered for his countrymen always recurs to my mind when I hear these 'women's conventions' alluded to: 'Because half-a-dozen grasshoppers under a fern make the field ring with their importunate chink, while thousands of great cattle repose beneath the shade of the British oak, chew the cud, and are silent, pray do not imagine that those who make the noise are the only inhabitants of the field; that, of course, they are many in number, or that, after all, they are other than the little, shriveled, meager, hopping, though loud and troublesome insects of the hour[89].'"

Edna continued. "I think, sir, that the noble and true women of this continent earnestly believe that the day which invests them with the power to vote would be the blackest in the annals of humanity, would ring the death-knell of modern civilization, of national prosperity, social morality, and domestic happiness. Women's suffrage would consign our nation to degradation and horror infinitely more appalling than a return to primeval barbarism. Then every exciting political canvass would witness the revolting deeds of the furies who assisted in storming the Tuileries; and repetitions of scenes enacted during the French Revolution, which mournfully attest how terrible indeed are female natures when once perverted.[90]"

"You must admit, Miss Earl, that your countrywomen are growing dangerously learned," answered Sir Roger, smiling.

"I am afraid, sir, that it is rather the quality than the quantity of their learning that makes them troublesome. One of your own noble seers has most gracefully declared: 'A woman may always help her husband, by what she knows, however little; by what she half knows or mis-knows, she will only tease him.'[91]"

Sir Roger bowed, and Mr. Manning said, "This is very true as a theory in sociology, but in an age when those 'strong-minded women' are becoming so alarmingly numerous, our eyes are rarely gladdened by a conjunction of cultivated intellects: loving

---

[89] *Reflections on the Revolution in France* – Edmund Burke. Side note: Do you know how much noise a thousand head of cattle can make? It ain't the grasshoppers that are the problem.
[90] America: Degradation, primeval barbarism, and guillotines since 1920!
[91] Sesame and Lilies – John Ruskin

hearts and womanly sensibilities. Can you shoulder the burden of proof?"

"Sir, that rests with those who assert that learning renders women disagreeable and unfeminine; therefore, the burden of proof remains for you."

"Permit me to lift the weight for you, Manning, by asking Miss Earl what she thinks of the comparative merits of the *Princess*, and of *Aurora Leigh*, as correctives of the tendencies she deplores?"

Hitherto the discussion had been confined to the trio, but now silence reigned around the table. When the Englishman's question forced Edna to look up, she saw all eyes turned upon her.

Embarrassment flushed her face, and her lashes drooped as she answered, "It has often been asserted that women are the most infallible judges of womanly virtues, and men of manly natures; but I am afraid that the poems referred to would veto this decision. While I greatly admire Mrs. Browning, and regard the first eight books of *Aurora Leigh* as vigorous, grand and marvelously beautiful, I cannot deny that a painful feeling of mortification seizes me when I read the ninth and concluding book, wherein Aurora, with most unwomanly vehemence, voluntarily declares her love for Romney. Tennyson's *Princess* seems to me more feminine and refined and lovely than *Aurora*; and it is because I love and revere Mrs. Browning, and consider her an ornament to the world, that I find it difficult to forgive the unwomanly inconsistency into which she betrays her heroine. Allow me to say that nothing in the whole range of literature so fully portrays a perfect woman as that noble sketch by Wordsworth, and the description in Rogers's 'Human Life.'"

Mr. Manning knitted his brows slightly "The first is, I presume, familiar to all of us, but the last, I confess, escapes my memory. Will you be good enough to repeat it?"

"Excuse me, sir; it is too long to be quoted here, and it seems that I have already monopolized the conversation much longer than I desired. Moreover, to quote Rogers to an Englishman would be equivalent to 'carrying coal to Newcastle,' or peddling 'owls in Athens.'"

Sir Roger smiled. "Indeed, Miss Earl, while you spoke, I was earnestly ransacking my memory for the passage to which you allude; but I am ashamed to say, it is as fruitless an effort as 'calling spirits from the vasty deep[92].' Pray be so kind as to repeat it for me."

At that instant little Hattie crept softly to the back of Edna's chair, and whispered, "Bro' Felix says, won't you please come back soon and finish that story where you left off reading last night?"

Very glad to possess so good an excuse, the governess rose at once; but Mrs. Andrews said, "Wait, Miss Earl. What do you want, Hattie?"

"Bro' Felix wants Miss Earl, and sent me to beg her to come."

"Go back and tell him he is in a hopeless minority, and that in this country the majority rule," said Grey Chilton, slyly pelting his niece with almonds. "There are fifteen here who want to talk to Miss Earl, and he can't have her in the schoolroom just now."

Edna looked imploringly at the lady of the house. "But Felix is really sick today, and if Mrs. Andrews will excuse me, I prefer to go." But Mrs. Andrews said nothing.

Sir Roger beckoned Hattie to him. "Pray, may I inquire, Mrs. Andrews, why your children do not make their appearance? You need not fear a repetition of the sarcastic rebuke of that wit who, when dining at a house where the children were unruly, lifted his glass, bowed to the troublesome little ones, and drank to the memory of King Herod. I am very certain 'the murder of the innocents' would never be recalled here, unless – forgive me, Miss Earl, but from the sparkle in your eyes, I believe you anticipate me. Do you really know what I am about to say?"

"I think, sir, I can guess."

"Let me see whether you are a clairvoyant."

"On one occasion when a sign for a children's school was needed, and the lady teacher applied to Charles Lamb to suggest a design, he meekly advised that of 'The Murder of the Innocents.' Thank you, sir. However, I am not surprised that you entertain such flattering opinions of a profession which in England boasts the schoolmaster 'Squeers' as its national type."

The young man laughed good-humoredly. "To protect the honor of my worthy countrymen, permit me to assure you that the aforesaid 'Squeers' is simply one of Dickens's caricatures."

[92] *Henry IV, Part I*, act 3, scene 1 -- Shakespeare

"Nevertheless, I have read that when *Nicholas Nickleby* was first published, six irate schoolmasters went immediately to London to thrash the author, each believing that he recognized his own features in the amiable portrait of 'Squeers.'"

She bowed and turned from the table, but Mrs. Andrews exclaimed, "Before you go, repeat that passage from Rogers; then we will excuse you."

With one hand clasping Hattie's, and the other resting on the back of her chair, Edna fixed her eyes on Mrs. Andrews's face, and gave the quotation.

> "His house she enters, there to be a light
> Shining within when all without is night;
> A guardian angel o'er his life presiding,
> Doubling his pleasures and his cares dividing;
> Winning him back, when mingling in the throng
> From a vain world we love, alas! too long,
> To fireside happiness and hours of ease,
> Blest with that charm, the certainty to please.
> How oft her eyes read his! her gentle mind
> To all his wishes, all his thoughts inclined;
> Still subject – ever on the watch to borrow
> Mirth of his mirth, and sorrow of his sorrow."[93]

---

[93] *Human Life* – Samuel Rogers

CHAPTER XXVII
A DRAMATIC RECONCILIATION

Flowery as Sicilian meadows was the parsonage garden on that quiet afternoon late in May, when Mr. Hammond closed the honeysuckle-crowned gate, crossed the street, and walked slowly into the church-yard, down the sacred streets of the silent city of the dead, and entered the enclosure where slept his white-robed household band.

The air was thick with perfume, as if some darting south wind had blown wide the mystic doors of Astarte's huge laboratory, overturned her potions, and deluged the world with her subtle fragrances.

Honey-burdened bees hummed their hymns to labor, as they swung to and fro. Numbers of Psyche-symbols, golden butterflies, floated dreamily in and around and over the tombs, now and then poising on velvet wings, as if listening for the clarion voice of Gabriel to rouse and reanimate the slumbering bodies beneath the gleaming slabs. Canary-colored orioles flitted in and out of the trailing willows, while a redbird perched on the brow of a sculptured angel guarding a child's grave and poured his sad, sweet, monotonous notes on the spicy air. Two purple pigeons with rainbow necklaces cooed and fluttered up and down from the church belfry. Close under the projecting roof of the granite vault, a pair of meek brown wrens were building their nest and twittering softly one to another.

The pastor cut down the rank grass and fringy ferns, the flaunting weeds and coreopsis that threatened to choke his more delicate flowers. Stooping, he tied up the crimson pinks, wound the tendrils of the blue-veined clematis around its slender trellis, and straightened the white petunias and the orange-tinted monarch crocuses, which the last heavy shower had beaten to the ground.

The small, gray vault was overrun with ivy, whose dark, polished leaves threatened to encroach on a plain slab of pure marble that stood very near it. As the minister pruned away the wreaths, his eyes rested on the black letters in the center of the slab: "Murray Hammond. Aged 21."

Elsewhere the sunshine streamed warm and bright over the graves, but here the rays were intercepted by the church, and its cool shadow rested over vault and slab and flowers.

The old man was weary from stooping so long. Now he took off his hat, passed his hand over his forehead, and sighed as he leaned against the door of the vault, where fine mosses were weaving their green arabesque immortelles.

Age was bending his body toward the earth with which it was soon to mingle. The ripe and perfect wheat nodded lower and lower day by day, as the Angel of the Sickle delayed; but Mr. Hammond's noble face wore that marvelous calm, that unearthly peace which generally comes some hours after death, when all traces of temporal passions and woes are lost in eternity's repose.

A symphony throbbed through the church, where the organist was practicing; out of the windows, and far away on the evening air, rolled the solemn waves of that matchlessly mournful Requiem which, under prophetic shadows, Mozart began on earth and finished in heaven. The sun had paused as if to listen on the wooded crest of a distant hill, but as the Requiem ended, he gathered up his burning rays and disappeared. The spotted butterflies, like "winged tulips,[94]" flitted silently away, and the evening breeze bowed the large yellow primroses, and fluttered the phlox; the red nasturtiums that climbed up at the foot of the slab shuddered and shook their blood-colored banners over the polished marble. A holy hush fell upon all things save a towering poplar that leaned against the church and rustled its leaves ceaselessly, and shivered and turned white, as tradition avers it has done since that day when Christ staggered along the Via Dolorosa bearing his cross, carved out of poplar wood.

[94] Zillah: A Tale of the Holy City – Horace Smith, 1828

Leaning with his hands folded on the handle of the weeding hoe, his gray beard sweeping over his bosom, his bare, silvered head bowed, and his mild blue eyes resting on his son's tomb, Mr. Hammond stood listening to the music. When the strains ceased, his thoughts travelled onward and upward till they crossed the sea of crystal before the Throne, and in imagination he heard the song of the four and twenty elders.

From this brief reverie some slight sound aroused him. Lifting his eyes, he saw a man clad in white linen garments, wearing oxalis clusters in his coat, standing on the opposite side of the monumental slab.

Mr. Hammond dropped the hoe. "St. Elmo! My poor, suffering wanderer! Oh, St. Elmo! Come to me once more before I die!"

The old man's voice was husky, and his arms trembled as he stretched them across the grave that stood between them both.

Mr. Murray looked into the tender, pleading countenance. Sorrow seized his own face, making his features writhe. He instinctively put out his arms, then drew them back, and hid his face in his hands.

In low, broken, almost inaudible tones, he said, "Sir, I am too unworthy. Dripping with the blood of your children, I dare not touch you."

The pastor tottered around the tomb to Mr. Murray's side. The next moment, the old man's arms were clasped around Mr. Murray, and his white hair fell on his pupil's shoulder.

"God be praised! After eighteen years' separation I hold you once more to the heart that, even in its hours of deepest sorrow, has never ceased to love you! St. Elmo! – "

He wept aloud and strained the prodigal to his breast.

After a moment Mr. Murray's lips moved, twitched. With a groan that shook his powerful frame from head to foot, he asked, "Will you ever, ever forgive me?"

"God is my witness that I fully forgave you many, many years ago. The dearest hope of my lonely life has been that I might tell you so, and make you realize how ceaselessly my prayers and my love have followed you in all your dreary wanderings. Oh, I thank God that, at last, at last you have come to me, my dear, dear boy! My poor, proud prodigal!"

A magnificent *jubilate* swelled triumphantly through church and churchyard, as if the organist up in the gallery knew what was happening at Murray Hammond's grave. When the thrilling music died away, St. Elmo broke from the encircling arms, and knelt with his face shrouded in his hands and pressed against the marble that covered his victim.

After a little while the pastor sat down on the edge of the slab and laid his fingers softly upon the bowed head.

"Do not dwell upon a past that is fraught only with bitterness to you, and from which you can draw no balm. Throw your painful memories behind you and turn resolutely to a future which may be rendered noble and holy. There is truth, precious truth in George Herbert's words:

> 'For all may have,
> If they dare choose,
> a glorious life or grave!'[95]

and the years to come may, by the grace of God, more than cancel those that have gone by."

"What have I to hope for – in time or eternity? None but Almighty God can ever know the dreary blackness and wretchedness of my despairing soul! The keen sleepless pain of my remorse! My utter loathing of my accursed nature!"

"And His pitying eyes see all, and Christ stretches out his hands to lift you up to Himself. His own words of loving sympathy and pardon are spoken again to you: 'Come unto Me, all ye weary and heavy laden, and I will give you rest.[96]' Throw all your galling load of memories down at the foot of the cross, and 'the peace that passeth all understanding[97]' shall enter your sorrowing soul, and abide there forever. St. Elmo, only prayer could have sustained and soothed me since we parted that bright summer morning eighteen long, long years ago. Prayer took away the sting and sanctified my sorrows for the good of my soul; and, my dear, dear boy, it will extract the poison and the bitterness

---

[95] "Perirrhanterium" – George Herbert
[96] Matthew 11:28
[97] Philippians 4:7

338

from yours. That God answers prayer and comforts the afflicted among men, I am a living attestation. It is by His grace only that I am fully resigned to His will. My only remaining cause of disquiet passed away just now, when I saw that you had come back to me. St. Elmo, do you ever pray for yourself?"

"For some weeks I have been trying to pray, but my words seem a mockery; they do not rise, they fall back hissing upon my heart. I have injured and insulted you, I have cursed you and yours, have robbed you of your peace of mind, have murdered your children – "

"Hush, hush! We will not disinter the dead. My peace of mind you have today given back to me; and I have long prayed for your salvation. Sometimes my faith grew faint, and as the years dragged on and I saw no melting of your haughty, bitter spirit, I almost lost hope; but I did not, thank God, I did not! I held on to the precious promise, and prayed more frequently, and, blessed be his holy name! At last, just before I go hence, the answer comes. As I see you kneeling here at my Murray's grave, I know now that your soul is snatched 'as a brand from the burning.' Oh, bless my merciful God, that in that day when we stand for final judgment, and your precious soul is required at my son's hands, the joyful cry of the recording angel shall be, 'Saved! Saved! For ever and ever, through the blood of the Lamb!'"

Overwhelmed with emotion, the pastor dropped his white head on his bosom. Once more silence fell over the darkening cemetery.

One by one the birds hushed their songs and went to rest. Only the soft cooing of the pigeons floated down now and then from the lofty belfry.

On the eastern horizon a thin, fleecy scarf of clouds was silvered by the rising moon. The western sky was a huge shrine of beryl whereon burned ruby flakes of vapor, watched by a solitary vestal star.

Mr. Murray rose and stood with his head uncovered, his eyes fixed on the nodding nasturtiums that glowed like bloodspots against the marble.

"Mr. Hammond, your magnanimity unmans me. I feel in your presence like a leper, and I should lay my lips in the dust, crying,

'Unclean! Unclean!' For all that I have inflicted on you, I have neither apology nor defense to offer. I could much better have borne curses from you than words of sympathy and affection. You amaze me, for I hate and scorn myself so thoroughly, that I marvel at the interest you still indulge for me. I cannot understand how you can endure the sight of my features, the sound of my voice. If I could atone! If I could give Annie back to your arms, there is no suffering, no torture that I would not gladly embrace! No penance of body or soul from which I would shrink!"

"My dear boy, (for such you still seem to me, notwithstanding the lapse of time,) let my little darling rest with her God. She went down early to her long home, and though I miss her sweet laugh, and her soft, tender hands about my face, and have felt a chill silence in my house where music once was, she has been spared much suffering and many trials. After a few more days I shall gather her back to my bosom in that eternal land where the blighting dew of death never falls; where

'Adieus and farewells are a sound unknown.[98]'

Atone? Ah, St. Elmo, you can atone. Save your soul, redeem your life, and I shall die blessing your name. Look at me in my loneliness and infirmity. I am childless; you took my idols from me, long, long ago; you left my heart desolate. Now I have a right to turn to you, to stretch out my empty arms, and say, 'Come, be my child, fill my son's place, let me lean upon you in my old age, as I once fondly dreamed I should lean on my own Murray!' St. Elmo, will you come? Will you give me your heart, my son! My son!"

He put out his trembling hands, and a tenderness shone in his eyes as he raised them to the stern man before him.

Mr. Murray bent forward and looked wonderingly at him.

"Do you, can you mean it? It appears so impossible, and I have been so long skeptical of all nobility in my race. Will you indeed shelter Murray's murderer in your generous, loving heart?"

"I call my God to witness, that it has been my dearest hope for dreary years that I might win your heart back before I die."

---

[98] "On Receipt Of My Mother's Picture" – William Cowper

"It is but a wreck, a hideous ruin, black with sins; but such as I am, my future, my all, I lay at your feet. If there is any efficacy in bitter repentance and remorse, if there is any mercy left in my Maker's hands, if there be saving power in human will, I will atone. I will atone!"

The strong man trembled like a wave-lashed reed as he sank on one knee at the minister's feet and buried his face in his arms. Spreading his palms over the drooped head, Mr. Hammond solemnly blessed him.

For some time both were silent, and then Mr. Murray stretched out one arm over the slab, and said brokenly, "Kneeling here at Murray's tomb, a strange, incomprehensible feeling creeps into my heart. The fierce, burning hate I have borne him seems to have passed away; and ah, something, mournfully like the old love toward him, comes back as I look at his name. Oh, idol of my youth, hurled down by my own savage hands! For the first time since that night, I feel that – that – I can forgive him. Murray! Murray! Oh, if I could give you back the life I took in my madness, how joyfully would I forgive you all my injuries. But his blood dyes my hands, my heart, my soul!"

"The blood of Jesus will wash out those stains. The law was fully satisfied when He hung on Calvary. There, ample atonement was made for just such sins as yours, and you have only to claim and plead his sufferings to secure your salvation. St. Elmo, bury your past here, in Murray's grave, and give all your thoughts to the future. Half of your life has ebbed out, and yet your life's work remains undone, untouched. You have no time to spend in looking over your unimproved years."

"'Bury my past?' Impossible, even for one hour. I tell you I am chained to it, as the Aloides were chained to the pillars of Tartarus, and the croaking fiend will not let me sleep in memory. Memory of sins that – that goad me sometimes to the very verge of suicide! Do you know, ha! how could you possibly know? Shall I tell you that only one thought has often stood between me and self-destruction? It was not the fear of death, no, no, no! It was not even the dread of facing an outraged God. It was the fear of meeting Murray! Not all eternity was wide enough to hold us both. The hate I bore him made me shrink from a deed which I felt would instantly set us face to face once more in the land of souls."

Mr. Hammond wept quietly. Mr. Murray took his hands in his, his lips trembling.

"Mr. Hammond, friend of my happy youth, guide of my innocent boyhood, if you could know all the depths of my abasement, how I wish I could atone for all I have done to you. But it is not enough to wish for forgiveness. My sorrow, however deep, will still not return your dear ones to your arms. Sometimes I think that if I ended my life, I could in some way make up for what I have taken from you."

"St. Elmo, do not upbraid yourself so bitterly – "

"Sir, your words are full of charity, and I thank you; but they cannot comfort me. Yesterday I read a passage which depicts so accurately my dreary isolation, that I have been unable to expel it; I find it creeping even now to my lips:

> "'O misery and mourning! I have felt –
> Yes, I have felt like some deserted world
> That God hath done with, and had cast aside
> To rock and stagger through the gulfs of space,
> He never looking on it any more;
> Unfilled, no use, no pleasure, not desired,
> Nor lighted on by angels in their flight
> From heaven to happier planets; and the race
> That once hath dwelt on it withdrawn or dead.
> *Could such a world have hope that some blest day*
> *God would remember her, and fashion her*
> *Anew?*'[99]"

"Yes, my dear St. Elmo, so surely as God reigns above us, He will refashion it, and make the light of His pardoning love and the refreshing dew of his grace fall upon it. Have faith, grapple yourself by prayer to the feet of God, and he will gird, and lift up, and guide you."

Mr. Murray shook his head mournfully, and the moonlight shining on his face showed it haggard, hopeless.

---

[99] "Afternoon at a Parsonage" – Jean Ingelow

The pastor rose, put on his hat, and took St. Elmo's arm.

"Come home with me. This spot is fraught with painful associations that open afresh all your wounds."

They walked on together until they reached the parsonage gate. As the minister raised the latch, his companion gently disengaged the arm clasped to the old man's side.

"Not tonight. After a few days I will try to come."

"St. Elmo, tomorrow is Sunday, and – "

Mr. Hammond paused, and did not speak the request that looked out from his eyes.

It cost Mr. Murray a severe struggle, and he did not answer immediately. When he spoke, his voice was unsteady.

"Yes, I know what you wish. Once I swore I would tear the church down, scatter its dust to the winds, leave not a stone to mark the site. But I will come and hear you preach for the first time since that sunny Sabbath, eighteen years dead, when your text was, 'Cast thy bread upon the waters; for thou shalt find it after many days.[100]' Sodden and worthless from the great deep of sin, it drifts back at last to your feet. Instead of stooping tenderly to gather up the useless fragments, I wonder that you do not spurn the stranded ruin from you. Yes, I will come."

"Thank God. Oh, what a weight you have lifted from my heart. St. Elmo, my son!"

There was a long, lingering clasp of hands. At last the pastor went into his home with tears of joy on his furrowed face, while his smiling lips whispered to his grateful soul, "In the morning sow thy seed, and in the evening withhold not thy hand; for thou knowest not whether shall prosper, either this or that, or whether they both shall be alike good.[101]"

Mr. Murray watched the stooping form until it disappeared, and then went slowly back to the silent burying ground and sat down on the steps of the church.

Hour after hour passed and still he sat there, almost as motionless as one of the monuments, while his eyes dwelt as if spellbound on the dark, dull stain where Annie Hammond had bled, heartbroken, in days long, long past. Remorse evoked from

---

[100] Ecclesiastes 11:1
[101] Ecclesiastes 11:6

the charnel house the sweet girlish face and delicate figure of the Annie Hammond, her sweet laugh. He remembered how Annie wept with joy when he asked her to marry him, and she had nestled happily in his arms as she'd planned their future together.

His pale face was propped on his hand. There in the silent watches of the moon-lighted midnight, he held communion with God and his own darkened spirit.

> "What hast thou wrought for Right and Truth,
> For God and man,
> From the golden hours of bright-eyed youth,
> To life's mid-span?"[102]

His almost Satanic pride was laid low as the dead in their moldering shrouds, and all the giant strength of his darkened nature was gathered up and hurled in a new direction. The Dead Sea Past moaned and swelled, and bitter waves surged and broke over his heart, but he silently buffeted them.

The moon rode in mid-heaven when finally he rose and went around the church. There he knelt and prayed with his forehead pressed to the marble that covered Murray Hammond's last resting-place.

> "Oh! that the mist which veileth my To Come
> Would so dissolve and yield unto mine eyes
> A worthy path! I'd count not wearisome
> Long toil nor enterprise,
> But strain to reach it; ay, with wrestlings stout…
> Is there such a path already made to fit
> The measure of my foot? It shall atone
> For much, if I at length may light on it
> And know it for mine own."[103]

---

[102] "My Soul and I" – John Greenleaf Whittier
[103] "Honors – Part II" – Jean Ingelow

CHAPTER XXVIII
AN ASTONISHING PROPOSAL

"Oh, how grand and beautiful it is. Whenever I look at it, I feel exactly as I did on Easter Sunday when I went to the cathedral to hear the music. It is a solemn feeling, as if I were in a holy place. Miss Earl, what makes me feel so?"

Felix stood in an art gallery, and, leaning on his crutches, looked up at Church's "Heart of the Andes."

"You are impressed by the solemnity and the holy repose of nature; for here you look upon a pictured cathedral, built not by mortal hands, but by the architect of the universe. Felix, does it not recall to your mind something of which we often speak?"

The boy was silent for a few seconds, and then his thin, sallow face brightened.

"Yes, indeed! You mean that splendid description which you read to me from *Modern Painters?* How fond you are of that passage, and how very often you think of it. Let me see whether I can remember it."

Slowly but accurately he repeated the eloquent tribute to "Mountain Glory," from the fourth volume of *Modern Painters.*

"Felix, you know that the poet John Keats said, 'A thing of beauty is a joy forever'[104]; and as I can never hope to express my ideas in half such beautiful language as Mr. Ruskin uses, it is an economy of trouble to quote his words. Last week you asked me to explain to you what is meant by 'aerial perspective,' and if you will study the atmosphere in this great picture, Mr. Church will explain it much more clearly to you than I was able to do."

---

104 "Endymion" – John Keats

Heart of the Andes -- Frederic Edwin Church

"Yes, Miss Earl, I see it now. The eye could travel up and up and never get out of the sky; and it seems to me those birds yonder would fly out of sight through that air in the picture. But, Miss Earl, do you believe that the Chimborazo in South America is as grand as Mr. Church's? I do not, because I have noticed that pictures are much handsomer than the real things they stand for. Mamma carried me last spring to see some paintings of scenes on the Hudson River, and when we went traveling in the summer, I saw the very spot where the artist stood when he sketched the hills and the bend of the river, and it was not half so pretty as the picture. And yet I know God is the greatest painter. Is it the far-off look that everything wears when painted?"

"Yes, the 'far-off look,' as you call it, is one cause of the effect you wish to understand; and it has been rather more elegantly expressed by Campbell, in the line:

"'Tis distance lends enchantment to the view.'[105]

I have seen this fact exemplified at a house in Georgia where I was once visiting. From the front door I had a very fine view of lofty hills, a dense forest, and a pretty little town where the steeples of the churches glittered in the sunshine. I stood for some time admiring the landscape; but presently, when I turned to speak to the lady of the house, I saw, in the glass sidelights of the

---

[105] "Hope" – Thomas Campbell

door, a miniature reflection of the very same scene that was much more beautiful. I was puzzled, and could not comprehend how the mere fact of diminishing the size of the various objects could enhance their loveliness. Were all far-off things handsomer than those close at hand?

In my perplexity I went as usual to Mr. Ruskin, wondering whether he had ever noticed the same thing; and of course he had, and has a noble passage about it in one of his books on architecture. I will see if my memory appreciates it as it deserves: 'Are not all natural things, it may be asked, as lovely near as far away? Nay, not so. Look at the clouds, and watch the delicate sculpture of their alabaster sides and the rounded luster of their magnificent rolling. They are meant to be beheld far away; they were shaped for this place, high above your head. Approach them, and they fuse into vague mists, or whirl away in fierce fragments of thunderous vapors.[106] (And here, Felix, your question about Chimborazo is answered.)

"Felix, in rambling about the fields, you will frequently be reminded of this. I have noticed that the meadow in the distance is always greener and more velvety, and seems more thickly studded with flowers, than the one I am crossing; or the hillside far away has a golden gleam on its rocky slopes, and the shadow spots are softer and cooler and more purple than those I am climbing and panting over. I hurry on, and after a little, turning to look back, lo, all the glory I saw beckoning me on has flown, and settled over the meadow and the hillside that I have passed, and the halo is behind. When we go home I will read you something which Emerson has said concerning this, for I can remember only a few words: 'What splendid distance, what recesses of ineffable pomp and loveliness in the sunset! But who can go where they are, or lay his hand, or plant his foot thereon? Off they fall from the round world forever.'[107]"

Edna's eyes went back to the painting and rested there. Little Hattie, who had been gazing up at her governess in curious perplexity, pulled her brother's sleeve and said, "Bro' Felix, do you understand all that? I guess I don't; for I know when I am hungry

[106] *The Stones of Venice*, Vol. 1 – John Ruskin
[107] "Nature" – Ralph Waldo Emerson

(and seems to me I always am); why, when I am hungry the closer I get to my dinner the nicer it looks! And then there was that hateful, spiteful old Miss Abby Tompkins, that mamma would have to teach you! Ugh! I have watched her many a time coming up the street, (you know she never would ride in stages for fear of pickpockets,) and she always looked just as ugly as far off as I could see her as when she came close to me – "

A hearty laugh cut short Hattie's observation. Coming forward, Sir Roger Percival put his hand on her head, saying, "How often children tumble down 'the step from the sublime to the ridiculous!108' Miss Earl, I have been watching your little party for some time, listening to your incipient art-lecture. You Americans are queer people. When I go home I shall tell Mr. Ruskin that I heard a little boy criticizing *The Heart of the Andes*, and quoting from *Modern Painters*. Felix, as I wish to be accurate, will you tell me your age?"

Felix, sure that he was being ridiculed, only reddened and frowned and bit his thin lips.

Edna laid her hand on his shoulder and answered for him. "He is thirteen years old. Though Mr. Ruskin is a distinguished exception to the rule that prophets are not without honor, save in their own country, I think he has no reader who loves and admires his writings more than Felix Andrews."

Here the boy raised his eyes and asked, "Why is it that prophets have no honor among their own people? Is it because they have to be seen from a great distance in order to seem grand? I heard mamma say the other day that if some book written in America had only come from England everybody would be raving about it."

"Some other time, Felix, we will talk of that problem. Hattie, you look sleepy."

"I think it will be lunch time before we get home," replied the yawning child.

Sir Roger took her by her shoulders and shook her gently. "Come, wake up, little sweetheart! How can you get sleepy or hungry with all these handsome pictures staring at you from the walls?"

---

108 qtd. by Napoleon upon the retreat of his army from Moscow.

The good-natured child laughed; but Felix, who had an unconquerable aversion to Sir Roger's huge whiskers, curled his lips, and exclaimed scornfully, "Hattie, you ought to be ashamed of yourself. Hungry, indeed! You are almost as bad as that English lady, who, when her husband was admiring some beautiful lambs, and called her attention to them, answered, 'Yes, lambs are beautiful – *boiled*!'"

Wishing to conciliate him, Sir Roger replied, "When you and Hattie come to see me in England, I will show you the most beautiful lambs in the United Kingdom; and your sister shall have boiled lamb three times a day, if she wishes it. Miss Earl, you are so fond of paintings that you would enjoy a European tour more than any lady whom I have met in this country. I have seen miles of canvas in Boston, New York, and Philadelphia, but very few good pictures."

"And yet, sir, when on exhibition in Europe this great work here before us received most extravagant praise from transatlantic critics, who are very loath to accord merit to American artists. If I am ever so fortunate as to be able to visit Europe, and cultivate and improve my taste, I think I shall still be very proud of the names of Allston, West, Church, Bierstadt, Kensett and Gifford."

She turned to leave the gallery, and Sir Roger said, "I leave tomorrow for Canada, and may possibly sail for England without returning to New York. Will you allow me the pleasure of driving you to the park this afternoon? Two months ago you refused a similar request, but since then I flatter myself we have become better friends."

"Thank you, Sir Roger. I presume the children can spare me, and I will go with pleasure."

Sir Roger bowed. "I will call at five o'clock."

He handed her and Hattie into the coupe, tenderly assisted Felix, and saw them driven away.

Presently Felix laughed, and exclaimed, "Oh, I hope Miss Morton will be in the park this evening. It would be glorious fun to see her meet you and Sir Roger."

"Why, Felix?"

"Oh! Because she meddles. I heard Uncle Grey tell mamma that she was making desperate efforts to catch the Englishman;

and that she turned up her nose tremendously at the idea of his visiting you. When Uncle Grey told her how often he came to our house, she bit her lips almost till the blood spouted. Sir Roger drives very fine horses, uncle says, and Miss Morton hints outrageously for him to ask her to ride, but she can't manage to get the invitation. So she will be furious when she sees you this afternoon. Yonder is Goupil's; let us stop and have a look at those new engravings mamma told us about yesterday. Hattie, you can curl up in your corner, and go to sleep and dream of boiled lamb till we come back."

Later in the day Mrs. Andrews went up to Edna's room, and found her correcting an exercise.

"At work as usual. You are incorrigible. Any other woman would be so charmed with her conquest that her head would be quite turned by a certain pair of brown eyes that are considered irresistible. Come, get ready for your drive; it is almost five o'clock, and you know foreigners are too polite, too thoroughly well-bred not to be punctual. No, no, Miss Earl; not that hat, on the peril of your life! Where is that new one that I ordered sent up to you two days ago? It will match this delicate white shawl of mine, which I brought up for you to wear. Come, no scruples if you please. Stand up and let me see whether its folds hang properly. You should have heard Madame De G – when she put it around my shoulders for the first time, '*Juste ciel!* Madame Andrews, you are a Greek statue.' Miss Earl, put your hair back a little from the left temple. There, now the veins show. Where are your gloves? You look charmingly, my dear; only too pale, too pale! If you don't contrive to get up some color, people will swear that Sir Roger was airing the ghost of a pretty girl. There is the bell. Just as I told you, he is punctual. Five o'clock to a minute."

She stepped to the window and looked down at the equipage before the door.

"What superb horses! You will be the envy of the city."

There was something in the appearance and manner of Sir Roger which often reminded Edna of Gordon Leigh, notwithstanding his whiskers. During the spring he visited her so constantly, sent her so frequently baskets of elegant flowers, that he succeeded in overcoming her reticence, and established himself on a friendly footing in Mrs. Andrews's house.

Now, as they drove along the avenue and entered the park, their spirits rose. Sir Roger turned very often to look at the fair face of his companion, which he found more and more attractive each day. He saw, too, that under his earnest gaze the faint color deepened, until her cheeks glowed like seashells. When he spoke, he bent his face much nearer to hers than was necessary to make her hear his words. They talked of books, flowers, music, mountain scenery, and the green lanes of "Merry England." Edna was perfectly at ease, and in a mood to enjoy everything.

They dashed on, and the sunlight disappeared. The gas streetlights glittered all over the city before Sir Roger turned his horses' heads homeward. When they reached Mrs. Andrews's door, he dismissed his carriage and spent the evening.

At eleven o'clock he rose to say good-bye. He clasped Edna's hand close to his chest. "Miss Earl, I hope I shall have the pleasure of renewing our acquaintance at an early day; if not in America, then in Europe. The brightest reminiscences I shall carry across the ocean are those that cluster about the hours I have spent with you. If I should not return to New York, will you allow me the privilege of hearing from you occasionally?"

She withdrew her hand, and her face flushed painfully as she answered. "Will you excuse me, Sir Roger, when I tell you that I am so constantly occupied I have not time to write, even to my old and dearest friends."

Passing the door of Felix's room, on her way to her own apartment, the boy called to her, "Miss Earl, are you very tired?"

"Oh, no. Do you want anything?"

"My head aches and I can't go to sleep. Please read to me a little while."

He raised himself on his elbow and looked up fondly at her. "Ah, how very pretty you are tonight! Kiss me, won't you?"

She stooped and kissed his poor parched lips. As she opened a volume of the Waverly Novels, he said, "Did you see Miss Morton?"

Edna's eyes glittered. "Yes. She was on horseback, and we passed her *twice*."

"Glad of it! She does not like you. I guess she finds it as hard to get to sleep tonight as I do."

Edna commenced reading. It was nearly an hour before Felix's eyes closed, and his fingers relaxed their grasp on hers. Softly she put the book back on the shelf, extinguished the light, and stole upstairs to her desk.

That night, as Sir Roger tossed restlessly on his pillow, thinking of her, recalling all that she had said during the drive, he would not have been flattered by a knowledge of the fact that she was so entirely engrossed by her manuscript that she had no thought of him or his impending departure.

When the clock struck three she laid down her pen. The mournful expression that crept into her eyes told that memory was busy with the past years. When she fell asleep she dreamed not of Sir Roger but of Le Bocage and its master, of whom she would not permit herself to think in her waking hours.

The influence which Mr. Manning exerted over Edna increased as their acquaintance ripened. With curious interest he watched the expansion of her mind. Now and then he warned her of some error into which she seemed inclined to plunge, or wisely advised some new branch of research.

Gradually she learned to lean upon his strong, clear mind, and to find in his society a quiet happiness. The antagonism of their characters was doubtless one cause of their attraction to each other, and furnished the balance-wheel which both required.

Edna's intense and dreamy idealism demanded a check, which the positivism of the editor supplied. His extensive and rigidly accurate information on almost all scientific topics constituted a valuable treasury of knowledge to which she always had access.

His faith in Christianity was like his conviction of the truth of mathematics, more an intellectual process and the careful deduction of logic than the result of some emotional impulse. His religion, like his dialectics, was consistent, irreproachable, unanswerable. Though he never sought a controversy on any subject, he never shunned one, and, during its continuance, his demeanor was invariably courteous, but unyielding.

Very early in life his intellectual seemed to have swallowed up his emotional nature, as Aaron's rod did those of the magicians of

Pharaoh. Only the absence of dogmatism, and the habitual suavity of his manner, atoned for his unbending obstinacy on all points.

Edna's fervid and beautiful enthusiasm surged and broke over this man's stern, flinty realism, like the warm, blue waters of the Gulf Stream that throw their silvery spray and foam against the glittering walls of sapphire icebergs sailing slowly southward.

Merciless as an anatomical lecturer, he would smilingly take up one of her metaphors and dissect it, and over the pages of her manuscripts for *Iconoclast* his gravely spoken criticisms fell withering as hoar frost.

They differed in all respects, yet daily they felt the need of each other's society. The frozen man of forty sunned himself in the genial presence of the lovely girl of twenty, and in the dawn of her literary career she felt a sense of security from his proffered guidance, even as an ambitious child, just learning to walk, totters along with less apprehension when the steady hand she refuses to hold is near enough to catch and save her from a fall.

One Saturday Edna sat with her bonnet on, waiting for Mr. Manning, who had promised to accompany her on her first visit to Greenwood. As she put on her gloves, Felix handed her a letter which his father had just brought up.

She gasped, recognizing Mrs. Murray's writing. Edna tore it open and read it immediately, and, while her eyes ran over the sheet, an expression, first of painful surprise came into her countenance.

"MY DEAR CHILD: Doubtless you will be amazed to hear that your former lover has utterly driven your image from his fickle heart; and that he ignores your existence as completely as if you were buried twenty feet in the ruins of Pompeii. Last night Gordon Leigh was married to Gertrude Powell. The happy pair, attended by that despicable mother, Agnes Powell, will set out for Europe early next week. My dear, it is growing fashionable to 'marry for spite.' I have seen two instances recently, *and know of a third which will take place ere long.* Poor Gordon will rue his rashness, and, before the year ends, he will arrive at the conclusion that he is an unmitigated fool, and has simply performed, with great success, an operation known as cutting off one's nose to spite one's face. Your rejection of his renewed offer piqued him beyond expression, and when he returned from New York he was in the most accommodating frame of mind that Mrs. Powell could desire. She immediately laid siege to him. Gertrude's preference for his society was extremely soothing to his vanity, which you had wounded, and the indefatigable maneuvers of the wily mamma, and the continual flattery of the girl, accomplished the result. I once credited Gordon with more sense than he has shown, but each year convinces me more firmly of the truth of my belief, that no man is proof against the persistent flattery of a beautiful woman.

"When he announced his engagement to me, we were sitting in the library, and I looked him full in the face, and answered: 'Indeed! Engaged to Miss Powell? I thought you swore that so long as Edna Earl remained unmarried you would never relinquish your suit?' He pointed to that lovely statuette of Pallas that stands on the mantelpiece, and said bitterly, 'Edna Earl has no more heart than that marble Athena.' Whereupon I replied, 'Take care, Gordon. I notice that of late you seem inclined to deal rather too freely in hyperbole. Edna's heart may resemble the rich veins of gold, which in some mines run not near the surface but deep in the masses of quartz. Because you cannot obtain it, you have no right to declare that it does not exist. You will probably live to hear some more fortunate suitor shout Eureka! over the treasure.' He turned pale as the Pallas and put his hand over his face.

"Then I said, 'Gordon, my young friend, I have always been deeply interested in your happiness. Tell me, do you love this girl Gertrude?' He seemed much embarrassed, but finally made his confession: 'Mrs. Murray, I believe I shall be fond of her after a while. She is very lovely, and deeply attached to me, (vanity you see, Edna,) and I am grateful for her affection. But I never expect to love any woman as I loved Edna Earl. I can adore Gertrude; but not as I have worshipped my first love, my proud, peerless Edna! She will never realize all she threw away when she coldly dismissed me.'

"Poor Gordon! Well, he is married; but his bride might have found cause of disquiet in his restless, abstracted manner on the evening of his wedding. What do you suppose was St. Elmo's criticism on this matrimonial mismatch? 'Poor devil! Before a year rolls over his head he will feel like plunging into the Atlantic, with Plymouth Rock for a necklace! Leigh deserves a better fate, and I would rather see him tied to wild horses and dragged across the Andes.' These pique marriages are terrible mistakes; so, my dear, I trust you will duly repent of your cruelty to poor Gordon."

As Edna put the letter in her pocket, she wondered if Gertrude really loved her husband, or if chagrin at Mr. Murray's heartless desertion had goaded the girl to accept Mr. Leigh.

"Perhaps after all, Mr. Murray was correct in his estimate of her character, when he said that she was a mere child, and was capable of earnest affection. I hope so – I hope so."

Edna's thoughts returned to that paragraph in Mrs. Murray's letter which seemed intentionally mysterious: "I know of a third instance which will take place ere long."

Did she allude to St. Elmo and Estelle? Edna could not believe this possible, and shook her head at the suggestion; but her lips grew cold, and her fingers locked each other as in a clasp of steel.

When Mr. Manning called, and assisted her into the carriage, he observed an unusual preoccupancy of mind; but after a few desultory remarks she rallied, gave him her undivided attention, and seemed engrossed by his conversation.

It was a fine, sunny day, bright but cool, with a stiffening west wind ripping the waters of the harbor.

The week had been one of unusual trial. Felix was sick, and even more than ordinarily fretful and exacting. Weary of writing and of teaching so constantly, the governess enjoyed the brief time of freedom.

Mr. Manning's long residence in the city had familiarized him with the beauties of Greenwood, and the history of many who slept dreamlessly in the costly mausoleums which they paused to admire. When at last he directed the driver to return, Edna sank back in one corner of the carriage and said, "Some morning I will come with the children and spend the entire day."

She closed her eyes, and her thoughts traveled to that pure white obelisk standing in the shadow of Lookout. Melancholy memories brought a sigh to her lips and a cloud to the face that for two hours past had been singularly bright and animated.

Greenwood Cemetery

The silence had lasted some minutes, when Mr. Manning, who was gazing out of the window, turned to Edna. "You look pale and badly today."

"I have not felt as strong as usual. It is a great treat to get away from the schoolroom and out into the open air, which is bracing and delightful. I believe I have enjoyed this outing more than any I have taken since I came North; and you must allow me to tell you how I thank you for your remembrance of me."

"Miss Earl, what I am about to say will perhaps seem premature, and will doubtless surprise you; but I beg you to believe that it is the result of mature deliberation."

He paused and looked earnestly at her.

Edna gasped. "You certainly have not decided to give up the editorship of *Iconoclast*, as you spoke of doing last winter. It would not survive your desertion six months."

"My allusion was to yourself, not to the magazine, which I shall edit as long as I live. Miss Earl, this state of affairs cannot continue. You have no regard for your health; you are destroying yourself. Let me take care of you and save you from the ceaseless toil in which you are wearing out your life."

"Sir?" Edna asked.

"To teach, as you do, all day, and then sit up nearly all night to write, would exhaust a constitution of steel. You are probably not aware of the change which has taken place in your appearance during the last three months. Hitherto circumstances may have left you no alternative, but one is now offered you. My property is enough to render you comfortable. I have already purchased a pleasant home, to which I shall remove next week. I want you to share it with me – to share my future – all that I have."

Completely bewildered, she sat looking wonderingly at him.

"You have known me scarcely a year, but you are not a stranger to my character, and I think that you have implicit confidence in me. Notwithstanding the unfortunate disparity in our years, I believe we are becoming dependent on each other, and in your society I find a charm such as no other human being possesses. I am not demonstrative, but my feelings are warm and deep. However incredulous you may be, I assure you that you are the first, the only woman I have ever asked to be my wife."

Now Mr. Manning took her cold hands in his. "I have known many who were intellectual, whose society I have enjoyed, but not one until I met you whom I would have married. To you alone am I willing to entrust the education of my little Lila."

Finally Edna was able to speak. "Your daughter?"

"My niece. She was but six months old when we were shipwrecked off Barnegat. In attempting to save his wife, my brother was lost. With the child in my arms I clung to a spar, and finally swam ashore. Since then, regarding her as a sacred treasure committed to my guardianship, I have faithfully endeavored to supply her father's place."

Edna could not help but admire him even more at that moment. But ... "But you wish to marry me?" she asked faintly.

"There is a singular magnetism about you, Edna Earl, which makes me wish to see your face always at my hearthstone. You are inordinately ambitious. I can lift you to a position that will fully satisfy you, and place you above the necessity of daily labor – a position of happiness and ease, where your genius can properly develop itself. Can you consent to be Douglass Manning's wife?"

There was no more tremor in his voice than in the measured beat of a bass drum. In his granite face not a feature moved, not a muscle twitched, not a nerve quivered.

So entirely unexpected was this proposal that Edna could not utter a word. The idea that he could ever wish to marry anybody seemed incredible, and that he should need her society appeared absurd. For an instant she wondered if she had fallen asleep in the soft, luxurious corner of the carriage, and dreamed it all.

"Miss Earl, you do not seem to comprehend me, and yet my words are certainly very explicit. Once more I ask you, can you put your hand in mine and be my wife?"

He laid one hand on hers, and with the other pushed back his glasses.

Withdrawing her hands, she covered her face with them, and answered almost inaudibly, "Let me think – for you astonish me."

"Take a day, or a week, if necessary, for consideration, and then give me your answer."

Mr. Manning leaned back in the carriage, folded his hands, and looked quietly out of the window.

For a half hour silence reigned.

Brief but sharp was the struggle in Edna's heart. Probably no woman's literary ambition had ever been more fully gratified than hers, by this most unexpected offer of marriage from one whom she regarded as the noblest ornament of her profession. Thinking of the hour when she sat alone, shedding tears of bitter disappointment over his curt letter rejecting her manuscript, she glanced at the stately form beside her, the calm, commanding face, the dark, finely molded hands, waiting to clasp hers for all time, and her triumph seemed complete.

To rule the destiny of that strong man, whose intellect was so influential in the world of letters, was a conquest of which, until this hour, she had never dreamed. The blacksmith's darling was, after all, a mere woman, and the honor dazzled her.

To one of her peculiar temperament wealth offered no temptation; but Douglass Manning had climbed to a grand eminence. Looking up at it, she knew that any woman might well be proud to share it.

He filled her ideal, he came fully up to her lofty moral and mental standard. She knew that his superior she could never hope to meet, and her confidence in his integrity of character was boundless.

She felt that his society had become necessary to her peace of mind; for only in his presence was it possible to forget her past. Either she must marry him, or live single, and work and die – alone.

Edna was weary of battling with precious memories of that reckless, fascinating cynic whom, without trusting, she had learned to love. Perhaps if she were the wife of Mr. Manning, whom without loving she fully trusted, it would help her to forget St. Elmo.

She did not deceive herself. She knew that, despite her struggles and stern interdicts, she loved St. Elmo as she could never hope to love anyone else.

Impatiently she said to herself, "Mr. Murray is almost as old as Mr. Manning, and in the estimation of the public is his inferior. Oh, why cannot my weak, wayward heart follow my strong, clear-eyed judgment? I would give ten years of my life to love Mr. Manning as I love – "

Mr. Manning seemed serene, majestic, and pure as the vast snowdome of Oraefa, glittering in the chill light of the midnight sun; while St. Elmo seemed fiery, thunderous, destructive as Izalco – one moment crowned with flames and lava-lashed – the next wrapped in gloom and dust and ashes.

She almost groaned aloud in her chagrin as she thought, "Surely, if ever a woman was infatuated – possessed by an evil spirit – I certainly am."

While she sat there wrestling as she had never done before, even on that day of trial in the church, memory, as if leagued with Satan, brought up the image of Mr. Murray as he stood pleading for himself, for his future. She heard his thrilling, passionate cry, "Oh, my darling! my darling! come to me!" Pressing her face to the lining of the carriage to stifle a groan, she felt again the close clasp of St. Elmo's arms, the throbbing of his heart against her cheek, the warm, tender, lingering pressure of his lips on hers.

When they had crossed the ferry and were rattling over the streets of New York, Edna took her hands from her eyes. There was a rigid paleness in her face and a mournful hollowness in her voice as she said, "No, Mr. Manning. I cannot be your wife. Sir, you cannot doubt that I do most fully and gratefully appreciate this honor, which I had not the presumption to dream of. My reverence and admiration are, I confess, almost boundless, but I find not one atom of love; and an examination of my feelings satisfies me that I could never yield you that homage of heart, that devoted affection which God demands that every wife should pay her husband. You have quite as little love for me. In pleasant and profitable companionship we can certainly indulge, and it would greatly pain me to be deprived of it, but this can be ours without marriage. Mr. Manning, we shall always be firm friends, but nothing more."

An expression of surprise and disappointment drifted across, but did not settle on, the editor's quiet countenance.

Turning to her, he answered with grave gentleness, "Judge your own heart, Edna; and accept my verdict with reference to mine. Do you suppose that after living single all these years I would ultimately marry a woman for whom I had no affection? You spoke last week of the mirror of John Galeazzo Visconte, which showed his beloved Correggia her own image. Though I am a proud and reticent man, I beg you to believe that could you look into my heart you would find it such a mirror. Permit me to ask whether you intend to accept the love which I have reason to believe Mr. Murray has offered you?"

Edna blushed deeply. "Mr. Manning, I never expect to marry anyone, for I know I shall never meet your superior, and yet I cannot accept your most flattering offer. You fill all my requirements of noble, Christian manhood; but after today this subject must not be alluded to."

"Are you not too hasty? Will you not take more time for reflection? Is your decision mature and final?"

"Yes, Mr. Manning – final, unchangeable. But do not throw me from you. I am very, very lonely. You surely will not forsake me?"

There were tears in her eyes as she looked up pleadingly in his face. The editor sighed and paused a moment before he replied, "Edna, if under any circumstances you feel that I can aid or advise you, I shall be exceedingly glad to render all the assistance in my power. Rest assured I shall not forsake you as long as we both shall live. Call upon me without hesitation, and I will respond as readily and promptly as to the claims of my little Lila. In my heart you are associated with her. You must not tax yourself so unremittingly, or you will soon ruin your constitution. There is a weariness in your face prophetic of failing health. Either give up your situation as governess or abandon your writing. I certainly recommend the former, as I cannot spare you from *Iconoclast*."

Here the carriage stopped at Mrs. Andrews's door. As he handed her out Mr. Manning said, "Edna, my friend, promise me that you will not write tonight."

"Thank you, Mr. Manning; I promise."

She did not go to her desk; but Felix was restless, feverish, querulous, and it was after midnight when she laid her head on her pillow. The milkmen in their noisy carts were clattering along the streets next morning before her heavy eyelids closed. She fell into a brief, troubled slumber over which flitted a Fata Morgana of dreams, where the central figure was always that tall one whom she had seen last standing at the railroad station with the rain falling over him.

CHAPTER XXIX
A LIFE IN THE BALANCE

"Let thy abundant blessing rest upon it, O Almighty God, else indeed my labor will be in vain. 'Paul planted, Apollos watered, but thou only can give the increase.'[109] It is finished; look down in mercy, and sanctify it, and accept it."

The night was almost spent when Edna laid down her pen, and raised her clasped hands over the manuscript, which she had just completed.

For many weary months she had toiled to render it worthy of its noble theme, had spared neither time nor severe trains of thought. By day and by night she had searched and pondered; she had prayed fervently and ceaselessly, and worked arduously, unflaggingly to accomplish this darling hope of her heart, and at last the book was finished.

The manuscript was a mental tapestry into which she had woven exquisite shades of thought, curious and quaint devices, and rich, glowing imagery that flecked the groundwork with purple and amber and gold.

But would the design be understood and appreciated by the great, bustling world, for whose amusement she had labored at the spinning-wheels of fancy – the loom of thought? Would they hang this tapestry of her mind along the walls of memory and turn to it tenderly, reading its ciphers and its illuminations? Or would it be torn and trampled underfoot?

Looking down at the mass of manuscript now ready for the printer, a tender, yearning expression filled the author's eyes. Her hands passed caressingly over its closely-written pages, as a mother's soft fingers might lovingly stroke the face of a child

---

[109] 1 Corinthians 3:6

about to be thrust out into a hurrying crowd of indifferent strangers, who perhaps would rudely browbeat her darling.

For several days past Edna had worked hard to complete the book, and now at last she could fold her tired hands and rest her weary brain.

But outraged nature suddenly swore vengeance, and her overworked nerves rose in fierce rebellion, refusing to be calm. She had so long anticipated this hour that its arrival was greeted by emotions beyond her control. As she contemplated the possible future of that manuscript, her heart bounded madly. Then once more, fearful agony seized her, and darkness and a sense of suffocation crushed her.

Rising, she strained her eyes and groped toward the window, but before she reached it, she fell and lost all consciousness.

The sound of the fall, the crash of a china vase which her hand had swept from the table, echoed startlingly through the silent house. Mrs. Andrews ran upstairs and into Felix's room, saw that he was sleeping soundly, and then she hastened up another flight of steps to the apartment occupied by the governess. The gas burned dazzlingly over the table where rested the roll of manuscript, and on the floor near the window lay Edna.

Ringing the bell furiously to summon her husband and the servants, Mrs. Andrews knelt, raised the girl's head, and rubbing her cold hands, tried to rouse her. Edna's heart beat faintly, and seemed to stop now and then. The pale, rigid face was as ghastly as if the dread kiss of the angel Samael had been pressed upon her still lips.

Finding all her restoratives ineffectual, Mrs. Andrews sent her husband for the family physician, and with the assistance of the servants, laid the girl on her bed.

When the doctor arrived and questioned Mrs. Andrews, she could furnish no clue to the cause of the attack, save by pointing to the table, where pen and paper showed that the sufferer had been at work.

Edna opened her eyes at last, and looked around at the group of anxious faces, but in a moment the spasm of pain returned. Twice she muttered something, and putting his ear close to her mouth, the doctor heard her whispering, "Never mind; it is done at last! Now I can rest."

An hour elapsed before the paroxysms entirely subsided. Then, with her hands clasped and thrown up over her head, Edna slept heavily, dreamlessly.

For two days she remained in her own apartment. On the morning of the third she came down to the schoolroom, with a slow, weary step, a bloodless face, and a feeling of hopeless helplessness.

She dispatched her manuscript to the publisher to whom she had resolved to offer it, and, leaning far back in her chair, took up Felix's Greek grammar.

Since the days of Dionysius Thrax, it had probably never appeared so tedious, so intolerably tiresome, as she found it now. She felt relieved, almost grateful when Mrs. Andrews sent for her to come to the library, where Dr. Howell was waiting to see her.

Seating himself beside her, the physician examined her countenance and pulse, and put his ear close to her heart.

"Miss Earl, have you had many such attacks as the one whose effects have not yet passed away?"

"This is the second time I have suffered so severely; though very frequently I feel a disagreeable fluttering about my heart, which is not very painful."

"What mode of treatment have you been following?"

"None, sir. I have never consulted a physician."

"Humph! Is it possible?"

He looked at her with the keen, incisive eye of his profession, and pressed his ear once more to her heart, listening to the irregular and rapid heartbeat.

"Miss Earl, are you an orphan?"

"Yes, sir."

"Have you any living relatives?"

"None that I ever heard of."

"Did any of your family die suddenly?"

"Yes, I have been told that my mother died as well as usual, while engaged in spinning; and my grandfather I found dead, sitting in his rocking-chair, smoking his pipe."

Dr. Howell cleared his throat, sighed and was silent.

A strange, startled expression leapt into Edna's shadowy eyes. Her mouth quivered, her wan face grew paler, and her thin fingers grasped each other; but she said nothing.

The physician had come like Daniel to the banquet of life, and solved for the Belshazzar of youth the hideous riddle scrawled on the walls.

Edna's voice sank to a whisper. "Dr. Howell, can you do nothing for me?" She leaned forward to catch his answer.

"Miss Earl, do you know what is meant by hypertrophy of the heart?"

"Yes, yes, I know." She shivered.

"Whether you inherited your disease, I am not prepared to say, but in your case there are some grounds for the belief."

Presently she said, "But grandpa lived to be an old man."

The doctor's eyes fell upon the mosaic floor of the library; and then she knew that he could give her no hope. Edna dropped her face in her palms.

"Miss Earl, I never deceive my patients. It is useless to dose you with medicine, and drug you into semi-insensibility. You must have rest and quiet; rest for mind as well as body; there must be no more teaching or writing. You are overworked, and incessant mental labor has hastened the approach of a disease which, under other circumstances, might have encroached very slowly. If latent, which is barely possible, it has contributed to a fearfully rapid development. Refrain from study, avoid all excitement, exercise moderately but regularly in the open air; and, above all things, do not tax your brain. If you carefully observe these directions you may live to be as old as your grandfather. Heart diseases baffle prophecy, and I make no predictions."

He rose and took his hat from the table.

"Miss Earl, I have read your writings with great pleasure, and watched your brightening career with more interest than I ever felt in any other female author. God knows it is exceedingly painful for me to tear away the veil from your eyes. From the first time you were pointed out to me in church, your countenance alarmed me, for its marble pallor whispered that your days were numbered. Frequently I have been tempted to come and expostulate with you, but I knew it would be useless. You have no reader who would more earnestly deplore the loss of your writings, but, for your own sake, I beg you to throw away your pen and rest."

She raised her head and a faint smile crept across her face.

"Rest? If my time is so short I cannot afford to rest. There is so much to do, so much that I have planned, and hoped to accomplish. I am only beginning to learn how to handle my tools, my life's work is as yet barely begun. When my long rest overtakes me, I must not be found idly sitting with folded hands. Since I was fifteen years old I have never once rested; and now I am afraid I never shall. I would rather die working than live a drone."

"But, my dear Miss Earl, those who love you have claims upon you."

"I am alone in this world. I have no family to love me, and my work is to me what I suppose dear relatives must be to other women. For six years I have been studying to fit myself for usefulness, have lived with and for books. Though I have a few noble and kind friends, do you suppose I ever forget that I am kinless? It is a mournful thing to know that you are utterly isolated among millions of human beings; that not a drop of your blood flows in any other veins. My God only has a claim upon me.

"Dr. Howell, I thank you for your candor. It is best that I should know the truth; and I am glad that, instead of treating me like a child, you have frankly told me all. More than once I have had a singular feeling, a shadowy presentiment that I should not live to be an old woman, but I thought it the relic of childish superstition, and I did not imagine that – that I might be called away at any instant. I did not suspect that just as I had arranged my workshop, and sharpened all my tools, and measured off my work, that my morning sun would set suddenly in the glowing east, and the long, cold night fall upon me, 'wherein no man can work'[110] – "

Her voice faltered. The physician turned away and looked out of the window.

"I am not afraid of death, nor am I so wrapped up in the mere happiness which this world gives; no, no. But I love my work. I

[110] John 9:4

366

want to live long enough to finish something grand and noble, something that will live when the hands that fashioned it have crumbled back to dust; something that will follow me across and beyond the silent valley; something that will echo in eternity! that grandpa and I can hear 'sounding down the ages[111],' making music for the people, when I go to my final rest.

"You know Glanville said, and Poe quoted, 'Man doth not yield himself to the angels, nor unto death utterly, save only through the weakness of his feeble will.[112]' My will is invincible; it will sustain me for a longer period than you seem to believe. Doctor, do not tell people what you have told me. I do not want to be watched and pitied, like a doomed victim who walks about the scaffold with a rope already around his neck. Let the secret rest between you and me."

He looked wonderingly at the electric face. Something in its chill radiance reminded him of the borealis light that waves its ghostly banners over a cold midnight sky.

"God grant that I may be in error concerning your disease; and that threescore years and ten may be allotted you, to embody the dreams you love so well. I repeat, if you wish to prolong your days, give yourself more rest. I can do you little good; still, if at any time you fancy that I can aid you, do not hesitate to send for me. I shall come to see you as a friend, who reads and loves all that has yet fallen from your pen. God help and bless you, child!"

As he left the room she locked the door, and walked slowly back to the low mantelpiece. Resting her arms on the black marble, she laid her head down upon them. Ambition and death stared face to face and held grim parley over the coveted prey.

Taking the probable measure of her remaining days, Edna fronted the future, and pondered the possibility of crowding into two years the work which she had designed for twenty.

To tell the girl to rest was a mockery; the tides of thought ebbed and flowed as ceaselessly as the ocean, and work had become a necessity of her existence. She was far beyond the cool, quiet palms of rest, far out on the burning sands. The mirage rippled and beckoned, and she panted and pressed on.

---

[111] "The Conquered Banner" – Abram Joseph Ryan
[112] Glanville's quote can be found in the story "Ligeia" – Edgar Allan Poe

One book was finished, but before she had completed it the form and features of another struggled in her busy brain, and she longed to put them on paper.

The design of the second book appeared to her eyes almost perfect, and the first seemed insignificant in comparison. Trains of thought that had charmed her, making her heart throb and her temples flush, and metaphors that glowed as she wrote them down, ah! how tame and trite all looked now, in the brighter light of a newer revelation. The achieved tarnished in her grasp; all before her was clothed with a dazzling glory, luring her on. If she could only live long enough to incarnate the new ideal!

Most of all, she knew that memory would spring up and renew its torture the moment that she gave herself to aimless reveries. Her sole hope of peace of mind, her only rest, was in unceasing labor. She worked late at night until her body was exhausted, because she dreaded to lie awake, tossing on her pillow, haunted by precious recollections of days gone by.

Now in her path rose God's Reaper, swinging his shining sickle, threatening to cut off and lay low her budding laurel wreath.

While she stood silent in the quiet library, Edna's soul was wrestling with God for permission to toil a little while longer on earth, to do some good for humanity, and in hopes of saving a darkened soul as dear to her as her own.

She never knew how long that struggle for life lasted; but when the prayer ended, and she lifted her face, the shadows and the sorrowful dread had passed away, and the old calm, the old patient smile reigned over her pale, worn face.

*****

Early in July, Felix's feeble health forced his mother to abandon her projected tour to the White Mountains. In accordance with Dr. Howell's advice, Mr. Andrews removed his family to a seaside summer-place, which he had owned for some years, but rarely occupied. Edna accompanied them, to watch the children.

The seaside house at the "Willows" was large and airy, the ceilings were high, windows wide. A broad piazza, stretching across the front, was shaded by two aged and enormous willows that stood on either side of the steps, and gave a name to the place.

The fresh matting on the floors, the light cane sofa and chairs, and the white muslin curtains and green blinds imparted an appearance of delicious coolness and repose to the rooms that Edna adored. While not one bright-hued painting was visible, the walls were hung with soft, misty engravings of Landseer's pictures, framed in carved ebony and rosewood and oak.

The gilded splendor of the Fifth Avenue house was left behind; here simplicity and quiet comfort held sway. Even the china wore no glitter, but was enameled with green wreaths of vine-leaves; and the vases held only plumy ferns, fresh and dewy.

Low salt meadowlands extended east and west, waving fields of corn stretched northward, and the slight knoll on which the building stood sloped smoothly down to the foam-fretted bosom of the blue Atlantic.

To the governess and her pupils, the change from New York heat and bustle to seaside rest was welcome and delightful. During the long July days, when the strong ocean breeze tossed aside the willow boughs, and swept through the rustling blinds, and lifted the hair on Edna's hot temples, she felt as if she had indeed taken a new lease on life.

For several weeks her book had been announced as in press, and her publishers printed most flattering circulars, which heightened expectation, and paved the way for its favorable reception. Save the first chapter, rejected by Mr. Manning long before, no one had seen the MS.

Finally, the book was bound; editors' copies winged their way throughout the country; the curious eagerly supplied themselves with the latest publication; and Edna's destiny as an author hung in the balance.

It was with strange emotions that Edna handled the copy sent to her, for it seemed indeed a part of herself. Her own heart throbbed in its pages, and she wondered whether the great world-pulses would beat in unison.

Instead of a preface she had quoted on the title-page those pithy lines in "Aurora Leigh":

"My critic Belfair wants a book
Entirely different, which will sell and live;
A striking book, yet not a startling book –
The public blames originalities.
You must not pump spring-water unawares
Upon a gracious public full of nerves –
Good things, not subtle – new, yet orthodox;
As easy reading as the dog-eared page
That's fingered by said public fifty years,
Since first taught spelling by its grandmother,
And yet a revelation in some sort:
That's hard, my critic Belfair!"[113]

Now, as Edna nestled her fingers among the pages of her book, a tear fell and moistened them. "Grandpa! Do you keep close enough to me to read my book? Oh! Do you like it? Are you proud of your poor little Pearl?"

The days were tediously long while she waited in suspense for the result of the weighing in editors' sanctums. A week dragged itself away; and then the severity of the decree might have entitled it to one of those slips of blue paper upon which Frederick the Great required his courts to inscribe their sentences of death.

Edna learned the full import of the words:

"He that writes,
Or makes a feast, more certainly invites
His judges than his friends; there's not a guest
But will find something wanting or ill-drest."[114]

Newspapers pronounced the book a failure. Some sneered in a gentlemanly manner, employing polite phraseology; others coarsely caricatured it. Many were insulted by its incomprehensible erudition; a few growled at its shallowness. Today there was a hint at plagiarism; tomorrow an outright, wholesale theft was asserted. Reviews poured in upon her thick and fast; all found grievous faults, but no two reviewers settled on

---

[113] Aurora Leigh – Elizabeth Barrett Browning
[114] from the Prologue to *The Surprisal* by Sir Robert Howard

the same error. What one seemed disposed to consider almost laudable the other denounced violently. One eminently shrewd, lynx-eyed editor discovered that two of her characters were stolen from a book which Edna had never seen; another found her entire plot in a work of which she had never heard; a third, shocked at her pedantry, indignantly assured her readers that they had been imposed upon, that the learning was all "picked up from encyclopedias[115]"; whereat the young author could not help laughing heartily, and wondered why, if her learning had been so easily gleaned, her insulted critics did not follow her example.

Edna was astonished. She knew that her work was not perfect, but she was equally sure that it was not contemptible. She was convinced, from the universal howling, that she had wounded more people than she dreamed were vulnerable.

Meanwhile, her book sold rapidly; the publishers could scarcely supply the demand.

At last Mr. Manning's Magazine appeared, and the yelping pack of Dandie Dinmont's pets – Auld Mustard and Little Mustard, Auld Pepper and Little Pepper, Young Mustard and Young Pepper[116], stood silent and listened to the roar of the lion.

The review of Edna's work was headed by that calm retort of Job to his self-complacent censors, "No doubt but ye are the people, and wisdom shall die with you[117]"; and it contained a withering rebuke to those who had so flippantly essayed to crush the young writer.

Mr. Manning handled the book with the stern impartiality which gave such value to his criticisms – treating it as if it had been written by an utter stranger.

He analyzed it thoroughly; and while pointing out some serious errors which had escaped all eyes but his, he bestowed upon a few passages praise which no other American writer had ever received from him, and predicted that they would live when those who attempted to ridicule them were utterly forgotten in their graves.

---

[115] He's ... not wrong.
[116] From *Guy Mannering* – Sir Walter Scott
[117] Job 12:2

The young author was told that she had not succeeded in her grand aim, because the subject was too vast for the limits of a novel, and her acquaintance with the mythologies of the world was not sufficiently extensive or intimate. But she was encouraged to select other themes more in accordance with the spirit of the age in which she lived. Some faults of style were gravely reprimanded, some beauties most cordially held up for the admiration of the world.

Gratefully and joyfully she accepted Mr. Manning's verdict, and turned her undivided attention upon her new manuscript.

While the critics snarled, the mass of readers warmly approved. Gradually the book took firm hold on the affections of the people; and a few editors came boldly to the rescue, and ably championed it.

During these days of trial, Edna could not avoid observing one humiliating fact that saddened without embittering her nature. She found that instead of sympathizing with her, she received no mercy from authors, who, as a class, out-Heroded Herod in their denunciations, and left her little room to doubt that –

> "Envy's a sharper spur than pay,
> And unprovoked 'twill court the fray;
> No author ever spared a brother;
> Wits are gamecocks to one another."[118]

---

[118] *Fables* – John Gay

CHAPTER XXX
THE TEETH OF THE STORM

Felix came hobbling up, a book in his hand. "Miss Earl, you promised that as soon as I finished the *Antiquary* you would read me a description of the spot which Sir Walter Scott selected for the scene of his story. We have read the last chapter; now please remember your promise."

"Felix, in your hunger for books you remind me of the accounts given of cormorants, who eat fish endlessly and never are sated. The 'Antiquary' ought to satisfy you for the present; still, if you exact an immediate fulfillment of my promise, I am quite ready to comply."

Edna took from her workbasket a new and handsomely illustrated volume of *The Harvest of the Sea* and read Bertram's glowing description of Auchmithie and the coast of Forfarshire.

Finding that her pupils were deeply interested in the "Fisher Folk," she read on and on; and when she began the story of the widow at Prestonpans, Hattie's eyes widened with wonder, and Felix's were dim with tears:

"We kent then that we micht look across the sea; but ower the waters would never blink the een that made sunshine around our hearths; ower the waters would never come the voices that were mair delightfu' than the music o' the simmer winds, when the leaves gang dancing till they sang. My story, sir, is dune. I hae nae mair tae tell. Sufficient and suffice it till say, that there was great grief at the Pans – Rachel weeping for her weans, and wouldna be comforted. The windows were darkened, and the air was heavy wi' sighin' and sabbin'.[119]"

---

[119] *The Harvest of the Sea* – James Glass Bertram

It was one of those rare and royal afternoons late in August, when summer, conscious that her reign is well-nigh ended, gathers all her gorgeous drapery, and proudly robes the world in regal pomp and short-lived splendor.

Pearly cloud islets, with silver strands, clustered in the calm blue of the upper air; soft, salmon-hued cumulus masses sailed solemnly along the eastern horizon – atmospheric ships freighted in the tropics with crystal showers for thirsty fields and parched meadows – with snow crowns for Icelandic mountain brows. Restless gulls flashed their spotless wings as they circled and dipped in the shining waves. In the magic light of evening, the swelling canvas of a distant sloop glittered like plate-glass smitten with sunshine.

A strong, steady, southern breeze curled and crested the bounding billows, over which a fishing-smack danced like a gilded bubble. As the aged willows bowed their heads, the wind whispered messages from citron, palm, and orange groves, gleaming far, far away under the white fire of the Southern Crown. Strange tidings these "winged winds" waft over sea and land. Today, listening to low tones that traveled to her from Le Bocage, Edna looked out over the ever-changing, wrinkled face of the ocean, and fell into a reverie.

Silence reigned in the sitting-room; Hattie fitted a new tarlatan dress on her doll, and Felix was dreaming of Prestonpans.

The breeze swept over the cluster of Tuscan jasmine and the tall, snowy phlox nodding in the green vase on the table, and shook the muslin curtains till light and shadow chased each other like waves over the walls. After a while Felix took his chin from the windowsill, and his eyes from the sparkling water, and his gaze sought the beloved countenance of his governess.

> The mouth with steady sweetness set,
> And eyes conveying unaware
> The distant hint of some regret
> That harbored there.[120]

---

[120] "Absent" from *The Letter L* – Jean Ingelow

Her dress was of white mull, with lace gathered around the neck and wristbands; a delicate fringy fern leaf was caught by the cameo that pinned the lace collar, and around the heavy coil of hair at the back of her head, Hattie had twined a spray of scarlet tecoma.

Save the faint red on her thin lips, Edna's face was as stainless as that of Mary, in a carved ivory "Descent from the Cross," which hung over the mantelpiece.

As the boy watched her, he thought her eyes were larger and deeper and burned more brilliantly, while the violet shadows beneath them seemed to widen day by day, telling of hard study and continued vigils.

"Yonder comes mamma and – Uncle Grey! No; that is not Uncle Grey. Who can it be? It is – Sir Roger!"

Hattie ran out to meet her mother, who had been to New York. Felix frowned, took up his crutches, and put on his hat.

Edna turned and went to her own room. In a few moments Hattie brought her a package of letters, and a message from Mrs. Andrews, asking her to come back to the sitting-room.

Glancing over the addresses, the governess saw that all the letters were from strangers, except one from Mrs. Murray, which she eagerly opened.

The contents of the letter were melancholy and unexpected. Mr. Hammond had been very ill for weeks, was not now in immediate danger, but was confined to his room; and the physicians thought that he would never be well again. He had requested Mrs. Murray to write, and beg Edna to come to him, and remain in his house. Mrs. Powell was in Europe with Gertrude and Gordon, and the old man was alone. Mrs. Murray and her son had been taking care of him thus far.

At the bottom of the page Mr. Hammond had scrawled almost illegibly: "My dear child, I need you. Come to me at once."

Mrs. Murray had added a postscript to tell her that if she would telegraph them upon what day she could arrange to start, Mr. Murray would come to New York for her.

Edna put the letter out of sight and girded herself for a desperate battle with her famishing heart, which bounded wildly at the tempting joys spread almost within react. The yearning to go back to the dear old parsonage, to the revered teacher, to cheer and brighten his declining days, and, above all, to see Mr. Murray's face, to hear his voice once more – oh! the temptation was strong indeed, and the cost of resistance bitter beyond precedent.

Having heard incidentally of the reconciliation that had taken place, she knew why Mr. Hammond so earnestly desired her presence in a house where Mr. Murray now spent much of his time. She knew all the arguments, all the pleadings to which she must listen, and she dared not trust her heart.

"Enter not into temptation!" was the warning which she uttered again and again to her own soul. Though she feared the pastor would be grieved, she hoped that he would not consider her ungrateful – hoped that his warm, tender heart would understand hers.

Though she had always studiously endeavored to expel Mr. Murray from her thoughts, there came hours when his image conquered; when the longing, the intense wish to see him overmastered her. She felt that she would give ten years of her life for one long look into his face, or for a picture of him.

Now, when she had only to say, "Come!" and he would be with her, she sternly denied her starving heart, and instead of bread gave it stones and serpents.

She took her pen to answer the letter, but a pang from her heart told her that she was not strong enough. Swallowing some medicine that Dr. Howell had prescribed, she snatched up a crimson scarf and went down to the beach.

The serenity of her countenance had broken up in a fearful tempest, and her face writhed as she hurried along to overtake Felix. Just now she dreaded to be alone, and the only companionship she could endure was that of the boy whom she had learned to love, as woman can love only when all her early idols are in the dust.

"Wait for me, Felix!"

The boy stopped, turned, and limped back to meet her, for there was a pleading intonation in her mournful voice.

"What is the matter, Miss Earl? You look troubled."

"I only want to walk with you, for I feel lonely this evening."

"Miss Earl, have you seen Sir Roger Percival?"

"No, no; why should I see him? Felix, my darling, my little brother! Do not call me Miss Earl any longer. Call me Edna. Ah, child, I am utterly alone; I must have somebody to love me. My heart turns to you."

She passed her arm around the boy's shoulders and leaned against him, while he rested on his crutches and looked up at her with fond pride.

"Edna! I have wanted to call you so since the day I first saw you. You know very well that I love you better than everything else in the world. If there is any good in me, I shall have to thank you for it; if ever I am useful, it will be your work. You do not need me - you are so great and gifted; whose writings everybody reads and admires. You cannot need anyone, and, least of all, a poor cripple. If I thought that you, Miss Earl - whose book all the world is talking about - if I thought you really cared for me - Oh, Edna! I believe my heart would be too big for my poor little body!"

"Felix, we need each other. Do you suppose I would have followed you out here, if I did not prefer your society to that of others?"

"Something has happened since you sat looking out of the window an hour ago. Your face has changed. What is it, Edna? Can't you trust me?"

"Yes. I received a letter which troubles me. It announces the feeble health of a dear and noble friend, who writes begging me to come to him, and nurse and remain with him as long as he lives. You need not start and shiver so - I am not going. I shall not leave you; but it distresses me to know that he has asked an impossible thing. Now you can understand why I did not wish to be alone."

She leaned her cheek down on the boy's head. Both stood silent, looking over the wide heaving waste of the sea.

A glowing orange sky overarched an orange ocean, which slowly became in turn ruby, and rose, and violet, and pearly gray, powdered with a few dim stars. As the rising waves broke along the beach, the stiffening breeze bent the spray till it streamed like silvery plumes; and the low musical murmur swelled to a monotonous moan that seemed to come over the darkening waters like wails of the lost from some far, far "isles of the sea."

Awed by the mysterious solemnity which ever broods over the ocean, Felix slowly repeated that dirge of Tennyson's, "Break, break, break!" When he commenced the last verse, Edna's voice, low and quivering, joined his.

Out of the eastern sea, up through gauzy cloud-bars, rose the moon, radiant, almost full, shaking off the mists, burnishing the waves with a ghostly luster.

The wind rose and fluttered Edna's scarlet scarf like a pirate's pennon, and the low moan became a deep, sullen, ominous mutter.

"There will be a gale before daylight; it is brewing down yonder at the southwest. The wind has veered since we came out. There! Did you notice what a savage snort there was in that last gust?"

Felix pointed to the distant waterline, where now and then a bluish flash of lightning showed the teeth of the storm raging far away under southern constellations, extinguishing for a time the golden flame of Canopus.

"Yes, you must go in, Felix. I ought not to have kept you out so long."

Reluctantly Edna turned from the beach. They had proceeded but a few yards in the direction of the house when they met Mrs. Andrews and her guest.

"Felix, my son! Too late, too late for you! Come in with me. Miss Earl, as you are so fond of the beach, I hope you will show Sir Roger all its beauties. I commit him to your care."

She went toward the house with her boy. As Sir Roger took Edna's hand and bent forward, looking eagerly into her face, she saw his pained and startled expression.

"Miss Earl, did you receive a letter from me written immediately after the perusal of your book?"

"Yes, Sir Roger, and your congratulations and flattering opinion were, I assure you, exceedingly gratifying, especially as you were among the first who found anything in it to praise."

"You have no idea with what intense interest I have watched its reception at the hands of the press. I think the shallow, flippant criticisms were almost as nauseating to me as they must have been to you. Your book has had a fierce struggle with these self-consecrated, red-handed, high priests of the literary gods; but its success is now established. I bring you news of its advent in England, where it has been republished. You can well afford to exclaim with Drayton:

> We that calumnious critic may eschew,
> That blasteth all things with his poisoned breath.
> Detracting what laboriously we do
> Only with that which he but idly saith.[121]

"Fortunately, Miss Earl, though the critics show their teeth, they are not strong enough to do much harm. Have you answered any of these attacks?"

"No, sir. Had I ever commenced filling the sieve of the Danaides, I should have time for nothing else."

She had crossed her arms on the low stone wall that enclosed the lawn. The moon shone full on her face, and her eyes and her thoughts went out to sea. Her companion stood watching her countenance, which recalled to his mind that vivid description:

---

[121] from Moses, His Birth and Miracles, Book II – Michael Drayton

And then she raised her head, and upward cast
Wild looks from *homeless eyes,* whose liquid light
Gleamed out between the folds of blue-black hair,
As gleam twin lakes between the purple peaks
Of deep Parnassus, at the mournful moon.[122]

After a short silence, Sir Roger said, "Miss Earl, I can find no triumph written on your features, and I doubt whether you realize how very proud your friends are of your success."

"As yet, sir, it is not assured. My next book will determine my status in literature; and I have too much to accomplish – I have achieved too little, to pause and look back, and pat my own shoulder. I am not so indifferent as you seem to imagine. Praise gratifies, and censure pains me; but I value both as mere gauges of my work, indexing the amount of good I may or may not hope to effect. I wish to be popular – that is natural, and, surely, pardonable; but I desire it not as an end, but as a means to an end – usefulness to my fellow-creatures:

'And whether crowned or crownless, when I fall,
It matters not, so as God's work is done.'"[123]

She seemed talking rather to herself, or to the surging sea where her eyes rested, than to Sir Roger.

As he noticed the pallor of her face, he sighed, and put his hands on hers.

"Come, walk with me on the beach, and let me tell you why I came back to New York, instead of sailing from Canada, as I once intended."

A half hour elapsed, and Mrs. Andrews, who was sitting alone on the piazza, saw the governess coming slowly up the walk. As she ascended the steps, the lady of the house exclaimed, "Where is Sir Roger?"

"He has gone."

---

[122] "Sappho" – Charles Kingsley
[123] by Alexander Smith

"Well, my dear, pardon me for anticipating you, but as I happen to know all about the affair, accept my congratulations. You are the luckiest woman in America."

Mrs. Andrews put her arm around Edna's waist, but something in the countenance astonished her.

"Mrs. Andrews, Sir Roger sails tomorrow for England. He desired me to beg that you would excuse him for not coming to bid you good-bye."

"Sails tomorrow! When does he return to America?"

"Probably never."

"Edna Earl, you are an idiot! You may have any amount of genius, but certainly not one grain of common sense. I have no patience with you! I had set my heart on seeing you his wife."

Edna drew back, hurt. "But, unfortunately for me, I could not set my heart on him. I am very sorry. I wish we had never met, for indeed I like Sir Roger. But it is useless to discuss what is past. Where are the children?"

"Asleep, I suppose. After all, show me 'a gifted woman, a genius,' and I will show you a fool."

Mrs. Andrews bit her lip and walked off. Stung by her words, Edna sighed and went upstairs to Felix's room.

The boy was sitting by the open window, watching gray clouds trailing across the moon, checkering the face of the mighty deep, now with shadow, now with sheen. So absorbed was he in his communing with the mysterious spirit of the sea, that he did not notice the entrance of the governess until he felt her hand on his shoulder.

"Ah, have you come at last? Edna, I was wishing for you a little while ago, for as I sat looking over the waves, a pretty thought came into my mind, and I want to tell you about it. Last week, you remember, we were reading about Antony and Cleopatra; and just now, while I was watching a large star yonder making a shining track across the sea, a ragged, hungry-looking cloud crept up, and nibbled at the edge of the star, and swallowed it. And I called the cloud Cleopatra swallowing her pearl!"

Edna looked wonderingly into the boy's bright eyes and drew his head to her shoulder.

"My dear Felix, are you sure you never heard that same thought read or quoted? It is beautiful, but this is not the first time I have heard it. Think, my dear little boy; try to remember where you saw it written."

"Edna, I am very certain I never heard it before. Do you recollect how it is written in the Englishman's poem? If you can repeat it, I shall know instantly, because my memory is very good."

"I think I can give you one stanza, for I read it when I was in great sorrow, and it made an impression upon me:

'The clouds, like grim black faces, come and go;
One tall tree stretches up against the sky;
It lets the rain through, like a trembling hand
Pressing thin fingers on a watery eye.
The moon came, but shrank back, like a young girl
Who has burst in upon funereal sadness;
One star came – Cleopatra-like, the Night
Swallowed this one pearl in a fit of madness!'[124]

"I never heard the poetry before, and I tell you, Edna, the idea is just as much mine as it is his."

"I believe you. Such coincidences are rare, and people are very loath to admit the possibility; but that they do occasionally occur, I have no doubt."

"Edna, I look at my twisted feet sometimes, and I feel thankful that it is my body, not my mind, that is deformed. If I am ever able to tell the world anything, it will be how much I owe you; for I trace all holy thoughts and pretty ideas to you and your music and your writings."

They sat there in silence, watching heavy masses of cloud darken the sea and sky. After a time, Felix lifted his face from Edna's shoulder and asked timidly, "Did you send Sir Roger away?"

"He goes to Europe tomorrow, I believe."

---

[124] "I Stand Beside Thy Lonely Grave" – John Stanyan Biggs

"Poor Sir Roger. I am sorry for him. I told mamma you never thought of him; that you loved nothing but books and flowers and music."

"How do you know that?"

"I have watched you, and when he was with you I never saw that great shining light in your eyes, or that strange moving of your lower lip, that always shows me when you are really glad; as you were that Sunday when the music was so grand; or that rainy morning when we saw the pictures of the 'Two Marys at the Sepulcher.' I hated poor Sir Roger, because I was afraid he might take you to England, and then, what would have become of me? The world seems so beautiful, so peaceful, as long as I have you with me. Everybody praises you, and is proud of you, but nobody loves you as I do."

He took her hand, passed it over his cheek and forehead, and kissed it tenderly.

"Felix, do you feel at all sleepy?"

"Not at all. Tell me something more about the animalcula that cause the phosphorescence yonder – making the top of each wave look like a fringe of fire."

"I do not feel well enough tonight to talk about animalcula. I am afraid I shall have one of those terrible attacks I had last winter. Felix, please don't go to bed for a while at least. If you hear me call, come to me quickly. I must write a letter before I sleep. Sit here, will you, till I come back?"

For the first time in her life she shrank from the thought of suffering alone and felt the need of a human presence.

"Edna, let me call mamma. I saw this afternoon that you were not well."

Edna shook her head. "No, it may pass. I want nobody about me but you."

Only a narrow passage divided her room from his. Leaving the door open, she sat down before her desk to answer Mr. Hammond's appeal.

As the night wore on, the wind became a gale. The fitful, bluish glare of the lightning showed fearful ranks of ravenous waves scowling over each others' shoulders. A roar as of universal thunder shook the shore, and in the coral-columned cathedral of the great deep, the wrathful ocean played a wild fugue.

Felix waited patiently, listening for the voice of his governess. But no sound came from the opposite room. At last, alarmed by the ominous silence, he took up his crutches and crossed the passage.

The muslin curtains, blown from their ribbon fastenings, streamed like signals of distress on the breath of the tempest, and the lamplight flickered and leaped to the top of its glass chimney.

On the desk lay two letters addressed respectively to Mr. Hammond and Mrs. Murray. Beside them were scattered half a dozen notes from unknown correspondents, asking for the autograph and photograph of the young author.

Edna knelt on the floor, hiding her face in the arms which were crossed on the lid of the desk.

Felix came close to her and hesitated a moment, then touched her lightly. "Edna, are you ill, or are you only praying?"

She lifted her head instantly, and her blanched, weary face reminded the boy of a picture of Gethsemane, which, having once seen, he could never recall without a shudder.

"Forgive me, Felix. I forgot that you were waiting – forgot that I asked you to sit up."

She rose, took Felix in her arms, and whispered, "I am sorry I kept you up so long. The pain has passed away. I think the danger is over now. Go back to your room and go to sleep as soon as possible. Good-night, my darling."

They kissed each other and separated; but the fury of the tempest forbade all idea of sleep. Thinking of the "Fisher Folk" exposed to its wrath, governess and pupil committed them to Him who calmed the Galilean gale.

> "The sea was all a boiling, seething froth,
> And God Almighty's guns were going off,
> And the land trembled."[125]

---

[125] "Wreck of 'The Grace of Sutherland'" – Jean Ingelow

CHAPTER XXXI
MRS. MURRAY INTERVENES

The Greek myth concerning Demophon embodies a valuable truth, which the literary career of Edna Earl was destined to exemplify. Harsh critics, like disguised Ceres, plunged the young author into the flames to burn away her mortal spirit. Fortunately for her, as no short-sighted, loving Metanira snatched her from the fiery ordeal, she ultimately obtained the boon of immortality. Her regular contributions to the magazine enhanced her reputation, and broadened the sphere of her influence.

Profoundly impressed by the conviction that she held her talent in trust, Edna worked steadily, looking neither to the right nor left, but keeping her eyes fixed upon that day when she should be called to render an account to Him who would demand His own with interest.

As the months rolled away, each magazine article seemed an improvement on the last, and lifted her higher in public favor.

The friendship between Mr. Manning and Edna strengthened, as each learned more fully the character of the other; and an affectionate, confiding frankness marked their conversations. As her popularity increased, she turned to him more frequently for advice, for success rendered her cautious. Day by day she weighed more carefully all that fell from her pen, dreading lest some error should creep into her writings and lead others astray.

In her publisher – an honorable, kind-hearted, and generous gentleman – she found a valued friend; and as her book sold extensively, her hope of an income was realized, and she was soon relieved from the necessity of teaching. She was a pet with the reading public; her pictures and autographs were eagerly sought after; and the little, barefooted Tennessee child had grown up to celebrity.

Sometimes, when a basket of flowers, or a handsome book, or a letter of thanks and cordial praise was received from an unknown reader, the young author was so overwhelmed with grateful appreciation of these little tokens of kindness and affection, that she wept over them, or prayed tremulously that she might make herself more worthy of the good opinion entertained of her by strangers.

Mr. Manning, whose cold, searching eye was ever upon her, could detect no exultation in her manner. She was earnestly grateful for every kind word uttered by her friends and admirers, for every favorable sentence penned about her writings; but she seemed only gravely glad, and was as little changed by praise as she had been by severe animadversion. The sweet, patient expression still rested on her face, and her beautiful eyes beamed with the steady light of resignation rather than the starry sparkle of extravagant joy.

Sometimes when the editor missed her at the literary reunions, he sought her in the schoolroom, he was often found her seated beside Felix, reading to him or listening to his conversation with a degree of interest which she did not always offer to the celebrities who visited her.

Her power over the young man was boundless. His character was as clay in her hands, and she was faithfully striving to model a noble, hallowed life; for she believed that he was destined to achieve distinction, and fondly hoped to stamp upon his mind principles and aims that would bear abundant fruit when she was silent in the grave.

Mrs. Andrews often told her that she was the only person who had ever controlled or influenced the boy – that she could make him just what she pleased; so she devoted herself to him, resolved to spare no toil in her efforts to correct his strong, obstinate, stormy nature. Few understood the sympathy which bound her so firmly to her broad-browed, sallow friend, who she loved dearly as a brother.

One December day, several months after their return from the seaside, Edna and Felix sat in the library. The boy had just completed Prescott's *Philip II,* and the governess had promised to read to him Schiller's *Don Carlos* and Goethe's *Egmont,* in order to impress upon his memory the great actors of the Netherlands revolution, just as Mr. Hammond had done in her studies. She took up the copy of *Don Carlos,* and, crossing his arms on the top of his crutches, as was his habit, the pupil fixed his eyes on her face.

The reading had continued probably a half-hour when Edna noticed Felix looking over his shoulder toward the door. He clumsily arose, suspicious but curious.

Looking up from her reading, Edna followed his gaze toward the door, to the stranger standing there.

Then her cry of joy rang through the room. Dropping the book, Edna sprang forward with open arms.

"Oh, Mrs. Murray! Mrs. Murray! dear friend!"

Edna buried herself in Mrs. Murray's arms. For some moments they stood locked in a warm embrace, and then Edna's chest heaved, and she burst out in sobs.

Mrs. Murray held the girl at arm's length, and as she looked at the wan, thin face. Edna half-laughed, half-sobbed, wiping away her tears.

Her dear friend exclaimed, "My poor Edna! My dear little girl, why did not you tell me you were ill? You are a mere ghost of your former self. My child, why did you not come home long ago? I should have been here a month earlier but was detained by Estelle's marriage."

Edna looked vacantly at Mrs. Murray. Her lips whitened. "Did you say Estelle – was married?"

"Yes, my dear. She is now in New York with her husband. They are going to Paris –"

"She married your –" Edna's head fell forward on Mrs. Murray's bosom.

As in a dream she heard Mrs. Murray say, "Estelle married that young Frenchman, Victor De Sanssure, whom she met in Europe. Edna, what is the matter? My child!"

She could not rouse Edna, and in great alarm called for assistance.

Mrs. Andrews promptly resorted to the remedies advised by Dr. Howell; but it was long before Edna fully recovered. Even then she lay with her eyes closed, and her hands clasped across her forehead.

Mrs. Murray sat beside the sofa weeping silently, while Mrs. Andrews briefly acquainted her with the circumstances attending former attacks. When Mrs. Andrews was summoned from the room and all was quiet, Edna looked up at Mrs. Murray. Tears rolled over her cheeks as she said, "I was so glad to see you, the great joy and the surprise overcame me. I am not as strong as I used to be in the old happy days at Le Bocage, but after a little I shall be myself. It is only occasionally that I have these attacks of faintness. Put your hand on my forehead, as you did years ago, and let me think that I am a little child again. Oh, the unspeakable happiness of being with you once more!"

"Hush! Do not talk now, you are not strong enough!"

Mrs. Murray kissed her and tenderly smoothed the hair back from her blue-veined temples, where the blood still fluttered irregularly.

For some minutes the girl's eyes wandered eagerly over her companion's countenance, tracing there the outlines of another and far dearer face, and finding a resemblance between mother and son which she had never noticed before. Then she closed her eyes again, and a half smile curved her trembling mouth, for the touch of the hand seemed indeed Mr. Murray's.

"Edna, I shall never forgive you for not writing to me, telling me frankly of your failing health."

"Oh! Scold me as much as you please. It is a luxury to hear your voice even in reproof."

Mrs. Murray huffed. "I knew mischief would come of this separation from me. You belong to me, and I mean to have my own, and take proper care of you in future. The idea of your working yourself to a skeleton for the amusement of those who care nothing about you is preposterous. I intend to put an end to such nonsense."

"Mrs. Murray, why have you not mentioned Mr. Hammond? I almost dread to ask about him."

"Because you do not deserve to hear from him. A grateful and affectionate pupil you have proved, to be sure. Oh, Edna, what has come over you, child? Are you so intoxicated with your triumphs that you utterly forget your old friends, who loved you when you were unknown to the world? At first I thought so. I believed that you were heartless, like all of your class, and completely wrapped up in ambitious schemes. But, my little darling, I see I wronged you. Your poor pale face reproaches me for my injustice, and I feel that success has not spoiled you; that you are still my little Edna – my sweet child – my daughter. Be quiet now, and listen to me, and try to keep that flutter out of your lips.

"Mr. Hammond is no worse than he has been for many months, but he is very feeble, and cannot live much longer. You know very well that he loves you tenderly, and he says he cannot die in peace without seeing you once more. Every day, when I go over to the parsonage, his first question is, 'Ellen, is she coming? – have you heard from her?' I wish you could have seen him when St. Elmo was reading your book to him. It was the copy you sent; and when we read aloud the joint dedication to him and to me, the old man wept, and asked for his glasses, and tried to read it, but could not. He – "

Edna put out her hand with a mute gesture, which her friend well understood, and she paused and was silent, while Edna turned her face to the wall and wept softly, trying to compose herself.

Ten minutes passed, and she said, "Please go on now, Mrs. Murray, and tell me all he said. You can have no idea how I have longed to know what you all at home thought of my little book. Oh, I have been so hungry for home praise. I sent the very earliest copies to you and to Mr. Hammond, and I thought it so hard that you never mentioned them at all."

"My dear, it was my fault, and I confess it freely. Mr. Hammond, of course, could not write, but he trusted to me to thank you in his name for the book and the dedication. I was angry with you for not coming home when I wrote for you; and I was jealous of your book, and would not praise it, because I knew you expected it. But because I was silent, do you suppose I was not proud of my little girl? If you could have seen the tears I shed over some of the eulogies pronounced upon you, and heard all the ugly words I could not avoid uttering against some of your critics, you could not doubt my thorough appreciation of your success.

"My dear, it is impossible to describe Mr. Hammond's delight as we read your novel to him. Often he would say, 'St. Elmo, read that passage again. I knew she was a gifted child, but I did not expect that she would ever write such a book as this.' When we read the last chapter he was completely overcome, and said, 'God bless my little Edna! It is a noble book; it will do good – much good!' To me it seems almost incredible that the popular author is the same little lame, crushed orphan, whom I lifted from the grass at the railroad track, seven years ago."

Edna had risen, and was sitting on the edge of the sofa, with one hand supporting her cheek, and a tender, glad smile shining over her features, as she listened to the commendation of those dearer than all the world beside. Mrs. Murray watched her anxiously, and sighed, as she continued.

"If ever a woman had a worshipper, you certainly possess one in Huldah Reed. It would be amusing, if it were not touching, to see her bending in ecstasy over everything you write, over every notice of you that meets her eye. She regards you as her model in all respects. You would be surprised at the rapidity with which she acquires knowledge. She is a pet of St. Elmo's, and repays his care and kindness with a devotion that makes people stare. You know my son is regarded as an ogre, and the child's affection for him seems incomprehensible to those who only see the rough surface of his character. She never saw a frown on his face or heard a harsh word from him, for he is strangely tender in his treatment of the little thing.

"Sometimes it makes me start when I hear her merry laugh ringing through the house, for the sound carries me far back into the past, when my own children romped and shouted at Le Bocage. You were always a quiet, demure, and rather solemn child; but this Huldah is a gay little sprite. St. Elmo is so astonishingly patient with her, that Estelle accuses him of being in his dotage. Oh, Edna, it would make you glad to see my son and that orphan child sitting together reading the Bible. Last week I found them in the library. She was fast asleep with her head on his knee, and he sat with his open Bible in his hand. He is so changed in his manner that you would scarcely know him, and oh, I am so happy and so grateful, I can never thank God sufficiently for the blessing."

Mrs. Murray sobbed, and Edna bent her own head lower in her palms.

For some seconds both were silent. Mrs. Murray seated herself close to the governess and clasped her arms around her.

"Edna, why did you not tell me all? Why did you leave me to find out by accident that which should have been confided to me?"

The girl trembled, and a fiery spot burned on her cheeks as she pressed her forehead against Mrs. Murray's bosom. "To what do you allude?" she asked hastily.

"Why did you not tell me that my son loved you, and wished to make you his wife? I never knew what passed between you until about a month ago, and then I learned it from Mr. Hammond. Although I wondered why St. Elmo went as far as Chattanooga with you on your way North, I did not suspect any special interest, for his manner betrayed none when, after his return, he merely said that he found no one on the train to whose care he could commit you. Now I know all – know why you left Le Bocage; and I know, too, that in God's hands you have been the instrument of bringing St. Elmo back to his duty – to his old noble self. Oh, Edna, my child, if you could know how I love and thank you. How I long to fold you in my arms – so – and call you my daughter. Edna Murray – St. Elmo's wife! When I took a bruised, homespun-clad girl into my house, how little I dreamed that I was sheltering unawares the angel who was to bring back happiness to my son's heart, and peace to my own!"

She lifted Edna's burning face and kissed her quivering lips repeatedly.

"Edna, my brave darling, how could you resist St. Elmo's pleading? How could you tear yourself away from him? Was it because you feared that I would not willingly receive you as a daughter? Do not shiver so – answer me."

"Oh, do not ask me! Mrs. Murray, spare me! This is a subject which I cannot discuss with you."

"Why not, my child? Can you not trust the mother of the man you love?"

Edna unwound the arms that clasped her, and rising, walked away to the mantelpiece. Leaning heavily against it, she stood for some time with her face averted. Beneath her veil of long, floating hair, Mrs. Murray saw the slight figure sway to and fro, like a reed shaken by the breeze.

"Edna, I must talk to you about a matter which alone brought me to New York. My son's happiness is dearer to me than my life, and I have come to plead with you, for his sake, if not for your own, at least to – "

"It is useless. Do not mention his name again. Oh, Mrs. Murray! I am feeble today; spare me! Have mercy on my weakness."

Edna put out her hand appealingly, but in vain.

"One thing you must tell me. Why did you reject him?"

"Because I could not respect his character. Oh, forgive me! You force me to say it – because I knew that he was unworthy of any woman's confidence and affection."

The mother's face flushed angrily, and she rose and threw her head back with the haughty defiance peculiar to her family.

"Edna Earl, how dare you speak to me in such terms of my own son? There is not a woman on the face of the broad earth who ought not to feel honored by his preference – who might not be proud of his hand. What right have you to pronounce him unworthy of trust? Answer me!"

"The right to judge him from his own account of his past life. The history which he gave me condemns him. His crimes make me shrink from him."

"Crimes? Take care, Edna. You must be beside yourself. My son is no criminal. He was unfortunate and rash, but his impetuosity was certainly pardonable under the circumstances."

"All things are susceptible of palliation in a mother's partial eyes," answered the governess.

"St. Elmo fought a duel, and afterward carried on several flirtations with women who were weak enough to allow themselves to be trifled with. I shall not deny that at one period of his life he was lamentably dissipated. But all that happened long

393

ago, before you knew him. How many young gentlemen indulge in the same things, and are never even reprimanded by society, much less denounced as criminals? The world sanctions dueling and flirting, and you have no right to set your extremely rigid notions of propriety above the verdict of modern society. Take care that you do not find yourself playing the Pharisee on the street corners."

Mrs. Murray walked up and down the room twice, then came to the hearth.

"Well, Edna, I am waiting to hear you."

"There is nothing that I can say which would not wound or displease you; therefore, dear Mrs. Murray, I must be silent."

"Retract the hasty words you uttered just now. They express more than you intended."

"I cannot. I mean all I said. Offences against God's law, which you consider pardonable – and which the world winks at and permits, and even defends – I regard as grievous sins. I believe that every man who kills another in a duel deserves the curse of Cain, and should be shunned as a murderer. My conscience assures me that a man who can deliberately seek to gain a woman's heart merely to gratify his vanity, or to wreak his hate by holding her up to scorn, or trifling with the love which he has won, is unprincipled, and should be ostracized by every true woman. Were you the mother of Murray and Annie Hammond, do you think you could so easily forgive this murderer?"

"Their father forgives and trusts my son. You have no right to sit in judgment upon him. Do you suppose that you are holier than that white-haired saint whose crown of glory is waiting for him in heaven?? Are you so much purer than Allan Hammond that you fear contamination from one to whom he clings?"

"No – no – no! You wrong me. If you could know how this breaks my heart, you would not taunt me so cruelly; you would only – pity me!"

The despairing agony in Edna's voice touched Mrs. Murray's proud heart. Tears softened the indignant expression of her eyes, as she looked at the feeble form before her.

"Edna, my poor child, you must trust me. One thing I must know – I have a right to ask – do you not love my son? You need not blush to acknowledge it to me."

She waited a while, but there was no reply as Edna bowed her head and a tear, then another, pattered on the hearth. Softly, Mrs. Murray's arm stole around the girl's waist.

"My daughter, you need not be ashamed of your affection for St. Elmo."

Edna lifted her face from the mantel, and clasping her hands across her head, exclaimed, "Do I love him? Oh, none but God can ever know how entirely my heart is his! I have struggled against his fascination –I have wrestled and prayed against it. But today – I do not deceive myself – I love him as I can never love any other human being. I fall asleep praying for him –in my dreams I am with him once more – that the first thought on waking is still of him. What do you suppose it cost me to give him up? Is it hard, think you, to live in the same world and yet never look on his face, never hear his voice? God only knows how hard! But to live with this great sea of silence between us – a dreary, cold, mocking sea, crossed by no word, no whisper, filled only with sailing ghosts of precious memories! Yes, despite all his unworthiness – despite the verdict of my judgment, and the upbraiding of my conscience – I love him. You can sympathize with me. Do not reproach me."

She put out her arms like a weary child and dropped her face on Mrs. Murray's shoulder.

"My child, if you had seen him the night before I left home, you could not have resisted any longer the promptings of your own heart," Mrs. Murray said tenderly. "He told me all that had ever passed between you; how he had watched and tempted you; how devotedly he loved you; how he reverenced your purity of character. Then he covered his face and said, 'Mother, if God would only give her to me, I could, I would be a better man!' Edna, I feel as if my son's soul rested in your hands. If you throw him off utterly, he may grow desperate, and go back to his old habits of reckless dissipation and blasphemy; and if he should! Oh! If he is lost at last, I will hold you accountable, and charge you before God with his destruction. Edna, beware! If you will not listen to your own suffering heart, or to his love, hear me! Hear a mother pleading for her son's eternal safety!"

The haughty woman fell on her knees before the orphan and wept.

Edna instantly knelt beside her and clung to her. "I pray for him continually. My latest breath shall be a prayer for his salvation. His eternal welfare is almost as precious to me as my own; for if I get to heaven at last, do you suppose I could be happy even there without him? But, Mrs. Murray, I cannot be his wife. If he is indeed conscientiously striving to atone for his past life, he will be saved without my influence. If his remorseful convictions of duty do not reform him, his affection for me would not accomplish it. Oh, of all mournful lots in life, I think mine is the saddest. To find it impossible to tear my heart from a man whom I distrust, whom I cannot honor, whose fascination I dread. I know my duty in this matter – my conscience leaves me no room to doubt – and from the resolution which I made in sight of Annie's grave, I must not swerve.

"I have confessed to you how completely my love belongs to him, how fruitless are my efforts to forget him. I have told you what bitter suffering our separation costs me, that you may know how useless it is for you to urge me. Ah, if I can withstand the wailing of my own lonely, aching heart, there is nothing else that can draw me from the path of duty; no, not even your entreaties, dear Mrs. Murray, much as I love you. God, who alone sees all, will help me to bear my loneliness. He only can comfort and sustain me; and in His own good time He will save Mr. Murray, and send peace into his troubled soul. Until then, let us pray patiently."

Flush and tremor had passed away, her features were locked in grieved sternness; and the unhappy mother saw that further entreaty would indeed be fruitless.

She rose and paced the floor for some moments. At last Edna said, "How long will you remain in New York?"

"Two days. Edna, I came here against my son's advice, in opposition to his wishes, to intercede in his behalf and to prevail on you to go home with me. He knew you better it seems than I did; for he predicted the result, and desired to save me from mortification; but I obstinately clung to the belief that you cherish some feeling of affectionate gratitude toward me. You have undeceived me. Mr. Hammond is eagerly expecting you, and it will be a keen disappointment to the old man if I return without you. Is it useless to tell you that you ought to go and see him? You need not hesitate on St. Elmo's account; for unless you wish to meet him, you will certainly not see him. My son is too proud to thrust himself into the presence of anyone, much less into yours, Edna Earl."

"I will go with you, Mrs. Murray, and remain at the parsonage – at least for a few weeks."

Mrs. Murray's face softened, but her voice was still hard. "I scarcely think Mr. Hammond will live until spring; and it will make him very happy to have you in his home."

Mrs. Murray wrapped her shawl around her and put on her gloves.

"I shall be engaged with Estelle while I am here, and shall not call again; but of course you will come to the hotel to see her, and we will start homeward day after tomorrow evening."

She turned toward the door, but Edna caught her dress.

"Mrs. Murray, kiss me before you go, and tell me you forgive the sorrow I am obliged to cause you today. My burden is heavy enough without the weight of your displeasure."

But the proud face did not relax; the mother shook her head, disengaged her dress, and left the room.

An hour after Felix came in, and approaching the sofa where his governess rested, said vehemently, "Is it true, Edna? Are you going South with Mrs. Murray?"

"Yes; I am going to see a dear friend who is probably dying."

"Oh, Edna! What will become of me?"

"I shall be absent only a few weeks – "

Felix clutched her arm and cried, "I have a horrible dread that if you go you will never come back. Don't leave me! Nobody needs you half as much as I do. Edna, you said once you would never forsake me. Remember your promise!"

"My dear little boy, I am not forsaking you; I shall only be separated from you for a month or two; and it is my duty to go to my sick friend. Do not look so wretched, for just so surely as I live, I shall come back to you."

"You think so now; but your old friends will persuade you to stay, and you will forget me, and – and – "

Felix turned around and hid his face on the back of his chair.

It was in vain that she endeavored, by promises and caresses, to reconcile him to her temporary absence. He would not be comforted. Felix's tear-stained, woebegone face, as she saw it on the evening of her departure, pursued her on her journey south.

CHAPTER XXXII
HOME AGAIN

The mockingbird sang as of old in the myrtle-boughs that shaded the study-window, and within the parsonage reigned the peaceful repose which seemed ever to rest like a benediction upon it. A ray of sunshine stealing through the myrtle-leaves made golden ripples on the wall; a bright wood fire blazed in the wide old-fashioned chimney; the white cat slept on the rug, with her pink paws turned toward the crackling flames; and blue and white hyacinths hung their fragrant bells over the gilded edge of the vases on the mantelpiece.

Huldah sat on one side of the hearth peeling a red apple. Snugly wrapped in his palm-leaf cashmere dressing-gown, Mr. Hammond rested in his cushioned easy chair with his head thrown far back and his fingers clasping a large bunch of his favorite violets. His snowy hair drifted away from a face thin and pale, but serene and happy. In his bright blue eyes there was a humorous twinkle, and on his lips a half-smothered smile, as he listened to the witticisms of his Scotch countrymen in *Noctes Ambrosianae*[126].

Close to his chair sat Edna, reading aloud from the quaint and inimitable book he loved so well. She paused now and then to explain some word which Huldah did not understand, or to watch for symptoms of weariness in Mr. Hammond's face.

The three faces contrasted vividly in the ruddy glow of the fire. That of the little girl, round, rosy, merry-eyed; the aged pastor's furrowed brow and streaming silver beard; and the carved-ivory features of the governess, borrowing no color from the soft folds of her rich merino dress. As daylight ebbed, the

---

[126] These are 71 witty colloquies collected in a book by John Wilson.

ripple of sunlight danced up to the ceiling and gradually vanished; the mockingbird hushed his vesper-hymn; and Edna closed the book and replaced it on the shelf.

Huldah tied on her scarlet-lined hood, kissed her friends good-bye, and went back to Le Bocage. The old man and the orphan sat looking at the flicker of the flames on the burnished andirons.

"Edna, are you tired, or can you sing some for me?"

"Reading aloud rarely fatigues me. What shall I sing?"

"That solemn, weird thing in the 'Prophet,' which suits your voice so well."

She sang 'Ah, mon fils!' and then, without waiting for the request which she knew would follow, gave him some of his favorite Scotch songs.

As the last sweet strains of "Mary of Argyle" echoed through the study, the pastor shut his eyes, and memory flew back to the early years when his own wife Mary had sung those words in that room, and his dead darlings clustered eagerly around the piano to listen to their mother's music. Five fair-browed, innocent young faces circling about the idolized wife, and baby Annie nestling in her cradle beside the hearth, playing with her waxen fingers and crowing softly. Death had stolen his household jewels; but recollection robbed the grave, and music's magic touch unsealed "memory's golden urn."

"Oh, death in life, the days that are no more!"[127]

Edna thought he had fallen asleep, he was so still, his face was so placid. She came softly back to her chair and looked into the fireplace at the ruby temples and towers, the glittering domes and ash-gray ruined arcades built by the oak coals.

A month had elapsed since her arrival at the parsonage, and during that short period Mr. Hammond had rallied and recovered his strength so unexpectedly that hopes were entertained of his entire restoration; and he spoke confidently of being able to reenter his pulpit on Easter Sunday.

---

[127] "Days That Are No More" – Lord Alfred Tennyson

The society of his favorite pupil seemed to render him completely happy, and his countenance shone in the blessed light that gladdened his heart. After a long, stormy day, the sun of his life was preparing to set in cloudless peace and glory.

Into all of Edna's literary schemes he entered eagerly. She read to him the manuscript of her new book as far as it was written and was gratified by his perfect satisfaction with the style, plot, and aim.

Mrs. Murray came every day to the parsonage, but Edna had not visited Le Bocage. Though Mr. Murray spent two mornings of each week with Mr. Hammond, he called at stated hours, and she had not yet met him. Twice she had heard his voice in earnest conversation, and several times she had seen his tall figure coming up the walk through the trees, but of his face she caught not even a glimpse. St. Elmo's name had never been mentioned in her presence by either his mother or the pastor, but Huldah talked ceaselessly of his kindness to her. Knowing the days on which he came to the parsonage, Edna, her heart aching, always absented herself from the invalid's room until the visit was over.

One afternoon she went to the church to play on the organ. After an hour of mournful enjoyment in the gallery so fraught with precious reminiscences, she left the church and found Tamerlane tied to the iron gate, but his master was not visible. She knew that he was somewhere in the building or yard, and denied herself the pleasure of going there a second time.

Neither glance nor word had been exchanged since they parted at the railroad station, eighteen months before. She longed to know his opinion of her book, for many passages had been written with special reference to his perusal; but she would not ask. It was a sore trial to sit in one room, hearing the indistinct murmur of his voice in the next, and yet never to see him.

Few women could have withstood the temptation; but the orphan dreaded his singular power over her heart, and dared not trust herself in his presence.

This evening, as she sat with the firelight shining on her face, thinking of the past, she could not realize that only two years had elapsed since she came daily to this quiet room to recite her lessons, for during that time she had suffered so keenly in mind and body that it seemed as if weary ages had gone over her young head. Involuntarily she sighed and passed her hand across her forehead.

A low tap at the door diverted her thoughts, and a servant entered and gave her a package of letters from New York. Every mail brought one from Felix. Now, opening his first, a tender smile parted her lips as she read his passionate appeal for her speedy return, and saw that the closing lines were blotted with tears. The remaining eight letters were from persons unknown to her, and contained requests for autographs and photographs, for short sketches for papers in different sections of the country, and also various inquiries concerning the time when her new book would probably be ready for press. All were kind, friendly, gratifying. One was eloquent with thanks for the good effect produced by a magazine article on a dissipated, irreligious husband and father, who, after its perusal, had resolved to reform, and wished her to know the beneficial influence which she exerted. At the foot of the page was a line penned by the rejoicing wife, invoking heaven's choicest blessings on the author's head.

"Is not the laborer worthy of his hire?" Edna felt that her wages were munificent indeed; that her coffers were filling, and though the "Thank God!" was not audible, the great joy in her uplifted eyes attracted the attention of the pastor, who had been silently watching her, and he laid his hand on hers.

"What is it, my dear?"

"The reward God has given me."

She read aloud the contents of the letter, and there was a brief silence, broken at last by Mr. Hammond.

"Edna, my child, are you really happy?"

"So happy that I believe the wealth of California could not buy this sheet of paper, which assures me that I have been instrumental in bringing sunshine to a darkened household; in calling the head of a family from haunts of vice back to his wife and children; back to the shrine of prayer at his own hearthstone. I will wear that happy wife's blessing in my inmost heart, and like those old bells in Cambridgeshire, it shall ring a silvery chime, exorcising all gloom, and loneliness, and sorrow."

The old man's eyes filled as he noted the radiance of the woman's lovely face.

"You have indeed cause for great joy, as you realize all the good you are destined to accomplish, and I know the rapture of saving souls, for, through God's grace, I believe I have snatched some from the brink of ruin. But, Edna, my child, there is a dreary look sometimes in your eyes, that reveals loneliness, almost weariness of life. I have studied your countenance closely; I read it I think without errors; and as often as I hear your writings praised, I recall those lines, written by one of the noblest of your own sex:

'To have our books
Appraised by love, associated with love,
While we sit loveless! is it hard, you think?
At least, 'tis mournful.'[128]

Edna, are you perfectly contented with your lot?"

A shadow drifted slowly over her marble face. "I cannot say that I am perfectly content, and yet I would not exchange places with any woman I know."

"Do you never regret a step which you took one evening, yonder in my church?"

"No, sir, I do not regret it. I often thank God that I was able to obey my conscience and take that step."

"Suppose that in struggling up the steep path of duty one soul needs the encouragement, the cheering companionship which only one other human being can give? Will the latter be guiltless if the aid is obstinately withheld?"

"Suppose the latter feels that in joining hands both would stumble?"

"You would not, oh, Edna! You would lift each other to noble heights. My child, will you let me tell you some things that – "

She threw up her hand, with that old, childish gesture which he remembered so well, and shook her head.

"No, sir. Please tell me nothing that will rouse a sorrow I am striving to drug. Spare me, for as St. Chrysostom once said of

---

[128] *Aurora Leigh* – Elizabeth Barrett Browning

Olympias the deaconess, I 'live in perpetual fellowship with pain.'"

"My dear little Edna, as I look at you and think of your future, I am troubled. I wish I could confidently say to you, what that same St. Chrysostom wrote to Pentadia: 'For I know your great and lofty soul, which can sail as with a fair wind through many tempests, *and in the midst of the waves enjoy a white calm.*[129]'"

She turned and took the minister's hand in hers. An indescribable peace settled on her countenance and stilled the trembling of her low, sweet voice. "Across the gray stormy billows of life, that 'white calm' of eternity is rimming the waterline, coming to meet me. Already the black pilot-boat heaves in sight; I hear the signal, and Death will soon take the helm and steer my little bark safely into the shining rest, into God's 'white calm.'"

She went to the piano and sang, as a solo, "Night's Shade No Longer," from Moses in Egypt.

While the pastor listened, he murmured to himself:

> "Sublime is the faith of a lonely soul,
> In pain and trouble cherished;
> Sublime is the spirit of hope that lives
> When earthly hope has perished."[130]

She turned over the sheets of music, hunting for a German hymn of which Mr. Hammond was very fond, but at this moment the doorbell rang. Soon after the servant brought in a telegraphic dispatch addressed to Mr. Hammond.

It was from Gordon Leigh, announcing his arrival in New York, and stating that he and Gertrude would reach the parsonage some time during the ensuing week.

Edna went into the kitchen to help with the preparation of the minister's supper. When she returned and placed the waiter on the table near his chair, she told him that she must go back to New York immediately after the arrival of Gordon and Gertrude, as her

---

129 Both quotes can be found in *Woman's Work in the Church: Historical Notes on Deaconesses and Sisterhoods* -- John Malcolm Forbes Ludlow
130 "The Isle of Palms" – John Wilson

services would no longer be required at the parsonage, and her pupils needed her.

Two days passed without any further allusion to a subject which was evidently uppermost in Mr. Hammond's mind.

On the morning of the third, Mrs. Murray said, as she rose to conclude her visit, "You are so much better, sir, that I must claim Edna for a day at least. She has not yet been to Le Bocage; and as she goes away so soon, I want to take her home with me this morning. Clara Inge promised me that she would stay with you until evening. Edna, get your bonnet. I shall be entirely alone today, for St. Elmo has carried Huldah to the town, and they will not get home until late. So, my dear, we shall have the house all to ourselves."

Edna could not deny herself the happiness offered. She knew that she ought not to go, but for once her strength failed her, and she yielded to the temptation.

During the drive Mrs. Murray talked cheerfully of various things, and for the first time laid aside entirely the haughty constraint which had distinguished her manner since they travelled south from New York.

They entered the noble avenue, and Edna gave herself up to the rushing recollections which were so mournfully sweet. As they went into the house and the servants hurried forward to welcome her, she could not repress her tears. This was her home, her heart's home; and as numerous familiar objects met her eyes, Edna was almost overpowered by her emotions.

"I wonder if there is any other place on earth half so beautiful," murmured Edna several hours later, as they sat looking out over the lawn where the deer and sheep were browsing.

"Certainly not to our partial eyes. And yet without you, my child, it does not seem like home. It is the only home where you will ever be happy."

"Yes, I know it; but it cannot be mine. Mrs. Murray, I want to see my own little room."

"Certainly; you know the way. I will join you there presently. Nobody has occupied it since you left, for I feel toward your room as I once felt toward the empty cradle of my dead child."

Edna went upstairs alone and closed the door of the apartment she had so long called hers, and looked with childish pleasure and affection at the rosewood furniture.

Turning to the desk where she had written much that the world now praised and loved, she saw a vase containing a superb bouquet, with a card attached by a strip of ribbon. The hothouse flowers were arranged with exquisite taste, and the orphan's cheeks glowed suddenly as she recognized Mr. Murray's handwriting on the card: "For Edna Earl." When she took up the bouquet a small envelope similarly addressed, dropped out.

For some minutes she stood irresolute, fearing to trust herself with the contents; then she drew a chair to the desk, sat down, and broke the seal.

"My DARLING: Will you not permit me to see you before you leave the parsonage? Knowing the peculiar circumstances that brought you back, I will not take advantage of them and thrust myself into your presence without your consent. I have left home today, because I felt assured that, much as you might desire to see 'Le Bocage,' you would never come here while there was a possibility of meeting me. You, who know something of my wayward, sinful, impatient temper, can perhaps imagine what I suffer, when I am told that your health is wretched, that you are in the next room, and yet, that I must not, shall not see you – my own Edna! Do you wonder that I almost grow desperate at the thought that only a wall – a door – separates me from you, whom I love better than my life? Oh, my darling! Allow me one more interview. Do not make my punishment heavier than I can bear. It is hard – it is bitter enough to know that you cannot, or will not trust me; at least let me see your dear face again. Grant me one hour – it may be the last we shall ever spend together in this world.

Your own, ST. ELMO."

Edna fought back tears. "Ah, my God! Why is it that I am tantalized with glimpses of a great joy never to be mine in this life? Why, in struggling to do my duty, am I brought continually to the very gate of the only Eden I am ever to find in this world, and yet can never surprise the watching Angel of Wrath, and have to stand shivering outside, and see my Eden only by the flashing of the sword that bars my entrance?"

Looking at the handwriting so different from any other which she had ever examined, her thoughts were irresistibly carried back to that morning when, at the shop, she saw this handwriting for the first time on the blank leaf of the Dante; and she recalled the shuddering aversion with which her grandfather had glanced at it, and advised her to commit it to the flames of the forge.

How many such notes as this had been penned to Annie and Gertrude, and to that wretched woman shut up in an Italian convent, and to others of whose names she did not know?

Mrs. Murray opened the door, looked in, and said, "Come. I want to show you something really beautiful."

Edna put the note in her pocket, took the bouquet, and followed her friend downstairs, through the rotunda, to the door of Mr. Murray's sitting-room. She inhaled deeply, smelling the cigar smoke that still lingered in the air, bringing his memory fully to tantalizing life in her heart.

"My son locked this door and carried the key with him; but after some search, I have found another that will open it. Come in, Edna. Now look at that large painting hanging over the sarcophagus. It is a copy of Titian's *Christ Crowned with Thorns*, the original of which is in a Milan church, I believe."

"It is very beautiful," Edna said faintly.

"While St. Elmo was last abroad, he was in Genoa one afternoon when a boat was capsized. Being a fine swimmer, he sprang into the water where several persons were struggling, and saved the lives of two little children of an English gentleman, who had his hands quite full in rescuing his wife. The father was so grateful to my son that last year he sent him this picture, which, though of course much smaller than the original, is considered a very fine copy. I begged to have it hung in the parlor, but fearing that its history might possibly be discovered (you know how he despises anything like a parade of good deeds), St. Elmo insisted on bringing it here to this Egyptian Museum, where, unfortunately, people cannot see it."

Christ Crowned with Thorns -- Titian

For some time they stood admiring it. Then Edna's eyes wandered away to the Taj Mahal, to the cabinets and bookcases. Her lip began to quiver as every article of furniture babbled of the By-Gone – of the happy evenings spent here – of that hour when the idea of authorship first seized her mind and determined her future.

Mrs. Murray walked up to the arch, over which the curtains fell touching the floor. Laying her hand on the folds of silk, said, "I am going to show you something that my son would not easily forgive me for betraying; for it is a secret he guards most jealously."

Edna put out her hands. "No, I would rather not see it. I wish to learn nothing which Mr. Murray is not willing to reveal."

"You will scarcely betray me to my son when you see what it is. Besides, I am determined you shall have no room to doubt the truth of some things he has told you. Do you recognize that face yonder, over the mantelpiece?"

Mrs. Murray held the curtains back. Despite her reluctance, Edna raised her eyes timidly, and saw, in a richly-carved oval frame, hanging on the opposite wall, a life-size portrait of herself.

"We learned from the newspapers that some fine photographs had been taken in New York, and I sent on and bought two. St. Elmo took one of them to an artist in Charleston, and superintended the painting of that portrait. When he returned, just before I went North, he brought the picture with him, and with his own hands hung it yonder. Since that day he always keeps the curtains down over the arch, and never leaves the house without locking his rooms."

Edna had dropped her crimsoned face in her hands, but Mrs. Murray raised it forcibly and kissed her.

"I want you to know how well he loves you – how necessary you are to his happiness. Now I must leave you, for I see Mrs. Montgomery's carriage at the door. You have a note to answer; there are writing materials on the table yonder."

She went out, closing the door softly, and Edna was alone with surroundings that pleaded piteously for the absent master. Oxalis and heliotrope peeped at her over the top of the lotos vases; one of a pair of gauntlets had fallen on the carpet near the cameo cabinet; two or three newspapers and a meerschaum lay upon a chair; several theological works were scattered on the sofa, and the air was heavy with lingering cigar-smoke.

Just in front of the Taj Mahal was a handsome copy of Edna's novel, and a beautiful morocco-bound volume containing a collection of all her magazine sketches.

She sat down in the crimson-cushioned armchair that was drawn close to the circular table, where pen and paper told that the owner had recently been writing, and near the inkstand was a handkerchief with German initials, *S. E. M.* She gently ran her hand over both, her heart aching.

409

There, too, was her own little Bible; and as she took it up it opened at the fourteenth chapter of St. John, where she found, as a book-mark, the photograph of herself from which the portrait had been painted. An unwithered geranium sprig lying among the leaves whispered that the pages had been read that morning.

Out on the lawn birds swung in the elm-twigs, singing cheerily, lambs bleated and ran races, and the little silver bell on Huldah's pet fawn, "Edna," tinkled ceaselessly.

"Help me, O my God! In this the last hour of my trial."

The prayer went up, and Edna took a pen and turned to write. Her arm struck a portfolio lying on the edge of the table, and in falling loose sheets of paper fluttered out on the carpet. One caught her eye. She picked it up and found a sketch of the ivied ruins of Phyle. Underneath the drawing, and dated fifteen years before, were traced, in St. Elmo's writing, those lines which Henry Soame is said to have penned on the blank leaf of a copy of the "Pleasures of Memory":

> "Memory makes her influence known
> By sighs, and tears, and grief alone.
> I greet her as the fiend, to whom belong
> The vulture's ravening beak, the raven's funereal song!
> She tells of time misspent, of comfort lost,
> Of fair occasions gone forever by;
> Of hopes too fondly nursed, too rudely crossed,
> Of many a cause to wish, yet fear to die;
> For what, except the instinctive fear
> Lest she survive, detains me here,
> When all the 'Life of Life' is fled?"

The lonely woman looked upward, appealingly, and there upon the wall she met – not as formerly, the gleaming, inexorable eyes of the Cimbrian Prophetess – but the pitying God's gaze of Titian's Jesus.

When Mrs. Murray returned to the room, Edna sat as still as one of the mummies in the sarcophagus, her head thrown back, her long, black eyelashes sweeping her colorless cheeks.

One hand was pressed over her heart, the other held a note directed to St. Elmo Murray. Her cold, fixed features made Mrs. Murray utter a cry of alarm.

As she bent over her, Edna opened her arms and said in a feeble, spent tone, "Take me back to the parsonage. I ought not to have come here; I might have known I was not strong enough."

"You have had one of those attacks. Why did you not call me? I will bring you some wine."

"No; only let me go away as soon as possible. I am ashamed of my weakness."

She rose, and her pale lips writhed as her sad eyes wandered in a farewell glance around the room.

She put the unsealed note in Mrs. Murray's hand, and turned toward the door.

"Edna! My daughter! You have not refused St. Elmo's request?"

"My mother, pity me! I could not grant it."

CHAPTER XXXIII
JUDGE NOT, THAT YE BE NOT JUDGED

"They have come. I hear Gertrude's birdish voice."

The words had scarcely passed Mr. Hammond's lips ere his niece bounded into the room, followed by her husband.

Edna was sitting on the chintz-covered lounge, mending a basketful of the old man's clothes that needed numerous stitches and buttons. Now, setting aside her sewing materials, she rose to meet the travelers.

At sight of her, Gordon Leigh stopped suddenly and his face grew instantly as bloodless as her own.

"Edna! Oh, how changed! What a wreck!"

He grasped her outstretched hand, folded it in his, which trembled violently. A look of anguish mastered his features, as his eyes searched her countenance.

"I did not think it would come so soon, passing away in the early morning of your life. Oh, my pure, broken lily!"

He did not seem to heed his wife's presence until Gertrude threw her arms around Edna, exclaiming, "Get away, Gordon! I want her all to myself. Why, you pale darling! What a starved ghost you are. Not half as substantial as my shadow, is she, Gordon? Oh, Edna, how I have longed to see you, to tell you how I enjoyed your delightful, noble book! To tell you what a great woman I think you are; and how proud of you I am." All this was uttered interjectionally between vigorous hugs and warm, tender kisses.

"I am happy to see you, too," Edna said, smiling.

Gertrude kissed her again. "A gentleman who came over in the steamer with us asked me how much you paid me per year to advertise your book. He was a miserable old bachelor who ridiculed all women unmercifully. At last I told him I would bet

412

both my ears that the reason he was so bearish and hateful, was because some pretty girl had flirted with him outrageously. He turned up his ugly nose especially at 'blue stockings'; said all literary women were 'hopeless pedants and slatterns,' and quoted that abominable Horace Walpole's account of Lady Mary Wortley Montagu's 'dirt and vivacity.'[131] I really thought Gordon would throw him overboard. I wonder what he would say if he could see you darning Uncle Allan's socks. Oh, Edna, dearie, I am sorry to find you looking so pale."

As Gertrude threw her bonnet and wrappings on the lounge, she added, "I wished for you just exactly ten thousand times while I was abroad, there were so many things that you could have described so beautifully. Gordon, don't Edna's eyes remind you very much of that divine picture of the Madonna at Dresden?"

She looked round for an answer, but her husband had left the room. Remembering a parcel that had been stowed away in the pocket of the carriage, she ran out to get it.

Presently she reappeared at the door with a goblet in her hand.

"Uncle Allan, who carries the keys now?"

"Edna. What will you have, my dear?"

"I want some brandy. Gordon looks very pale, and complains of not feeling well, so I intend to make him a mint-julep. Ah, Edna! These husbands are such troublesome creatures."

She left the room jingling the bunch of keys, and a few moments after they heard her humming an air from "Rigoletto," as she bent over the mint-bed, under the study window.

Mr. Hammond, who had observed all that passed, saw the earnest distress clouding the orphan's brow. "She has not changed an iota; she never will be anything more than a beautiful, merry child, not a companion in the true sense of the word. Unless Gordon learns more self-control, he will ere long betray himself. I expostulated with him before his marriage, but for once he threw my warning to the winds. I am an old man, and have seen many phases of human nature, and I have found that these pique

---

[131] Horace Walpole: "Lady Mary Wortley is arrived; I have seen her; I think her avarice, her dirt, and her vivacity are all increased: her dress, like her language, is a galamatias of several countries, the groundwork rags, and the embroidery nastiness." But nobody has time for Horace Walpole's stupid opinions.

marriages are always mournful – always disastrous. In such instances I would with more pleasure officiate at the grave than at the altar. Once Estelle and Agnes persuaded me that St. Elmo was about to wreck himself on this rock of ruin, and even his mother's manner led me to believe that he would marry his cousin; but, thank God! He was wiser than I feared."

"Mr. Hammond, are you sure that Gertrude loves Mr. Leigh?"

"Oh, yes, my dear. Of that fact there can be no doubt. Why do you question it?"

"She told me once that Mr. Murray had won her heart."

It was the first time Edna had mentioned his name since her return, and it brought a faint flush to her cheeks.

"That was a childish whim which she has utterly forgotten. A woman of her temperament never remains attached to a man from whom she is long separated. I do not suppose that she remembered St. Elmo a month after she ceased to meet him. I feel assured that she loves Gordon as well as she can love anyone."

The outline of Edna's mouth hardened. "I will go away at once. This is Saturday, and I will start to New York early Monday morning. Mr. Leigh is weaker than I ever imagined he could be." Into her eyes crept an expression of scorn that very rarely found a harbor there.

"Yes, my dear. Although it grieves me to part with you, I know it is best that you should not be here, at least for the present. Agnes is visiting friends at the North and when she returns, Gordon and Gertrude will remove to their new house. Then, Edna, if I feel that I need you, if I write for you, will you not come back to me? Dear child, I want your face to be the last I look upon in this world."

She drew the pastor's shrunken hand to her lips and shook her head.

"Do not ask me to do that which my strength will not permit. There are many reasons why I ought not to come here again. Moreover, my work calls me to a distant field. My physical strength seems to be ebbing fast, and my vines are not all purple with mellow fruit. Some clusters, thank God, are fragrant, ripe, and ready for the wine-press, when the Angel of the Vintage comes to gather them in; but my work is only half done."

The splendor of the large eyes seemed almost unearthly as she looked out over the fields, where in summers past the shout of the merry reapers rose like the songs of Greek harvesters to Demeter.

Edna sat silent for some time, with her slender hands folded on her lap, and the pastor heard her softly repeating, as if to her own soul, those lines on "Life":

> "A cry between the silences,
> A shadow-birth of clouds at strife
> With sunshine on the hills of life;
> Between the cradle and the shroud,
> A meteor's flight from cloud to cloud!"[132]

Several hours later, when Mr. Leigh returned to the study, he found Edna singing some of the minister's favorite Scotch ballads. Gertrude rested on the lounge, half propped on her elbow, leaning forward to dangle the tassel of her chamber robe within reach of an energetic little blue-eyed kitten, which, with its paws in the air, rolled on the carpet, catching at the silken toy. Edna left the piano and resumed her mending of the contents of the clothes-basket.

In answer to some inquiries of Mr. Hammond, Mr. Leigh gave a brief account of his travels in Southern Europe; but his manner was constrained, his thoughts preoccupied. Once his eyes wandered to the round, rosy, dimpling face of his beautiful child-wife, and he frowned, bit his lip, and sighed; while his gaze, earnest and mournfully anxious, returned and dwelt upon the weary but serene countenance of the orphan.

In the conversation Gertrude took no part; now and then glancing up at the speakers, she continued her romp with the kitten. At length, tired of her frolicsome pet, she rose with a half-suppressed yawn, and sauntered up to her husband's chair. Softly and lovingly she passed her palms over her husband's darkened brow, and her fingers drew his hair now on one side, now on the other, while she peeped over his shoulder to watch the effect of the arrangement.

---

[132] "Questions of Life" – John Greenleaf Whittier

The caresses were inopportune, her touch annoyed him. He shook it off, and, stretching out his arm, put her gently but firmly away, saying, coldly, "There is a chair, Gertrude."

Edna's eyes looked steadily into his, with an expression of grave, sorrowful reproof – and the flush deepened on his face as his eyes fell before her rebuking gaze.

Perhaps the young wife had become accustomed to such rebuffs; at all events she evinced neither mortification nor surprise, but twirled her silk tassel vigorously around her finger, and exclaimed, "Oh, Gordon, have you not forgotten to give Edna that letter written by the gentleman we met at Palermo? Edna, he paid your book some splendid compliments. I fairly clapped my hands at his praises – didn't I, Gordon?"

Mr. Leigh drew a letter from the inside pocket of his coat. As he gave it to Edna, said with a touch of bitterness in his tone, "Pardon my negligence; probably you will find little news in it, as he is one of your old victims, and you can guess its contents."

The letter was from Sir Roger. While he expressed great grief at hearing, through Mr. Manning's notes, that her health was seriously impaired, he renewed the offer of his hand, and asked permission to come and plead his suit in person.

As Edna hurriedly glanced over the pages, and put them in her pocket, Gertrude said gaily, "Shame on you, Gordon. Do you mean to say that all who read Edna's book are victimized?"

He looked at her from under thickening eyebrows, and replied with undisguised impatience, "No; your common sense ought to teach you that such was not my meaning or intention. Edna places no such interpretation on my words."

"Common sense? Oh, Gordon, dearie, how unreasonable you are. Why, you have told me a thousand times that I had not a particle of common sense, except on the subject of juleps; and how, then, in the name of wonder, can you expect me to show any? I never pretended to be a great shining genius like Edna, whose writings all the world is talking about. I only want to be wise enough to understand you, dearie, and make you happy. Gordon, don't you feel any better? What makes your face so red?"

She went back to his chair, and leaned her lovely head close to his, while an anxious expression filled her large blue eyes.

Gordon Leigh realized that his marriage was a terrible mistake which only death could rectify; but even in his wretchedness he blamed only himself. Had he not wooed the love of which, already, he was weary? Having deceived her at the altar, was there justification for his dropping the mask at the hearthstone? Nay, there must be no rattling of skull and crossbones to freeze the blood in the sweet laughing face of the trusting bird.

Now her clinging tenderness, her affectionate humility, upbraided him as no harsh words could possibly have done. With a smothered sigh he passed his arm around her and drew her close to his side. "At least my little wife is wise enough to teach her husband to be ashamed of his petulance."

"And quite wise enough, dear Gertrude, to make him very proud and happy; for you ought to be able to say with the sweetest singer in all merry England:

> 'But I look up and he looks down,
> And thus our married eyes can meet;
> Unclouded his, and clear of frown,
> And gravely sweet.'"[133]

As Edna glanced at the young wife, a mist gathered in her own eyes, and collecting her sewing utensils she went to her room to pack her trunk.

During her stay at the parsonage she had not attended service in the church, because Mr. Hammond was lonely, and her Sabbaths were spent in reading to him. But her old associates in the choir insisted that, before she returned to New York, she should sing with them once more.

Thus far she had declined all invitations; but on the morning of the last day of her visit, the organist called to say that a distinguished divine from a distant state would fill Mr. Hammond's pulpit. As the leading soprano in the choir was disabled by severe cold, and could not be present, he begged that Edna would take her place, and sing a certain solo in the music which he had selected for an opening piece. Mr. Hammond, who was pardonably proud of his choir, was anxious that the stranger

---

[133] "Present" from *The Letter L* – Jean Ingelow

should be greeted and inspired by fine music, and urged Edna's compliance with the request.

Reluctantly she consented. For the first time Duty and Love signaled a truce, and shook hands over the preliminaries of a treaty for peace.

That Sunday morning, as she passed through the churchyard and walked up the steps where a group of Sabbath-school children sat talking, her eyes involuntarily sought the dull brown spot on the marble.

Over it little Herbert Inge had spread his white handkerchief, and piled thereon his Testament and catechism, laying on the last one of those gilt-bordered pictorial cards, containing a verse from the Scriptures, which are frequently distributed by Sabbath-school teachers.

Edna stooped and looked at the picture covering the bloodstain. It represented our Savior on the Mount, delivering the sermon, and in golden letters were printed his words:

"Judge not, that ye be not judged. For with what judgment ye judge, ye shall be judged; and with what measure ye mete, it shall be measured to you again."[134]

The eyes of the Divine Preacher seemed to look into hers, and the outstretched hand to point directly at her.

She trembled, and hastily kissing the sweet red lips which little Herbert held up to her, she went in and hurried up to the gallery.

The congregation assembled slowly. Almost all the faces were familiar to Edna, and each arrival revived something of the past. Here the flashing silk flounces of a young belle brushed the straight black folds of widow's weeds; on the back of one seat was stretched the rough brown hand of a poor laboring man; on the next lay the dainty fingers of a matron of wealth and fashion, who had entirely forgotten to draw a glove over her sparkling diamonds.

In all the splendor of velvet, feathers, and sea-green moiré, Mrs. Montgomery sailed proudly into her pew, convoying her daughter Maud, who was smiling and whispering to her escort. Just behind them came a plainly-clad young carpenter, clasping to

---

[134] Matthew 7:1-3

his heart the arm of his sweet-faced wife, and holding the hand of his three-year-old boy, who toddled along, staring at the brilliant pictures on the windows.

When Mr. Leigh and Gertrude entered there was a general stir, a lifting of heads and twisting of necks, in order to see what new styles of bonnet, lace, and mantle prevailed in Paris.

A moment after Mrs. Murray walked slowly down the aisle. Edna's heart stood still as Mr. Murray's powerful form followed his mother. He stepped forward, and while he opened the door of the pew and waited for his mother to seat herself, his face was visible. Edna drank in the profile, water for her thirsty heart; then he sat down, closing the door.

The minister entered, and as he ascended the pulpit, the organ began to breathe its solemn welcome. When the choir rose and commenced their chorus, Edna stood silent, with her book in her hand, and her eyes fixed on the Murrays' pew.

The strains of triumph ceased, the organ only sobbed its sympathy to the thorn-crowned Christ, struggling along the Via Dolorosa. Edna's quivering lips parted, and she sang her solo.

As her magnificent voice rose and rolled to the arched roof, people forgot propriety, and turned to look at the singer. She saw Mrs. Murray start and glance eagerly up at her. For an instant her grand, pure voice faltered slightly, as Edna watched the mother whispered something to the son. But he did not turn his proud head. He only leaned his elbow on the side of the pew next to the aisle, and rested his temple on his hand.

When the preliminary services ended, and the minister stood up in the shining pulpit and commenced his discourse, Edna felt that St. Elmo had enlisted angels in his behalf; for the text was contained in the warning whose gilded letters hid the blood-spot, "Judge not, that ye be not judged."

As far as two among his listeners were concerned, the preacher might as well have addressed his sermon to the mossy slabs visible through the windows. Both listened to the text, and neither heard any more. Edna sat looking down at Mr. Murray's massive, finely-poised head, and she could see his profile contour of features, regular and dark, as if carved and bronzed.

During the next half-hour her vivid imagination sketched and painted a vision of enchantment – of what might have been, if St. Elmo, there in the crimson-cushioned pew, had kept his soul from grievous sins. A vision of a happy, proud wife reigning at Le Bocage, shedding the rosy light of her love over the lonely life of its master; adding to his clear intellect and ripe experience, the silver flame of her genius; borrowing from him broader and more profound views of the world on which to base her ideal aesthetic structures; softening, refining his nature, strengthening her own; helping him to help humanity; loving all good, being good, doing good; serving and worshipping God together; walking hand and hand with her husband with peaceful faces full of faith, looking heavenward.

> "God pity them both! and pity us all,
> Who vainly the dreams of youth recall.
> For of all sad words of tongue or pen
> The saddest are these, 'It might have been!'"[135]

At last, with a faint moan, which reached no ear but that of Him who never slumbers, Edna withdrew her eyes from the spot where Mr. Murray sat, and raised them toward the pale Christ, whose wan lips seemed to murmur:

"Be of good cheer! He that overcometh shall inherit all things. What I do, thou knowest not now, but thou shalt know hereafter."[136]

The minister, standing beneath the picture of the Master whom he served, closed the Bible and ended his discourse by hurling his text as a thunderbolt at those whose upturned faces watched him:

"Finally, brethren, remember under all circumstances the awful admonition of Jesus, 'Judge not, that ye be not judged!'"

The organ peals and the doxology were concluded; the benediction fell like God's dew, on sinner and on saint, and amid the solemn tones of the gilded pipes, the congregation turned to quit the church.

---

[135] "Maud Muller" – John Greenleaf Whittier
[136] Matthew 14:27; Revelation 21:7; John 13:7

With both hands pressed over her heart, Edna leaned heavily against the railing.

"Tomorrow I go away forever. I shall never see his face again in this world. Oh! I want to look at it once more."

As he stepped into the aisle, Mr. Murray threw his head back, and his eyes swept up to the gallery and met hers. It was a long, eager, heart-searching gaze. She saw a countenance more fascinating than of old; for his sardonic glare had gone. His bitterness, the "dare-man, dare-brute, dare-devil" expression had given place to a stern mournfulness. Now the softening shadow of deep contrition and manly sorrow hovered over features where scoffing cynicism had so long scowled.

The magnetism of St. Elmo's eyes was never more marvelous than when they rested on the beautiful face of the woman he loved so well, whose calm, holy eyes shone like those of an angel as they looked sadly down at his. In the mystic violet light with which the stained glass flooded the church, Edna's pallid, suffering face, sublime in its meekness and resignation, hung above him like one of Perugino's saints over kneeling medieval worshippers.

As the moving congregation bore him nearer to the door, she leaned farther over the mahogany balustrade. A snowy crocus she wore at her throat snapped its brittle stem and floated down till it touched his shoulder. He laid one hand over it, holding it there.

While a prayer burned in his splendid eyes, hers smiled a melancholy farewell.

The crowd swept the tall form forward, under the arches, beyond the fluted columns of the gallery, and the long gaze ended.

> "Ah! well for us all some sweet hope lies
> Deeply buried from human eyes;
> And in the hereafter, angels may
> Roll the stone from its grave away."[137]

---

[137] "Maud Muller" – John Greenleaf Whittier

CHAPTER XXXIV
THE VOYAGE

"I am truly thankful that you have returned!" Mrs. Andrews said when Edna arrived. "I am quite worn out trying to humor Felix's whims. He has actually lost ten pounds; and if you had stayed away a month longer I think it would have finished my poor boy. He almost had a spasm last week, when his father told him he had better reconcile himself to your absence, as he believed that you would never come back to the drudgery of the schoolroom. I am very anxious about him; his health is more feeble than it has been since he was five years old."

"Oh, no," Edna said softly.

Mrs. Andrews prattled on. "My dear, you have no idea how you have been missed. Your admirers call by scores to ascertain when you may be expected home. I do not exaggerate in the least when I say that there is a champagne basketful of periodicals and letters that have arrived recently for you. You will find them piled on the table and desk in your room."

"Where are the children?" asked Edna, glancing around the sitting-room into which Mrs. Andrews had drawn her.

"Hattie is spending the day with Lila Manning, who is just recovering from a severe attack of scarlet fever. Felix is in the library trying to sleep. He has one of his nervous headaches to-day. Poor fellow, he tries so hard to overcome his irritable temper and to grow patient, that I am growing fonder of him every day. How travel-spent and ghastly you are. Sit down, and I will order some refreshments. Take this wine, my dear, and presently you shall have a cup of chocolate."

"Thank you, not any wine. I only want to see Felix."

Edna went to the library, cautiously opened the door, and crept softly across the floor to the end of the sofa.

The boy lay looking through the window, and up beyond the walls and chimneys, at the sapphire sky where rolled the sun. Casual observers thought the boy's face ugly and disagreeable; but the tender, loving smile that lighted Edna's face as she leaned forward, told that some charm lingered in the sharpened features overcast with sickly sallowness.

But in his large, deep-set eyes, over which the heavy brows arched like a roof, Edna saw now a strange expression that frightened her. Was it the awful shadow of the Three Singing Spinners at the wedding of Peleus, whom Catullus wrote about? As the child looked into the blue sky, did he catch a glimpse of their trailing white robes, purple-edged – of their floating rose-colored veils?

The governess was seized by apprehension as she watched her pupil. Bending down, she said, fondly, "Felix, my darling, I have come back! Never again while I live will I leave you."

The almost bewildering joy that flashed into his countenance eloquently welcomed her. Kneeling beside the sofa, she wound her arms around him, and drew his head to her shoulder.

"Edna, is Mr. Hammond dead?"

"No, he is almost well again, and needs me no more."

"I need you more than anybody else ever did. Oh, Edna, I thought sometimes you would stay at the South that you love so well, and I should see you no more; and then all the light seemed to die out of the world, and the flowers were not sweet, and the stars were not bright, and oh, I was glad I had not long to live."

"Hush! You wring my heart, for I have missed you too. My dear little boy, in all this wide earth, you are the only one whom I have to love and cling to, and we will be happy together. Darling, your head aches today?"

She pressed her lips twice to his hot forehead.

"Yes; but the heartache was much the hardest to bear until you came. Mamma has been very good and kind, and stayed at home and read to me; but I wanted you, Edna. I do not believe I have been wicked since you left; for I prayed all the while that God would bring you back to me. I have tried hard to be patient."

With her cheek nestled against his, Edna told him many things that had occurred during their separation and noticed that his eyes brightened suddenly.

"Edna, I have a secret to tell you; something that even mamma is not to know just now. You must not laugh at me. While you were gone I wrote a little manuscript, and it is dedicated to you. and some day I hope it will be printed. Are you glad, Edna?"

"Felix, I am very glad you love me sufficiently to dedicate your little story to me, and yes, I am glad you wrote it."

"If you had been here, it would not have been written, because then I should merely have talked out all the ideas to you; but you were far away, and so I talked to my paper. After all, it was only a dream. One night I was feverish, and mamma read aloud those passages that you marked in that great book, Maury's *Physical Geography of the Sea,* that you admire and quote so often; and of which I remember you said once, in talking to Mr. Manning, that 'it rolled its warm, beautiful, sparkling waves of thought across the cold, gray sea of science, just like the Gulf Stream it treated of.' Two of the descriptions which mamma read were so splendid that they rang in my ears like music. When at last I went to sleep, I had a funny dream about madrepores and medusae, and I wrote it down as well as I could, and called it 'Algae Adventures, in a Voyage Round the World.'"

"My dear, ambitious authorling, my little round-jacket scribbler!" Edna gave him a sideways hug.

"Edna, I should like above all things to write a book of stories for poor, sick children; little tales that would make them forget their suffering. If I could even reconcile one lame boy to being shut up indoors, while others are shouting and skating in the sunshine, I should not feel as if I were so altogether useless in the world. Edna, do you think that I shall ever be able to do so?"

"Perhaps so, dear Felix; certainly, if God wills it. When you are stronger we will study and write together, but today you must compose yourself and be silent. Your fever is rising."

"The doctor left some medicine yonder in that goblet, but mamma has forgotten to give it to me. I will take a spoonful now, if you please."

His face was much flushed. As she kissed him and turned away, he cried, "Where are you going?"

"To my room to take off my hat."

"Do not be gone long. I am so happy now that you are here again. But I don't want you to get out of my sight."

On the following day, when Mr. Manning called to welcome her home, he displayed an earnestness and depth of feeling which surprised the governess. Putting his dark hand on her arm, he said in a tone that had lost its metallic ring, "How fearfully changed since I saw you last. I knew you were not strong enough to endure the trial. If I had had a right to interfere, you should never have gone."

"Mr. Manning, I do not quite understand your meaning."

"Edna, to see you dying by inches is bitter indeed. I believed that you would marry Murray – and I felt that to refuse his affection would be a terrible trial, through which you could not pass with impunity."

Oh! It has been, she thought.

"I have conferred with your physician. He reluctantly told me your alarming condition, and I have come to plead with you for the last time not to continue your suicidal course, not to destroy the life which, if worthless to you, is inexpressibly precious to a man who prays to be allowed to take care of it. Once more I hold out my hand to you and say, give me the wreck of your life. Give me the ruins of your heart. I will guard you tenderly; we will go to Europe – to the East; and rest of mind, and easy traveling, and change of scene will restore you."

"Mr. Manning, I beg your pardon, but I cannot--"

He caught her hands in his. "Edna, I do not ask for your love, but I beg for your hand, your confidence, your society – for the right to save you from toil, and perhaps to save your life. Will you go to the Old World with me?"

Looking suddenly up at him, she was astonished to find tears in his searching and usually cold eyes.

Scandinavian tradition reports that seven parishes were once overwhelmed in avalanches, and still lie buried under snow and ice, and yet occasionally those church-bells are heard ringing clearly under the glaciers of the Folge Fond.

So, in the frozen, crystal depths of this man's nature, his long silent, smothered affections began to chime.

A smile trembled over Edna's face, touched by his generosity and concern for her. "No, no, my dear, noble friend. I can not go to the Old World with you. I know how peculiarly precarious is my tenure of life, and how apparently limited is my time for work in this world, but I try to labor faithfully. I can say truly, I am not troubled, neither am I afraid, and my faith is –

'All as God wills, who wisely heeds,
To give or to withhold,
And knoweth more of all my needs
Than all my prayers have told.'"[138]

The editor took off his glasses and wiped them, but the dimness was in his eyes. After a minute, during which he recovered his old calmness, and hushed the holy chime, he said gravely, "Edna, one favor, at least, you will grant me. The death of a relative in Louisiana has placed me in possession of an ample fortune. I wish you to take my little Lila and travel for several years. You are the only woman I ever knew to whom I would entrust her and her education, and it would gratify me beyond expression to feel that I had afforded you the pleasure which can not fail to result from such a tour. Do not be too proud to accept a little happiness from my hands."

"Thank you, my generous, noble friend. I gratefully accept a great deal of happiness at this instant, but your kind offer I must decline. I can not leave Felix."

He sighed, took his hat, and his eyes ran over the face and figure of the governess.

"Edna Earl, your stubborn will makes you nearly akin to those gigantic fuci which are said to grow and flourish as submarine forests in the stormy channel of Terra del Fuego, where they shake their heads defiantly, always trembling, always triumphing, in the fierce lashing of waves that wear away rocks. You belong to a very rare order of humans, rocked and reared in the midst of tempests that would either bow down, or snap asunder, or beat

---

[138] "My Psalm" – John Greenleaf Whittier

out most natures. As you will not grant my petition, try to forget it; we will bury the subject. Good-bye. I shall call tomorrow afternoon to take you to drive."

With renewed zest Edna devoted every moment stolen from Felix to the completion of her new book. Her first had been a "bounteous promise" and she felt that the second would determine her literary position, would either place her reputation as an author beyond all cavil, or utterly crush her ambition.

Of one intensely gratifying fact she could not fail to be thoroughly informed, by the avalanche of letters which almost daily covered her desk; she had at least ensconced herself securely in a citadel, whence she could smilingly defy all assaults – in the warm hearts of her noble countrywomen. Safely sheltered in their sincere and devoted love, she cared little for the arrows that rattled and broke against the rocky ramparts, dropping out of sight in the moat below.

So with many misgivings, and much hope, and great patience, she worked on, and early in summer her book was finished and placed in the publisher's hands.

In the midst of her anxiety concerning its reception, a new and terrible apprehension took possession of her, for it became painfully evident that Felix, whose health had never been good, was slowly but steadily declining.

Mrs. Andrews and Edna took him to Sharon, to Saratoga, and to various other favorite resorts for invalids.

Feeble as Edna was, she always sat up whenever there was any medicine to be given during the night. While he was ill at Sharon, she did not close her eyes for a week.

During one of the midnight watches, Mrs. Andrews came to sit next to Edna, who sat next to Felix's pillow, watching him sleep. His hand was grasping hers, as it always had.

"I can't help feeling jealous of my son's affection for you," said Mrs. Andrews. "You must understand how trying it is for me, his mother, to see my child's whole heart given to a stranger, to hear morning, noon, and night, 'Edna,' always 'Edna,' never once 'mamma.'"

A strange, suffering expression came into Edna's pale face. Her lips trembled so that she could scarcely speak, but she said meekly, "Oh, forgive me if I have won your child's heart; but I love him. You have your husband and daughter, your brother and sister; but I – oh! I have only Felix! I have nothing else to cling to in all this world!" She kissed his fingers and wept as if her heart would break.

The visits to the various springs showed no encouraging results, and they came home almost disheartened.

Dr. Howell finally prescribed a sea-voyage, and a stay of some weeks at Eaux-Bonnes in the Pyrennes, as those waters had effected some remarkable cures.

Eaux-Bonnes

As the doctor left the parlor, where he held a conference with Mr. and Mrs. Andrews, she turned to her husband, saying, "It is useless to start anywhere with Felix unless Miss Earl can go with us; for he would fret himself into even worse health. Really, Louis, it is astonishing to see how devoted they are to each other. She is the strangest woman I ever knew. Sometimes, when she is sitting by me in church, I watch her calm, cold face, and she makes me think of a snow statue; but if Felix says anything to arouse her feelings and call out her affection, she is a volcano. While I confess I am jealous of her, her kindness to my child makes me love her more than I can express. Louis, she must go with us. Poor thing, she seems to be failing almost as fast as Felix. I verily believe if he should die, it would kill her. Did you notice how she paced the floor while the doctors were consulting in Felix's room? She loves nothing but my precious lame boy."

"Certainly, Kate, she must go with us. I quite agree with you, my dear, that Felix is dependent upon her, and would not derive half the benefit from the trip if she remained at home. Kate, will you tell her that it is my desire that she should accompany you? Speak to her at once, that I may know how many staterooms I shall engage on the steamer."

"Come with me, Louis, and speak to her yourself."

They went upstairs together and paused on the threshold of Felix's room to see what was passing within.

The boy was propped by pillows into an upright position on the sofa, and was looking curiously into a small basket which Edna held on her lap.

She was reading to him a touching little letter just received from an invalid child, who had never walked, who was confined always to the house, and wrote to thank her for a story which she had read in the Magazine, and which made her very happy.

The invalid stated that her chief amusement consisted in tending a few flowers that grew in pots in her windows; and in token of her gratitude, she had made a nosegay of mignonette, pansies, and geranium leaves, which she sent with her letter.

In conclusion, the child asked that the woman whom, without having seen, she yet loved, would be so kind as to give her a list of such books as a little girl ought to study, and to write her "just a few lines" that she could keep under her pillow, to look at now and then.

As Edna finished reading the note, Felix took it, to examine the small, indistinct characters, and said, "Dear little girl. Don't you wish we knew her? 'Louie Lawrence.' Of course, you will answer it, Edna?"

"Yes, immediately, and tell her how grateful I am for her generosity in sparing me a portion of her lovely flowers. Each word in her sweet little letter is as precious as a pearl, for it came from the very depths of her pure heart."

"Oh, what a blessed thing it is to feel that you are doing some good in the world! Edna, how happy you look. See, there are tears shining in your eyes. They always come when you are glad. What books will you tell her to study?"

"I will think about the subject, and let you read my answer. How deliciously fragrant the flowers are. Only smell them, Felix. Here, my darling, I will give them to you, and write to the little Louie how happy she made both of us."

She lifted the delicate bouquet so daintily fashioned by the child's fingers, inhaled the perfume, and, as she put it in Felix's thin fingers, she bent forward and kissed his fever-hot cheek.

At this instant Felix saw his parents standing at the door and held up the flowers triumphantly.

"Oh, mamma, come smell this mignonette. Why can't we grow some in boxes in our window?"

Mr. Andrews leaned over his son's pillows, softly put his hand on the boy's forehead, and said, "My son, just now I can not leave my business, but mamma intends to take you to Europe next week. I want to know whether Miss Earl will leave all her admirers here and go with you and help mamma to nurse you. Do you think she will?"

Mrs. Andrews stood with her hand resting on Edna's shoulder, watching the varying expression of her child's countenance.

"I think, papa – I hope she will; I believe she – "

Felix paused, and, struggling up from his pillows, he stretched out his poor little arms to her. "Oh, Edna, you will go with me? You promised you would never forsake me. Tell papa you will go."

His head was on her shoulder, his arms were clasped tightly around her neck. She laid her face on his and was silent.

Mr. Andrews placed his hand on the orphan's bowed head.

"Miss Earl, you must let me tell you that I look upon you as a member of my family; that my wife and I love you almost as well as if you were one of our children. I hope you will not refuse to accompany Kate on the tour she contemplates. Let me take your own father's place; and I shall regard it as a great favor to me and mine if you will consent to go, and allow me to treat you always as I do my Hattie. I have no doubt you will derive as much benefit from traveling, as I certainly hope for Felix."

"Thank you, Mr. Andrews, I appreciate your generosity, and I prize the affection and confidence which you and your wife have shown me. I came, an utter stranger, into your house, and you kindly made me one of the family circle. Felix is not merely my dear pupil, he is my brother, my companion, my best friend! I can not be separated from him. I will travel with him anywhere that you and Mrs. Andrews think it best he should go. I will never, never leave him."

In the midst of prompt preparations for departure Edna's new novel appeared. She had christened it *Shining Thrones on the Hearth*, and dedicated it "To my countrywomen, the Queens who reign thereon."

The aim of the book was to discover the only true and allowable sphere of feminine work. Though the theme was threadbare, she picked up the frayed woof and rewove it.

The tendency of the age was to equality, and this, she contended, was undermining the golden thrones shining in the hallowed light of the hearth, whence every true woman ruled the realm of her own family.

Regarding every pseudo "reform" which struck down the social and political distinction of the sexes as a blow that crushed one of the pillars of woman's throne, she earnestly warned of the danger to be apprehended from deluded female malcontents, who, dethroned in their own realm, roamed as pitiable exiles, threatening to usurp man's kingdom.

Most carefully she sifted the records of history, tracing in every epoch the sovereigns of the hearth-throne who had reigned wisely and contentedly, ennobling and refining humanity; and she proved by examples that the borders of the feminine realm could not be enlarged without rendering the throne unsteady, and subverting God's law of order. Woman reigned by divine right only at home. If married, in the hearts of husband and children, and not in the gilded palace of fashion, where thinly veiled vice and frivolity hold carnival. If single, in the affections of brothers and sisters and friends, as the golden scepter in the hands of parents. If orphaned, she should find sympathy and gratitude and usefulness among the poor and the afflicted.

Consulting the statistics of single women, and familiarizing herself with the arguments advanced by the advocates of that "progress," which would indiscriminately throw open all professions to women, she entreated the poor of her own sex, if ambitious, to become sculptors, painters, writers, teachers in schools or families; or else to remain mantua-makers, milliners, spinners, dairymaids; but on the peril of all womanhood not to meddle with scalpel or red tape.

To married women who thirsted for a draught of the turbid waters of politics, she said, "If you wish to serve the government under which you live, recollect that it was neither the speeches thundered from the forum, nor the prayers of priests and augurs, nor the iron tramp of glittering legions, but the potent, the pleading 'My son!' of Volumnia, the mother of Coriolanus, that saved Rome."

To discontented spinsters, who travelled over the land, haranguing audiences that secretly despised them, she pointed out that quiet, happy home at "Barley Wood," whence immortal Hannah More sent forth those writings which did more to tranquilize England, and bar the hearts of its yeomanry against the temptations of red republicanism than all the eloquence of Burke, and the cautious measures of Parliament.[139]

From the day of its appearance it was a success; and she had the gratification of hearing that some of the seed she had sown fell upon good ground, and promised an abundant harvest.

*****

Many who called to bid her good-bye on the day before the steamer sailed found it impossible to disguise their apprehensions that she would never return. Some who looked tearfully into her

---

[139] Editor's Note: Oh, Edna! I'm a woman, and I used to work as a horticulturist. I drove a skid loader and planted hundreds of trees and it was great! As a woman, I like being able to own property! and vote! and have a bank account! and wear pants! FUN FACT: In Edna's time, women could be arrested for wearing pants. It's true!

Modern women can go to college too. I have a master's degree and so do all my sisters! I'd keep going to college just for fun if it didn't cost so dang much.

Still love ya, Edna.

face and whispered "God-speed!" thought they saw the dread signet of death set on her brow.

To Edna it was inexpressibly painful to cross the Atlantic while Mr. Hammond's health was so feeble. Over the long farewell letter which she sent him, with a copy of her new book, the old man wept. Mrs. Murray had seemed entirely estranged, since that last day spent at Le Bocage and had not written a line since the orphan's return to New York. But when she received the new novel, and the mournful, meek note that accompanied it, Mrs. Murray laid her head on her son's bosom and sobbed aloud.

Dr. Howell and Mr. Manning went with Edna aboard the steamer. A persistent young book-vender with his arms full of copies of Edna's own book, stopped her on deck and extolled its merits, insisting that she should buy one to while away the tedium of the voyage. Both men laughed heartily at Edna's efforts to disengage herself from him.

Dr. Howell gave final directions concerning the treatment of Felix, and then came to speak to Edna.

"Even now, sadly as you have abused your constitution, I shall have some hope of seeing gray hairs about your temples, if you will give yourself unreservedly to relaxation of mind. You have already accomplished so much that you can certainly afford to rest for some months at least. Read nothing, write nothing – except long letters to me – and you will come back improved to the country that is so proud of you. Otherwise I fear that you will find an early grave, far from your native land, among strangers. God bless you, dear child, and bring you safely back to us."

As he turned away, Mr. Manning took her hand. "I hope to meet you in Rome early in February; but something might occur to veto my program. Edna, promise me that you will take care of your precious life."

"I will try, Mr. Manning."

He looked down into her worn, weary face and sighed. Then for the first time he took both her hands, kissed them, and left her.

Swiftly the steamer took its way seaward, through the Narrows, past the lighthouse. The wind sang through the rigging, and the purple hills of Jersey faded from view.

One by one the passengers went below. Edna and Felix remained on deck with stars burning above and blue waves bounding beneath them.

As Felix sat looking over the ocean, awed by its brooding gloom, did he catch in the silvery starlight a second glimpse of the rose-colored veils and purple-edged robes of the Fates, spinning and singing as they followed the ship across the sobbing sea?

He shivered, and clasping tightly the hand of his governess, said, "Edna, we shall never see our home again."

She leaned her head against his. "God only knows, dear Felix. His will be done."

> "How silvery the echoes run –
> Thy will be done – Thy will be done."[140]

---

[140] "An Island" – Elizabeth Barrett Browning

CHAPTER XXXV
A SPOTLESS WHITE PIGEON

St. Elmo Murray stood leaning against the mantelpiece at the parsonage. "Worthy? No, no! Unworthy, most unworthy. But was Peter worthy to preach the Gospel of Him whom he had thrice indignantly denied? Was Paul worthy to become the Apostle of the Gentiles, teaching the doctrine of Him whose disciples he had persecuted and slaughtered? If the repentance of Peter and Paul availed to purify their hands and hearts, ah, God knows my contrition has been bitter and lasting enough to fit me for future usefulness.

"Eight months ago, when the desire to become a minister seized me, I wrestled with it, tried to crush it. My remorse, my repentance, has been inexpressibly bitter; but the darkness has passed away, and today I can pray with all the fervor and faith of my boyhood, when I knew that I was at peace with my Maker."

Mr. Hammond clutched his hand as St. Elmo continued. "Oblivion of the past I do not expect, and do not desire. What I have done to you, my old friend, and to your children, I will never forget," he said, gently shaking Mr. Hammond's hand in emphasis. "I do this to atone. For years I fled from this reckoning, knowing that there is nothing I can do to bring back your darling dead. I have fled this reckoning across the whole world. But now, I feel that perhaps now I can atone through my ministry for all that I have taken for you. Now surely, upon my lonely, long-tortured heart, I feel peace falling like dew. Thank God! I have found peace after much strife and great weariness."

Mr. Murray could no longer control his voice. He dropped his head on his hand.

"St. Elmo, my heart can scarcely contain its joy when I look forward to your future, so bright with promise, so full of usefulness," Mr. Hammond said. "The marked change in your manner during the past two years has prepared this community for the important step you are to take today, and your influence with young men will be incalculable. Once your stern bitterness rendered you an object of dread; now I find that you are respected, and people here watch your conduct with interest. Ah, St. Elmo, I never imagined earth held as much pure happiness as is my portion today. To see you one of God's anointed, to see you ministering in the temple! To know that when I am gone to rest you will take my place, guard my flock, do your own work and poor Murray's, and finish mine. This, this is indeed the crowning blessing of my old age."

For some minutes, Mr. Hammond sobbed. Mr. Murray warmly pressed his handkerchief into his old friend's hand, and Mr. Hammond smiled through his tears.

Lifting his face, Mr. Murray answered, "As I think of the coming years consecrated to Christ, passed peacefully in endeavoring to atone for the injury and suffering I have inflicted on my fellow-creatures – especially you and Annie – the picture of a holy future rises before me. I feel indeed that I am unworthy, most unworthy of my peace; but, thank God!

'Oh! I see the crescent promise of my spirit hath not set;
Ancient founts of inspiration well through all my fancy yet.'"[141]

It was a beautiful Sabbath morning, just one year after Edna's departure, and the church was crowded to its utmost capacity, for people had come for many miles around to witness a ceremony, the announcement of which had given rise to universal comment. As the hour approached for the ordination of St. Elmo Murray to the ministry of Jesus Christ, even the doors were filled with curious spectators. When Mr. Hammond and St. Elmo walked down the aisle, there was a general stir in the congregation.

The officiating minister had come from a distant city to perform a ceremony of more than usual interest; and when he stood up in the pulpit, and the organ thundered through the

---

[141] "Locksley Hall" – Lord Alfred Tennyson

arches, St. Elmo bowed his head on his hand, and sat thus during the hour that ensued.

The ordination sermon was solemn and eloquent, and preached from the text in Romans: "For when ye were the servants of sin, ye were free from righteousness. But now being made free from sin, and become servants to God, ye have your fruit unto holiness, and the end everlasting life."[142]

The minister came down before the altar and commenced the services; but Mr. Murray sat motionless, with his countenance concealed by his hand. Mr. Hammond approached and touched him, and, as he rose, led him to the altar, and presented him as a candidate for ordination.

There, before the shining marble pulpit which he had planned and built in the early years of his life, stood St. Elmo. The congregation, especially those of his native village, looked with admiration and pride at the powerful form, clad in its suit of black – at his noble head, where gray locks were visible.

"But if there be any of you who knoweth any impediment or crime, for the which he ought not to be received into this holy ministry, let him come forth, in the name of God, and show what the crime or impediment is."

The preacher paused, the echo of his words died away, and perfect silence reigned.

St. Elmo raised his eyes from the railing of the altar, and, turning his face slightly, looked through the eastern window at the ivy-draped vault where slept Murray and Annie. The world was silent, but conscience and the dead accused him. Intolerable pain crossed his features, then his hands folded themselves tightly together on the top of the marble balustrade, and he looked appealingly up to the pale Jesus staggering under his cross.

At that instant a spotless white pigeon from the belfry found its way into the church through the open doors, circled once around the building, fluttered against the window, hiding momentarily the crown of thorns, and, frightened and confused, fell upon the fluted pillar of the pulpit.

---

[142] Romans 6:20, 22

437

An electric thrill ran through the congregation. As the minister resumed the services, he saw on St. Elmo's face a light, a great joy, such as human countenances rarely wear this side of the grave.

When Mr. Murray knelt and the ordaining hands were laid upon his head, a sob was heard from the pew where his mother sat. The voice of the preacher faltered as he delivered the Bible to the kneeling man, saying, "Take thou authority to preach the word of God, and to administer the holy sacraments in the congregation."

There were no dry eyes in the entire assembly, save two that looked out, coldly blue, from the pew where Mrs. Powell sat like a statue between her daughter and Gordon Leigh.

Mr. Hammond tottered across the altar, and knelt down close to Mr. Murray; and many who knew the history of the pastor's family wept as the gray head fell on the broad shoulder of St. Elmo, who threw his arm was around the old man's form and supported him. The ordaining minister, with tears rolling over his face, extended his hands in benediction above them.

"The peace of God, which passeth all understanding, keep your hearts and minds in the knowledge and love of God, and of His Son Jesus Christ our Lord; and the blessing of God Almighty, the Father, the Son, and the Holy Ghost, be among you, and remain with you always.[143]"

And all hearts and lips present whispered "Amen!" and the organ and the choir broke forth in a grand *Gloria in excelsis.*

Standing there at the chancel, purified, consecrated henceforth unreservedly to Christ, Mr. Murray looked so happy, so noble, so worthy of his high calling, that his proud, fond mother thought his face was fit for an archangel's wings.

Many persons who had known him in his boyhood came up with tears in their eyes and wrung his hand silently.

At last Huldah pointed to the white pigeon that was now beating its wings against the gilded pipes of the organ, and said in that singularly sweet, solemn tone with which children approach sacred things, "Oh, Mr. Murray! When it fell on the pulpit, it nearly took my breath away, for I almost thought it was the Holy Ghost."

---

[143] This service is from The Book of Common Prayer.

Tears, which till then he had bravely kept back, rolled down his face, as he stooped and whispered to her, "Huldah, the Holy Spirit, the Comforter, came indeed; but it was not visible, it is here in my heart."

The congregation dispersed. Mrs. Murray and the preacher and Huldah went to the carriage; and, leaning on Mr. Murray's arm, Mr. Hammond turned to follow. But, observing that the church was empty, St. Elmo said, "After a little I will come."

The old man walked on. Mr. Murray went back and knelt, resting his head against the beautiful glittering balustrade, within which he hoped to officiate through the remaining years of his earthly career.

The sexton, who was waiting to lock up the church, looked in, saw the man praying alone there at the altar, and softly stole away.

When St. Elmo came out, the churchyard seemed deserted. But as he crossed it, going homeward, his thoughts crowded with what he needed to do next in his holy work, a woman rose from one of the tombstones and stood before him – the blonde-haired Jezebel, with sapphire eyes and soft, treacherous red lips, who had goaded him to madness and blasted the best years of his life.

At sight of her he recoiled, as if a hooded cobra had started up in his path.

"St. Elmo, my beloved! In the name of other days stop and hear me. By the memory of our early love, I entreat you."

She came close to him, and her face was marvelous in its expression of remorseful sweetness.

"St. Elmo, can you never forgive me for the suffering I caused you in my giddy girlhood?"

Agnes took his hand and attempted to raise it to her lips; but he pulled it free from her touch. He stepped back, and steadily they looked in each other's eyes.

"Agnes, I forgive you. May God pardon your sins, as He has pardoned mine!"

He turned away, but she seized his coat-sleeve and threw herself before him, standing with both hands clasping his arm.

"If you mean what you say, there is happiness yet in store for us. Oh, St. Elmo, how often have I longed to come and lay my head down on your bosom and tell you all. But you were so stern and harsh I was afraid. Today when I saw you melted, when the look of your boyhood came dancing back to your dear eyes, I was encouraged to hope that your heart had softened also toward me. Is there hope for your poor Agnes? Once I preferred my cousin Murray to you; but think how giddy I must have been, when I could marry before a year had settled the sod on his grave? I did not love my husband, but I married him for the same reason that I would have married you then. It was to save my father from disgrace that I sacrificed myself; for money entrusted to his keeping – money belonging to his orphan ward – had been used by him in a ruinous speculation, and only prompt repayment could prevent exposure. St. Elmo, love me, take me back to your heart! God is my witness that I do love you entirely now."

She tried to put her arms up around his neck and to rest her head on his shoulder; but he put her at arm's length from him.

Holding her there, he looked at her with a cold scorn in his eyes, and a heavy shadow darkening the brow that five minutes before had been so calm, so bright.

"Agnes, how dare you attempt to deceive me after all that has passed between us? Oh, woman! In the name of all true womanhood I could blush for you."

She struggled to free herself, to get closer to him, but his stern grasp was relentless. As tears poured down her cheeks, she clasped her hands and sobbed, "Oh, do not look at me so harshly! I am not deceiving you; as I hope for pardon and rest for my soul – as I hope to see my father's face in heaven – I am not deceiving you! I do – I do love you, Oh, St. Elmo, you ought to know that I am terribly in earnest when I can stoop to beg for the ruins of a heart, which in its freshness I once trampled on."

He had seen her weep before, when it suited her purpose. He only smiled and answered, "Look you, woman! When you overturned the temple, you crumbled your own image that was set up there. I long, long ago swept out and gave to the hungry winds the despised dust of that broken idol. Over my heart you can reign no more. The only queen it has known since that awful night eighteen years ago, when my faith, hope, charity were all strangled in an instant by the velvet hand I had kissed in my doting fondness – the only queen my heart has acknowledged since then is – Edna Earl."

"Edna Earl! – a puritanical fanatic! A cold prude, a heartless blue! St. Elmo, are you insane? Did you not see that letter from Estelle to your mother, stating that she, Edna, would certainly be married in February to the celebrated Mr. Manning, who was then on his way to Rome to meet her? Did you see that letter?"

"I did."

"And discredit it? Blindness, madness, equal to my own in the days gone by! Edna Earl exists no longer; she was married a month ago. Here, read for yourself, lest you believe that I fabricate the whole."

She held a newspaper before his eyes. A paragraph, "Marriage in Literary Circles," was marked with a circle of ink:

"A reliable correspondent writes from Rome that the Americans now in that city are on the *qui vive* concerning a marriage announced to take place on Thursday next at the residence of the American Minister. The very distinguished parties are Miss Edna Earl, the gifted and exceedingly popular young authoress, whose works have given her an enviable reputation even on this side of the Atlantic, and Mr. Douglass G. Manning, the well-known and able editor of the *Iconoclast* Magazine. The happy pair will start, immediately after the ceremony, on a tour through Greece and the Holy Land."

Mr. Murray opened the paper, glanced at the date, and his swarthy face paled as he put his hands over his eyes.

Mrs. Powell came nearer, and once more touched his hand.

With a gesture of disgust, he pushed her aside.

"Away! Not a word – not one word more. I have lost her, I know; but if I never see her dear angel face again in this world, it will be in consequence of my sins. With God's help I mean to live out the remainder of my days so that at last I shall meet her in eternity. Leave me, Agnes! In future, keep out of my path, which will never cross yours; do not rouse my old hate toward you, which I am faithfully striving to overcome. The first time I went to the communion-table, after the lapse of all those dreary years of sin and desperation, I asked myself, 'Have I a right to the sacrament of the Lord's Supper? – can I face God and say I forgive

Agnes Powell?' Finally, after a hard struggle, I said, from the depths of my heart, 'Even as I need and hope for forgiveness myself, I do fully forgive her.' Mark you, it was my injuries that I pardoned, your treachery that I forgave. But – *there is no pardon for desecrated ideals!* Once, I selected you as the beau ideal of beautiful, perfect womanhood; but you fell from that lofty pedestal where my ardent, boyish love set you for worship, and through my acts I, too, fell down, down, almost beyond the pale of God's mercy! I forgive your wrongs, but 'take you back, love you?' I can never love anyone as I love my pure darling, my own Edna."

"A useless love for a cold-hearted prude," Agnes said, clutching his sleeve.

He quietly disengaged her fingers. "Do not touch me, Agnes. Several times you have thrust yourself into my presence; but if there remains any womanly delicacy in your nature you will avoid me henceforth. Agnes, go yonder to the church, and pray for yourself, and may God help you." He turned quickly and walked away.

Her mournful eyes, strained wide and full of tears, followed him till his form was no longer visible. Then, sinking down on the monument – whence she had risen at his approach – she shrouded her fair, delicate features, and rocked herself to and fro.

"Lost, lost!" she wailed. "Oh, St. Elmo! Your loathing is more than I can bear. Once he hung over me adoringly, wearying me with his caresses; now he shudders at my touch. And I – what is there that I would not give for just one of his kisses, which twenty-three years ago I put up my hand to ward off. God grant that Edna Earl may indeed be in her grave! Or that I may go down into mine before he sees her again. How I hate her! Oh, hold her fast in your icy grasp, grim death! For to see that girl in St. Elmo's arms would drive me wild! Oh, sleep in peace, Murray Hammond, for you are indeed avenged."

Agnes drew her veil closely around her tear-stained face and fled.

CHAPTER XXXVI
THERE IS NO NIGHT THERE

"How lovely! I did not think there was any place half so beautiful this side of heaven."

With his head on his mother's bosom, Felix lay near the window of an upper room, looking out over the Gulf of Genoa.

The crescent curve of the olive-mantled Apennine Mountains girdled the city in a rocky clasp, and mellowed by distance and the magic enameling of evening light, each peak rose against the sky like a pyramid of lapis lazuli, around whose mighty base rolled soft waves of golden haze.

Over the glassy bosom of the gulf, where boats filled with cheery Italians, floated the merry strains of a barcarole, keeping time with the silvery gleam of the dipping oars.

> "And the sun went into the west, and down
> Upon the water stooped an orange cloud,
> And the pale milky reaches flushed, as glad
> To wear its colors; and the sultry air
> Went out to sea, and puffed the sails of ships
> With thymy wafts, the breath of trodden grass."[144]

"Lift me up, mamma! Higher, higher yet. I want to see the sun. There! It has gone – gone down into the sea. I can't bear to see it set today. It seemed to say good-bye to me just then. Oh, mamma, mamma! I don't want to die. The world is so beautiful, and life is so sweet up here in the sunshine and the starlight, and it is so cold and dark down there in the grave. Oh, where is Edna? Tell her to come quick and sing something to me."

---

[144] "Brothers, and a Sermon" – Jean Ingelow

Felix shuddered and shut his eyes. He had wasted away until he looked a mere shadow of himself, lying there in his mother's arms.

"Edna, talk to me. Oh, don't let me get afraid to die. I – "

She laid her lips on his, and the touch calmed their shivering. After a moment, she began to repeat the vision of heaven from the book of Revelations: "And there shall be no night there; and they need no candle, neither light of the sun; for the Lord God giveth them light; and they shall reign for ever and ever."[145]

"But, Edna, the light does not shine down there in the grave. If you could go with me – "

"A better and kinder Friend will go with you, dear Felix."

She sang with strange pathos "Motet," that beautiful arrangement of "The Lord is my Shepherd."

As she reached that part where the words, "Yea, though I walk through the valley of the shadow of death," are repeated, the weak, quavering voice of the sick boy joined hers; and, when she ceased, the emaciated face was placid, the great dread had passed away forever.

Genoa – Franz Richard Unterberger

---

[145] Revelation 22:5

Anxious to divert his thoughts, she put into his hand a bunch of orange flowers and violets, which had been sent to her that day by Mr. Manning; and taking a book from the bed, she resumed the reading of *The Shepherd of Salisbury Plain,* to which the invalid had never wearied of listening.

But she soon saw that he was indifferent. Understanding the expression of the eyes that gazed out on the purple shadows shrouding the Apennines, she closed the volume, and laid the sufferer back on his pillow.

While she was standing before a table, preparing some nourishment to be given to him during the night, Mrs. Andrews came close to her and whispered, "Do you see much change? Is he really worse, or do my fears magnify every bad symptom?"

"He is much exhausted, but I trust the stimulants will revive him. You must go to bed and get a good sound sleep, for you look worn out. I will wake you if I see any decided change in him."

Mrs. Andrews hung for some time over her child's pillow, caressing him, saying tender, soothing, motherly things. After a while, she and Hattie kissed him, and went into the adjoining room, leaving him to Edna's care.

It was late at night before the sound of laughter, song and chatter died away in the streets of Genoa. While the human tide ebbed and flowed under the windows, Felix was restless, and his companion tried to interest him by telling him the history of the Dorias, and of the siege during which Massena won such glory. The boy's fondness for history showed itself even then, and he listened attentively to her words.

At length silence reigned through the marble palaces, and Edna rose to place the small lamp in an alabaster vase.

As she did so, something flew into her face, and fluttered to the edge of the vase. As she attempted to brush it off, she started back, smothering a cry of horror. It was a Death's Head Moth; and there, upon its back, appallingly distinct, grinned a ghastly, gray human skull. Twice it circled rapidly round the vase, uttering strange, stridulous sounds, then floated up to the canopy overarching Felix's bed, and poised itself on the carved frame, waiting and flapping its wings, vulture-like. Shuddering from head to foot, notwithstanding the protest which reason offered

445

against superstition, the governess sat down to watch the boy's slumber.

His eyes were closed, and she hoped that he slept; but presently he feebly put out his skeleton hand and took hers.

"Edna, mamma cannot hear me, can she?"

"She is asleep, but I will wake her if you wish it."

"No, she would only begin to cry, and that would worry me. Edna, I want you to promise me one thing – " He paused a few seconds and sighed wearily.

"When you all go back home, don't leave me here; take me with you, and lay my poor little body in the ground at 'The Willows,' where the sea will sing over me. We were so happy there. I always thought I should like my grave to be under the tallest willow, where our canary's cage used to hang. Edna, I don't think you will live long – I almost hope you won't – and I want you to promise me, too, that you will tell them to bury us close together; so that the very moment I rise out of my grave, on the day of judgment, I will see your face. Sometimes, when I think of the millions and millions that will be pressing up for their trial before God's throne, on that great, awful day, I am afraid I might lose or miss you in the crowd, and never find you again; but, you know, if our coffins touch, you can stretch out your hand to me as you rise, and we can go together. Oh, I want your face to be the last I see here, and the first – yonder."

He raised his fingers slowly, and they fell back wearily on the coverlet.

"Don't talk so, Felix. Oh, my darling, God will not take you away from me. Try to sleep, shut your eyes; you need rest to compose you."

She knelt, kissed him repeatedly, and laid her face close to his on the pillow.

Felix tried to turn and put his thin little arm around her neck.

"Edna, I have been a trouble to you for a long time, but you will miss me when I am gone, and you will have nothing to love. If you live long, marry Mr. Manning, and let him take care of you. Don't work so hard, dear Edna; only rest, and let him make you happy. Before I knew you I was always wishing to die; but now I hate to leave you all alone, my own dear, pale Edna."

"Oh, Felix, darling! You wring my heart."

Her sobs distressed him, and, feebly patting her cheek, he said, "Perhaps if you will sing me something low, I may go to sleep, and I want to hear your voice once more. Sing me that song about the child and the rose-bush, that Hattie likes so much."

"Not that! Anything but that. It is too sad, my precious little darling."

"But I want to hear it. Please, Edna."

It was a painful task that he imposed, but his wishes ruled her; and she tried to steady her voice as she sang, in a very low, faltering tone, the beautiful, but melancholy ballad. Tears rolled over her face as she chanted the verses; and when she concluded, he repeated very faintly:

> "Sweetly it rests, and on dream-wings flies,
> To play with the angels in paradise!"[146]

He nestled his lips to hers, and, after a little while, murmured, "Good-night, Edna."

"Good-night, my darling."

She gave him a stimulating potion and arranged his head comfortably. Ere long his heavy breathing told her that he slept. Stealing from his side, she sat down in a large chair near the head of his bed and watched him.

For many months he had been failing, and they had travelled from place to place, hoping against hope that each change would certainly be beneficial.

Day and night Edna had nursed him, had devoted every thought, almost every prayer to him; and now her heart seemed centered in him. Scenery, music, painting, rare manuscripts., all were ignored. She lived only for her friend, and knew not a moment of peace when separated from him. She had ceased to study aught but his comfort and happiness, had written nothing save letters to friends; and notwithstanding her anxiety about Felix, the frequent change of air had surprisingly improved her own health. For six months she had escaped the attacks so much dreaded, and began to believe her restoration complete, though

---

[146] "The Rose-Bush" – translated from the German by William W. Caldwell

the long-banished color obstinately refused to return to her face. Still, she was very grateful for the immunity from suffering, especially as it permitted more unremitting attendance upon Felix.

She knew that his life was flickering out. Now, as she watched the pale, pinched features, her own quivered, and she clasped her hands and wept, and stifled a groan.

She had prayed so passionately and continually that he might be spared to her; but it seemed that whenever her heart-strings wrapped themselves around an idol, a jealous God tore them loose, and snatched away the dear object, and left the heart to bleed. If that boy died, how utterly desolate and lonely she would be; nothing left to care for and to cling to, nothing to claim as her own, and anoint with the tender love of her warm heart.

She had been so intensely interested in the expansion of his mind, had striven so tirelessly to stimulate his brain, and soften and purify his heart; she had been so proud of his rapid progress, and so ambitious for his future, and now the mildew of death was falling on her fond hopes. She had borne patiently many trials, but this appeared unendurable. She had set all her earthly happiness on Felix, and as she gazed through her tears at his sallow face, so dear to her, it seemed hard that God denied her this one blessing. What was the praise and admiration of all the world in comparison with the loving light in that child's eyes, and the tender pressure of his lips?

The woman's ambition had long been fully satisfied, and even exacting conscience, jealously guarding its shrine, saw daily sacrifices laid thereon, and smiled approvingly; but the woman's hungry heart cried out, and fought fiercely, famine-goaded, for its last vanishing morsel of human love and sympathy.

Felix lay so motionless that Edna crept nearer and leaned down to listen to his breathing. Her tears fell on his thick, curling hair, and upon the orange-blossoms and violets.

Standing there she threw up her clenched hands and prayed sobbingly, "My Father! Spare the boy to me! I will dedicate anew my life and his to thy work. I will make him a minister of thy word, and he shall save precious souls. Oh, do not take him away! If not for a lifetime, at least spare him a few years. Even one more year, O my God!"

She walked to the window, rested her forehead against the stone facing, and looked out. The wonderful witchery of the solemn night wove its spell around her. Great, golden stars clustered in the clear heavens, and were reflected in the calm, blue waters of the Mediterranean, where not a ripple shivered their shining images. A waning crescent moon swung high over the eastern crest of the Apennines and threw a weird light along the Doria's marble palace, and down on the silver-gray olives, on the glistening orange-groves, snow-powdered with fragrant bloom. In that wan, mysterious, and most melancholy light –

> "The old, miraculous mountains heaved in sight,
> One straining past another along the shore
> The way of grand, dull Odyssean ghosts,
> Athirst to drink the cool, blue wine of seas,
> And stare on voyagers."[147]

From some lofty campanile, in a distant section of the silent city, sounded the angelus bell. From the deep shadow of olive, vine, and myrtle that clothed the amphitheatre of hills, the convent bells caught and reechoed it.

> "Nature comes sometimes,
> And says, 'I am ambassador for God';"[148]

and the splendor of the Italian night spoke to Edna's soul as the glory of the sunset had done some years before, when she sat in the dust in the pine glades at Le Bocage. She grew calm once more, while out of the blue depths of the starlit sea came a sacred voice that said to her aching heart:

"Peace I leave with you, my peace I give unto you; not as the world giveth, give I unto you. Let not your heart be troubled, neither let it be afraid."[149]

The cup was not passing away; but courage to drain it was given by Him who never calls his faithful children into the gloom

---

[147] *Aurora Leigh* – Elizabeth Barrett Browning
[148] *Aurora Leigh* – Elizabeth Barrett Browning
[149] John 14:27

of Gethsemane without having first stationed close at hand some strengthening angel. The governess went back to the bed, and there, on the pillow, rested the moth, which at her approach flew away with a humming sound, and disappeared.

After another hour she saw that a change was stealing over the boy's countenance, and his pulse fluttered more feebly against her cold fingers. She sprang into the next room, shook his mother, and hastened back, trying to rouse the dying child, and give him some stimulants. But though his large, black eyes opened when she raised his head, there was no recognition in their fixed gaze; for his soul was preparing for its final flight, and was too busy to look out of its windows.

In vain they resorted to the most powerful restoratives. Felix remained in his heavy stupor, with no sign of animation, save his low irregular breath, and the weak flutter of his thread-like pulse.

Mrs. Andrews wept aloud and wrung her hands. Hattie cried passionately as she stood in her long white nightgown at the side of her brother's bed; but there were no tears on Edna's cold, gray face. She had spent them all at the foot of God's throne; and now that He had seen fit to deny her petition, she silently looked with dry eyes at the heavy rod that smote her.

The night waned, and Felix's life with it. Now and then his breathing seemed to cease, but after a few seconds a faint gasp told that the clay would not yet forego its hold on the soul that struggled to be free.

The poor mother seemed almost beside herself, as she called on her child to speak to her once more.

"Sing something, Edna. Perhaps he will hear! It might rouse him."

Edna shook her head and dropped her face on his.

"He would not hear me. He is listening to the song of those whose golden harps ring in the New Jerusalem."

Out of the whitening east rose the new day, radiant in bridal garments, wearing a star on its pearly brow. The sky flushed, and the sea glowed, while silvery mists rolled up from the purple mountain gorges, and rested a while on the summits of the Apennines, and sunshine streamed over the world once more.

The first rays flashed into the room, kissing the withered flowers on Felix's bosom, and falling warm and bright on the boy's cold eyelids and the pulseless temples.

Edna's hand was pressed to his heart, and she knew that it had given its last throb; knew that Felix Andrews had crossed the sea of glass, and in the dawn of the eternal day wore the promised morning-star, and stood in peace before the Sun of Righteousness.

****

During the two days that succeeded the death of Felix, Edna did not leave her room; and without her knowledge Mrs. Andrews administered opiates that stupefied her.

Late on the morning of the third she awoke, and lay for some time trying to collect her thoughts.

Her mind was clouded, but gradually it cleared, and she strained her ears to distinguish the low words spoken in the apartment next to her own. She remembered, as in a feverish dream, all that passed on the night that Felix died. Pressing her hand over her aching forehead, she rose and sat on the edge of her bed.

The monotonous sounds in the neighboring room swelled louder for a few seconds, and now she heard very distinctly the words:

"And I heard a voice from heaven, saying unto me, Write, Blessed are the dead which die in the Lord from henceforth."[150]

She shivered and wrapped around her shoulders a bright blue shawl that had been thrown over the foot of the bed. Walking across the floor, she opened the door, and looked in.

The boy's body had been embalmed and placed in a coffin which rested in the centre of the room. An English clergyman, a friend of Mr. Manning's, stood at the head of the corpse, and read the burial service.

Mrs. Andrews and Hattie were weeping in one corner. Mr. Manning leaned against the window with his hand on Lila's curls. As the door swung open and Edna entered, he looked up.

Her dressing gown of gray merino trailed on the marble floor, and her bare feet gleamed as one hand caught up the soft merino folds sufficiently to enable her to walk. Over the blue shawl

---

[150] Revelation 14:13

streamed her beautiful hair, making the wan face look even more ghastly by contrast with its glossy jet masses.

She stood irresolute, with her calm, mournful eyes riveted on the coffin, and Mr. Manning saw her pale lips move as she staggered toward it. He sprang to meet and intercept her, and she stretched her hands in the direction of the coffin, and smiled strangely, murmuring like one in a troubled dream, "You need not be afraid, little darling, 'there is no night there.'"

She reeled and put her hand to her heart, and would have fallen, but Mr. Manning caught and carried her back to her room.

For two weeks Edna hovered on the borders of eternity. Often the anxious friends who watched her, felt that they would rather see her die than endure the suffering through which she was called to pass.

She bore it silently, meekly. When the danger seemed over, and she was able to sleep without the aid of narcotics, Mr. Manning could not bear to look at the patient pale face, so hopelessly calm.

No allusion was made to Felix, even after she was able to sit up and drive. Once, when Mr. Manning brought her some flowers, she looked sorrowfully at the snowy orange-blossoms, whose strong perfume made her turn paler. She said faintly, "I shall never love them or violets again. Take them away, sir, out of my sight. They smell of death."

From that day Edna made a vigorous effort to rouse herself. The boy's name never passed her lips; though she spent many hours over a small manuscript which she found among his books, directed to her for revision. "Tales for Little Cripples," was the title he had given it, and she was surprised at the beauty and pathos of many of the sentences. She carefully revised and rewrote it, adding a brief sketch of the young writer, and gave it to his mother.

About a month after Felix's death the governess seemed to have recovered her physical strength, and Mrs. Andrews announced her intention of going to Germany. Mr. Manning had engagements that called him to France.

On the last day of their stay at Genoa, he came as usual to spend the evening with Edna. A large budget of letters and papers had arrived from America; and when he gave her the package containing her share, she glanced over the directions, threw them unopened into a heap on the table, and continued the conversation in which she was engaged, concerning the architecture of the churches in Genoa.

Mrs. Andrews had gone to the vault where the body of her son had been temporarily placed, and Edna was alone with the editor.

"You ought to look into your papers; they contain very gratifying intelligence for you. Your last book has gone through ten editions, and your praises are chanted all over your native land. Surely, if ever a woman had adulation enough to render her perfectly happy and pardonably proud, you are the fortunate individual. Already your numerous readers are inquiring when you will give them another book."

She leaned her head back against her chair, and the little hands caressed each other as they rested on her knee, while her countenance was eloquent with humble gratitude for the success that God had permitted to crown her efforts; but she was silent.

"Do you intend to write a book of travels, embracing the incidents that have marked your tour? I see the public expect it."

"No, sir. At present, I expect to write nothing. I want to study some subjects that greatly interest me, and I shall try to inform and improve myself, and keep silent until I see some phase of truth neglected, or some new aspect of error threatening mischief in society. Indeed, I have great cause for gratitude in my literary career. At the beginning I felt apprehensive that I was destined to sit always under the left hand of fortune, whom Michelangelo designed as a lovely woman seated on a revolving wheel, throwing crowns and laurel wreaths from her right hand, while only thorns dropped in a sharp, stinging shower from the other; but, after a time, the wheel turned, and now I feel only the soft pattering of the laurel leaves.

"God knows I do most earnestly appreciate His abundant blessing upon what I have thus far striven to effect; but books seem such holy things to me, destined to plead either for or against their creators in the final tribunal, that I dare not lightly or hastily attempt to write them. I dare not, even if I could, dash off articles and books as the rower shakes water-drops from his oars; and I humbly acknowledge that what success I may have achieved is owing to hard, faithful work. I have received so many kind letters from children, that some time, if I live to be wise enough, I want to write a book especially for them. I am afraid to attempt it just now; for it requires more mature judgment and experience, and greater versatility of talent to write successfully for children than for grown persons. In the latter, one is privileged to assume native intelligence and cultivation; but the tender, untutored minds of the former permit no such margin; and this fact necessitates clearness and simplicity of style, and power of illustration that seem to me very rare[151]."

At length when Mr. Manning rose to say good night, he looked gravely at the governess, and asked, "Edna, can not Lila take the vacant place in your sad heart?"

"It is not vacant, sir. Dear memories walk to and fro therein, weaving garlands of immortelles – singing sweet tunes of days and years – that can never die. Hereafter I shall endeavor to entertain the precious guests I have already, and admit no more. The past is the realm of my heart; the present and future the kingdom where my mind must dwell, and my hands labor."

With a sigh he went away, and she took up the letters and began to read them. Many were from strangers, and they greatly cheered and encouraged her.

Finally she opened one whose superscription had until this instant escaped her cursory glance. It was from Mr. Hammond and contained an account of Mr. Murray's ordination.

She read and re-read it, with a half-bewildered expression in her countenance, for the joy seemed far too great for belief. She looked again at the date and signature, and passing her hand over her brow, wondered if there could be any mistake. The paper fell into her lap, and a cry of delight rang through the room.

"Saved – purified – consecrated henceforth to God's holy work? A minister of Christ? O most merciful God! I thank Thee! My prayers are answered with a blessing I never dared to hope for, or even to dream of. Can I ever, ever be grateful enough? A pastor, holding up pure hands! Thank God! My sorrows are all

---

[151] This is true.

ended now; there is no more grief for me. Ah, what a glory breaks upon the future. What though I never see his face in this world? I can be patient indeed; for now I know, oh! I know that I shall surely see it yonder."

Edna sank on her knees at the open window and wept for the first time since Felix died. Happy, happy tears mingled with broken words of rejoicing that seemed a foretaste of heaven.

Her heart was so full of gratitude and exultation that she could not sleep, and she sat down and looked over the sea while her face was radiant and tremulous. The transition from patient hopelessness and silent struggling – this most unexpected and glorious fruition of the prayers of many years – was so sudden and intoxicating, that it completely unnerved her.

She could not bear this great happiness as she had borne her sorrows. Now and then she smiled to find tears gushing afresh from her beaming eyes.

Once, in an hour of sinful madness, Mr. Murray had taken a human life, and ultimately caused the loss of another; but the waves that were running high beyond the mole told her in thunder-tones that he had saved, had snatched two lives from their devouring rage. And the shining stars overhead grouped themselves into characters that said to her, "Judge not, that ye be not judged"[152]; and the ancient mountains whispered, "Stand still, and see the salvation of the Lord!"[153] and the grateful soul of the lonely woman answered:

> "That all the jarring notes of life
> Seem blending in a psalm,
> And all the angels of its strife
> Slow rounding into calm."[154]

---

[152] Matthew 7:1
[153] Exodus
[154] "My Psalm" – John Greenleaf Whittier

CHAPTER XXXVII
THE BEST OF ALL POSSIBLE WORLDS

Immediately after her return to New York, Edna resumed her studies with renewed energy, and found her physical strength renewed and her mind invigorated by repose. Her fondness for Hattie induced her to remain with Mrs. Andrews in the capacity of governess, though her position in the family had long ceased to resemble in any respect that of a hireling. Three hours of each day were devoted to the education of the little girl, who was an engaging and exceedingly affectionate child, fully worthy of the love which her gifted governess lavished upon her. The remainder of her time Edna divided between study, music, and an extensive correspondence, which daily increased.

She visited little, having no leisure; but she set apart one evening in each week for the reception of her numerous kind friends, and of all strangers who desired to call upon her. These reunions were brilliant and delightful, and it was considered a privilege to be present at gatherings where eminent men and refined, cultivated Christian women assembled to discuss ethical and aesthetic topics.

Painful experience had taught her the imprudence of working until very late at night. In order to take care of her health, she resorted to a different system of study, which gave her much more sleep, and allowed her some hours of daylight for her literary labors.

Mr. Hammond wrote begging her to come to him, as he was now hopelessly infirm and confined to his room; but she shrank from a return to the village so intimately associated with events which she wished to forget. Though she declined the invitation, she proved her affection for her venerable teacher by sending him every day a long, cheerful letter.

Since her departure from the parsonage, Mrs. Murray had never written to her; but through Mr. Hammond's and Huldah's letters, Edna learned that Mr. Murray was the officiating minister in the church which he had built in his boyhood. Now and then the old pastor painted pictures of life at Le Bocage that brought happy tears to the orphan's eyes.

She heard from time to time of the good the new minister was accomplishing among the poor; of the beneficial influence he exerted, especially over the young men of the community; of the charitable institutions to which he was devoting a large portion of his fortune; of the love and respect and the golden opinions he was winning from those whom he had formerly estranged by his sarcastic bitterness.

While Edna fervently thanked God for this most wonderful change, she sometimes repeated exultingly:

> "Man-like is it to fall into sin,
> Fiend-like is it to dwell therein,
> Christ-like is it for sin to grieve,
> God-like is it all sin to leave!"[155]

She felt now that, should she become an invalid, and incapable of writing or teaching, the money made by her books, which Mr. Andrews had invested very judiciously, would at least supply her with the necessities of life.

One evening she held her weekly reception as usual, though she had complained of not feeling quite well that day.

A number of carriages stood before Mrs. Andrews's door and many friends who laughed and talked to the governess little dreamed that it was the last time they would spend an evening together in her society. The pleasant hours passed swiftly; Edna had never conversed more brilliantly, and the auditors thought her voice was richer and sweeter than ever, as she sang the last song and rose from the piano.

The guests took their departure – the carriages rolled away.

---

[155] An epigram from *Sinngedichte*—Baron Friedrich von Logau

Mrs. Andrews ran up to her room. Edna paused in the brilliantly lighted parlors to read a note, which had been handed to her during the evening.

Standing under the blazing chandelier, the face of this woman could not fail to excite interest in all who gazed upon her.

She was dressed in plain black silk, which exactly fitted her form, and in her hair glowed clusters of scarlet geranium flowers. A spray of red fuchsia was fastened by the beautiful stone cameo that confined her lace collar; and, save the handsome gold bands on her wrists, she wore no other ornaments.

Felix had given her these bracelets as a Christmas present, and after his death she never took them off; for inside he had his name and hers engraved, and between them the word "Mizpah."

Tonight the governess was weary, and her sweet face wore its old childish expression of mingled hopelessness and perfect patience. As she read, the weariness passed away, and over her pallid features stole a faint glow such as an ivory Niobe might borrow from its fluttering crimson folds of silken shroudings.

Her low voice was full of pathos as she said, "How very grateful I ought to be. How much I have to make me happy, to encourage me to work diligently and faithfully. How comforting it is to feel that parents have sufficient confidence in me to be willing to commit their children to my care. What more can I wish? My cup is brimmed with blessings. Ah, why am I not entirely happy?"

The note contained the signatures of six wealthy gentlemen, who requested her acceptance of a tasteful and handsome house, on condition that she would undertake the education of their daughters, and permit them to pay her a liberal salary.

While she could not accept the position, she appreciated most gratefully their generosity.

Twisting the note between her fingers, her eyes fell on the carpet. She thought of all her past; of the sorrows, struggles, and heartaches, the sleepless nights and weary, joyless days – first of adverse, then of favorable criticism; of toiling, hoping, dreading, praying. Now, in the peaceful zenith of her triumph, she realized

"That care and trial seem at last,

Through Memory's sunset air,
Like mountain ranges overpast,
In purple distance fair."[156]

The note fluttered to the floor. Her hands folded themselves together, and she raised her eyes to utter a humble, fervent "Thank God!"

But the words froze on her lips; for as she looked up, she saw Mr. Murray standing a few feet from her.

His face was almost as pale as hers, and his low voice trembled as he extended his arms toward her.

"God has pardoned all my sins and accepted me as a laborer worthy to enter His vineyard. Is Edna Earl more righteous than the Lord she worships?"

She stood motionless, looking up at him with eyes that brightened until their joyful radiance seemed indeed unearthly. The faint, delicate blush on her cheeks deepened and burned. With a quivering cry of gladness that told volumes, she hid her face in her hands.

He came nearer, and the sound of his rich, mellow voice thrilled her heart as no other music had ever done.

"Edna, have you a right to refuse me forgiveness, when the blood of Christ has purified me from the guilt of other years?"

She trembled and said brokenly, "Mr. Murray – you never wronged me – and I have nothing to forgive."

"Do you still believe me an unprincipled hypocrite?"

"Oh! No, no, no!"

"Do you believe that my repentance has been sincere, and acceptable to my insulted God? Do you believe that I am now as faithfully endeavoring to serve Him, as a remorseful man possibly can?"

"I hope so, Mr. Murray."

"Edna, can you trust me now?"

Some seconds elapsed before she answered, and then the words were scarcely audible.

"I trust you."

"Thank God!"

---

[156] "My Psalm" – John Greenleaf Whittier

There was a brief pause, and she heard a heavily-drawn sigh escape him.

"Edna, it is useless to tell you how devotedly I love you, for you have known that for years; and yet you have shown my love no mercy. But perhaps if you could realize how much I need your help in my holy work, how much more good I could accomplish in the world if you were with me, you might listen, without steeling yourself against me, as you have so long done. Edna, can you, will you trust me fully? Can you be a minister's wife, and aid him as only you can? Oh, my darling, my darling! I never expect to be worthy of you – but you can make me less unworthy. My own darling, come to me."

He stood within two feet of her, but he was – too humble? Nay, nay, too proud to touch her without permission.

Edna's hands fell from her crimson cheeks, and she looked up at the countenance of her king.

In her fond eyes he seemed noble and sanctified, and worthy of all confidence. As he opened his arms once more, she flew into them and laid her head on his shoulder, whispering, "Oh, I trust you! I trust you fully!"

Standing in the close, tender clasp of his strong arms, she listened to a narration of his grief and loneliness, his hopes and fears, his desolation and prayers during their long separation. Then for the first time she learned that he had come more than once to New York, solely to see her, having exacted a promise from Mr. Manning that he would not betray his presence in the city. He had followed her at a distance as she wandered with the children through the Park. Once in the ramble, he'd stood so close to her that he put out his hand and touched her dress. Mr. Manning had acquainted him with all that had ever passed between them during his unsuccessful suit; and during her sojourn in Europe, had kept him advised of the state of her health.

At last, when Mr. Murray bent his head to press his lips again to hers, he exclaimed in the old, pleading tone that had haunted her memory for years, "Edna, with all your meekness you are willfully proud. You tell me you trust me, and you nestle your dear head here on my shoulder – why won't you say what you know so well I am longing to hear? Why won't you say, 'St. Elmo, I love you'?"

Her glowing face was only pressed closer.

"My little darling!"

"Oh, Mr. Murray! Could I be here."

"Well, my stately Miss Earl! I am waiting most respectfully to allow you an opportunity of expressing yourself."

No answer.

He laughed as she had heard him once before, when he took her in his arms and dared her to look into his eyes.

"When I heard your books extolled; when I heard your praises from men, women, and children; when I could scarcely pick up a paper without finding some mention of your name; when I came here tonight, and paced the pavement, waiting for your admirers to leave the house; whenever and wherever I have heard your dear name uttered, I have been exultingly proud, for I knew that the heart of the people's pet was mine. I gloried in the consciousness which alone comforted me, that, despite all that the public could offer you, despite the adulation of other men, and despite my utter unworthiness, you never loved anyone but St. Elmo Murray! As God reigns above us, His world holds no man so resolved to prove himself worthy of his treasure.

"Edna, looking back across the dark years that have gone so heavily over my head, and comparing you, my pure, precious darling, with that woman, whom in my boyhood I selected for my life-companion, I know not whether I am most humble, or grateful, or proud!

'Ah I who am I, that God hath saved
Me from the doom I did desire,
And crossed the lot myself had craved
To set me higher?
What have I done that he should bow
From heaven to choose a wife for me?
And what deserved, he should endow
My home with THEE?'"[157]

---

[157] from "The Letter L" – Jean Ingelow

****

As Mr. Hammond was not able to take the fatiguing journey North, and Edna would not permit anyone else to perform her marriage ceremony, she sent Mr. Murray home without her, promising to come to the parsonage as quickly as possible.

Mr. and Mrs. Andrews were deeply pained by the knowledge of her approaching departure, and finally consented to accompany her on her journey.

The last day of Edna's stay in New York was spent at the quiet spot where Felix slept his last sleep. It caused her keen grief to bid good-bye to his resting-place, which was almost as dear to her as the grave of her grandfather. Their affection had been so warm, so sacred, that she clung fondly to his memory as if he had been her own brother.

It was not until she reached the old village depot, where the carriages were waiting for the party, and Edna threw her arms around Mrs. Murray and even old Henry, that the shadow of that day entirely left her countenance.

In accordance with her own request, Edna did not see Mr. Murray again until the hour appointed for their marriage, but stayed at the parsonage, talking with much joy with Mr. Hammond and all her old friends.

The next day, on a bright, beautiful afternoon warm with sunshine, she permitted Mrs. Murray to lead her into the parsonage study where the wedding party had assembled. Edna, shaking with joy, saw Mr. and Mrs. Andrews, Hattie, Huldah, and the white-haired pastor all there. As Edna entered, Mr. Murray advanced to meet her, and her eyes leapt to his as he received her hand from his mother. A great heart-pang leapt through her as their hands met. His face was serious, grave, and filled with love.

Halfway through the service, Edna's eyes were bent to the floor, and never once lifted, even when the trembling voice of her beloved pastor pronounced her St. Elmo Murray's wife. The intense pallor of her face frightened Mrs. Andrews, who watched her with suspended breath, and once moved eagerly toward her.

Mr. Murray felt her lean more heavily against him during the ceremony. Now, turning to take her in his arms, he saw that her eyelashes had fallen on her cheeks – Edna had lost all consciousness of what was passing.

Two hours elapsed before she recovered fully from the attack. When the blood showed itself again in lips that were kissed so repeatedly, Mr. Murray lifted Edna from the sofa in the study, and passing his arm around her, said, "Today I snap the fetters of your literary bondage. There shall be no more books written! No more study, no more toil, no more anxiety, no more heartaches. That dear public you love so well, must even help itself, and whistle for a new pet."

Edna leaned into his strong arms, nearly giddy with happiness. "My dear husband, it seems a shame that I should be surrounded by books in your most wonderful library, where I spent so many happy hours, and not spend a little time in study. Perhaps that would be acceptable?"

St. Elmo smiled. "Perhaps, my ambitious darling. You belong solely to me now, and I shall take care of the life you have nearly destroyed in your inordinate ambition. Come, the fresh air will revive you."

They stood a moment under the honeysuckle arch over the parsonage gate, where the carriage was waiting to take them to Le Bocage – now to be her home forever.

Mr. Murray asked, "Are you strong enough to go to the church?"

Edna gazed into the face she adored, which she'd longed for so many years. "Yes, my dear; the pain has all passed away. I am perfectly well again."

They crossed the street. To Edna's surprise and delight, Mr. Murray lifted her up in his arms and carried her up the steps and into the grand, solemn church. Once inside, he set her back down on her feet, where the soft, holy, violet light from the richly-tinted glass streamed over gilded organ-pipes and sculptured columns.

Neither Edna nor St. Elmo spoke as they walked down the aisle. In perfect silence both knelt before the shining altar, and only God heard their prayers of gratitude.

After some moments St. Elmo put out his hand, took Edna's, and holding it in his on the balustrade, he prayed aloud, asking

God's blessing on their marriage, and fervently dedicating all their future to His work.

The flush of the dying day was reflected on the window high above the altar. It burned through the red mantle of the Christ and fell upon the marble shrine like sacred, sacrificial fire.

Edna felt as if her heart could not hold all its measureless joy. It seemed a delightful dream to kneel at St. Elmo's side and hear his voice earnestly consecrating their lives to the service of Jesus Christ.

Edna knew from the tremor in his tone, and the tears in his eyes, that his dedication was complete. Now, to be his companion through all the remaining years of their earthly pilgrimage, to be allowed to help him and love him, to walk heavenward with her hand in his; this – this was the crowning glory and richest blessing of her life.

When his prayer ended, Edna laid her head down on the altar-railing and sobbed with joy. He gave her his handkerchief and kissed the top of her head.

In the orange glow of a wintry sunset they came out and sat down on the steps, while a pair of spotless white pigeons perched on the bloodstain. St. Elmo put his arm around Edna, and she rested her face upon his bosom, as she'd so long dreamed of doing.

"Darling, do you remember that once, in the dark days of my reckless sinfulness, I asked you one night, in the library at Le Bocage, if you had no faith in me? And you repeated so vehemently, 'None, Mr. Murray!'"

"Oh, sir!" Edna cried, lifting her head to gaze at him. "Oh, do not think of it. Why remember what is so painful and so long past? Forgive those words and forget them. Never was more implicit faith, more devoted affection, given to any human being than I give now to you, my dear St. Elmo; you, who are my first and my last and my only love."

His arm tightened around her waist as he bowed his face to hers, his splendid dark eyes smiling into hers.

"Forgive? Ah, my darling, do you recollect also that I told you then that the time would come when your dear lips would ask pardon for what they uttered that night, and that when that hour arrived I would take my revenge? My wife! My pure, noble, beautiful wife! Give me my revenge, for I cry with the long-banished Roman:

'Oh! a kiss – long as my exile
Sweet as my revenge!'"[158]

He put his hand under her chin, drew the lips to his, and they kissed repeatedly.

Down among the graves, in the brown grass and withered leaves, behind a tall shaft around which coiled a carved marble serpent with hooded head – there, amid the dead, crouched a woman with a stony face and blue eyes that glared with murderous hate at the sweet countenance of the happy bride. When St. Elmo tenderly kissed the lips of his wife, Agnes Powell smothered a savage cry. Nemesis was satisfied as the wretched woman fell forward on the grass, sweeping her blonde hair over her eyes to shut out the vision that maddened her.

Then and there, for the first time, as she sat enfolded by her husband's arm, Edna felt that she could thank him for the monument erected over her grandfather's grave.

The light faded slowly in the west and the pigeons ceased their fluttering about the belfry. As Edna and St. Elmo turned to leave the church, so dear to both, he stretched his hand toward the ivy-clad vault, and said solemnly, "I throw all mournful years behind me. By the grace of God, our new lives, beginning on this hallowed day, shall make noble amends for the wasted past. Loving each other, aiding each other, and serving Christ, through whose atonement alone I have been saved from eternal ruin -- to Thy merciful guidance, O Father, we commit our future!"

Edna looked reverently up at his beaming countenance, whence the shadows of hate and scorn had long since passed. As his splendid eyes came back to hers, reading in her beautiful, pure face all her love and confidence and happy hope, he drew her close to his bosom, and laid his dark cheek on hers, saying fondly and proudly:

---

[158] Coriolanus, act 5, scene 3 -- Shakespeare

"My wife, my life. Oh! we will walk this world,
Yoked in all exercise of noble end,
And so through those dark gates across the wild
That no man knows. My hopes and thine are one;
Accomplish thou my manhood, and thyself,
Lay thy sweet hands in mine and trust to me."[159]

The End

Read on to Get a Free Book

---

[159] *The Princess,* Part 7 – Lord Alfred Tennyson

In 1998, I wrote a short story about the time I fell in love with the fellow who ended up being my husband, and I pulled a lot of inspiration (and quotes) from *St. Elmo* to use in the story. This story was published in *Cicada* magazine in 1999, and then I published it as a little book a couple of years back.

It's called *Why Can't My Life Be a Romance Novel?* Go to https://claims.prolificworks.com/free/bouHr, sign up for my newsletter, and you can get your own free copy. Thank you for reading, and enjoy!

Please leave a review!

If you enjoyed *St. Elmo*, please leave a review on Amazon or Goodreads. Any and all reviews are welcomed. Thank you!

Made in the USA
Columbia, SC
22 April 2022

59330579R00288